RED HOUSE

Fiction. Perhaps.

KENT KILLMER

iUniverse, Inc.
New York   Bloomington

Red House
Fiction. Perhaps.

iUniverse books may be ordered through booksellers or by contacting:

iUniverse
1663 Liberty Drive
Bloomington, IN 47403
www.iuniverse.com
1-800-Authors (1-800-288-4677)

ISBN: 978-1-4502-6038-1 (pbk)
ISBN: 978-1-4502-6039-8 (cloth)
ISBN: 978-1-4502-6040-4 (ebk)

Library of Congress Control Number: 2010914029

Printed in the United States of America

iUniverse rev. date: 11/4/2010

For my wife and kids.

PROLOGUE

Fort Bragg, California
February 2011

UPSIDE DOWN. HE WAS SUSPENDED in the chair and hanging upside down. Held in place by the small dolly lift, which was keeping his nose but two inches above the incoming sea, he had been left to dangle, inverted in the chair, upside down. Discarded without ceremony, he had been abandoned to cough, spit and choke—choke on the water that was becoming deeper each minute as the foaming tide rushed in.

Had they given up? he wondered. Were they simply going to drown him? Pain. Dull, throbbing pain in his right lower jaw. An aching nausea overcame his every fiber. Had they roughed him up some more while he was out? The acrid ammonia odor from the capsules they'd used repeatedly to revive him still filled his sinuses. Throbbing—he turned his head to its maximum ability and looked down and out the corner of his eye in the direction from whence the ache came. There was a half inch-thick, steel cable with six flat, oblong hooks that could slide freely up and down. One, however, had been pushed up and through his chin, up through the bottom of his jaw, alongside his teeth and then back out of his open mouth. A stringer. They had put him on a stringer.

Like a fish.

He ran his tongue along the multistrand cable, discovering this was the root cause of the newfound metallic taste in his mouth. The steel clicked against his teeth. Not being able to close his chops for hours had made them as dry as cotton. He was parched and filled with phlegm. He glanced again skyward—toward the ceiling. The dark, moss-laden canopy over him continued to trickle down moisture and left a gritty film in his eyes. He smelled the lichen-coated rocks and heard the dripping overhead just before a large drop hit him in the eye. His head reeled back. Blinking out the residue, he saw the half inch-thick, stainless steel cable was anchored firmly overhead. It continued back deeper and ultimately disappeared into the pitch-black bowels of the cave.

There were other objects, blurry objects—other things hanging on oblong hooks behind him. He had to strain. Without a clear visual he had to arch his back and twist his neck whereupon he felt the immediate electric shock of level-ten pain in his mouth reminding him that he had been impaled. He arched, bounced once and turned again spasmodically in the other direction.

That stench—what is that god awful stench? he wondered. The odor was so pungent and oppressive it almost blocked out all others.

And there—there he saw six more oblong hooks, suspending six more oblong things, six more forms. They reminded him of the butcher's shop in Menlo Park where his father had taken him as a child to have the salmon they'd caught steaked out for their barbecue. They were all gently swaying together in the cold. Swaying in the moist, numbing cold, as if on display. There were no fingers, no hands, no feet, no heads. But they were all moving gracefully together in the sea breeze that was gliding into the cave.

Squinting to focus his eyes better, again he turned his head sideways and struggled to blink out the ceiling's excess moisture, which mixed with the blood running in a small rivulet down his face. He spat out more clots. The headless body nearest him had something on the small of its back—a marking of sorts. *It's a skinny triangle*, he thought, as he strained to get a better look. No, it was a skinny triangle with ragged edges. *What in the hell is that?* He knew the image. But what he had gone through seemed to have stripped him of his cognitive powers.

He looked further up the stringer, where the light was very low. It was misty. He saw five more pieces of meat, all gently swinging in metronome unison, with no sound other than the occasional creak from their mounting brackets. All appendages that could offer up any keys to identification forensically had been removed. Bolt cutters for the fingers, tin snips for the feet, machetes for the heads.

The adrenalin coursed through his veins. He flushed. He felt strangely reinvigorated. For a moment, he felt like he could tear the cable in two and bolt to freedom. That attempt would be a mistake, however and he knew it. Flesh and bone would not prevail, the cable would win out. While fantasizing, he choked again on the seawater, which was rushing in through the cave's narrow entrance. Foaming and rushing, it pushed up into his nose and mouth, as the Venturi effect commanded it to. Its velocity increased in these constricted spaces due to this unforgiving law of physics. He struggled to remain calm. To reason.

He attempted to swing himself. First, he moved to and fro to get the momentum going, creating but a modest arc. He'd contort his mouth just enough to get a small, sideways breath between each pendulum's swath above the water. It was a fervent attempt at negotiation with the incoming tide, which was lapping in his face. To live.

He was doing well until the apex, the high point of his arc, where the stringer once fully extended, snapped his face back sharply around in the opposite direction of travel. It jerked him back smartly at the jaw, right where he was impaled. He spat out another mouthful of blood. The jolt sharpened his memory's focus as to his plight. The reminder came with the sharpest of pain emanating from the entry point of the puncture wound where the baseline cable was tied off. Its stanchions at ceiling and floor were anchored in permanently.

"Shit," he said.

Again he tried his hands. Nope, seriously too tight and the rope was just too strong. He was out of options, out of strength. His face was blowing bubbles in the tide's rising waters. He choked. Wanted to breathe. He ached for air but instead aspirated and gagged on the slurry. Each time he'd move for another breath, the stringer would jerk him back promptly into place. First he'd feel the pain, then he'd realize the unyielding authority that only a twenty seven hundred psi tensile strength cable can evoke. No negotiation.

The omnipresent stringer piercing his jaw reminded him any motion at all was going to be magnified one hundredfold. First through the jaw, then to the face and on to his neck, which was grotesquely swollen with a large, purple and yellow hematoma from the internal blood that pooled as he hung upside down.

After ten more minutes of hellish swinging punctuated by the last-minute snapping back of his jaw, he realized his options were constricting. He would either drown, or pass out—then drown. Guess this was it. Lights out. Good night, nurse.

ONE

Menlo Park, California
October 2008

ORIGINALLY, FRANCIS HAD NO INTENTION of staying that late. As a Menlo Park venture capitalist, he knew God had put hands on the clock for others. Not for him. He did what it took. He did what came next. Deals were his life and his wife, a mistress whose passion knew no bounds. Francis had become a deal junkie. Initially, the transformation was intentional, for the green and for the glory. Now, the process was the cause and he was the effect.

Holding the flaming cedar shard to the end of his seven inch-long, fifty-two ring Ashton Churchill cigar, he rotated the thin, earthen-colored cylinder slowly, first to warm and then to ignite. This action consummated the plural marriage of nicotine, tar and fire, which his mother had warned him repeatedly was so wrong and yet his mouth, nose and palate knew to be oh so right.

Mr. Francis Scott Key—after *the* Francis Scott Key (a shirttail relative)—was a right wing, conservative, Regan-Constitutionalist who was a card carrying member of the Silent Majority. A man of means, Key was always impeccably dressed while working. Urban legend reported of the time his shirt cuffs' excessively starched razor edged, actually drew blood from his wrists. Although he'd always denied the story, those who knew him saw just a fleeting glint of pleasure in his eyes when the tale was rebuffed. His mouth would draw slightly thinner, his eyes would narrow to a squint and a sardonic smile would appear and then flit away just as quickly.

A master of appearances, deception and distance, Mr. Key allowed few to become acquaintances and no one to become close. When not working, he found comfort sandwiching his apparel and styling in that natty niche between über-casual and squalor that is best known by young men in their teens and wharf rats.

Late thirties, six feet two, tanned and sinewy, he had maintained the gritty physique acquired from prior years as a Navy SEAL. Arrestingly handsome, he'd honed his craft extracting a small measure of pleasure from each black ops experience. Somewhat self-absorbed, his gait and carriage made him appear more like a short stop than a high-powered executive, with his age just starting to make its appearance in the occasional fine line on his face.

Key's hair was coal black with the obvious exception of the forward leaning *My Friend Flicka* shock of gray. This appeared as so much frontal festooned plumage, hanging à la Elvis, raucously from fatigue, or cantilevered out just slightly over his forehead.

"Don't do it all in one day, Mr. Key," quipped the office janitorette. She whisked behind him brushing her torso ever so gently against his arms—arms linked to hands, which were finger-laced behind his head. The brush was so masterfully slight it could be confusing to the uninitiated as to whether it was deliberate or not.

Key, on the other hand, was anything but uninitiated. He had lost any degree of ambiguity as to her intentions some six brushes ago. Promptly following the veiled touching arrived a wall of aromas—a plaid smorgasbord of odors, which was an elegant blending of Lysol, DDT and the finest perfume offered up on aisle sixteen at the Dollar Store. Her skin was tighter than the surface of an overinflated volleyball. And her eyes were so large they would make Bambi's appear beady. And yet …

Something isn't there, he thought. Oh yes. It was the ability to initiate and retain a single cogent thought. Yet again. Who cares? He knew a real man wouldn't. In his ill-spent youth, he and his expatriates would do the town, then they'd do the women. After all, it was their due. They were manly men—hairy-chested, meat-eating, trans fat-binging, seegar-smoking, drink-till-you-puke, sport-fucking men. Ah yes. Those were the days. Tie into a bad piece of livestock? Not to worry. Sashay on down to your local OBGY-MEN and a shot of penicillin about the size of a Red Bull would fix that runny nose and any other body parts that might be similarly affected. But now? Now he had likened the current sexual lollapalooza and its buffet of infections to going to Vegas and betting your Johnson at the roulette wheel. He just didn't like the odds.

"Mr. Key?" again questioned the cleaning lady.

"Yes?" said Scotty.

"Should I put the cat out? Or are you commming?" she asked with the guttersnipe flirtatious style consistent with her youth and a HUD housing upbringing.

While all the obvious double entendres raced through Key's mind as to an appropriately testosterone-charged comeback, he responded quietly instead, "No. You go ahead." He did not lift his eyes or his head.

The cigar smoke curled up languidly skyward from the pale green, crystal, octagonal ash tray. The crystal was inset into a thirty-inch-high, wrought iron stand that continued over the top of the glass. It prominently displayed two dogs on their hind legs holding hoops up with their tiny front paws, joined at the apex, as if celebrating the doggie Olympics—perhaps the smoking doggie Olympics. The ash tray had been his grandfather's, then his fathers and ultimately his. The relic was over a hundred years old. The dogs were Scotties.

Still. If her teeth were just a *little* straighter, she had perhaps just slightly better posture and her blouse's polka dots were just half as large, she might be an appealing onesy in a *Daisy Mae Meets the Wolf-Man Behind the File Cabinet* kind of way. But then, he mused, he worked there. He'd see her again. Awkward.

And then, there was this whole breath thing. Her breath was registered in three states. It could stop a London Cabbie at full throttle well in advance of a shrill bobby's whistle. He knew that breath anywhere. A fifty-five gallon drum of Listerine, followed up with the white hot cleansing of a small nuclear device could not neutralize that odor.

Key harkened back to his childhood. He recalled the omnipresent goldfish that lived in an opalescent bowl, centered upon a dusty doily on the dark walnut nightstand, right by his bed. Over time, the bowl had etched a small ring into the furniture. The fish had been his little buddies. The bowl's pungent, brown green moss-laden, oppressive odor which wafted heavenward, had the moist night air spiriting it into his nostrils as he slept. It was eerily reminiscent of the cleaning lady's breath. Yes. She had aquarium breath. It was a deal killer.

It has been said that nothing fails like success, as in too much success. Francis, while being acutely aware of this phenomenon, was beginning to become numb from his prior accomplishments. Sometimes he'd form, not so much the words but rather, the concept in his mind: Is this it? Is this all there is? Am I not going to make a difference? A real difference? Am I going to be but a pimple on the buttocks of life? He reflected on the impact his long removed great-great-great-uncle had wrought on the national stage with the anthem. Pretty cool. He wanted to do some good as well, to effect something bigger than himself. To be remembered.

He found he was staring into his computer screen with the look of a walleye who'd just been introduced to a fisherman's mallet. Sometimes, he'd fantasize about being physically pulled into the screen—going into a world where he would make a difference on a grander stage. The thought intrigued him.

Whaaap! The office door slammed behind Daisy Mae, snapping him back into reality.

Scotty Key was demanding. He was a perfectionist. And he was Oxford-educated in economics and math. Normally right, as an intellectual property venture capitalist, Key had learned early and well how to quickly don his game face. A sardonic smile peppered with just enough pleasantries to feign true California sincerity offered up the illusion of caring. This was an acquired skill stamped onto his admission ticket ages ago in the Menlo Park firm where he plied his craft. While this facade had served him well for years in the venture business, the mantel on which he carried it was beginning to become a bit heavy. It had become less important, now that he had his demons mostly under control.

TWO

"YO! SCOTTY!" CAME A CRY from the next office. The voice belonged to another of the firm's partners and Scotty's best friend—Cornelius Brandon III, esquire, also known as Pig.

Blazing from around the corner of the rich walnut wainscoted corridor by the art deco sculptures and clean-lined, euro-glass walled conference room emerged a fireplug of a man on rails. "Go home, man!"

A product of Stanford, Pig was in his late twenties. He sported fire engine hair, complexion, temper, drive and delivery. He enjoyed carrying a set of business cards that proclaimed:

Introducing
The Son of a Bitch from the Bay
With All the Answers

Humility was not one of Pig's strengths. Incandescently bright, Pig had been a linebacker in school. That "caring and sensitive" delivery had served him well on the gridiron and was symptomatic of his approach to work and life. A blistering IQ, Pig used to notch his locker by biting off a hunk of the multi-yellow-stained pine top shelf every time he broke an opponent's limb. His collegiate football nickname was "Bonecrusher."

He still liked to break things. He liked to bust junior MBA's balls when they made a funding request from his firm, PacRim Ventures. While the "Pac" stood for Pacific, Pig took delight in claiming he traded this in his compensation package in honor of the Pac 10 Conference of which he was a proud alumnus.

"Scotty! Scotty! Scotty!" roared Pig.

"What?" responded Key.

"Did you see me squash those Nipponese empty suits today? They're bugs! What Pussies!"

"No. I missed that. My loss."

"You couldn't have. Not possible. You were in the room!" Pig's volume and magenta pigmentation were both elevating.

Scotty spun around in his chair to give Pig his full attention, realizing any attempt at feigning disinterest would be futile.

"Didn't you see Mr. Sushi's face when I asked him about the international patent rights?" Pig was screwing up his face into an overly leering oriental pout. "Like he's going to parade in here with his pursed lips, anchovy up the ass, oily haired, Brandon-San *bullshit* and expect us to drop a twenty million dollar-dime on him."

"He's negotiating, Pig. Relax," said Key.

"Okay, so we get the US and oh, by the way, he and the rest of his slipper footed centipede get the rest of the fucking *planet*!" In so saying, Pig slammed the rich, purple heart wood and abalone inlaid conference table violently with his bulbous hands. His ring finger had struck the corner so aggressively it made a slight indentation. A notch.

"Does it say fucking *stupid* under here?" he asked sarcastically as he raised his bangs up to expose his forehead. Pig started coughing, twice in quick succession. He coughed again, more furiously the third time. He coughed uncontrollably. Pig was a smoker and he liked to chew. His teeth were as yellow as the tops of his laceless Chuck Taylor tennis shoes. He was simultaneously laughing, choking and wheezing.

In an effort to clear his throat, he leapt to his feet with such ferocity that the studded leather chair flipped over backward. Attempting to keep his balance, he inadvertently backhanded his beer. It became a high-speed, foaming, spewing projectile vomiting ale four feet heavenward and a good third of the way across the twenty-five thousand-dollar conference table.

Ignoring the carnage he'd just created, Pig continued, "Those guys come over here, get degrees out the wazoo, go to one Giant's game and think they've got us all figured out. They come prancing in here, all heel-toe, nose in the air, heads bobbing like pigeons, throw me a gang sign with two 'sup, bros' and think they own us!"

"As a matter of public record, they do own 56 percent of all the triple A office space in downtown Los Angeles," said Key.

"Scotty, you're such an asshole. You know what I mean. And don't give me any of that namby-pamby, pinkie-ringed, I'm so very très-très European Oxford-educated and above all this shit either!" demanded Pig.

"You're right. It eats at me too sometimes. In particular, politically it is becoming more troubling as of late. But hey, it's a changing world. Handle it, or it will handle you," said Key.

"I knew I could count on you for some philosophical bull droppings," fumed Brandon.

"The guy's just doing his job," said Key.

"Exactly the problem with you, Key. Nothing bothers you anymore. You got no soul. You should call a spade a spade, or in this case, a greedy slope a greedy slope," bemoaned Pig.

"Has anyone ever told you how articulate you can be when you're upset?" taunted Key as he ran his forefinger across the top of his desk's inlaid filigree perimeter.

"Fuck you," said Pig.

"Good comeback. I'll place it in 'the journal of rapid retort, moderately droll, yet mindless comebacks'," said Key, while turning and reaching for his Mont Blanc, collecting his Blackberry and turning his computer off.

"Jag-off." Not looking back, Pig walked out in mock disgust, while making two rapid, up and down gestures high in the air with his right hand.

Key stopped half way home at one of his favorite haunts—the Jack-Daniels Hookah & Fern Bar Dojo. The fluorescent sign, but two thirds illuminated, sputtered noisily as it burned insects and filled an entire window due to the copy length. Approaching the entry way through the alley, one was first greeted by the stifling aroma of the sweaty mats and the unmistakable, sugary sweet and smoky odor of Jack Daniels whiskey. The rather eclectic blend was the amalgamation of a contemporary karate school and an '80s throwback of a touchy-feely watering hole juxtaposed against a new millennium hookah bar, with a Jack Daniels finish.

This combination offered an exceptional spot to get in touch with your feminine side, while driving your colleague's sternum back three-sixteenths of an inch into his chest cavity with the heel of your foot. It had it all. Scotty had many times suggested adding the trailing phrase "and Car Wash." The Owner would quietly smile and bow the notion away.

The Korean owner who had refitted the failed fern bar had found many of the prior green residents so restive he'd decided to keep a few. Okay, he'd kept them all. Subsequently, he'd reopened the establishment with the plants bearing brass and walnut individualized nameplates. This allowed the opportunity to raise endowments for and on behalf of a patron's favorite plant. Customarily, the creativity and checkbooks came out after the fourth Jack.

Scotty liked to personally name some of the more striking examples of flora. His favorite three nameplates, which he sponsored were:

1. Ulysses S. Plant   Boston fern
2. Robert E. Leaf   Squatty palm
3. Dwight D. Eisenflower   Who knew?

The owner simply went by "Master Dihm." Dihm was one of the most Americanized, Californicated Asians one could ever come across. He and Key were tight. Master Dihm abhorred sake as it made him sweat and loved Jack Daniel's Green Label neat. He could always be found stretching, performing his kata (karate dance routine for those with grace yet no rhythm) his *teiso*, or at the corner stool with a double Jack. He explained that he ingested the latter solely to help him relate better to his Western clientele.

Key liked Manhattans when it was cool but favored a gin and tonic in the warmer months. Due to this switching, Master Dihm affectionately referred to Scotty as "Flask Hopper." Key returned the riposte by calling the owner "Master Dihm Bulb." Key came through the locker room to the bar and promptly sat next to Master Dihm.

"Hi," said Key while pulling up a tall highly lacquered bar stool and resting the soles of his shoes on the bar's strong and long, four-inch diameter brass, foot rail.

"Height!" snapped Dihm. The greeting was such a crisp pronunciation of the word *hi*, it sounded like *height*.

"Six two," responded Key without emotion, as he made a toasting gesture toward Dihm.

"Scotty-san, your trousers are at half-mast," said Dihm.

Key looked down.

"April Fools!" exclaimed Dihm gleefully even though months early, unintentionally sparking a flood of unpleasant memories rushing back for Scotty.

April first every year, Scotty tried to wish that page away on his calendar. On this day, Scotty had wrestled a demon every year. On a much earlier April 1, he, along with his older brother and best friend, had attended Barnum & Bailey's Circus for the very first time. The threesome was excited, anxious to watch the tigers jump through the flaming hoops, hear the lions roar, see the man get shot out of the cannon and guffaw at the garishly large, red-footed clowns squirting each other with seltzer. Most of all, they were excited to be out on their own.

On his first outing without parental oversight, Scotty had been proud to just be hanging with the guys. His brother, Taylor, was fourteen, Scotty was nine and Oliver was eight. In his mind, they were grown-ups and they could handle anything that came along.

Ambling down the ill-lit, narrow, long, sloping, dark gray concrete ramp that linked the massive coliseum floors, they found themselves completely alone. Alone until a gang of five punks in their late teens who were in the business of shaking down younger, smaller children—just like them—confronted the trio from the rear.

Click-clack. Click-clack. Click-clack. One thug's boots telegraphed the gang's approach. The three quickened their pace. As their heels struck against the sparkly, mottled gray concrete, they could hear parroted heel sounds behind them picking up speed as well. After a brief pause, the three broke out into a dead run. Scotty ran as fast as his nine-year-old legs could carry him. It didn't take long for the older teens to catch them.

Precisely what happened next was still a bit of a blur. Scotty believed he was lifted off his feet and forcefully thrown against the concrete wall such that his head snapped back and cracked open upon impact. Dazed, he looked around to discover Taylor and Oliver receiving similar treatment.

He recalled possessing four dollars and seventy-six cents in his pocket. Undoubtedly, he would have to surrender this. But the five larger toughs did not make that demand. Instead, they kept hitting the three youths in the face, kicking them in the groin and throwing them up against the hard concrete wall for sport. The larger thugs didn't want the boy's popcorn or jackets. They simply wanted to inflict pain. They didn't stop. The pummeling continued. Were they going to kill him?

Blood running down his face, Taylor was the first to break free. A sprinter later in school, Taylor had always been fast. Wiry and nail tough, Scotty kicked one attacker and poked him in the eye as he managed to wiggle free. He ran ten steps and saw his brother had made it to the top of the ramp twenty yards away. Taylor waved wildly, screaming, "Come on! Let's go!"

Scotty tasted the blood on his lip. The hooligans still had Oliver pinned up against the wall. Were they going to continue to hit him? Surely they weren't going to kill him.

What chance did he, a nine-year-old, stand against five older teenagers? It would be stupid to reenter the fray. He had no shot—but Oliver was his best friend. Two of the older teens, witnessing his escape, turned and came roaring up the ramp to engage little Scotty yet again.

He stopped. Scotty hesitated. And then …

He ran.

He ran as fast as his little drumsticks could motor him up the ramp to safety. The older youths were closing in on Scotty and his brother for a second time when two overweight cops showed up. They blew their whistles, pulled their nightsticks and ran the other five off. Oliver had lost a tooth and walked with a limp for months later until he and his family moved away. He'd told Scotty publically he understood and would have done the same thing if roles were reversed. He would have run too. He said so. In private, however, Scotty felt a distance, a different vacant faraway look in Oliver's eyes. Thereafter, their relationship was never quite the same.

Scotty had always been ashamed of his actions on that day. He'd felt responsible—nine or not. Had he exercised cowardice or common sense when he'd chosen flight versus fight? His brother told him repeatedly later it was their only option. He said neither he nor Scotty had any shot against the five. They were never going to get murdered, they'd just avoided a sound thrashing.

Still, Scotty had ducked the call to action.

He'd shrunk from it.

The call when his friend had needed him to engage, practical or not.

His father reasoned later this might have been the motivating force for him to learn karate and become a SEAL. Regardless, he was hardwired now with this emotional baggage. He would not set idly by again when things were heading south, regardless of the odds.

"Ah, Flask Hopper, you're looking for the most part weak, slovenly, unfocused, pale and in general, very Western this evening."

Dihm's remarks snapped Scotty back to the present. "And you, Master Dihm Bulb, are quite fastidious, yet still a fat fuck who can't pronounce his Ls and is in constant search of bubble tea and a Beach Boys concert."

They both bowed—gently, melodically, rolling their heads together—and solemnly toasted each other with the sicky-sweet insincerity which only kindred spirits from separate corners of the globe and very drunk fraternity brothers come to truly understand.

Without warning, they both simultaneously leapt to their feet in feigned rage and started circling each other in a catlike, cobra-mongoose, taunting fashion. Master Dihm grabbed a pair of nunchucks and whipped them into a blurring frenzy behind his head, under each bicep, catching the estranged end with the opposite hand in front of his opponent. "I will crack your thin-shelled Western head easier than a rotten lychee nut, you white breaded, unprincipled cracker," threatened Dihm. "And I, Dihm Limb, will push these two fingers three inches into your naval." Dihm jumped up on the bar in a single motion, unintentionally shattering a glass with his spinning weapon and rapping the other wooden baton smartly against his shin.

"Leg conditioning?" queried Key.

"Hurrrumph," said Dihm not looking up while he rubbed his smarting shin.

"You should stick to growing your gut and ferns," said Scotty as he patted Dihm's protruding paunch.

"And you, imperialist Yankee dawg, should go stretch and prepare for your kata."

"Weight!" bowed Key somberly.

"Height!" shouted Dihm as he bowed.

Then, they both concomitantly performed an about face and exited the room. Key retired to the area that was covered with wall to wall mats. This venue had limited ventilation and smelled as though it needed a good disinfecting. Patrons performed teisos, katas and sparring here.

Key's form was less than perfect. He used a combination of karate and the Israeli's Krav Maga. More of an urban street brawler, he'd use whichever vehicle best suited him at the moment. Dihm accused his blended style of being akin to "a Shaolin monk in search of a broken beer bottle."

Stretching, Key groaned forward, placing his head to his knee. There, as usual, he saw the large almond-eyed oriental girl staring back at him in the mirror. Her eyes were like a Disney character's. When he'd turn to catch her gaze directly, she would glance away. She was a truly lithe, lean and muscular, smooth-legged beauty. When he'd seen her before, he hadn't been able to break away his stare. It wasn't simply her raw natural beauty. She looked as though she had many tightly held secrets, crisscrossed between rice paper and wrapped perfectly in satin ribbons—all hidden away in her puzzle box.

THREE

Detroit, Michigan
November 2008

"GET OUTTA THE FUCKIN' CAH," demanded Mr. U.

Skylar Bluebird, current stretch limo back seat resident, did not feel obliged to accommodate Mr. U. Fog enveloped the sepia-toned bridge abutment they were tucked in under.

In lieu of the current proposal, Bluebird leaned closer to the raised window and spoke through the glass in a rather shrill voice, "I can hear you just fine, thank you very much."

It was 3:05 am in the Six Mile area of Detroit. Only fools or individuals looking to do those same fools harm would loiter here. The fences had two parallel curly queues of razor wire atop and the Kentucky Fried Chicken franchise had bulletproof glass. Most dogs were mottled pit bulls and the cops didn't come this far down. A relentless mist was saturating all things still. The ground's spalling concrete was uneven and littered with broken glass, bits of trash, feces and needles.

Mr. U was a very thick individual, in his early fifties. He had at least two chins from all the high-end red meat dinners with his DC, K-Street lobbying crowd. He had a thick neck, thick fingers and forearms the size of hams. He spent half his time in DC and the other half in Detroit. Mr. U—that was all that people ever called him. No one knew his real name. Mr. U was a doer. He was the guy who got things done. He was the guy who got things done for the union. And the mob.

His pie face and heavy jowls bore hundreds of tiny exploding blood vessels whose pattern was eerily reminiscent of the New Jersey Turnpike. He sported a very tall-brimmed, charcoal fedora, which while not period appropriate was nonetheless color-metrically in alignment. Resting on his nose were unusually prominent, thick, black, horn-rimmed glasses, which would have been the envy of Truman Capote. His robust nose was cartoon-esque in proportion. Jowls and nose alike had mushroomed and were exacerbated by years of heavy drinking. His man boobs were large and quite probably lactating.

Although intelligent and ivy league-educated, Mr. U had hung on to his Philly accent, which made him sound less so and a bit foreboding and thug-like. On this occasion he was outfitted with a heavy, gold nugget chain necklace, comically large, gold cuff links, a black Armani suit and an exceedingly shiny silver tie.

"I'm a patient man. But you're trying my patience," he said.

"I can hear you just fine," said Bluebird remaining put.

"This ain't no fuckin' hearing test!" shouted U as he smashed the window with a single rap from his tire iron.

"Jesus!" exclaimed Bluebird. He recoiled and shrank back farther into the limo, as the plate glass nuggets exploded in all over his suit.

U bent over, grabbed Bluebird by the lapels and quite literally pulled him through the window. While Bluebird was still horizontal, U relaxed his grip so Skylar fell, hitting his face on the cracked and crumbled concrete below.

"Can we not engage in civil discourse like the grown-ups, Ape-zilla?" asked Bluebird, wiping blood off his lip after hitting the street. Skylar Bluebird was a diminutive form who shook before he had good reason to shake. He now, however, had a bona fide reason to be anxious. His blond wavy hair was meticulously coiffed with just a hint of ducktail in the back. Gaunt, with light pasty skin, he was dressed dapperly in a shiny, sharkskin gray suit, silk square, Allen Edmonds shoes and a pink tie which coordinated perfectly with his kerchief.

"I asked you nicely," said U.

Skylar pulled himself up off the ground, looked in horror at the hole in the knee of his two thousand-dollar suit trousers. "You animal. What is it you require of me at this dreadful hour?"

"A report. I *require* a report."

"What report?"

"The one that's a week late. Dat one."

"Of course. It's simply been frenetically hectic and …," said Skylar as he cast his eyes heavenward, waving both hands energetically in a rather limp-wristed manner.

"Save it." Mr. U put the palm of his hand up while dropping his head down.

"Well. I put in motion the things we discussed to the north and to the south."

"Good. And?"

"It didn't work out. It just didn't work out. There were issues."

"Issues? What issues?"

"My God, man, these entities have entire armies at their disposal. Do you understand me? You can't just waltz in there, do your business and saunter out like you're on a Paris runway! Which fairytale did you read last?"

"I'm talking to the fairy and hearing his tale right now," said U. He flicked a large glowing ember from his seven-inch, torpedo maduro toward Bluebird. A small, red penlight appeared and then flitted away.

"Oh heavens. Here now. There's no reason to be abusive. We set up a thoughtful plan. We hired professionals. We executed the plan with precision. The *plan* was flawed. It just didn't work out. You need to have patience," said Bluebird.

"Yeah, well, I need growth in 'dat area." In so saying, he placed his right thumb under his chin and rested his forefinger against the rightmost side of his large, prominent eyeglass stem and pressed. The last word had barely left his mouth when a muffled *boompf* sound came from under his hat.

A sawed-off, custom-made .38 dampened with silencer was concealed in the tall brim of Mr. U's hat. His glasses provided a faint crosshair and laser sighting vehicle. His eyeglasses' rightmost stem was the wireless triggering mechanism and an internal hat frame spread the recoil through the back of his head. The slug shot out the front of his hat and burrowed deep into Bluebird's left knee, right by the trouser tear. Exploding the joint, it dropped him like a pair of dirty socks.

"Again. How we gonna get this done?" asked U, more patiently this time as he lowered his voice.

"My knee! Shit! Look at my knee. You cur dog. You're not going to get it done!" sniffled Skylar, whimpering, cradling his knee. "They have fucking armies! Do you hear me? Armies! You can't get within two hundred yards of them without passing through three checkpoints, two metal detectors and brandishing ambassador credentials. You may conscript anyone you like into this folly, however it is a complete and utter waste of time, you no-necked Neanderthal."

"Now, see, you hurt my feelings," Mr. U said dispassionately.

The next muffled *boompf* was followed quickly by Skylar's lifeless form slumping to the ground with a small hole in the front of his face and a much larger one in the back.

"Was that really necessary?" came a calm, rich, baritone voice from deep inside the backseat of the limo. Briefly illuminated with the momentary glow of a cigarette, the silhouette of a tall, elderly, emaciated man with stooped shoulders leaned slightly forward just out of view. His hat was pulled down so low its brim blocked his face from recognition. The man had an Earle Nightingale, uncannily pleasant voice, almost announcer-like in quality.

"Napoleon, I didn't see you back there. You gave me a start. Why are you up dis late?" asked U.

"Just watching over my assets, which, I might add, you are chewing through like a McCormick Reaper."

"Hey. He was rude to me. He offended me."

"I think he had a point."

"We gotta get this done. We're gonna get this done. This is what I do."

"Yes. Yes, I understand. However we're going to have to consider other methods that are a bit less parochial in nature."

"My people have no flexibility on this, you understand."

"Neither do mine. And neither does our boss's new boss, who is about to be anointed."

"It's gonna happen? He's the chosen one for this town?" asked U.

"This town and all towns. The franchise is expanding. It's been over three decades since we've been this close—had an opportunity like this. We're going global."

"Is he that good? Pretty smooth?" asked Mr. U.

"Smooth as cum on a bride's ass."

"Charming?"

"If he tells you to go to hell, you'll look forward to the trip."

U chuckled. "And quite dah salesman I bet."

"He could sell you a white black bird."

FOUR

Menlo Park, California
March 2009

THE BLUE BLACK-HAIRED BEAUTY SCOTTY had been admiring at Jack Daniels Hookah & Fern Bar Dojo was named Ali Woo. Dihm affectionately liked to call her "Ali Ooop." A late twenties clothes-horse tomboy with piano perfect teeth, she was howl-at-the-moon beautiful. Her lineage was the byproduct of an Anglo father and an Asian mother. This gave her the unusual combination of fair skin, a squared jaw, large Asian eyes, lean limbs and a prominent set of pouting breasts. The juxtaposition of the cultures played well off of each other. The features, though different, were not antagonistic. With fawn-like frailty and grace, Ali was lean enough to tread water in a garden hose.

Ali Ooop nimbly and methodically went about the business of lengthening her tendons in preparation for combat. Key admired what a delicate creature she was—delicate, but nail tough. Once limbered, she could take on any opponent twice her size due to her quick, feline-like movements and location-specific striking ability. Her motions were rhythmic, fluid and expressed with an economy of energy. It was if she had studied the physics of each and every strike and deliberately expended only the minimum motion necessary to execute it. This made for crisp, clean, surgically targeted punches.

As the class began practicing their hand strikes, they moved over to a series of vertically upstanding four by fours that had been tapered at the top and wrapped tightly with rope.

Rap, rap. Ratta-tat, rap. Rap. Pop! Ali Ooop quickly chattered out her hand combinations without any facial expression. She rotated her elbow and then her wrist at the very last instant when delivering the knife edge of her hand strike to multiply its subsequent impact. It was all about physics—the timing and perfect rotational release as if uncoiling a bullwhip, rather than attempting to overpower. She peppered the hand conditioning board with a maniacal ferocity one would not expect from such a lithe figure.

"Nice series," said Key. He was gently trying to engage her, as in the past she'd quickly shied away from these overtures, as if a flushed quail.

"Thank you," acknowledged Ali. She smiled faintly and glanced downward, avoiding Key's impish half grin.

"You're Miss Woo?"

"Yes. Ali Woo."

"Can I interest you in a lemonade after your routine?"

"Why, yes," grinned Ali shyly with blindingly white teeth. She wiped her brow with her gi. It was difficult for Key to stop looking at her. Recognizing this tendency midway through the exchange, he broke off his gaze, so as to not be nominated into "stalker" status.

It was unclear how old she might be, not that he cared. Probably late twenties, he guessed. He found her demure mannerisms appealing. Many of the women he'd met recently were narcissistic, money-grubbing trollops who had lost any grounding in comporting themselves as ladies long ago.

Ali's timidity was just about to return when a gruff, growl-like grunt came from the northeast entryway. The new entrant snapped her hair back out of her face, slammed her street shoes in the holding cubby and took the mat.

The newcomer was a somewhat rotund and quite muscular Chinese woman. She normally performed her routines at a neighboring dojo and to Ali's knowledge, had rarely come to Mr. Dihm's dojo to spar.

Thick Body stared menacingly from the sparring room's center mat, where

25

she had just forcefully pushed her way by others as if through a human car wash. This positioned her at the front. She should have taken her rightful place at the end of the queue, however she was making a conscious effort to spar with Ali.

This pairing typically was a random selection based on where one ended up in the two lines on either side of the mat. One line fed in from the north and the other, from the south, by the plastic-beaded curtain and the bonsai trees.

While the newcomer's expression was blank, her eyes were glowing embers resolutely fixated upon Ali. She furrowed her deep, thick brow. Upon pulling her gi up in preparation to spar, she displayed an unusual personalized monogram—ESE—on her left forearm and both calves. Key thought it a strange place to inscribe one's initials but dismissed it.

Coming to the center of the mat to referee, Master Dihm was oblivious to the position-juggling that had just occurred. However, it had not escaped Miss Woo, who was calmly and icily returning the gaze. The two were now the logical next pairing in line to fight. Dihm pointed crisply at each woman, signaling them to commence sparring with each other. The muscular woman stood perfectly still while glaring at her opponent. Both sides slipped into their hand and foot pads without lowering their heads or averting their glare upon the other.

Other than the mitigating measures of the four pads each, the sparring was at top speed and full contact. Points were given for successful strikes above the waist, stomach, underarm and chest. Unless pulled at the last moment, no hard strikes to the face were allowed. Strikes below the waist, to the kidney or groin would result in a foul. No other areas of contact were awarded points.

"You know the rules. Legs and joints are out of bounds," said Dihm.

While kicks were encouraged, an opponent was warned with a foul and ultimately disqualified for kicking or attempting to strike the other's knee from the side of the joint. This could cause a reversal, resulting in a permanently crippling blow. A match was decided by the earlier of two minutes or the first to three points. Dihm brought his hand down so smartly between the two to convene the event his gi made a popping sound. He shouted, "Fight!"

The larger Chinese woman lunged toward Ali, delivering a forward kick and a back-fisted hand strike, followed up quickly with a spinning kick. The initial highly practiced, blurring, three-strike combination was well executed. Ali deflected the first two, but while she blocked down the last away from her face, the kick struck Ali squarely in the chest. The force of this single blow lifted Woo's body from the mat, sent her careening four feet through the air and slammed her against the wall. The back of her head struck the padded wall with a resonant thud.

"Point!" shouted Dihm, motioning toward the Thick One.

Ali eyeballed her challenger more closely—a worthy opponent indeed. She had underestimated the jaguar-like speed of this Tonka truck. She would not slight her competitor's skill again.

Key felt there was some additional background music, but he couldn't put his finger on it. He slid his Blackberry into his pocket and watched now with his full attention. Undaunted by the prior wall smacking, Ali-Oop did a crisp kip up and returned to her feet.

"Fight!" Dihm's gi snapped again as the two came together, circling while looking for an opportunistic sign of weakness.

This time, Ali was the aggressor. Advancing smartly, she drove the bulbous Chinese opponent backward. Cornered, the stockier stranger attempted a leg sweep, missed and then lunged out with a side kick, deliberately targeted toward the side of Ali's left knee. Nimbly raising her outboard leg to avert the blow, Ali concluded her opponent had a different agenda and she was going to have to pull the choke out to defend herself.

"Foul!" cried Dihm as he threw up a yellow cautionary flag. "Again and you're done!" He took the stranger aside and sternly warned her while wagging his finger that another such infraction would disqualify her.

She bowed much too deeply, as if in mock acquiescence to Dihm's request.

"Fight!" The gi popped again as Dihm's hand snapped down.

The cobra and mongoose came back together. While many of the stranger's motions were legal, the ferocity with which they were delivered, veritably exploding from her body, caused others nearby to stop stretching and take notice. The crispness of her attack caused her gi to snap and pop with each strike. A deadly calm came over the balance of the room as onlookers tried to sort out just exactly what they were witnessing.

After missing the first time, the muscular one successfully swept Ali and delivered a hand strike, which, although diverted, splintered the top of an adjoining four-by-four tapered hand-conditioning post. An eleven-year-old girl in the back gasped. Now all eyes were on this event. Other sparring had stopped. The room had become silent, save the muffled back and forth shuffling of the combatants' feet and the occasional shout of the aggressor as she delivered a blow. This was no routine sparring match.

Scotty's hands were on his hips and he was toying with the notion of stopping the match. While he did not want to insult his good friend, Dihm, by intervening, he was confident someone was going to get seriously hurt.

The heavier stranger lunged forward, diverting three crisp combinations of spinning elbows, a back fist and back kick by Ali. Squatty Body then successfully got behind Ms. Woo and was choking her with what appeared to Key to be a cross between Krav Maga and the classic SEAL sleeper hold. He knew it was difficult to extricate oneself from this and Ali would either soon pass out or have her wind pipe crushed. Ali's face flushed, went pale and then flushed again.

Fuck it, he thought. He was going to stop it. He strode toward the mat.

FIVE

JUST THEN, ALI RACED TO the adjacent wall and ran straight up it with the stranger's grip still intact around her throat. At the apex of her wall run, she snapped her head backward smartly against her opponent's face. The motion splattered the Chinese woman's nose and produced precisely one tooth on the mat which promptly covered Pie Face in blood. The move was legal, as it was not a hand or foot strike to the face, but rather an attempt to free herself from a match-ending hold. Head butts, per se, were frowned upon however.

Upon impact, the bulkier contender relaxed her grip and Ali fell to the mat. Woo twisted on the floor and swept the Chinese woman's stubby, thick legs. As the woman fell, Ali attacked with a fusillade of blows. Her contender deflected the first one. But Ali grabbed her opponent's gi with her left hand and air mailed her right elbow crisply across the woman's jaw. A crack reverberated around the room. Ali coiled, cocked and fired a bone-crunching, bladed hand strike to the side of the neck, rabbit punched the back of her neck and followed up by pulling a flat palm strike to the face. The quick, successive "point" blows won Ali the match.

This last hit was reminiscent of the final blinding blow taught in World War II training, where the nose was first broken with one hand and the fragments were then sent up to the optic nerve with the other. At a minimum, it blinded the opponent. At a maximum, it caused death. Inasmuch as the first nose-breaking blow was not delivered and the second was pulled, the nominal effect was less terminal in this case.

Whoompf! The stumpy woman hit the mat completely flat, obviously dazed. For a moment, she was in the seven-point stance—hands, knees and forehead all on the mat. She rose to her knees, shook her head doglike and stumbled to her feet, disoriented.

Dihm intervened. He pointed to Ali and shouted, "Foul." This was for not pulling the shot to her opponent's jaw. He then grabbed Ali's arm and raised it, declaring, "Match!" in recognition of the other three point blows she had delivered successfully.

Ali bowed to the Chinese woman but would not take her eyes off of her opponent. The other didn't return her bow. Rather, she wiped the blood from her mouth onto her right index finger and put the bloody finger into her mouth. She sucked it off while casting a primal, furtive glance out from under her thick brow towards Ali. She then spat on the mat.

"You," Dihm pointed straight at the muscular one solemnly, "you are not welcome back here."

The stout Chinese woman pushed her way past the balance of the class, amidst the onlookers' murmurings. En route, she blew her bloody nose with one finger, spraying blood on the light gray mats and deliberately walked through a cosmetic, paper-screened wall without slowing her pace. She went straight out the front door to the street without a shower. She even left her shoes in the cubby. She did not look back. She did not return. Ever.

Scotty went over to Dihm. "Was she the one you called Ali-Oop?" asked Key.

"Yes."

"I don't think the order is right. The Ali should go at the end."

"Oh?"

"And place 'Muhammad' at the beginning."

"I understand," responded Dihm, bowing with a gentle smile.

Key turned and walked over to Ali. He deadpanned, "So. You two. You're close?"

Ali simply smiled, looked down and shook her head. She wiped the perspiration from her face and felt the back of her head knotting up, smarting from the encounter with the wall. An egg sized hematoma was growing there.

"She's a pig."

"I had a feeling this was more than just a simple don't-go-out-with-my-guy, sorority sister thing," quipped Scotty. "I saw her initials on her forearm and calves. What's her name?"

"I don't know. She comes in here rarely," whispered Ali, as she rubbed her right big toe, which had jammed when she'd run up the wall.

"Oh?"

"She's from a neighboring dojo, across town. She believes her blood to be most pure—from royalty. She likes to come over now and then and strut."

"So. It's all about bloodlines? Similar to white supremacist Aryan skinheads?"

"Exactly. The only thing she holds sacred is her ancestor's point of view, which she is in the process of disgracing. She's stuck in the 1500s."

"And she's upset with you because?" asked Key. He turned and signaled a thumbs-up to Dihm to bring an ice pack over for the back of her head.

"Uncertain. I believe it's because I'm from a mixed marriage. My mother was Asian and my father was Caucasian. They feel I have disgraced my race and do not deserve to live."

"That's it? Just like that?"

"Just like that." She glinted a smile as she winced from pain.

"So there's no feud per se, other than your having the audacity of rolling down the birthing canal?"

Ali looked up at him with the largest of eyes, without raising her head.

"I'm sorry," Scotty said. "I could have phrased that better."

"No. Actually, you're right," she said, flashing those teeth again. "Those are the extent of my crimes."

"Still up for some lemonade?"

"Could we add some Jack and a lot more ice?" she asked, rubbing her head.

"I believe we have that technology," grinned Key.

The two of them saddled up to the bar, ice bag and all and listened to precisely how and what Master Dihm would have done in that same confrontation—blow by blow. Key would glance over at Ali, who'd occasionally roll her eyes.

As Ali sipped her poor-man's whiskey sour, she looked at him pensively over the top of her drink. Inwardly she was thinking, if this goes anywhere— *when do I tell him? How do I tell him?*

Six

IN THE DEEP CARPET SECTION of Key's office, the next morning's schedule came with a full complement of presenters. They were attempting to curry favor and kiss up to PacRim Venture's senior-most partners in hopes of separating them from their buckets of cash. The players knew this was de rigueur and while it was a frenetic pace, they had become accustomed to it. Late in the afternoon the firm was introduced to a young Berkley graduate student in his late twenties.

"Gentlemen, welcome, please, Mr. Milo Butterfield." This introduction was made by PacRim Venture's Managing Partner, Stanley Wentworth.

Wentworth was a small, unassuming figure. It was difficult to guess his age. He was somewhat rotund, always overdressed and prone to profuse periods of sweating. Sartorially resplendent he was draped in an all black wool garment. He had slicked-back, oily, thinning, blue-black dyed hair and he wheezed when he spoke. Infected black ingrown hairs on large moles upon his face made one never want to get too close. These tended to offer up a malevolent hue when he rubbed his face with both hands, which he was prone to do.

On balance, he was quite reminiscent of a high sheen, large oily beetle, draped in an Armani suit. Adorned with thick, yet exceedingly small diameter, black, horned rim glasses that rested prominently on the end of his nose,

Wentworth had the habit of licking his lips after most statements. You could almost visualize two large beetle-esque pincers preening small mites and saliva away from his mouth to make way for a cleaner next bite.

It wasn't Wentworth's nerves. It was almost as if this was his way to ever more punctuate the profound thought that had just left his mouth. This allowed a moment of dramatic pause for the words to either drip off or soak in, depending on the listener's inclination.

Wentworth went on with his introduction. Still standing, he placed all ten fingers straight on the conference table, shifted his weight and leaned forward for emphasis. "Mr. Butterfield has been good enough to share a concept with us today. That notion, succinctly stated, is a much tidier method of mining. In fact, the method is so tidy it employs the use of a small, surgically focused nuclear device. But of course, I do not want to steal any more of his thunder, so please, Mr. Butterfield, share your thoughts."

Butterfield rose to his feet and moved to the white board tentatively. Milo Butterfield appeared to be a holdover from the sixties. Not only were his clothes "period" appropriate, but perhaps even some soil from that era had affectionately remained attached to his garments as well. He was exceedingly lean, a scrawny individual reminiscent of Ichabod Crane, with extraordinarily cobalt blue, piercing eyes. Strong in hue, yet cold, they weren't necessarily attractive, they were simply intense and penetrating. Key mused his father used to have camping cookware of that shade, only with white and black flecks.

The young presenter had a raspy voice, which encouraged him to communicate with an economy of speech, although in fact he rarely did so. It would also frequently spike to a screech-like tone as he became more nervous. Then again, he was always nervous. His delivery, while reeking with sincerity, was halting, as if every tenth neuron's synapse didn't quite fire or he was constantly reflecting on something far more interesting. He also possessed right-knee-gyration syndrome. Seemingly impossible to arrest its motion when seated, the knee vibrated up and down at the same frequency as a squirrel's hind leg scratching away mites from its ear.

A Rhodes Scholar, yet still very anxious, he was not comfortable presenting. He picked up a blue dry erase marker and dropped it, then picked up another black marker and dropped it promptly as well. Leaning over to pick them both up, he returned to the erect position with just a hint of color in his ghostly pale complexion.

Jesus, thought Pig. *This is going to be painful.*

"Thank you, Mr. Wentworth. I appreciate your ... introduction. Actually, you did an excellent job of encapsulating what I am about today. I've come across, in theory, what could be an astonishing way to revolutionize mining for the next century. It involves a small nuclear device, which is both a concept strength and weakness. My purpose today is to share the idea with you at a high level in an attempt to impart some of my enthusiasm. Quite frankly, public funding at the university level has all but dried up with the recent budget cutbacks in California due to the faltering economy." He hesitated.

"Go on," said Beetleman.

"As a result, the university and I have been exploring potential joint ventures with the private sector. My objective, if successful in my bid for your involvement, would be for you to agree to extend a joint, private grant of three million dollars to the University of Cal Berkeley and me for the express purpose of making a prototype of the device ... with the intention of a sharing in international intellectual property patents and profits thereafter."

"We're listening," said Beetleman.

Scotty was actively listening, although he glanced at his watch, recalling he'd admonished Butterfield to get it done inside of forty minutes so as to allow twenty minutes for questions.

"Without taking this initial discussion to three significant digits, the notion is one of a small, controlled nuclear device that makes rapidly sequential repetitive explosions and contractions as it burrows through the earth."

In so saying, Butterfield brandished a large poster-sized engineering drawing with accompanying calculations, which was entitled *Throughput*.

"These explosions are, alternately, expansive then constrictive. This is the first time we have the unique blending of these actions in disciplined, quick succession. Although seemingly defying physics, it's accomplished by having a small nuclear device at the leading edge of the canister that employs fission. As you're aware, this technology of f particles is what created the original thermonuclear explosions at Hiroshima and Nagasaki. This was the first generation of nuclear devices."

Pig yawned while scanning the room for an errant cookie or fruit cup that had not been previously consumed during a prior meeting.

"At the rear of the tube, detailed in the engineering drawings to be about four feet in length, is another nuclear device. This end employs explosions that are used for burrowing, or mining, as the canister chews forward."

"Mr. Butterfield?" inquired Beetleman as he pushed his black spectacles further up his nose with his left forefinger while flipping through the back pages of the previously passed out pro forma with his right.

"Yes, sir."

"As we shared with you in advance, a key part of our process is to devil's advocate and second-guess your concept, budget and feasibility every step of the way, to safeguard our investor's capital."

"I recall that admonishment."

"To that end, with your permission, I will be encouraging my staff to ask questions and gently challenge along the way."

"You have my permission, enthusiasm and encouragement to do so. Good, constructive push back demonstrates interest!" said Butterfield.

"Mr. Butterfield." Key had raised but his right forefinger. "While I realize at the onset you mentioned you were not going to take this discussion to—in your words, 'three significant digits'—would you be so good as to expand on the additional technology required to keep this genie in the bottle?"

"I'd be glad to." Butterfield walked forward to throw over the next two pages of his flip chart.

Regrettably, in the same motion, Butterfield's left foot hooked a stray extension cord. What proceeded next could not have been choreographed better by Chaplin himself. The initial trip put Milo into a slo-mo, Karo-syrupy free fall. His gaunt pterodactyl-esque limbs pinwheeled in a wild, staccato, herky-jerky fashion. He flailed through space in an awkward effort to regain balance, decorum and some degree of composure. The effect was not unlike that of the Scarecrow in Oz being electrocuted while learning to ice skate. His right arm hit the computer in the middle of the conference table and drug it eight inches, making the dreaded fingernails-on-chalkboard screech while gouging the richly inlaid wood one-thirty-second of an inch.

The travesty continued, as Milo's spinning left arm, in an effort to counter his fall, drove wildly to the left, striking a prominently displayed, richly framed watercolor of Yosemite's El Capitan. This sent the painting and the brass presentation light mounted above it crashing to the floor.

The room was a morgue. Butterfield's face flushed then drained, flushed and then went pale again. His jaw muscles tightened, relaxed and then tightened again in humiliation.

SEVEN

"HOLY SHIT," EXCLAIMED PIG, CLEARLY straining to hold back a belly laugh. Cornelius fidgeted to the right and left in his chair while looking up and down the table as if to say, *Is anyone else seeing this?* The two word exclamation came out mumbled, as his mouth was three-quarters full of two stale macadamia nut cookies scrounged from a pile of leftovers in the kitchen. The pile had "basura" scrawled all over it.

"It happens," said Key dryly, trying to restore order and exhibit some compassion.

"Perhaps this would be a good time for a break," said Wentworth, while rubbing his face with both hands. "Ten minutes. Tops."

Butterfield turned his piercing porcelain blue eyes to Pig and said nothing. He walked out the door to the rest room and splashed cold water on his face to compose himself. Entering the bathroom stall, he vomited, toweled off and washed his face and hands again.

Precisely ten minutes later, the room reassembled .

"I believe, Mr. Butterfield, you were going to field Mr. Key's question with regard to controlling these repetitive explosions," led off Wentworth, as he snapped his suit coat jacket downward with both hands somewhat perfunctorily.

"Thank you. Yes." Milo's knee vibrations were at warp speed. "As an aside, you can see my experience as a presenter is sorely lacking. It is my sincere hope this in no way erodes your confidence in the topic at hand. I have a great deal more knowledge and experience on the topic than in my ability to hawk it. I want to assure you that, while we currently have no working prototype, the device will work."

"No one's on trial here. We need to scrutinize in detail the ideas you put forth to us prior to endorsing and proffering them further up the food chain. It's all good. Pray continue," said Key with a compassionate tone.

"Thank you for those kind remarks, Mr. Key. Continuing. The question on the floor is: How do we keep the genie in the bottle? I assume that refers to keeping the device limited to a planned, tight burrowing pattern, with a disciplined series of explosions and implosions, if you will, rather than an all-out, uncontained nuclear explosion."

"Bingo."

"An excellent question, which deserves an equally thoughtful response. It truly gets at the heart of the matter. The technology is so very contemporary that I've trusted it to no one. There are no files, no hard drive. In fact, I keep it with me at all times."

Butterfield opened his mouth wider than a Missouri mule and, pointing deep into the cavity, proudly displayed his rearmost left molar. "I've imprinted the formulas, their derivations, algorithms and source codes all on a single flash memory chip and sealed it under this tooth. They say you can't take it with you. Well, I can." Butterfield laughed nervously out loud—a shrieking, goofy, over-the-top laugh. His knee continued fluttering as fast as a hummingbird's wing, striking the underside of the table every tenth flap.

Pig leaned forward and looked down the conference table at Key again. He raised his right eyebrow three-eighths of an inch. Cornelius then cocked his head forty-five degrees clockwise and held it—as the RCA Victor dog logo. He leaned back and said nothing. Pig then bent back even further in his chair, interlaced his fingers behind his head and redirected his attention toward a golden finch, which was busily constructing a nest outside of the western window. He was thinking about taking a shit.

Butterfield continued. "There are four governing mechanisms that keep the nuclear eruptions at a manageable level. First, there is the yen and the yang of a fission detonation being promptly followed up and complemented, or mitigated, if you will, by a fusion detonation. While it's not in fact an implosion, or vacuum-creating technique, it does materially strip off a goodly portion of the radically excited protons and neutrons. This, in turn, keeps them from becoming agitated to an out-of-control chain reaction. Are you familiar with how a fire can be extinguished through suffocation with an adjacent explosion? The concept is a loose analogy. The second controlling element is a hardened micro-laser at the midpoint of the device, which acts like a traffic cop or the timing light used to tune older cars. It directs the sequencing and priority of explosions."

Pig was fidgeting into hyperdrive. His eyes were darting from the finch to the restroom to his watch. Finch. Restroom. Watch. He spoke up. "Not unlike a cheese slicer, cutting one to the next?" Pig smiled impishly to himself, as he realized he had finally just legitimately used the phrase "cut the cheese" in a business meeting.

Wentworth gave him a glare of disapproval, looking to rebuke him for the crack and in hopes of tamping down another.

"Precisely. One that cuts cheddar, then Swiss back again, all in less than a third of a nanosecond."

"Leave it to Brandon to think of a food comparable," mused Wentworth as he fussed with and refolded his silk square. Beetleman licked his lips thoughtfully, pulling at his blood red suspenders. He pulled them out, relaxed them and pulled them out again.

Scotty reached over, sipped his steaming hot coffee from a PacRim Ventures logoed cup and continued listening.

"The third controlling element is akin to a fuel injector, or an anti-fuel injector. This component is installed to mitigate, moderate and control the eruptions so they remain manageable – manageable, in a cylinder, as is the case in an automobile."

"Well you are surely not using water to squelch that puppy," Pig said.

"Most correct you are, sir. Do you recall how nuclear reactors were controlled by the insertion of cadmium rods? Depending on how many, how frequent the spacing, how deep those rods penetrated, the reactor controlled the rate of the chain reaction, or explosion. Our anti-fuel injectors are, in fact, spritzing liquid cadmium to control the rate of this explosion."

"Hmmm," Beetleman grunted. He wasn't doubting. He was just grunting and rubbing his face with both hands again.

"Fourth, the last control agent is the canister itself," said Milo as he slapped his pointer with uncharacteristic vigor against the graphic in an attempt to steady his nerves. "It is made out of a nine-inch thick zircon oxide-ceramic and titanium composite, which is a derivative harder than that used in the nose cone of the last space shuttle. This, additionally, is interlaced with micro-fine strands of cadmium to not only make it forty times stronger than diamond, but to allow it to serve as a stabilizing agent as well."

"Thank you. You've answered my question," said Key.

Butterfield continued. "We hold the view that this burrowing device will go through the Earth's crust like a hot knife through butter—hence, the name 'Throughput.' As you can imagine, it would be extraordinarily cost effective in contrast to the equipment-intensive environment today. Mining industry machines can be twenty stories tall and weigh four thousand tons each."

"Very impressive," said Key. "As these things go, the notion is intriguing. Please speak a minute to risk. What is not yet solved? What shouldn't but could go wrong?"

"We want to know about the snakes and lizards. How many and where they are buried?" added Pig, leaning forward over the conference table in a pose reminiscent of a bull dog.

"Currently there are but two issues left unsettled. They revolve around getting it started and then shutting it off with some degree of dignity."

The words had barely left Butterfield's mouth when Pig pounced. "Did I hear you correctly? The singular problem is starting and stopping it?!"

"Hear him out," clipped Key.

Butterfield was clearly becoming more nervous, as he was starting to squeak. "With regard to the first blast, it is important that the canister's heat not exceed twenty-seven hundred degrees centigrade, or it could experience hairline cracks and a follow-on meltdown. After it gets going, it is self-cooling, as it tends to propel itself away from its own markedly high heat refuse. It would veritably take an ocean of water to cool the device down from the initial blast temperatures, however. We've looked at surrounding it with liquid hydrogen, yet the hydrogen appears to make it too unstable. We do, however, feel this is a solvable problem.

'Lastly, we have not yet devised a method to shut the reaction down with confidence each and every time."

"What does *that* mean?" Wentworth asked. "Does it mean we have to endure a one hundred megaton blast during the Beta?"

"No. That's the beauty of the canister. It will allow a cocktail-sized explosion to be surgically focused and contained. We're in the 0.25 to 0.4 megaton range. While this is, in fact, two hundred fifty to four hundred thousand pounds of dynamite, true, it could be controlled with industrial blast curtains and a thermal nuclear blanketing device to suffocate fallout and keep it deep in the earth.

"Won't that approach then contaminate the soil so it could not be mined thereafter?" asked Key.

"To be certain, there are contamination and remediation aspects to be dealt with. These will be mitigated due to the small size of the charges. Nevertheless, the site should not be mined for at least six months thereafter or until the radiation level subsides to an acceptable Roentgen reading. In conclusion, this process should revolutionize mining for fifty years."

Cornelius Brandon III, esquire, then in painstaking Stanford detail, explored the initial capital outlays, cash advances required, the project's performance milestones, overall budgets, pro formas and EBITDA (earnings before interest, taxes, depreciation and amortization) his investors could expect. It was also determined that a working model was approximately one year away from production.

Another hour passed, whereupon Wentworth suggested the meeting be adjourned while PacRim Ventures huddled and floated a trial balloon to their investors. They wanted to determine if there was an appetite for a future discussion on any basis before they invested any more time. The meeting concluded shortly thereafter, with Mr. Butterfield making his exit.

Pig, Wentworth and Scotty remained.

"Well. What do you chaps think?" inquired Wentworth, licking his lips thoroughly, as if to clean away a few more mites. He ran both hands backward through his dyed black, oily hair, exposing a ruby centered university ring that could have doubled as a door stop.

"If he can produce just one-third of what he claims, then he's got a home run. What do you think, Brandon?" asked Key.

"I think he's more full of shit than a Christmas goose," said Pig. "If just one-third of what he claims doesn't work, then he's got a *run home*!"

Wentworth lowered his glasses with disdain and turned to Key. "Scotty?"

"What's this? Overhead smash my back court? Goading me on to return 'Dr. No's' volley? Pass." Key straightened up in his chair and spoke in measured, metered tones. "I believe we're losing sight of why we're here. We are not holding ourselves out as some weighty caldron of pedantic knowledge, whose purpose is to instantly decide on the scientific merits of a presentation claim at first blush. Rather, we are businessmen. We make deals. We take risks. We package. We present the opportunity, fairly and objectively. In exchange for those risks, we make a great deal of money when we are very, very right and we try to mitigate loss and protect our investor's downside when we are very, very wrong. End of line."

"Scotty is correct," said Wentworth solemnly.

"You're right," said Pig. "God I hope I can be that self-righteous when I get to be grown up. I particularly liked the part about 'the caldron of pedantic knowledge.' That made my dick hard."

"Hey, at least I didn't say quodlibetic," deadpanned Scotty.

"I'd been all right with that. Yeah, my Maserati has one of those in chrome. Yeah. I'm pretty sure it does."

Wentworth pushed his large black glasses back from the end of his nose, stood up as if popped from a toaster and said disgustedly, "Good night, gentlemen!" He strode out of the room, snapping his coat downward again smartly to formalize the meeting's conclusion.

EIGHT

Menlo Park, California
April 2010

OVER A YEAR HAD PASSED since Butterfield had pitched PacRim Ventures. Key had just gone for a long run and was at his breakfast table during the morning cool of the Bay's marine layer. Still sweating, he was preparing his orange juice, fruit, English muffin and burnt bacon, as he did most mornings. Burning himself on the toaster, he uttered a brief obscenity. Grabbing a large BBQ fork, he feigned a fencing riposte to extract the maximum revenge against the overly aggressive appliance.

Scotty was half-listening to an editorial radio broadcast announcing the new administration had increased the budget deficit over sixfold, from just over $200 billion when they took over to $1.4 trillion currently and there were questions mounting as to how it would ever be paid off.

A dollar borrowed is a dollar earned, he thought as he shook his head in amazement at the direction the country was headed. Then, an urgent bulletin interrupted the normal broadcasting to report a small localized earthquake in Mexico City. He stopped chewing his breakfast long enough to better hear the tail end of the report.

"While a relatively few number of deaths, it appears the president of

Mexico and some of his staff were among the ones killed." the announcer reported.

Curious, Key thought as he walked to the restroom to lather up in the shower.

Key was distracted by a Satan's fetus, aka a potato bug of epic proportions. *Ugly mother*, thought Scotty. With his sandal in hand, he leaned over and reduced the bug from three dimensions to two, refocused and turned the hot water on.

Scotty hadn't given the report a great deal more thought until he arrived at his office. Over coffee, Wentworth remarked, "Curious Mexico quake wasn't it?"

"Yes. Yes indeed," said Scotty. "Odd thing was the fissure resembled a single cavity with lines extending in each direction, rather than a uniform crevasse or crack—most peculiar."

"Odd thing to notice, Francis. More importantly, where in the hell are we on Raptor?" Beetleman was asking about an important code-named account, which was heating up.

"All good, chief. All good."

"Quit shining my apple and get that thing done will you?" Wentworth wiped the beads of perspiration from his oily nose and cleaned his Polo glasses with the same cloth. He was nattily attired, yet sweating nonetheless, as he did every day. "Sketchy details. Fewer than two dozen individuals killed," he added.

"Yup. Odd they were all only in the immediate area of the Mexican president."

Today was the drop-dead date Scotty needed to have his report completed on a new supply chain venture. He booted his computer and was mousing around through the pro forma's pivot tables when he heard the constant chirping reminder of his database calendar. It was doing that inexorable, never-ending background beeping, which only total grid failure, a five megaton, low frequency magnetic impulse, or a targeted brush of his forefinger could ever abate.

He minimized the current application and maximized the background program, which was impatiently awaiting his attention. Ah yes, it was reminding him to take his scuba regulator in for a checkout. While Key truly loved diving, it had been a couple of years since he had gone down.

He knew his regulator and gauges would need to be recalibrated, inspected for salt water corrosion and have their O-rings replaced. Desirous he was that every breath he'd draw would be of compressed air, as opposed to a choking slurry of air and salt water, which could be the byproduct of farting this maintenance off. He headed towards the door and shouted to the receptionist, "Tell Wentworth I'm off."

"To where?"

"Make up someplace that sounds important."

"Doing what?"

"Some of that high-powered executive stuff."

The buxomly receptionist giggled and dismissed him with a hand wave, wagging her finger at him with the other hand as he walked out.

Getting into his car, he reflected upon his fascination with the ocean. The water had strong curative powers for him. He'd battled sinus problems, which the salt water had remediated in the past. It aided in his snorting out all mucus, clearing the sinus cavities and enhancing his respiratory system. Extruding a veritable nasal placenta, he felt like he could then rightly breathe—so well in fact, it was if he was breathing through his nose, sinuses and ears, all at the same time.

He loved the water. He also respected it. Possessing a weight of 62.4 pounds per cubic foot, water weighed over 40 percent the weight of concrete. When this mass was put in motion, the strength and momentum was enormous. He knew many underestimated it. It could buoy you up and gently place you on top of the next rock shelf, or indiscriminately and with impunity, slam you face down while body surfing and snap your backbone like a twig. It just depended on Neptune's temperament, the phase of the moon and your personal juju on that day.

The sounds of the waves lapping, rising and falling were therapeutic for

Key's nerves. Almost hypnotic, "downstairs," or underwater, was literally a different world. While Key had stayed away from drugs, he envisioned the electric blues and luminescent yellows witnessed below had to be akin to some seventies form of LSD "tripping," without that pesky aftereffect.

Scotty liked the absolute quiet this environ afforded, save and except for the gurgling sound of his own breath with the occasional tank ping. The ping reminded him that every thirty-three feet he descended, he was subjecting himself to yet another "atmosphere" of 14.7 pounds per square inch of pressure. He didn't feel squat, however—no difference.

He downshifted and roared around the corner, en route to the dive shop. He mused, perhaps the greatest joy in diving in clear waters with visibility from one hundred to one hundred seventy-five feet was the total control in all three dimensions. Man could effectively achieve conditions of independent flight while underwater. Albeit all was dependent on his thirty minutes of air—depending on the depth. He loved to float out over a hundred fathom shelf and suspend spread eagle, roll a couple of somersaults and hang completely upside down while examining the cracks and crevices. These were the magical locations where many of the sea's most precious bounty hid.

They could be as small as a barber pole shrimp or as colorful as a bright red sponge, which appeared totally black until an intense underwater beam of light hit it. Sometimes the menacing-looking, yet reticent moray eel appeared. The moray, unprovoked, could glide fluid-like over your outstretched wand or, if cornered, could remove two fingers with no more effort then clipping a couple of French fries.

Scotty, while relatively fearless, always felt a strong dose of respect was needed for these creatures. He recalled a Puerto Rican's story of a large municipal aquarium in Florida. The aquarium had an abundant supply of sharks, nothing too terribly aggressive. Their prize animal was a large aging nurse shark, which was twelve feet in length and about thirty-four inches in diameter.

Nurse sharks were known to be some of the most docile of their species. To the crowd's delight, on the other side of the Plexiglas, the trainer had a daily ritual of swimming to the bottom and pulling the nurse shark out from under her rock by the tail. This sandy "sleeping bag" was where she had been resting quite serenely, wanting to be unmolested, wanting to be left alone.

To the crowd's continued glee, the trainer would, in mawkish drama, violently thrash the poor shark back and forth while tugging on her tail. This would throw the shark's head twenty inches up and to the right and then down and to the left to counteract the explosively unnatural and unwelcomed physics taking place to her southern extremity.

This "shark-wrangling" had the elderly viewers' mouths gaping and the young children jumping up and down, screaming and pointing for their parents to see. Some with glee, some with abject horror. They were all clamoring for yet one more assault on the nurse's nerves. At the conclusion of this seemingly amazing feat of courage, the diver would throw the nurse an eighteen-inch Yellowfin, swim to the edge of the tank and make a large bow to his audience. Then he'd swim even closer to the glass, remove his regulator from his mouth and smile a triumphant ringmaster smile of bravado, while waving once more to the clapping crowd as he took his bows.

On one spring day when the aquarium was packed, the trainer commenced his routine as usual, just as he had done hundreds of times before. As customary, at the end of his abuse, he glided a yellowfin over to his aqueous puppet as reward. On this singular day, however, the smaller fish hung suspended, unattended and alone. The entire crowd, as usual, was screaming in glee, laughing and pointing at the feeder's shenanigans.

Then, with no fanfare or advance warning, the nurse calmly turned a pirouette—a perfect one hundred eighty degrees—and ever so gently bit the trainer's head off cleanly at his C5 vertebra. The bleeding, severed head and smaller yellowfin lay side by side in the tank. Suspended. Motionless. Each employing a Karo syrup-esque, eerily morbid, slo-mo race to the bottom of the tank.

They descended serenely, side by side. The nurse, with a degree of boorish, pedestrian indifference as to what had just occurred, glided back under her rock, quite probably to belch. Key's Puerto Rican friend had summed it up nicely: "Just remember, when you are down there, you are a guest in their home."

Key recalled his first awareness of how vulnerable he was in that environment. If one carried himself arrogantly or aggressively, then the sea was a great equalizer.

Before trading in his speargun for a camera in his youth, he'd dispatch a parrotfish here, a boxfish there. He remembered how angry this made his father. His dad enjoyed hunting many things. Killing was okay, as long as you ate your kill. He was strongly against wanton waste or killing just for the sake of killing. Not hypocritical, he admitted freely he enjoyed the sport, but felt it wrong not to eat your kill.

Scotty reflected on one sultry afternoon when he had been developing his skills with his double-banded speargun. He'd become quite proficient at dispatching his target. He recalled the thirty-two-inch barracuda that would "hang dog" him in his blind spot as he went about carrying out his business of death.

Normally in groups of at least three, barracudas would hang just out of sight, off his backside, awaiting the flight of the spear's conclusion. They'd anxiously anticipate a small morsel of fish being left over. And, if the diver wasn't careful or flashed a shiny watch in a glinty aluminum flash, it would quickly reverse the hunter-hunted roles.

As a young man with limited patience, this began to annoy Key. He set about the task of eliminating the aluminum nuisance. One less silver shadow would be all. No big deal. He remembered turning and eyeing the menacing, forward-jutting jaw, where inside lay scores of razor-sharp teeth. The teeth didn't have any attitude about them. They were simply doing their job. It was instinctual. After all, they couldn't change ten thousand years of genetic programming.

His victim had a depth of eight inches and should have been an easy kill. It was about thirty-six inches long and within four feet of his gun—no problemo, well within range. He had taken much smaller fish from further away many times before.

He aimed and fired. The next image his mind has seared in his memory forever—he saw his speargun line stretched out horizontally taut, to its maximum, laying suspended out in front of him and nothing else. The barracudas had literally disappeared. Although he physically had not seen them swim away, they were there one minute and then, poof, gone. It was as if one had leaned over to the other and said, "Hey, Larry, see the fool with the gun? Let's have lunch, dust, vacuum and get out of here."

He'd learned those animals, the "aluminum ghosts," had a completely different sense of time and space. From that time forward, Key was no longer concerned about barracudas. In fact, he became more relaxed around them. He knew that, if they wanted him or body parts thereof, he was flat there for the taking. No amount of juking or posturing would forestall the inevitable.

He'd be lunch.

He dropped the regulator off, quickly leapt into his car over the closed-door-top-down opening and returned to the office.

Pig burst into his office, leveling the large walnut door with a single forearm shiver, which rattled all pictures on the adjoining two walls.

"So. Hey, Aquaman, when is splashdown?"

"Ten days from Monday."

"How long are you on reprieve?"

"A nine dayer—a week with two ears."

"Where you headed?"

"Thought I'd do Cozumel."

"Say. Listen here now. You don't have to go that far to hear Spanish. Just come over to my place while it's being cleaned. Comprende?"

"I'm looking forward to this—the going and the leaving," said Scotty, smirking while scratching his nose with just his middle finger.

Key's mind wandered back to the breakfast radio bulletin surrounding the freakishly localized earthquake and the death of the Mexican president.

NINE

Pig glanced at Key. "Whatcha say we put our pencils and rulers away real neat like, sneak out the back so the nuns don't catch us and get shit-faced?"

"I accept—with conditions. Could the location be something different than the crusty Petri dish you normally frequent?" Key was recalling the last restaurant Pig suggested where they both ended up with food poisoning.

"For instance?"

"Well, say a stadium for instance."

"A Giant's game? Aces! I'm in."

"Close. An A's game." Scotty was not a fan of the Giants.

"But that's across the water."

"I know. There are however other, more civilized, alternatives to simply swimming. Put the big-boy pants on and let's cross the bridge."

"The Giants."

"Athletics."

"Giants."

"A's."

"Giants. And I'll drive," traded Pig.

"A's. I'll drive."

"It's raining."

"Pussy. I'll drive—and pay," countered Key.

"You sweet-talker. I could become a closet A's fan," smirked Pig.

Key glanced at his watch. It was 5:20 pm and he hadn't eaten since his breakfast meeting. Only now was the pace winding down enough for him to listen to his stomach growling. He begin placing everything neatly away at his desk. Turning "piles into files." He was a bit compulsive with regard to organization and tidiness.

Neat and tidy. Neat and tidy. These words rung in his ears from his youth. His father had possessed the same proclivity for fastidiousness, which he had ridiculed at the time and ten years later was now emulating. Key finished the reorganization of his desk. He looked at the expanse of gleaming mahogany where, once before, Everest-esque piles of paper had resided, where transactional chaos previously had reigned.

"Wood," muttered Key. "That's what you look like." It was a great sense of relief to see again the clear, open expanse of hand-rubbed hardwood rising up from the battlefield of contractual phraseology and phone notes. His traps were starting to relax and fall away from his earlobes.

Key grabbed his putty-colored London Fog raincoat and bounded for the door. He was a man possessed with milking sixty-one seconds out of every minute. At full stride, he was quite nimble and quick. Others had threatened to install those convex shoplifting mirrors customarily found in 7/Elevens to see him coming around corners. More than once, he had hit his unsuspecting prey headlong at full stride in a blind intersection. They would be left looking up at the ceiling, their clothing decoupaged with their own coffee, while hearing Scotty's mumbling voice trailing off à la Doppler effect in the distance, "Sorry."

Key raced down the back hall toward the exit, attempting to beat Pig to his car. With the alacrity of an octopus in the decathlon, he slipped his rain coat from the coat tree into the crook of his right arm, swiped his ID card and armed the alarm—all in a single, fluid motion.

Making his way toward the door, Key remembered his hat. While not a hard-core hat man, Key felt it did make him look rather rakish. Key's spring-loaded "derby popper" was considered great sport in the office. To work, it required a basket from a five-inch, soft, yellow, rubber basketball—all air, no rim. When perfectly executed, it would send a large counterbalance down with a resounding *whumpf!* resulting in one's hat catapulting four feet in the air.

It was considered "average" to be able to make the shot and catch the hat. After all, there had been countless hours of practice around the Black Mountain Spring water cooler. An "above average" mark was awarded to those who could make the shot, duck and catch the hat atop their head in a single motion. Bonus points were given to participants for any additional creative stylings added.

In this event, Scotty had scored high in the office Olympics. Donning the hat while executing a moonwalk delivery with inline skates had earned him serious bonus points the prior year. Regrettably, skates had subsequently been disallowed and he'd been stripped of his title due to some incessant board room whining regarding the scarring of Italian foyer marble.

Rubbish. What drivel. If God didn't want inline skates in the front lobby, he wouldn't have etched in such wonderfully tempting inlaid slalom patterns. It was as though Picasso had painted a bejeweled, glistening paisley, humping the world's largest garden slug, all in a vat of Vaseline. It simply had to be skated.

Scotty took on a new persona outside the office. He stiff-armed the revolving door without breaking stride, with the vengeance of a Heisman candidate. Outside, the steps glistened with one of those misty-moisty California drizzles, which on one side of the Bay was considered fog and on the other was considered rain.

Key and Pig folded their bodies into Scotty's restored British Racing Green MGB GT, whose top was down and Key jettisoned them out of the parking lot. His exhaust barked out the throaty tones emblematic of that model. In the street, traffic was moving at a wake-like pace. Key had many attributes. Patience was not among them. He kept muttering to himself and alternately squeezing the steering wheel—first with his right hand, then with his left.

This kneading motion gave him the false sense of doing something when there was nothing that could be accomplished at this moribund pace. This continued for but two or three minutes, however, it seemed like an eternity. After a moment, he gently leaned forward, whereupon the mini rivulets that had gathered unnoticed on top of his tan Filson, waxed duck rain hat, surged forward. After a twenty-seven-inch free fall, the cool rainwater coalesced once again. This time in his crotch.

"Perfect," muttered Key.

While his slacks were dark, fortunately enough, they still enveloped his groin and leather seat with that coolish, squishy feeling, which was not welcome nor easily shaken.

"Shit," muttered Key.

"Problem?" teased Pig, even though he saw exactly what the situation was and was taking keen delight in being there to witness it.

"Nope. Benjamin Franklin said it's okay to talk to yourself, as you'll always have a brilliant speaker and an attentive audience," said Key.

Pig snorted.

Key downshifted in disgust and squirted through a back ally. By adding a mere five turns, he could save almost thirty-seven seconds if all turns were performed on no more than two wheels. The trade was more than fair, considering the potential rewards.

They crossed the San Mateo Bridge and breathed the salt-laced air. They could see the outcroppings of the Transamerica Building in the distance, as well as Coit Tower. Scotty left the top down as it had started to clear up. Although it felt good to be alive, he noticed a large, dark cloud hanging atop Mt. Diablo in the distance.

The odd thing was that it was a solitary dark cloud and the balance of the sky was clear. Scotty wondered if it was a foreshadowing. Key knew Mt. Diablo meant "Devil Mountain." He had trekked to the top with his parents and read the story about the Spanish explorers who, upon conquering its apex, saw the devil from the top of the mountain.

TEN

Oakland, California
April 2010

AT THE OAKLAND COLISEUM, AN ocean of aromas and sounds greeted the pair. The smells in Scotty's nostrils returned warm memories of relaxed Sunday afternoons with the old man at the ballgame. Those were good times. Nothing was complicated then. The Coliseum was sunny, always sunny. He could count the rain-out days on three fingers. Back in the day, you could smell the dogs, the grass and hear the constant hawking of the concessionaires. "Frosty malt! Malts here!" yelled the young black man who was gangly, tall and thin, with a prominent protruding gold tooth.

"Doggy-doggy-doggy-doggy—*dawg*-EEEEEZE!" shrilled an overweight red-headed Irishman, who snapped Scotty back to present day. The man carried his concession wares on a roll of protruding intestinal flesh. This approach pulled up the back of his red and white striped shirt to expose three-quarters of an inch of ass crack.

Then there was the omnipresent peanut vendor, who could throw the goods fifteen seats across and three rows up. Occasionally, he'd throw with a good deal of panache, flipping the nuts from behind his back and forward as he bowed to the patron. He could flat deliver the mail.

One should not forget the fabled "banjo man." Uncertain origin and festooned with propellered beanie, Kelly green and gold cape, beard and banjo, he was as much a part of the Coliseum as was Scotty's hero back in the day—Tony La Russa. La Russa was the ice man, totally unflappable—the King of Cool. This guy made Buckingham Palace Guards look maniacal by comparison. Scotty truly admired La Russa's self-control, he felt that ability was an excellent measure of a man. All coach's after Tony left paled in comparison, as had the A's record.

Scotty liked that the Coliseum regularly employed the physically or mentally challenged in vending positions. Bravo. Another thing that amazed Key was a crowd this size moving with a reasonable amount of grace and decorum. There were occasional unrulies to be certain, but en masse, everyone was there for a good time and not to unload too much garbage on his fellow man. The Mediterranean climate provided an unparalleled clime for baseball's Mecca. No wonder the San Ramon Valley consistently produced so many national prodigies.

Scotty and Pig ambled over to their seats, after both grabbing the largest beers allowed for consumption without personally holding a vendor's license. The size of Alhambra Water bottles, the beers begged for the accompaniment of a baked pretzel of gardening hose proportions with a "foot-long" dog slathered with mustard and relish.

Heaven.

The crowd noise ebbed and flowed with the hits, as if in rhythm with the not-too-distant bay. The high point of the evening for Pig was "dot racing." This was Oakland's answer to pari-mutuel betting à la the large Diamond Vision scoreboard. It was an animated race between three video dots. All-American colors of red, white and blue had the crowd going berserk betting amongst themselves. Crowds wildly cheering for their colored dot of choice in an unremarkable event defined California camp.

Then, a rather statuesque brunette caught Brandon's attention. His head swiveled around, owl fashion, following her every move.

"I think I'm having a heart attack," mumbled Pig.

"I believe your affliction is somewhat lower," said Key.

"That's what I said—a 'hard attack,'" said Pig as he twisted the other way to gain a better view from the small, green, confining ball park seat.

Although young Brandon had been married twice previously, he attributed his "mulligans" (as he called them) to scoring low marks in "mate selection." In actual fact, his raging temper was only superseded by his pigheadedness, which he considered a resolute virtue. This made his relationships mercurial, tempestuous and brief at best.

Scotty and Pig settled into their field level seats, which were equidistant between third and home, three rows back.

Pig queried, "Do you think I could still command her respect if I told her I was a zillionaire venture capitalist who needed her to wear a bejeweled dog collar and bark upon my every command?"

Scotty paused. "Perhaps. But only if you left out the part about the venture capitalist."

Pig guffawed. Popcorn flew from his lap as he violently lurched backwards, shamelessly destroying the man's shins behind him. Cornelius was enjoying himself, as was Key. Scotty pulled out an Ashton Churchill cigar that was about the size of a donkey's extremities, preparing to go up to the smoking area, while Pig did the Skoal 'I've got a dead mouse hiding under my lip' thing. They ordered another round of beers and continued to tell each other how smart they were.

Pig's eyes returned again to the brunette goddess to his upper left. He was visually drinking her in, consuming her, limb by limb. She was with another woman, an Asian girl.

"Mine's the brunette. Too bad yours is a Slope," said Pig.

"I'm going out on a limb here, but I'm thinking she may not care for that moniker."

"Oooooooh. Righteous indignation from his Oxfordness."

Key turned to look. The brunette's partner was Ali Woo, whom he'd lost touch with and hadn't seen for over a year since her animated sparring match at Master Dihm's.

"Deal." returned Key as he put the cigar away. They headed up towards the ladies.

As Scotty and Cornelius approached the seated women, Scotty broke out in a grin. "Small world," he quipped to Ali.

"As it would seem," smiled Ms. Woo.

"You two know each other?" asked Pig incredulously.

"Sort of," answered the two, almost in unison.

Key paused momentarily and admired Ali's legs. In high heels, they looked like they had been lopped off the back end of a young colt.

"Well," started Ali, I'd like you to meet a very good friend of mine, Donna Corona. And no cracks please. She's heard them all." Ali motioned to the voluptuous brunette, who was in knee-high Jimmy Choo boots and a blouse cut low enough to invite further advances while eliminating any ambiguity as to what lay beyond.

"How do you brew? I'm Cornelius Brandon, although you can call me Pig."

"Charming. I hope it's not a hygiene commentary," grinned the curvy brunette as she crossed her legs coquettishly.

"Well no. It's more of an indication of how he trades his deals. When medicated, hobbled and muzzled, he's really quite harmless," added Key.

"So, ugh, where's the smart money?" asked Pig.

"I like the A's," answered Donna-the-beautiful.

"Oh no, no, no. I mean on dot racing?" asked Pig.

"Oh," giggled Donna. "Red. Definitely red."

"Sorry. Red is unavailable this evening," Pig said, pointing to his hair. "It's a magenta-man thing—Stanford Cardinal. I'm sorry, but it's out of my hands. You can be white."

Ms. Corona looked aghast in mock sternness, wagging her finger at him defiantly. "I'll be blue. And I get two dot lengths for your being pigheaded."

"Oooooh. She's tough," taunted Scotty, shaking his head.

"Okay. Okay. But only if you'll join us in our seats"—he motioned to the field level"—and we procure for you the finest foot-longs money can buy."

"As long as it's not death by pork buns!" chimed in Ali. "The worst!" She made an *X* by crossing her two forearms and fake gagged herself with her finger.

The four laughed and moved down to PacRim Venture's VIP seats. Ali and Scotty both reached their inner arms toward their common armrest. When their hands met, neither jerked back or apologized. Key let his remain on bottom and Ali gently folded hers over the top of his while interlacing her smallest finger through his and into his palm. Nothing was said.

Pig and Donna were going at it verbally a mile a minute. Key and Ali on the other hand were communicating without speaking. At first it was the hands. Later she turned toward him ever so slightly, so her foot rested behind his calf. Key was feeling the need to order a larger box of popcorn.

"So what do you two guys do when you're not rescuing maidens from the cheap seats?" asked Donna, with gum in her mouth.

"We sell plastic explosives to a left-wing guerrilla group," said Pig.

"If truth be known, we teach a barbershop quartet to trill like Shiite clerics," aped Key.

The ball game started. Key realized how long it had been since he had allowed himself to let his hair down with the fairer sex. It was nothing short of a pluperfect evening. Quite dry and just a little warm when the game started, the temperature promptly moved into the 70s. After the fifth inning, the usual chill came in and it felt good to be sitting close to one another.

Key learned that Ali was a legal secretary, for an entity that dealt with import and export tariffs concerning international trade agreements. She was cerebral, without being pedantic or too impressed with herself. He enjoyed her. She kept conversation light and bubbly, however, never empty-headed. With a strong wit, she had the ability to speak to contractual agreements and licensing matters and yet still make goofy jokes. Secure and comfortable with herself, she made others feel at ease around her. Ali was a thoughtful listener.

Scotty had grown weary of the never-ending fish ladder of hucksters hawking their deals based on inflated claims. Talking, the incessant talking.

The vast majority of the time, the initial deal pitches degenerated into an endless stream of babbling over-promises. Sometimes he felt he was dealing with professional conversationalists.

When hearing another speak, Ali would wait patiently until the end of their remarks. She'd then pause for a moment and nod reflectively, as if to marinate or drink in the significance of what the other had just said. In so doing, she honored and elevated the importance of the other's speech, no matter how trivial. She'd honed courteous listening to an art form. Key was taken with this trait, as people who constantly interrupted were a pet peeve of his.

ELEVEN

THE GAME ENDED WITH THE A's losing, which had become a pattern this season. The couples exchanged pleasantries and went to be alone with their newfound baseball pals. Upon reaching Scotty's townhome, Key opened the door for Ali, directed her to the sofa and brought her a warm brandy. She took off her four and a half-inch spiked heels. Her jeans were so tight you could read the dime's date in her back pocket.

"Nice shoes," said Key, admiring her hoof wear.

"Thanks."

"Louboutins? Manolos?"

"Nope. Casadei. My favorite."

"French?"

"Nope. Italian. Via Zappos—my personal Goddess." She then opened her third roll of Mentos that evening and threw the first in the series high in the air, leaned her head back and caught it with her open pouting lips.

"You know. Those aren't sugar free …"

"Yeah. And neither were those dogs and brewskies you and your fire engine-haired buddy were knocking back!"

"Touché." Key clinked his brandy up against hers, as Ali applied another coat of Burt's Bees lip gloss.

She saw an understated marble entranceway at Scotty's place, the use of heavy woods throughout with deep dental moldings and stonework used liberally. While the evening did not get too cold, sitting out for hours had given them a bit of a chill, which was just fine for canoodling. They had exchanged small talk for a little over two hours. Reaching for the nearby afghan, which was covered with mallard ducks and trout, Ali twisted herself into what appeared to be a very uncomfortable position.

"Does that hurt?" asked Key.

"What?" responded Ali, not sure where he was taking this.

"Is the sofa uncomfortable? You look like … well, like you're not comfortable," answered Key, motioning with his hand up and down as to her contorted state.

"Oh no. This is years of yoga and a breech birth on display. This first pose, or position if you will, is yoga based." She then showed him step one in arriving at her pretzelesque state. "Then," she paused and arched her back so severely it made Key wince, "you simply add these few movements for the complete effect." As she moved, she looked like a small, furry animal—who'd just been struck by an automobile and jettisoned to the side of the road.

"Fascinating." Key swallowed from his snifter, inhaling deeply the rich aromas wafting off his drink.

"So. Why haven't you ever been married?" asked Ali.

"Never a priority." Scotty reflected on his parent's divorce and wondered again if this had stunted his appetite for that science project.

"Priority? Or preference?" asked Ali, gently drilling down.

"Well, at the risk of going all Zen on you, I'm a fairly private guy, who tends to move slowly in relationships, sometimes too slow for the other side," said Key.

"Why do you suppose that is?" asked Ali.

"Nothing terribly mystical. Just a little socially backward." He set his drink down on the massive coffee table of wrought iron and weathered barn wood. It was constructed stoutly enough to shoulder his drink and, perhaps, a John Deere tractor.

In truth, there was some background music to Scotty's quip. Key's parents had divorced when he was young. While that, in itself, wouldn't have scarred Scotty, the ensuing rage that Key's mother leveled toward his father had had an indelible effect. He can remember the many times his mother had denigrated his father, blocked his dad's phone calls and in general, made his father out to be an ogre in his formative mind.

Scotty's mom had gone on to ruin her ex-husband financially and harangue many of his employers in a scathing rage. It wasn't until Scotty was twelve that he started to put it together. As a result, he and his mother had drifted a bit and his relationship with his father had become closer. For a period of time in his youth, whenever a fresh negative accusation was made about his father, he would say in unison with his dad, "another chapter in *Bad Dad.*"

"And what do you have to confess about your sordid past?" teased Key.

"It's not so sordid."

"Been married?"

"Yup. Once."

"What happened?" asked Key softly.

"Nothing. Everything. We had different likes and dislikes. He liked to hit. And I didn't like to be hit."

"Ahhhhhhhhhhh …"

"I don't want you to take this wrong, but today has been wonderful. I'd rather not soil it with a rehash of a marital … marital Odyssey. I'd be happy to share it with you in another setting. Why don't we plan time when you've already gotten me upset over something trivial and both of us are already really pissed off. You know? Then we won't be wasting a perfectly good evening." Ali smiled in an attempt to foreclose the exchange.

"Deal," said Key, not requiring any more paint by numbers.

"So tell me," she asked, "what's the secret of the cosmos? What is the reason so many relationships end up in the dumpster these days?"

"Well, I may not be able to answer that question, but perhaps one similar."

"Okay." After placing her drink next to his on the coffee table, she slid over and cuddled up next to him. She listened thoughtfully while looking out the window at the retail lights in the distance.

"I hold a view that I call the bottom-line-theory of relationships."

"I'm listening."

"Well, like this evening, when a couple hasn't been out before, they don't know each other from a load of coal ..." Scotty spoke almost in a whisper and was motioning with his hand dismissively.

"Uh-huh."

"Neither expects anything from the other. They each respect, maybe even slightly fear, the other party. They take nothing for granted. Their relationship is 'framed' at the lowermost 'bottom line.'" He lowered his hand and drove it left to right to graphically simulate his concept.

"Okay," chimed in Ali.

"As a result, at that point in time, their expectations and graphically speaking, the coordinates of these expectations are in the pristine-virginal state of zero-zero."

"Zero-zero?"

"Yes. The x-axis and the y-axis are both at zero, their lowest respectively— no expectations, no promises. Nada. Zip." Scotty drew lines horizontally and vertically in the air with his hand to make his point. "When we came up here, I opened up your car door. Do you recall?"

"Yes."

"How did you feel about that?"

"I felt good about it. That made me think you were a *gentleman*." She nudged him playfully in the lower ribs as she elongated her last word.

"Exactly. Most people (I genuinely don't believe this is the case with you)"—he feigned a guttural hurrumphing noise while rolling his eyes— "but most ladies will, from the first door opening thereafter always, always, always expect their door to be opened and their man always, always, always to be a *gentleman. Kkkkkritch.*" Scotty raised the bottom line on his graph ceremoniously by raising his forearm in concert with the sound effect.

"We have now created a de facto new standard. Her man must always perform to this level, just to get to back to *zero*. To make her happy in the future, he must always go *way* above this."

Ali nodded.

"Let's say you and I go out seven days in a row and on the seventh date, I send you seven long-stemmed red roses. How would you feel about that?"

"I hate roses. They remind me of funerals. Can we make it gladiolas?"

"Gladiolas it is. Done. So what do you think?"

"You're a sweet guy. You're … well, you're thoughtful."

"Mento?" she asked as she offered him one while throwing the other high in the air for her next Willie Mays-like oral catch.

"Pass. That's right. *Kkkkritch*. The bottom line just got raised again by her, higher still. Even less of the 'happiness field' remains for this couple to navigate in because she now always, always, always expects her man to be a gentleman *and* thoughtful. Every time. That's just for openers. He gets no points for these, as they are *expected*, in fact, demanded. A new, higher zero-zero has been established by her once again raising the bar." He paused and glanced at her to see if this was sinking in or just pissing her off.

"No way. Are you suggesting this is a sexist thing?"

"Not at all. Although it does seem to have a propensity to hover around the more vocal of the two sexes."

"You're doing most of the talking," said Ali, as she sent another Mento skyward.

"Yes. Tonight I am. So the line continues to raise, restrict and constrict, until it snuffs out the remaining sliver of the 'happiness field' completely. The two are habitually unhappy, as their minimum, bottom-line baseline expectations of each other are so elevated they both walk around in a constant state of disappointment. Ergo, they split. Then a new, larger, wide-open happiness field is re-birthed with another suitor and the cycle repeats itself."

"Lord, Scotty that's depressing. You didn't appear to be that jaundiced. Are you a closet misanthrope?" winced Ali as she backed away from him a bit, all the while searching his face for a faint smile to offer up some form of humorous relief.

"I'm not. I just want to leave our happiness field in its virginal state. If you make me dinner, it's because you *want* to. I should say 'thank you' *each and every time* for an act of kindness. You're doing it because you want to—you chose to—not because you have to, not because you owe me. You're doing it by choice, every time. You owe me nothing. Even when people are married, other than fidelity, they owe each other nothing. They do things by conscious choice and should be thanked, *every time*. I believe that's the key to keeping a relationship fresh and vibrant."

Ali gave her head a whimsical toss. Her shiny, blue black hair flopped first to the right, than the left. Any gelding show-pony would have been envious of the grooming and how her hair cascaded down her shoulders. Her skin was absolutely flawless and her eyes were the size of Gatorade lids. They were a hybrid between Anglo and Asian. While they carried the characteristic slant, they were enormous, Nordic or Slavic in proportion.

"You're staring," she mused.

"I am," Key responded, not averting his gaze as he reached to cup her face.

Key was uncertain how they had become closer on his blood-red, eight-way-tied, Italian leather couch. But they had. Maybe it was the smoky scent of the roaring fire he had built earlier or the crackling of the cured oak logs that encouraged companionship on the crisp evening. He moved closer to her as she spoke softly. She slowly sipped her Courvoisier. At a glacial pace, they found themselves moving nearer to each other—brushing, touching. Her leg was half draped over his.

They were so near in fact, he could pick up her scent. It was a faint mixture of vanilla and peach, which had him hearkening back to the corner fountain in his youth. His father had religiously given him fifty cents for a large peach sundae, his favorite. He was struggling with the name of the place. Bickleys. Yes, the drug store and old-timey fountain was called Bickleys.

After Church he would be taken there by his folks. He remembered the aisles of candy and the smiling face of the oppressively heavy woman behind the counter. Her small, white cap was almost comically small in proportion to her pie face. This was juxtaposed against her billowing, surgery room appearing, green and white frock, a bit reminiscent of a playing card Queen in *Alice in Wonderland*. Her hair was knotted tightly. It was suffocated with such purpose by a hair net that a small cyclone would certainly have become exhausted attempting to unseat it.

He recalled her arms—those large soggy arms, always in motion, which were comforting to a small child while hugging him. Her arms would swing, as if a pendulum's counterweight against the greater, centered fulcrum of her body mass. And he recalled the smell of fresh peaches being sliced for the topping. The quarter peaches were meticulously placed at the corner points of the hulking globs of vanilla ice cream. He used to ask for a bowl full of "glaciers" referring to his exacting specification for the size of the vanilla lumps soon to be birthed. She'd grin, as she knew exactly what Scotty wanted. They were close.

The scent of peaches would arrive seventeen seconds before the goods—he used to count them down under his breath. Flo. That was her name, Flo. She could talk a blue streak. They used to say she was vaccinated with a phonograph needle.

Scotty wrote a rigid specification. Not only must the ice cream be mounded to a comical height, but the peach quarters were to be spread carefully as petals surrounding the obelisk in the center. As if praying to it. The crushed peach syrup was in a colloidal suspension, whose gooey topping was spread evenly about the bowl, inviting spoon and gnats alike. The crowning glory was the five-inch, conical whipped cream presentation with a glorious maraschino cherry at the summit. Scotty maintained at this very fountain stool (devouring a sundae) is where he experienced his first climax.

To complete the gastronomical orgasm, Scotty would accompany the treat with a Coke—a double vanilla coke. He had not thought of the Coke and heavy vanilla extract until this moment when the faint aromas flooded his mind with the older comfort-food odors of his youth.

"Drifting?" asked Ali.

"Sorry. Don't mean to be. You reminded me of a pleasant memory I had from my ill spent youth."

Ali smiled.

What a great lady. She was wise enough to know that, if he wanted to share the story, he would, but no pressure. She never interrupted. She was relaxed, confident and at peace with herself. While her mouth might only mention a word or two, her eyes signaled warmth and volumes of understanding.

"Well, "began Key, "I guess we're getting to that awkward staring-into-the-campfire stage of the evening." He put it out there to see which way she'd run with it.

She smirked. Ali bowed her head and smiled broadly without speaking. She stood up slowly, took Key's hand and brought him to his feet.

"I would like to stay, but it's time for me to go." She slipped away little by little from his touch.

Key reached for his floppy, scrunched-up hat from the brass coat tree and guided her toward his MGB-GT. Driving back to her apartment, they did not speak. She touched his hand and rested her head on his shoulder.

Parking, he pointed over to the bright, clown red Toyota Yaris in her driveway. "Yours?"

"Yes. And do *not* make any rice burner cracks. That's my 'vitamin,'" said Ali referring to the car's shape.

Key felt it looked more like a suppository, but he thought better about sharing that and let the observation slide. "Oh no. I was simply going to ask if it was difficult breaking the middle pole out of that bumper car ride before liberating it."

"Cute. I'll reflect on that as you return your grandfather's Model T to assisted living."

"Guess I deserved that," said Key.

"I enjoyed tonight," said Ali.

Key came to her side to open her door. As he did, Ali's head remained down. Then she looked up, grinned and said, "*Kkkkritch.*"

She tossed her luxurious mane like a toddler who'd just gotten away with something. They walked together up to her door.

Holding both her hands, he looked at her for seconds and said nothing. Finally he uttered, "I'd like to do this again."

"Me too," was her soft reply, which came as she looked down shyly at the ground, like a reticent schoolgirl. The door closed slowly, each peering at the other through the last inch of the opening between door and jamb.

Damn, I'd like to carry her books, thought Scotty to himself as he walked back to his car. He drove off.

TWELVE

THE TWO CONTINUED TO SEE each other and became even closer. One of the first things Ali shared with him was she had a daughter from her prior brief marriage. Scotty learned, in large measure, the marriage is what had prompted her to learn karate and jujitsu.

Ali's daughter's name was Happi—Happi Woo. She had just turned five when she met Scotty. Happi was an adorable little thing—a "wee poppet," as her Scottish neighbor called her. She frequently wore dog ears. Her long, blue black hair draped her shoulders like her mother's and bounced as she walked. Happi possessed the same large, black, button eyes as her mom and she surrounded those beacons with an extraordinarily large, circular pair of black, Wally Cox meets Andy Warhol set of glasses. This, drew even more attention to her already beautiful orbs. As custom had it for young Asian girls, she wore the cramming, frenetic mash-up of competing plaids layered over garish stripes with alarmingly bright, knee-high stockings. The style was outrageous, yet at the same time, it worked. She looked like she belonged on a key chain.

Happi was an excellent gymnast, tumbler and hip-hop dancer. She loved to dance and like Michael Jackson, she learned to shake her groceries, gyrating to the rhythm of a washing machine. With excellent frame and posture, she would strike poses and hold them in a frozen manner, sometimes for lengthy periods—amazingly so for a five-year-old. Due to her fondness for hip-hop and the manner in which she popped from rock to rock at the neighborhood pond, her nickname soon became "Hoppy."

Her animation was exacerbated by another condition, which was not completely understood. Hoppy was mute. Ali had taken her to the doctor repeatedly, doctor after doctor, specialist after specialist, shrink after shrink, all reached the same conclusion. There was nothing wrong with Hoppy's physical ability to form and execute words. She was simply *choosing* not to speak at this point in time, or it was perceived safer and more comfortable for her not to. Rather, she chose to "speak" and express herself in a more physical, animated manner through mime speak. They thought she'd grow out of it.

Though mute, Hoppy found great enjoyment in lip-synching almost daily to the wooden end of a mop in her front yard. Normally her boom box perched atop the fire hydrant and in full voice accompanied her. Her choice of artists seemed to center around a Fergie, Gwen Stefani, or Lady Gaga genre.

Very large, Farm Aid-style, sold-out events (in her mind) would find her moving her act to the front porch, where she'd balance precariously on top of the intersection of the fence railing and a small porch banister. The railing would creak, groan and complain under each gyration, sometimes even threatening structural failure. The structure's complaining would, in no way, assuage the harmonic, thumping onslaught she punished it with.

"Hoppy! Get your buns down off that banister, pronto!" Ali would shout.

This venue's platform (although pleasing to the audience in Hoppy's view) met swiftly with squint-eyed disapproval from mom with the follow-on singular loud clap, signaling time for the final bow and dismount. Hoppy always stuck the dismount.

Key and Hoppy got along famously. She enjoyed mugging at him by puckering her face up behind the convex, dime-store, opalescent glass of the fish bowl to make it all the more distorted. In like fashion, when Scotty was inside and she was outside, she taunted him by knocking on the window to first get his attention. Then she'd turn her head coyly and open her mouth to its absolute carp-like widest, while at the same time pushing it against the glass and blowing loudly.

In addition to making a very odd sound, the effort filled her already large cheeks with air, which gave her the appearance of a rather large bullfrog—or funhouse puffer fish. This image was amped up further by her large glasses, from which her eyes appeared to be bugging out. It was difficult not to laugh at the visual onslaught, which was the desired outcome. As her mother, Hoppy grew fonder of Scotty by the month.

In addition to her mom and Scotty, two other objects were the center of Hoppy's time and affection. First, there was the ten-year-old who lived next door—Alex.

Alex was twice Hoppy's size. Possessing a haystack shock of thick, red hair, he had a strong upper body with legs thinner than a chicken's. Dimples and freckles, freckles and dimples. He drug a large, purple and green, plastic dinosaur around by a six-foot, corn-hued piece of twine for the better part of the day. Wherever he went, the Paleozoic-era beast accompanied him, as did the 49ers cap he wore at a rakish gangsta angle.

Alex would do his staccato combination of limping and skipping around the neighborhood with dinosaur in tow. Unceremoniously and with no foreshadowing, he would break into his familiar rant of: "Motherfucker! Motherfucker! Motherfucker!"

"I told you not to do it!" He would exclaim repeatedly, with energy and volume well in excess of what was required. Alex was retarded. Of course, this in no way stood in the way of his forging a strong relationship with Hoppy. In many ways, it helped. With his energy and total lack of inhibition, he could provide enough audio for both of them.

He had a rich history of relentlessly going into the local Shell station, which had a mini-mart. There, he would pile six bags of Cheetos, chips and four candy bars atop the counter as he requested two packs of Camels. Then he'd put a dollar down with confidently expectant eyes that this would surely culminate the transaction.

"Here you go, Alex," the station manager would say, worn down through mind-numbing repetition. He'd alternately give Alex a candy bar or bag of chips. The manager would tell Alex he'd keep the rest for him behind the counter, making the rest up out of the penny jar.

Lastly, Hoppy had a pet—a pet ferret. The animal was purchased after a two-month negotiation with Ali. From the onset, Ali never stood a chance. Hoppy would present Ali each morning at breakfast with a new ferret picture. Normally these were cut out neatly along the borders from some magazine or online article and she'd Scotch Tape hearts around it. This signified her ardent and undying affection for the rodent. Hoppy customarily made this presentation to Mom with both hands after Hoppy's last bite of cereal. Still possessing a milk moustache, bowl cupped in hands, Hoppy would stare intently with eyes wide open, up at Ali. Hoppy reasoned this approach seemed to add gravity to the presentation. Ali explained that pet ferrets were illegal in California in a useless effort to dismiss the notion.

After twenty some consecutive rejections, one month, for Ali's birthday, Hoppy gave her mom a cigar box purse, which was decoupaged and laminated. The purse was functional, trendy and cute. It was, however, completely laminated and covered with ferrets, every inch ferrets.

That weekend, Ali owned up to the inevitable and secured a ferret from an undisclosed underground venue for Hoppy, who was ecstatic. She laughed, tumbled and performed many frozen poses in exaltation. She sang loudly (albeit silently) in celebration to her mop, both on the hydrant and banister. And she hopped.

There was a fleeting period of time when Hoppy was attempting to convince Ali to dye Hoppy's hair blonde, to be more "in concert" with some of her rocker idols. That was not going to happen. Hoppy must have sensed the impenetrable stone wall on this proposal. On this sole issue, the youngster ultimately yielded to the fusillade of rejection, right about the time the ferret showed up.

Originally, it was a rather large, black ferret. As if to satisfy her urges, Hoppy introduced her new pet to the CVS Clairol bottle of blonde hair coloring. And voilà, it was "rocker orange." Problem solved.

Although initially shocked, Ali quickly concluded this was a good compromise. Better an orange rodent than an orange daughter. This episode, in fact became the seminal birthing for the animal's name, which quite naturally became—Tang.

"Let's call him Tang. That suits," said Ali.

Hoppy nodded enthusiastically.

If not cavorting with Alex, making monkey faces outside the window, or expanding her face to Disney proportions behind the fish bowl, Hoppy would spend her time playing hide-and-seek with Scotty and Tang. Ferrets have a voracious appetite for snatching items of food or smallish things and then promptly scurrying off and hiding their newfound treasures. Cute at first, this trait soon became problematic, when items of value started disappearing in areas which made them hard to retrieve, like inside walls. To combat this propensity, Key taught the animal (by rewarding it with veterinarian approved "Pill Pockets) to hide its booty inside Hoppy's book bag.

This accomplished a couple of things. First, it made the disappearing items—car keys, Bluetooth earbuds, cell phones and the like—easier to find. Second, it cut down on having to spackle closed a new hole in the wall every other week. The holes were normally in the corners, down low, right above the baseboard. If food items were not promptly found, the room started to smell quite moldy and musty.

Pill Pockets were originally designed to envelope medication for animals and mask any potential unpleasant pill taste with a more appealing one, thereby making the meds go down more easily. Tang was gaga for them, they were ferret crack. Tang played the game with a passion, a fervent indefatigable purpose and gusto known only to ferrets and meth addicts. She even chewed through one end of the couch's thick, floor-length fabric to secure a Pill Pocket that Hoppy had inadvertently dropped in an otherwise unobtainable corner. Tang's primary residence was a three-by-two-by-two-foot cage. She chose to "summer" in Hoppy's book bag when retrieving her bounty, was feeling stressed, or if she wasn't getting enough attention.

After months of developing a closeness to each other, Ali broached another subject with Scotty one evening.

"Say you," whispered Ali.

"Mmmm?"

"I've got to come clean with you on something." She put her book down and folded her hands solemnly, suggesting more would soon unfold.

"Shoot."

"You know how I mentioned I was a 1099 contractor, aka technical writer, for some Tier 1s?"

"Yup."

"Well, while still certainly true, it's just I also have a little hobby on the side."

"I have hobbies too. I love to fly fish, scuba dive and snow ski."

"Yesssss." She was squirming a bit as she tugged nervously at her long, black mane. "Well … Well, this one is a bit more than a hobby. It's actually a part-time job—an *important* part-time job."

"Okaaaaaay."

"I work for the NSA," said Ali perfunctorily. There. She'd spat it out. Expressionless, she stopped talking. Awaiting his reaction she extended her hand. "Mento?" Her head cocked back as she let one fly for herself.

"No. No, thank you. Like black ops? Like *spooks?* National Security Agency? That kind of NSA?"

"Yes. That one," said Ali demurely, while she glanced to the side coyly. She crossed her legs languidly in jeans that were so tight she looked like a pair of pliers walking down the street.

"Wow. I'm honored you'd share this with me. I guess at this point, we officially trust each other … with our lives." Scotty put his book down and sat up a bit straighter.

"You know I like you a lot, Scotty. And, well, like last week for instance, you remarked about some of the odd hours I've been keeping, early in the morning..

"I didn't want you to think it involved another guy and I didn't want to deceive you. You and I are solid, aces, from my point of view anyway.

"You're not saying anything. Stop with the not saying anything," implored Ali as she literally wrung her hands like a housefly.

"I'm not trying to wig out on you. It's just that, being a prior SEAL, I understand that organization better than most. I know what they do. And I know what they don't do."

"Like talk?" she asked.

"Precisely. There's the natural curiosity piece of, 'How'd your day go, dear? Overthrow any third-world regimes who were trying to down our grid?' And yet I know completely that you can never tell me just how your day did go. I'm not sure it's an issue, however. I'm just drinking it all in," mused Scotty as he looked up in the air, searching out distant ceiling corners and then did a back and forth visual shoeshine, awestruck at what he'd just learned.

During all of this, Ali had been rolled up in a ball with her head on her knees, eyes down, both arms wrapped around her shins, all closed up. She leaned back on the sofa, raised her hands over her head and stretched out long and leisurely, in a catlike yawn. She interlaced her fingers, rested her chin on them in front of her and stared off into space pensively. "To tell him or not to tell him. I labored long and hard on this one. It is truly a case of what sucks the least," grumbled Ali.

"Yeah. I get that. I do. Well—wow. Well, *wow!*" said Scotty, while scrubbing his face, stunned with disbelief. He was realizing that the fleas come with the dog. She wasn't asking for his approval, nor was it a topic up for negotiation. "I say that, with all the real problems out there, let's not make up any when we don't have any!"

"Makes sense!" said Ali, throwing her arms around him with a broad smile.

She jumped in his lap and wrapped her legs around his waist.

Thirteen

The Scotty–Ali love connection continued to blossom, so much so that he invited her on his diving trip, which he'd scheduled previously. He called his travel agent to add another seat for her and additionally booked an interim stop for them through Mexico City en route to Cozumel. The Mexican president's bizarre death was still an itch he had to scratch.

"Not the most direct route," mumbled the travel agent.

"True, it is rather circuitous. I've just always wanted to experience Mexico City—the filth, the looting, the begging. And now with illegal immigration out of control and borderline martial law, the combo is just too much to resist."

"Mmm-hmmm," grunted the agent, not looking up as she ferociously attacked her keyboard with French nails with inlaid rhinestones.

The flight down was uneventful. Scotty always felt his mother had bred with a cocker spaniel due to his propensity of gluing his mug to the window. The sea's turquoise and aqua marine hues bleached, as the shallows rose up to meet the light, sandy beaches.

The California topography was engaging. It was reminiscent of his father's Army blanket, all crumpled up when they used to play "fort", when Scotty was a kid. The Sierras peppered with snow were a glorious sight. He could make out the ski runs, almost like a large high school graduating class had marked their numerals there. He thought he saw class of 2018. As the plane popped through the clouds, the sun bounced off the water and iluminated the darker cloud's underbelly, as if a large lantern were contained therein.

Although not a part of this trip, Scotty's personal favorite was flying over Lake Tahoe. When the sun was just right, it looked like God's watercolor. One could see down forty feet into the water where steep mountain walls cascaded down sharply to the edge of Emerald Bay. High-country pocket lakes abounded.

As he and Ali headed on south the tension started to leave his rhomboids. He was reviewing with her some of the diving procedures, as she had just become certified.

"I remember my first breath underwater," said Key. "I felt like I was really getting away with something. Like I was breaking all of the rules—nature's in particular. It wasn't completely out of the question that there could be payback later."

"Like what?"

"Oh, you know, my regulator could flood with water suddenly. It was though I was cheating death a little bit. So. I felt just a little bit more alive. Make sense?"

"I suppose so."

"Stab your forefinger down your throat when this gets just too goofy."

Ali hit him.

" I'd like to be a fish. Really. Ideally, it would just be all upside with no downside. You know, none of that whole scaly-skin-never-being-able-to-sleep-and-having-to-stay-in-school-forever-thing. That piece would suck."

"Absolutely," she deadpanned as she opened and closed her extended lips in a faux carp-like manner while cupping her hands to open and close slowly on the side of her face.

"Mento?" said Ali as she was trying to cajole Key to propel one toward her mouth.

"You're killing me."

The plane's engines droned on and lulled her back to sleep. Key's shoulder became a conveniently close pillow. Her blue black hair hung limp straight, like water. It flowed over his shoulder and then spread uniformly upon his chest. Then there was her mouth, perfectly sculpted, bow shaped, from the smoothest porcelain the deity could serve up from his color palette. As they landed in Mexico City, Ali awoke.

"Tell me again why we're here?" asked Ali as they made their way by taxi through the abject poverty, filth and squalor.

"Well the shopping of course, the tequila, oh and the heartburn and follow-on gas. And perhaps a little morbid curiosity."

"Oh?"

"Did you read about the death of the Mexican president, his consulate and most of his staff?" asked Scotty.

"Yes, yes I did—a tragedy. A freak earthquake wasn't it?"

"So it would seem."

"You're doubting. I've seen that look," said Ali.

"Why do you say that?"

"The inflection in your voice. I'm familiar with that uptick at the end."

"Well, I don't have anything to be doubtful about. I just wanted to see the site."

"Okay. But … But what for?"

"I just need to satisfy a couple of nagging questions."

"Yes, dear," caved Ali.

"Ah yes. My two favorite words of connubial bliss. Stick with those and you'll see diamonds as big as horse turds."

Upon landing, Scotty and Ali drove to the earthquake site. It was unsettling how localized the damage was. There appeared to be very little disturbance but four blocks from the actual event. The surrounding area didn't show any leading or indicating fissures as would be customary with a temblor of this magnitude.

"In my experience, earthquakes are not like tornadoes," said Key.

"How so?"

"They're not normally this surgically precise."

"So, what are you saying? Mother Nature cheated?"

"I wouldn't phrase it that way. I just wanted some piece of mind that it was really Mother Nature's doing."

"You're overreacting," said Ali. "You've been reading too many conspiracy theory novels. Sometimes, shit just happens."

"Mmmmm," said Key, turning his gaze to Ali. He raised his chin slightly and arched his right eyebrow while he squinted to avoid gazing directly into the sun. "Aren't you somewhat surprised there are Federales still hanging out here? As opposed to Mexico's answer to FEMA?"

"You're serious. You're not going to let this go. You are like a dog with a bone! I thought this was a vacation for you and me! The earthquake was over ten days ago. You're suggesting there's more to this?"

"Precisely."

"Seen too many CSIs, Scotty."

"Perhaps. But it is entirely too antiseptic, too neat and tidy. It's the tidiest earthquake scene I've ever witnessed. And yet it is surrounded with crime-scene tape."

"Really. Give it a rest," said Ali.

"It's more than a little convenient. If it's perceived to be a natural disaster, then everyone writes it off as bad luck. And like you said, people automatically check the 'shit happens' box."

"Okay. Let's say it wasn't a natural disaster. How does one cook something up like this at home? An earthquake isn't exactly something you get out of a vending machine. One can't saunter into Terrorists "R" Us and politely request their Earthquake-in-a-Drum."

"No. You're right. There is clearly more deep-fissure damage here than could be inflicted by a few dollops of C-4. And there's not a cavernous blast hole suggesting a missile was involved."

Key leaned over the opening, which literally seemed to have no bottom. He reached down, picked up a large piece of rubble and motioned with his forefinger to his lips for Ali to remain silent. He then hurled the hunk of concrete into the abyss, as close to the center as his arm would allow. He quickly glanced down at his watch's second hand.

After a few seconds, his eyes became quite large.

"Did you hear that?"

"Hear what?" answered Ali.

"Nothing—absofuckinglutely nothing." Key's eyes opened wider. "Gravity has this whole habit of accelerating objects at thirty-two feet per second per second."

"Fascinating."

"Actually it is. A human, for example, reaches a terminal velocity of about one hundred thirty-five miles per hour depending on their specific gravity and mass."

"Wait," said Ali. "I think I heard something." She craned her neck toward the opening while pulling her hair back into a knot.

"Are you sure?"

"No."

One of the Federales was suddenly now paying more than a little attention to them. They noticed what Key was doing. He watched them intently, as if he might walk over to learn of their business requirements for site attendance, or perhaps ask for their passports.

"Well. Did you not *not* hear that?" asked Key.

"I don't understand," said Ali, a bit befuddled.

"My point is, given the significant elapsed time, it's pretty amazing if you heard something during the time frame, or even if you didn't."

"Ummm."

"With the average free-falling body accelerating at thirty-two feet per second per second until it gets up to one hundred thirty-five miles per hour …"

"Uggggghhhh," groaned Ali.

"If sixty miles per hour is eighty-eight feet per second, then terminal velocity at one hundred thirty-five is a bit more than twice that speed—say two hundred feet per second, to make the math easy …"

"There's a point coming up real soon, I hope?"

Key ignored the jab. "It was some twenty seconds before you said you might have heard something. That's a four thousand-foot deep hole, or over three-quarters a mile down without hitting any obstruction. Doesn't that strike you as odd?"

"Yes, but what really strikes me odd, however, is that you retain all that useless information in your head."

"Useless suggests never being used. I just used it. In a quake, it would seem to me that the fissures from a subsequent fault would rarely be perfectly straight down."

"Check please," said Ali, walking back toward the taxi stand in disgust.

"Hold on," said Key, grabbing her forearms to arrest her flight. "They would ordinarily be at some gentler slope parallel to and following a fault line. That would cause the rock to rattle and bang around on the way down. *This rock didn't make a sound*," he whispered.

"Okay. We have a quirky quake. Whose fault is that?" queried Ali with both hands outstretched, palms up, becoming more exasperated with Scotty's obsessive tedium.

"Humor right?" asked Scotty as he winked.

"Definitely. It's coming at you at thirty-two feet per second per second," said Ali.

"You'll tell me in the future? Maybe hold up a couple of fingers, so I'll know?"

"I can do that," Ali saluted. "Is there a point here?"

"I'm not sure yet. Something simply ain't kosher. It just doesn't pass the smell test." Scotty again was squinting and shading his eyes to see better. An emaciated, hungry dog with eight exposed ribs and dragging three tin cans that had been tied to his tail clattered by, going through the trash. Sniffing for any organic matter to consume, the dog rubbed his ten-inch patch of skin where mange had taken hair previously up against a fence post for some temporary relief.

"Well," said Ali, "here's some more 'given' information to process. You're 'given' me a headache. If you're done acting like a holy rock and roller, let's go vacate—if this is *truly* a vacation." Although said sternly, Ali hid her face shyly behind the two fingers she was holding up and looked coyly between the fingers with but one eye.

"You're right. You are absolutely right. We came. We saw. We dropped dirt clods. Hey, I'm a happy guy. We're off like a prom dress."

The two made their way back out of the rubble, away from the quake site. Watching their every move were the prior Federales and a gentleman of Iraqi extraction, turban and all. Key could not tell if they were together however, both were laying down the stink eye.

FOURTEEN

Cozumel, Mexico
August 2010

THE TWO MADE THEIR WAY back to the airport and secured their connection to Cozumel. As the purplish pink sun set into the ocean, Scotty craned his neck in an attempt to discern a glimmer of the famous green flash. No luck, not this time.

He had seen one before in Australia while diving the Great Barrier Reef. He'd gotten up prior to daybreak to ensure the best conditions, the flattest seas, right as the sun was rising. He could see clear to the horizon line. He recalled how he'd possessed a yearning to see it and had wondered if he'd seen it at all. He slid the window shade closed, leaned back in his seat and flipped through the in-flight magazine.

Scotty decided he was going to run the whole Mexico City phenomena by a "shirttailed" relative of his in Cozumel to vet it. His second "cousin" and prior SEAL buddy, Vincent Rodriguez, was a dive master at Dive Paradise, a local dive shop. Dive Paradise had lost as many divers as the next outfitter, true. But hey, they would take you to the best walls and always put you onto the best pelagics.

The back island dive master vocation was attractive to Rodriguez, as it allowed him to keep a low profile under the radar. At times, one hundred fifty feet under the radar. Rodriguez' past was checkered and he needed to keep his comings and goings low key. He had day jobs and he also had a night job. His day jobs were full-time dive master and part-time weed peddler to the locals. The quantities were small.

He used to refer to himself as 'the Cupbearer,' as he sampled as much as he sold. His nighttime job was dabbling in ad hoc projects for the Central Intelligence Agency as an informant to supplement his income. These projects were normally arranged by the Agency summoning him with a large chalked "X" marked upon the mailbox at 4th and Beach. Rodriguez would signify agreement to the meet by tying an obscure piece of kite string around the very base of the town's flagpole with a half deflated yellow balloon attached. It had to be yellow.

Scotty didn't think Vinnie was into taking folks all the way out on a black op, however, he was never certain. Vinnie was very accomplished in putting the hurt on people. Highly trained and very skilled, he was surgically precise in making people uncomfortable. He was commissioned to have the "Prince of Pain" come visit as necessary. While he characterized himself as being quite persuasive, he alleged he always tried to avoid sending his clients on the ultimate "dirt nap." Scotty was never clear as to how much of this was fraternal puffery and how much was true.

They checked in to La Ceiba. This was a spot he had frequented before and it seemed to work. Key liked the older units right on the water. He'd have his rich mocha coffee in one of those handmade pottery cups, which were never quite perfect in shape, while staring straight out to sea. The sliding door opened out onto the sand beach, right to the rinse tanks and the water beyond. This availed him the opportunity to have two and three dives a day with the lattermost being a shallow beach dive to outgas the earlier dive's nitrogen. Without an appropriate surface interval, he'd be potentially confronted with nitrogen narcosis, or "the bends."

Down by the beachside rinse tank, five blistered, spalling concrete steps signaled the path to an easing of the entry into the water. *Lap. Lap. Lap.* The sound of the water's rhythm tended to wash away any troubles.

"This the best entry point?" asked Ali.

"Yup. This is it." Key stared straight ahead, out across the azure seas, cup of coffee in hand.

Between the large gull and pelican droppings, one could gingerly pick his or her way into the surf. The stepped entry point lessened the likelihood of being body slammed by a wave or suffering the indignity of laying one's ankle wide open against an obscured coral head. All the while, two-inch crabs were scampering in and out of the rocks with enormous energy, speed and ferocity.

"Wow those guys are speedy," exclaimed Ali.

Their tireless toil made it seem as if they were clamoring, perhaps signaling a Paul Revere warning to the other marine life: *"Scatter! Two More Giant Sea Monsters Coming!"* They'd burst out from under a rock and disappear in the blink of an eye. The *shhhh-shhhh* of the small, lapping waves encouraged all to keep their voices down in the morning quiet. The crabs obliged obediently and went about their business in complete silence.

An alternative entry was a quarter mile down the beach. One could take a fifteen-foot free fall from the commercial dock ramp, which led to where the cruise ships moored. This was appropriate when the surf was nasty in an El Niño year. For the uninitiated diver, however, this second approach availed the additional bonus of ripping one's mask from his face or cracking the back of her head against the top of her tank, due to the impactful force of the water upon entry.

The couple smelled the sea and the salt. The hush hushing of the wind through the palm leaves patterned against the sound of the lapping waves, *Hush-hush, Shhhh-shhhh.*

"What's your favorite time of day here?" asked Ali.

"I like the morning. The seas are the most calm for diving and the animals are easier to see up top. No nervous water." Key relished getting up for early morning dives and going to the edge of the sea wall. Occasionally, he'd just barely make out the dorsal fin of a small shark cruising, as it completed his feeding in the shallows from the night before. Yellow and blue tangs abounded, darting as jets in formation.

"Look at those guys go!" shrieked Ali, pointing playfully.

The shape of the sergeant major's black and gray chevrons amplified their quick darting and swooping motions while the infrequent trumpet fish would stand on his head, waving slowly back and forth to camouflage amongst the reeds.

"Staying for just nine days?" inquired the clerk at the registration desk. He was scanning the itinerary Scotty had presented him upon arrival.

Key mused to himself that it seemed like there was always an initial "problemo." But then, whatever it was always seemed to get solved because *Scotty* was so important. Whether this was incompetence or a ruse on the part of the clerks to make the guest feel special enough to part with a larger tip was always a bit unclear.

"Nine it is," responded Key.

"If you really loved me, we'd stay two weeks," mused Ali.

"Well. I do really love you. But I also really love my job and for it to love me back requires this whole attendance thing."

After registration, the two made their way past colorful papier-mâché parrots and frogs. Turtles of hammered brass and bright, hand-rubbed copper were hung helter-skelter throughout the local's shop. There was this rhythm, even while you were off the water, as if you were still at sea. It was a constant undercurrent. A gentle faux-motion rhythm. The sea had a tremendous hold over Key, whether he was on it or just near it. He was uncertain if this was because he bore an astrological water sign or that it simply made him always want to pee.

En route to his room, his memory was flooded with visuals and aromas of prior trips. Always present (never to disappoint) was the strong, searing, steamy, almost pungent odor of half-digested Mexican beef decoupaging the splattered bowl in the baños. This was infamously endemic of any Mexican vacation. It was tantamount to a brown badge of courage, traumatically tattooed on turístas. Regrettably, the odor-masking agent was so equally obnoxious the cure was frequently worse than the problem. Key thought it strange that memories had such sharp, little corners to stick in one's mind.

They unpacked. They took a quick snork and followed up with a beach dive. This was a bit of a ritual for Scotty—de rigueur. He'd always make his first dive of the trip shallow and from the beach—about thirty feet, tops. Certainly no decompression stops required. At that depth, he could stay down long enough to read a book.

This additionally allowed him to be within "free-ascent" range. If his gear did crap out, he'd just dump it and follow his bubbles slowly to the surface, thereby avoiding an air embolism. This approach allowed him to iron out any equipment bugs in a more stress-free environment than a deeper dive would allow. Moreover, Ali Ooop, ever the good sport, was not nearly as comfortable in the water as "Aquaman"—the nickname she'd adopted for Key on the trip, knowing his penchant for all things aqueous. This practice round availed her the chance to get her sea legs.

A drift dive from a small fast boat could find one in a four or five-knot current. This is fast for a diver. The experience was effortless and fun with full-functioning equipment. You barely even felt the need to swim, it was as if you were flying. With arms folded beneath your chest, you'd just tweak your fins as ailerons to subtly change direction, being shuttled by the corals and palegics, as if on "the mother-of-all-people-movers."

Key recalled one dive master who used to urge caution about being separated on a drift dive from the boat by saying, "No problemo. Next stop, Cancun." It was the fast (think small) boat driver's job on top to follow the diver's bubbles. Key could not resist an earnest look into the diver's eyes before each adventure to determine clarity, to gain insight into just how many cervezas the captain had ingested the night before—because, "Next stop. Cancun."

He was also intrigued how during an ascent, air seemed to be magically manufactured in his lungs, as he came under fewer and fewer atmospheres of pressure. It was an interesting phenomenon.

As Scotty and Ali motored their little drumsticks out away from the beach, they came across a good view of the small, sunken plane beneath them. Floating above it, the gin clear water gave it an opalescent sheen, as it appeared to be gently wiggling a bit below their gaze. It was submerged in but sixty feet of water, so it afforded many marine life condominiums.

"How clear is the water going to be?" asked Ali.

"It'll range from ninety up to one hundred sixty feet on a good day. Today's pretty good, not great, but pretty good."

The wreck beneath them attracted scores of gray french angels and the brilliant iridescent blue and yellow queen angels. Some were the size of dinner plates. They were unfazed by the divers around them. Pulling their way down the anchor line, Key and Ali stopped at a twenty-foot depth. They hung suspended over the wreck forty feet below them. It was quiet.

Deliberately adjusting their buoyancy compensators to be slightly (gravity) negative made it so they would not have to struggle to stay submerged. They continued descending very slowly. It was completely silent, save the sound of their breathing through their regulators. In and out, in and out, sounding more then a little like Darth Vader.

On the way out, Ali had asked, "Anything in particular downstairs to look for?"

"You bet. We're in search of Waldo'"

"Waldo?"

"Yup. He's the local seven-foot two-inch green moray eel, whose residence used to be in the coral at sixty feet. If you rapped three times on the largest rock near his home, he'd come out to be hand fed."

"Kidding, right?"

"Fed him for years."

Not urban legend, Key had fed the eel in years past but had not seen his friend's long, olive drab, slinky, undulating body for the last few visits. He allowed a little water into his mask, tasting the salt and tilted his head back slightly, to exhale through his nose to reclear it. He motioned to Ali to start their descent.

On the way down, he was thinking he still had a healthy respect for the animal's thirty-two inch girth. Apart from being keenly aware of its swiftness and efficiency underwater, he'd heard of one gal who, while hand feeding Waldo, had had her glove half shredded. To add insult to injury, Waldo then deftly slithered up her buoyancy compensator (as she had hidden more bread to feed tangs) and slithered out the top of her BC. And, as if in righteous indignation, Waldo chomped down on her earlobe on the way out.

After searching for Waldo to no avail and making their inspection of the plane standing on their heads, the couple completed their first dive. They looked at each other's gauges at sixty feet, saw three hundred pounds and decided it was time to ascend. Scotty and Ali followed their bubbles up slowly to the surface and rolled over on their backs. Although not mandatory, they still hung at ten feet to "clean up" for three minutes as a safety stop. Upon surfacing, they popped out their regulators, put in their snorkels, flipped over on their backs and gently kicked their fins to propel them back to shore.

"What's your pleasure?" asked Key.

"I don't want to be a drag, but I'm down to my last calorie. I feel like some ceviche with abalone. How about you?" In actual fact, Ali was not only interested in food, she was keen on hand-feeding bread to the scores of multicolored parrot fish, some of which were up to two feet long. This was done at the bar, which was cantilevered out completely over the ocean.

"I may just amble down to the dive shop to check out where we can see the best animals tomorrow," said Key.

Key finished showering himself off outside and then rinsed his gear. He slipped on a light amber, cheesecloth shirt, which made his lean, muscular, dark tan body look even darker. He grabbed the keys to the moped they'd rented and put-putted his way into town. Key had to slow down for the world-class speed bumps the community had imposed. As a courtesy, each was preceded by a sign with the word *topes*, or *bump*, to warn the uninitiated that his or her ass was about to be assaulted.

On the way to the shop, Scotty passed front yards with rusted-out washing machines, shoeless children and dozens of chickens, endlessly pecking their way through the gravel. He'd always marveled at the Gatling-gun speed with which they'd hit the gravel directly with their beaks and bounce up for more. He thought this swift, deliberate, striking motion was surely what spawned the expression "come down on you like a chicken on a June bug." But they seemed happy. Happy that they had work, which was more than many back in the United States could say, given the new economy.

Arriving at Dive Paradise, Scotty found Vincent in the back of the shop, filling tanks and speaking pidgin Spanish to the help. The shop's exterior walls' paint had faded long ago and many of the structure's corners were out of square.

All entering were greeted by the ploddingly slow ceiling fan, which almost as a blood pressure sheriff, seemed to dictate a laidback, mañana cadence for all who entered. Vinnie was around Key's age, he had a raisin-wrinkled face and was exceedingly thin, with skin the color of pecan pie. This made for stark contrast up against his stringy, greasy, bleached blond hair hanging just off of his shoulders. He bore a single "Don't Tread On Me" tattoo, resplendent with serpent, on his right forearm.

FIFTEEN

"Hola!" shouted Vinnie.

"Hey, bubble peddler!" cried Key.

"Is that you, Scotty me lad? Bien! Bien!" shouted Rodriguez.

"Revolting," said Key, throwing his head back laughing, "simply revolting. There's nothing worse than a Mexican trying to fake an Irish accent."

"Well a top of the burrito to you! Glory be, it is. Well, Scotty, let's see if they've kilt what's under your kilt! You just pull up a chair and tell me your life's story. But for God's sake, make it interesting will you?"

Rodriguez went over, grabbed Scotty's hand and then drew him closer to give him a bear hug with both arms. They both grinned with the familiarity of friends who had seen "the shit," caused their share of shit and been through the shit together.

"Married?" asked Vincent.

"Nope. Practice, practice, practice," said Key.

"Good to see you haven't lost your sense of humor. Killed anyone lately?" inquired Vinnie.

"Haven't made a practice of it, at least no blood relatives of yours I'm owning up to," said Key with a crooked smile, as he struck a three-inch-long wooden kitchen match against a post to light his cigar. The smell of sulfur filled the air.

"But, amigo, you're letting all that valuable education go to waste. Trained killers should practice their craft now and then, or they get … they get …"

"Respectable?"

"No, Oh, nooo. Worse—they're just not as 'broom' worthy."

"Okay, I'll bite. What's broom worthy?"

"Glad you asked." Vinnie was delighted Key took the bait. "See, all our lives we're going to the bathroom with a broom. At first, all big, hard, maintaining-your-craft, SEAL types, you got to put it *under* a broom to keep from peeing on yourself." Vinnie motioned with both hands below his belt to ensure the message was understood. "Now you out-of-shape, no-account, resort-vacationing, expense account-traveling puuussy types, you have to put it *over* a broom to keep from peeing on yourself."

"What a terrible thing to say. That just hurts. Really, you just placed a permanent dent in my Qui."

Rodriguez shakes his head to the left and right. "Chinca te. I'll bet it's been almost ten years since I've seen you, five years since we've talked and two years since I've cared. Don't tell me you came all the way from … from …"

"San Francisco."

"All the way from San Francisco just to get a bottle of bubbles from the 'Prince of Pain'? What's on your mind? If you haven't been married, then you haven't been divorced. Soooo, I guess it means my Starlight nightscope stays in the case?"

"To be certain. In addition to setting up a dive for tomorrow, I wanted to run something by you," said Key, pointing up high to the blackboard that published the date, time, location and duration of each upcoming dive.

"Lay it on me, you bleached out, sushi-sucking gringo. You know, Scotty, if your skin were a pocito shade lighter it would remind me of mi madre's undone apple pie." Vinnie opened his eyes and mouth garishly wide to make his point.

"Always a kind word," mumbled Key.

"We do Palancar Reef tomorrow for the deep dive. Mondo palegics, mas grande animals. Some of them even shave. A few have balls the size of church bells. The second downer is in the shallows near the Eel Gardens. It's about thirty feet, so the whole thing is like a slow deco hang to off-gas. Other than that, how can I help your narrow, Anglo ass? Diga me."

"Are you still working with Mother?" inquired Scotty, after first glancing around to ensure they were alone.

"My mother died."

"You know what I mean, asshole. The Agency," repeated Scotty, a bit agitated.

"You cut right to the chase, don't you? I was expecting more verbal foreplay from someone I loved." Vincent leaned over and capped off one of the dive bottles. Sweat, hardly abated by the room's overhead fan, ran down his back. He drug another heavily faded steel tank just over the edge and accidentally blew off an O-ring. "Shit! Who's asking?"

"I'm asking," said Scotty.

"Reason?" With a visible change in countenance, Vinnie dropped the tank's elevated butt to the floor, deliberately allowing it to bang loudly on the concrete, as if to emphasize there needed to be a damn good reason for this question.

Key knew what his friend's newfound attitude was all about. With the new administration prosecuting those with a CIA or SEAL stripe who had interrogated terrorists without their kid gloves on, active members and alumni were personally flirting with prosecution themselves.

Unbelievable, thought Key, *just plain goofy*. Some recent headlines were even suggesting a new policy of Mirandizing enemy combatants, essentially encouraging them to lawyer up before their "known associates," or links to other deadly cells, could be extracted. *Next they'll have us coat our bullets with KY Jelly so they don't hurt so much when they go in,* he thought. The current political environment amazed Key and he understood Vinnie's reluctance to be forthcoming. It was becoming Superman's ethereal comic book Bizzaro World. Many things were starting to feel upside down and backward.

"Hey, I don't have to know how many villages you've burned and how many ears are on your necklace. I just need some high-level G-2 on a … on a thing."

"I'm listening." Rodriguez had stopped working, stood straighter and folded his arms.

"Did the CIA have any involvement with the Mexican president's death?"

"No. I believe that was a higher authority."

"Who?"

"God."

"So, you genuinely believe it was an earthquake?"

"Why not? They happen. In fact, they happen frequently in Mexico. It's our form of urban renewal." Vinnie, now relaxing, thoroughly enjoyed his last crack and laughed heartily out loud.

"Vinnie, I made a stopover at the quake site on the way here. Something smells, it didn't look right."

"Por qué?"

"There were guards, Federales, still surrounding the fissure, almost like they're investigating a crime scene and there were a couple of lower life forms there skulking about—ragheads."

"Okay. And that's a big deal becauuusse?" asked Vincent, in mock horror as he contorted his face, swinging his head in slow, sarcastic circles while pursing his lips.

"Yeah. All right, I know it's a stretch. But when I threw a stone in, it either never hit bottom, or it's over three-quarters a mile deep."

"Your point?"

"I don't believe it was a *natural* disaster."

"So, some evil, swarthy-skinned, third-world, pinko-faggot junkie just happened to throw a large hole at the Mexican president? Amigo, please. Just how many times did you see Oliver Stone's *JFK*? Sometimes shit just happens."

"You're starting to sound like my girlfriend. So you think I'm starting to sound a little delusional, eh?"

"No. You're starting to sound a lot delusional. But, hey, you're kin. At least we've humped the same donkeys, that almost makes us kin. I'll sniff around with some of the 'fraternity brothers' and see what's belched up. Are there any other puzzle pieces you haven't given me? Anything, my amigo, to add just a shred of substance to this thin bullshit? Un Pocito más?"

"Well, seventeen, eighteen months ago, the firm I work for looked at a proposal that, perhaps, might qualify as a possible explanation."

"What was this group's name?"

"Vinnie, I don't want to lie to you. I simply would rather not tell you. Remember what the Russians used to say. The less you know, the better you sleep. Snoop around and let me know if I need to change my medication."

"I'll keep an ear to the rail, Scotty."

"Thanks." He smiled and slapped Rodriguez's back in appreciation.

"As long as you're here, let me show you a superbad rebreather we got in a week ago," extolled Vinnie.

"Pass. I've got to get back to the 'delicate little flower.' But please, give me a heads up if you find anything, as we'll be here for just a few days."

"That's not hardly enough time to get bent—even if you were down the whole time."

"You're right. See ya." Scotty turned and waved as he headed out of the dive shop.

It was a humid afternoon. Grass and palm frond seedlings were in the air. It smelled as though Scotty were deep in a pollen bong. He picked his way down the dark, musty, rotten, wooden steps out of the shop. He avoided the dog with all ribs visible. As he grabbed the rail's soft, moist, putty-like wood with nail heads raised from lightning, he noticed an individual of Middle Eastern descent, perhaps Iraqi. The man was leaning up against the peeling stone wall. One could just barely make out the bleached-out Dos Equis beer ad painted on the wall's surface behind him.

While the man's head was wrapped in a turban, Scotty was unsure as to his nationality. Key's observer was a short, gaunt, swarthy man who was sucking on one of those smallish Turkish cigars the size of a cigarette.

Cigarillo tobacco drool had permanently stained his beard on the right side of his mouth, a bit like a grasshopper.

The man kept his eyes averted, down and away from Key. But then, just for a brief instant, those dark, piercing eyes flashed up and into Key's. Just as quickly, they darted away and back down at the pavement. Key could tell from the cadence of the eye sweep those eyes had been on him before. He had absolutely given Key the stink eye and clearly had an agenda.

Sixteen

Good Lord, he thought, *what a menacing-looking fuck. We need him at our next party.*

An ominous mixture of feelings flooded Key and made his face overly warm, for no good reason. It perplexed him. Just having recently been bitch-slapped by Vinnie for spiking levels of estrogen and potentially violating the SEAL's unwritten code (or Pussy Index), he elected not to obsess over it.

"You wuss," he mumbled to himself, as he walked away. "You can take out three armed foreign assets with two quick moves and you're letting this … this insect, who'd have his hands full controlling the back pressure from your Water Pic, concern you. It's nothing. He's nothing." But then again, machismo aside, Key knew all too well that innocent-appearing ten-year-old boys in Iraq could give you a warm, toothy grin, just prior to letting a fragmentation grenade roll silently from their robe's concealed pocket into an unsuspecting GI's jacket and they'd keep smiling at you.

Right up until the blast.

Nevertheless, he ignored his apprehension. Key continued off toward his bike and paused in one of the shops, where a goodly number of brass and clay pots were displayed, hanging in the entrance way. They were all hung independently, softly swaying in the warm breeze. The shopkeeper greeted him with a warm smile as she motioned to the recent arrivals. She had been peddling goods to the cruise ship tourists and was highly confident these would catch his eye.

"Cuánto cuesta?"

"Veinte dólares. Fixed prices. Good shop."

As he stood there feigning a shopper's interest, he rotated one plate ninety degrees to get a reflected hammered brass, rough and distorted 'fun house' view of the streetscape behind him.

"Well, the gnarly little shit followed me. Maybe he's in the area to shop a bit for the wife, kids and camel mistress," muttered Key to himself. Not completely convinced, he left, backtracked and went into another shop. After going all the way in, he strolled clear to the back of the shop, fondling a couple of papier-mâché parrots along the way. He took his time, being careful not to poke his eye out with the end of a mariachi singer's guitar neck.

Scotty quickened his pace. He returned to the front of the shop, only at the opposite side from where he'd entered. He slowly pushed back and opened an exceedingly dusty, wooden shutter, which complained vigorously with a creak as it was asked to do something it obviously had not performed in years. There. On the other side of the street, perched three-quarters behind a dusty straw, red and green mat was his trailing Gila monster. He was squatting in the opposite alley. This allowed him full view of both the entrance and the side door of the shop.

"The game's afoot," whispered Key to himself.

Key walked outside, unapologetically, without flinching, straight over to his shadow. The Iraqi was bent over in a compacted manner. He averted Key's gaze. His chin was not far from the ground, whilst his elbows remained on his knees, as if his neck and upper spine were unhinged. Key sauntered over close to the small, squatting man, deliberately uncomfortably close. He could smell the man's acrid, biting, jerk-your-head-back body odor.

He moved closer, close enough to make out the small, hairy moles on his tail's left ear and the large blood mole on his lower lip. He could see the man's yellowed, fungus-infected, untrimmed toenails. They were a half inch longer than his toes and most were already curling back. Key had seen stray dogs practice better grooming habits. He brushed two of his neighbor's flies away from his face. Scotty moved closer still and gently bent over. He was within ten inches of his shadow's turban.

Scotty was standing and staring straight down at the top of his stalker's bonnet. He watched the man's hands intently, anticipating any quick movement. None came. The tiny little man sat motionless, staring straight ahead, as if focusing on a single blade of grass growing out of the opposite wall. Key pulled out his own cigar. His Ashton Churchill was much larger than his prey's. Seven inches long, fifty two ring diameter and bearing a Connecticut Shade natural wrapper, this bad boy could fumigate a warehouse, or make a large wetland area insect free.

They both sat there, smoking. Perhaps this passive-aggressive confrontation was how the phrase *Mexican standoff* was coined. The location was spot-on. Key continued to loom. All the while, Scotty deliberately blew smoke downward toward Stink Eye's face. With the oppressive Mexican humidity, a small cloud completely enveloped and lay hanging in his eyes. The short man's eyes watered. After a few minutes of complete silence, Key's ash on the end of his cigar became lengthy and weighty. With a flick of his thumb, he deftly sent it skyward.

Surgically launched, half came to rest on Stink Eye's bonnet and the other half tumbled down into his beard. The Iraqi did not move—not a twitch. Stink Eye was caught in Key's headlights. He knew it. Key knew it. He knew Key knew he knew it. Key took his cigar out of his mouth and looking downward, he slowly, deliberately and very softly said one word:

"Why."

The inflection in his voice was absent. The word was not framed in the form of a question. Rather, it was a clinical, pedestrian demand for a response.

No response came. The man made no reaction. Two more minutes passed. Key's cigar had a new one and a quarter-inch ash, half of which was cool and gray and half of which was still a red-hot glowing ember. He pulled the toothpick from his mouth and picked off a hot ember the size of his watch's date window. He flicked this one down at Stink Eye saying:

"Por qué."

The red coal hit the man's garment on his thigh, burning through the material and dropped hot onto his leg. Stink Eye flinched. Visibly singed, he was struggling to show no pain, motion, or emotion.

"Por qué?" Scotty said again, this time with gentle inflection.

Suddenly, quick as a cobra who's been taunted too long by a mongoose, the Iraqi reached up his left flowing linen sleeve and retrieved an eight-inch, knifelike spike from a concealed wrist sheath. In a single motion, he went from his left forearm over his right knee and violently stabbed the ground where Key's foot had just resided.

With good anticipation and catlike reflexes, Scotty jumped straight up and onto a thirty-two-inch high counter just before the spike hit the ground. The ferocity of the strike caused the spike to penetrate the earth a full two inches.

"So we're going to dance?" asked Key rhetorically.

As Stinkeye reached for a throwing knife concealed in his tall, soiled, scrunched-down socks, Key chose not to give him another opportunity. He adroitly snapped off a side kick to the right side of Stink Eye's face with the outward blade of his left foot.

A crisp crack signified he had broken his opponent's jaw. The short man lay on the hard-packed, red brown clay and plucked a loose gold tooth from the upper right hand side of his mouth. He placed it in his pocket carefully, as if this had occurred before, as if he needed a vivid reminder to revisit this confrontation. He then scowled and spat a large mouthful of blood at Key as he lunged toward him.

SEVENTEEN

SCOTTY DROPPED TO THE GROUND on his hip, while deftly performing a leg sweep with the other. He sent his adversary slamming flat on his back. The rear of the man's head struck the stone-hard dirt with a resounding thud. Stink Eye grabbed Key's ankle and bit out a chunk of consequence. He spat Scotty's hide to the soil. Blood ran heavily from Key's ankle. To this point, Scotty had been toying with him, though admittedly, this last act just flat pissed him off.

"Going to fight like a woman?" taunted Key sarcastically. "Well, let's just see if this bitch has any balls."

Key did a no-hands cartwheel, avoiding the smaller man's next lunge. In midflight, he grabbed Stink Eye's genitals firmly with his right hand and turned them clockwise ninety degrees as he completed the move. The Iraqi shrieked a painful religious curse. Key then grabbed his shadow's throat with his other hand. Keeping hold of the initially engaged important parts in concert with the other, he slid Stink Eye's entire body down a long table, which was adorned with clay pots and other novelties. As a cricket scampering, the shopkeeper wasted no time in shuttling out of the way of the mêlée.

The clay pots broke alternately against the Iraqi's head and each other, as the copper figurines clanged and banged, until he came to rest against an enormous, hammered brass platter at the end of the slide. His head made a gonging sound as it struck the orb—a tone not unlike the commencement of a Chinese ritual.

The swarthy man rose groggily to his feet, groping for yet another throwing knife in his robe. In so doing, he exposed a small *ESE* tattoo on his forearm. Without hesitation, Key lunged forward and slapped both sides of the man's head with his open palms. This caused one ear drum to burst and disoriented him. Out of desperation, Stink Eye threw the knife anyway. Speed without course rarely wins and this was no exception as the knife missed Key by a good margin.

Then, Stink Eye reached inside his other sleeve for what appeared to be a small, hammerless gun.

Shit, thought Key, *Who is this guy? The Banana Man?* In the next motion, Key pulled the bad guy's knife from the post from which it had stuck. He whirled quickly, executing a fluid spinning kick, which caught his opponent again in the jaw, breaking the other side of his mandible. The force of the kick sent him flying four feet backward through the air. He crashed hard against a grass mat and its supporting vertical post. Chickens clucked. Feathers flew. Dust billowed.

Stink Eye lay on the ground, groggy. Being a little ornery, Scotty went over and untied the bottom portion of the man's turban. He laced it under his neck, sucked it up and cinched it around tightly to the post behind his head. He then took the bound one's knife. Key was positioned with his forearm pressed forcefully against the small man's throat, pinning him firmly against the four-by-four post behind him. He assumed the "kill" position. The shopkeeper stood by motionless, from a distance, silent. Her eyes grew ever wider.

The ruckus had attracted a small crowd outside. A brief moment, which seemed like an eternity, passed with Key poised above Stink Eye. Then, with panther quickness and ferocity,

Key drove the knife deeply.

His lunge went clean through the turban, a full inch of cloth and deeply penetrated the wooden post behind it. He deliberately missed the man's head, just slightly skinning the scalp as a reminder not to fuck with him again. This effort effectively pinned the perpetrator to the post, not unlike the manner in which an entomologist would mount a prized beetle. Scotty reached for a nearby burning hurricane lamp and said to the evildoer, "You know, I'm going to miss the time we've had together. I mean it, to let you know I mean it, I'm going to keep a light burning for you."

Scotty lit the top of his turban, which was pinioned firmly to the post and wrapped so tightly under Stink Eye's neck it was choking him.

The bound one was unsure exactly what was happening. As Scotty rose to leave, he heard the desperate screaming and violent twisted thrashings of his prized beetle trying to free himself. The air was filled with the smell of burning sackcloth with an earthy scalp finish.

His adversary pinwheeled violently while trying to free himself, drubbing and thumping against the support posts with his sandals, while stretching with both hands for the other side of the post—just out of reach. As Key exited, the crowd gave him wide berth and quietly mumbled an instant replay for other Johnny-come-latelies.

Key limped back to Dive Paradise with his ankle wound soaking his trouser, sock and tennis shoe with blood. Away now from the heat of battle, he winced with each step he took, as the throbbing pain had him anticipating and dreading the next. His awareness as to the bite's depth increased as his shoe filled up with blood. Every third step, the blood squished between his toes and out onto the parched, sandy road, which soaked it up quickly.

Key reentered Dive Paradise as Vinnie's eyes trailed from Key's sweating and chalk-colored countenance down to his blood-soaked jeans and shoe.

"You know," Vinnie glanced up into Key's eyes rather blasé and said, "it's customary here on the island to take your clothes off before diving with the sharks."

"Well," responded Key, "this was a land shark. No disrobing required." He slumped to one side, grabbed a large display of buoyancy compensators to steady himself and pulled them all down on top of himself as he collapsed to the floor.

"Come here," said Vinnie. "Let me see that. Shit! You really were bit! You need a doc, or at least a vet, to see this, amigo."

Rodriguez went to the back of his shop to retrieve his corroded first aid kit. He beat on the rusty clasp twice to open it with the end of his tipless dive knife. He swabbed the wound with alcohol, packed it tightly with gauze and applied a compression wrap in an effort to slow the bleeding.

"There. That should hold you until a doc can look at it," said Vinnie.

"Thanks," said Key. "Looks like my delusions just went and got all real on me."

Scotty related to Vinnie what had just happened. At the conclusion, Vinnie pulled a long drag off of his Royal Jamaican cigar, turned to Key and said, "You may have gone and just stepped in something. I'll get back to you."

Scotty gingerly pulled himself up and hopped on one leg out of the shop to his moped. It took him two tries to get it off of its stand. "Thank God for electric starters," he mumbled to himself. As he putt-putt-putted back to La Ceiba, every bump and washed-out gully in the hard-packed earth reverberated up his leg and caused his ankle to throb. His foot was getting tight in his shoe, as it continued to swell. Sweating profusely, he was beginning to feel nauseated.

As he wiped perspiration from his brow, he realized he was becoming dizzy and a bit woozy. It sneaked up on him. He slowed down so he could better manage the new pinball game his eroded senses had just placed him in. Arriving back at the hotel, when he reached for the opposite handlebar to pull the bike back onto its rest, he missed and the moped fell to the walk with a clatter. Ignoring it, he staggered to his room. He opened the door and Ali gasped.

"My God! What happened to you?" she cried, with lines of horror on her face.

"Routine check-out dive stuff. But I am ready for that nap now." Falling onto bed, Key passed out.

EIGHTEEN

KEY AWOKE SIXTEEN HOURS LATER in a small island hospital. His wound had been packed, stitched and cleaned. Regrettably, the hospital had not. The facility's lights were blinking on and off and there was a yellowish cast throughout. An errant dog and chicken made their way leisurely down the corridors in quest of food. A dizzying array of bugs had taken up residence in the corners of the drapes and underneath the mats. Key's foot was elevated to help drain the synovial fluid and blood that had built up on his ride back to the hotel. He had an IV in his left hand and blood going into his right forearm. Ali was there as he opened his eyes.

"Thank God, you're awake!"

"Where are we?" asked Key.

"You're on a Vulcan spacecraft hurtling toward Saturn," answered Ali, relaxing after seeing he was his old self.

"Uh-huh. Give me some good news."

"Upon arrival, people, very small people, will steal body parts, many body parts. But they will be particularly fond of your spleen. When pureed with pork, this becomes a delicacy that is treasured as their national dish." Ali never cracked a smile. She asked, "Maybe I should make the dive reservations in the future?"

"Maybe so. Damn, I'm hungry. I don't suppose there's a cheeseburger to be had?"

"No. But I could get you favorable terms on fajitas."

"Fajitas it is. Then let's get the hell out of here."

"Not so fast. The doctor wants you to stay off the leg for at least two more days before you fly," admonished Ali.

"So. How are you liking your vacation so far?" said Scotty.

"Memorable. Quite memorable." She dropped her head and buried her face into his chest shaking it back in forth in amazement.

Key lay flat out for the better part of their vacation. After the third day down, he was going stir crazy and opted for an unscheduled voluntary checkout. He had heard stories of guys going in for a case of the bends and a spinal tap being performed. Really? He was out of there.

He accomplished his escape with a modicum of fanfare, bounding out of bed and knocking over the large, brittle mother-in-law's tongue in the foyer. It was time, as two-thirds of the plant was already dead and the rest was on life support. With his gauze bandages slowly unwrapping as he shuffled, Key made his way toward the front door. Throbbing, his foot still throbbed every time he went from horizontal to vertical. Shortish, overweight, baggy-armed Mexican nurses trailed him while verbally admonishing him with musical tonality against his escape plan.

They vociferously urged him to return to bed. They were doing their job and Scotty wasn't doing his. He considered ordering a large peach sundae with scoops of vanilla ice cream the size of glaciers. He thought better. First he dealt them respectfully kind comments, which degenerated into muttered Spanish obscenities, due to the pain as he made his way to the exit. Not at them mind you, as Scotty was, if anything, courteous. His muttering was more a commentary on the entire affair. He went back to Dive Paradise to determine whether Vinnie had learned anything more in his absence. Key asked Ali to remain at the hotel for her own safety. If they remained separate, her face would not be associated with his.

"Whatcha got for me?" Scotty snapped as he entered the shop.

"Later tonight would be better, Señor," uttered Vinnie, in a very real Mexican accent this time without his familiar jocularity. He physically ushered Scotty out the door. "Diga me later. Mas grande tanks to be filled, amigo," whispered Rodriguez as he motioned toward all the empty tanks. Vinnie always prided himself in sounding American. Clearly, Rodriguez was not striving for humor this time.

Without further objection, Key left.

Three hours later, after nightfall, Key returned. It was a soggy, muggy evening. He heard the faint strains of the strolling mariachis. Their acoustic tunes were juxtaposed against a gyrating nearby discoteca pounding out Latin rhythms for half the town to hear. He could see the pale lanterns lighting the shops along the way. Most of the lights were dim—dim purposefully with low wattage and exacerbated as a third were partially filled with bugs making them dimmer still.

The night's stillness was punctuated by tourists screaming what little broken Spanish they had acquired at the top of their lungs. This was in part due to ingesting mass quantities of alcohol, in part to affirm an understanding of the native tongue and in part to confirm to all within earshot their turista IQ was below room temperature.

"Diga me," said Scotty again to Vinnie in the dive shop.

Vinnie did not respond initially. Rather, silently placing his forefinger to his lips to shush Scotty, he first walked Key outside, clear to the end of the dock where he kept his dive boat named *Atsa-Moray*.

"These puppies will take the light of just the stars and magnify it thirty thousand times," he said, motioning down to a duffel bag full of night vision goggles. The boat was moaning as it gently rubbed against its moorings with every other wave. Large spider webs were on every piece of structure that bore a right angle.

"Ain't technology grand?" said Key.

Rodriguez gazed quietly through the telephoto night vision lens at the greenish coastlines. Shimmering images were cast from magnification, heat, and the light drunk in from the inky darkness.

"My friend, I have no clue if there's a connection, but there has been some recent chatter about 'Red Mercury.' Are you familiar with that shit?" asked Vinnie.

"Nope. School me up."

"Supposedly, it's a dangerous substance that allows the production of cheaper nuclear bombs. Worse, they can be made very, very small—like between a softball and a bowling ball."

"Perfect."

"If this crap is for real, it could also produce antiradar coatings and serve as fuel for smaller reactors, not to mention fit nicely into a suitcase."

"Hiroshima in a drum. Wait, I think I saw this on an infomercial. Does it clean carpet stains too?" asked Key.

"Are you done? Shut the fuck up and listen," barked Rodriguez as he looked around again furtively, feeling Key's humor was ill timed.

"Apologies."

"Chemically, it's a complex blending of mercury and oxidized antimony. If true, it means a new age of supermetals. Some suggest it's being made secretly in the Urals. A group called Promekologia in Russia produces it."

"So, the 'big red threat' is back upon us? Is that the bottom line? They've just been lying in the weeds, waiting for our defenses to go down?"

"I've not said that. I'm simply telling you what I heard," Vinnie rubbed his gaunt and craggy face with both his hands. The sea, salt spray, women, cigars and tequila (not necessarily in that order) had aged his face beyond its years. His form factor, however, was still taught and athletic. He continued, "Legend has it, in Yekaterinburg, behind heavy steel doors with armed guards, this stuff is cooked up in small quantities. It's fenced through an international black market for $300,000 to $3 million per kilogram. Whatever the market will bear."

"Hmmmm ..."

"*Wall Street Journal* said 'Western experts don't believe it. But five minutes before plastic was first cooked up, scientists didn't believe that possible either.'

"I heard the same thing." Key's hands were on his hips and he had lost all tendency for humor.

"The *Journal* produced a classified decree from Yeltsin and Putin. It grants Promekologia the exclusive license to manufacture and export this for three years tax free."

"Who do they contract with?"

"The usual suspects; Iran, Iraq, Syria and North Korea. To date however, their largest contract is a group out of your backyard. Their code name is ESE.

"I know those initials. Is it for real?"

"No one is certain. The article felt Yeltsin's—now Putin's—decree was real and even interviewed Promekologia's director, Oleg Sadgkov. While ole Oleg is a learned scholar, every now and then he'll go off to where you think he's a couple of olés short of a bullfight."

"How so?" asked Key.

"Well, for example, the article says 'But for a man of science, he has quirks. He turns white even when a visitor pulls out a camera and says, "We've done research that proves that extrasensory experts can kill a living being from one thousand kilometers just by taking their photo. In fact, I myself, can do this."

"Priceless."

"In any event, I don't know if this is tied to your little ankle biter, but Red Mercury has been in deep, deep cover for awhile. All of a sudden, it's getting a lot of daylight. There will be a fair number out there whose jaws will get real tight about this topic seeing el sol."

"Sometimes daylight is the best disinfectant."

"Further, here's some of what I pulled off the net after researching it. Cohen, the 'father of the neutron bomb,' has been claiming for some time that Red Mercury is a powerful, explosive-like chemical known as a ballotechnic.

The energy released during its reaction is enough to directly compress the secondary without the need for a fission primary."

"Some of this is déjà vu all over again," said Scotty.

"He learned the Soviet scientists perfected the use of Red Mercury and produced a number of softball-sized 'pure fusion' bombs, weighing as little as ten pounds, which he claims were produced in large numbers. He alleges the reason this is not more widely known is that elements within the US power structure are deliberately keeping it 'under wraps' due to the scary implications such a weapon would have on John Q. Public."

"That's all we need, yet another real or unreal reason to wring our hands and raise the threat level."

"Since a Red Mercury bomb would require no fissile material, it would be impossible to protect against its widespread proliferation. Therefore, they simply claim it doesn't exist, while acknowledging its existence privately."

"Their version of don't ask, don't tell."

"Exactly. Cohen claims when Yeltsin took power, he secretly authorized the sale of Red Mercury on international markets and fake versions were sometimes offered to gullible buyers."

"So much for honor among thieves," quipped Scotty.

"Cohen's claims appear tough to support. However, the amount of energy released by the fission primary is thousands of times greater than conventional explosives."

"Puurrrfect."

"Ballotechnic materials do not explode. So it's difficult to know how their energy could be used for compression. There is no confirmation of Cohen's claim of Red Mercury's existence. Those in labs where it's been made have publicly refuted claims, including Edward Teller."

"So why does anyone believe it at all?"

"Cohen says nuclear weapon designer Dr. Frank Barnaby had secret interviews with Russian scientists. They said Red Mercury was made by dissolving mercury antimony oxide in mercury, heating and irradiating it and then removing the excess through evaporation."

Key brought his forefingers pensively up against his lips as his elbows rested on the dock's paint spalling railing. He said nothing.

"One thing I do know," whispered Vinnie.

NINETEEN

"IF I WERE YOU, I would shag ass out of here RFN," said Vinnie.

"Right Fuckin' Now?"

"Bingo. I'm talking next-flight RFN. And even though it is muy bueno to see your blanco ass after all these años, do me a favor and don't come around for at least tres más. In fact, don't write or call me either. If I get any more dope on this thing, I'll get in touch with you. This got real hot real fast. And I don't see an asbestos diaper on either one of us."

"Makes sense," said Key, as he and Vinnie headed back to the end of the dock, shook hands and headed off into the night in separate directions.

Key took Vinnie's warning to heart. He and Ali left on the next plane to SFO. In fact, they did not even return to the hotel for their things. He paid a policeman at the airport two hundred US dollars to ship the goods COD and promised to send another two hundred upon receipt.

Upon arrival in San Francisco, the two went to their own dwellings. Scotty's ankle was just getting to the point, as he changed elevation from seated to standing, it wouldn't exhibit the dreadful throbbing that took ten seconds to settle down. Originally it was so pronounced his face would flush and he'd grind his back molars until he thought he'd cracked enamel.

He grabbed his gear, bid Ali adieu as she hailed a cab and he bailed into his bottle green MGB. While Ali was initially slow to warm to the cab idea, she knew, as Scotty persisted, not traveling together made the most sense.

Key revved up the rpm to seven thousand on the way back to his office. He had a nagging feeling this recent ordeal was not going to be the final chapter. The voices in his head lamented that he was getting too personally involved. Maybe he should just back off, as Ali suggested.

"Pig!" shouted Scotty as he rounded the corner from his office.

"Francis! Man, what have you gone and done to yourself? Why are you hobbling around? I told you not to take that Chinese basket stuff to heart, it'll make an old man of you!"

Key considered sharing with Cornelius the whole ordeal but decided better. For awhile, discretion made the most sense.

"Dog bite—baaad dog bite." responded Key.

"Dog bite. Right," taunted Pig. "Maybe from that lust-crazed sex poodle of yours! Bow wow wooowwwwww!" Cornelius shook both hands in front of himself and opened his eyes and mouth wide for effect.

"Hey! Hey! Hey!" shouted Key.

"So, did you dive much?"

"Not as much as we'd have liked," grimaced Key.

For the next few weeks, Key's thoughts would drift back and forth to the events in Cozumel. Had it not been for the painfully ugly scab healing on his right ankle, he would have been able to dismiss the entire episode as a bad dream.

At the office's coffee island in the kitchen the next afternoon, Key bumped into Wentworth.

"Stanley?"

"Yes, Francis."

"Did you ever hear back from Mr. Butterfield?" asked Key, as he motioned for Wentworth to join him out on their meticulously landscaped exterior deck.

"Butterfield, Butterfield," muttered Wentworth, his eyes rolling up and to the right in an effort to recall just who Key was talking about.

"That young lanky Berkeley grad student who came in here a year or so ago with a concept to revolutionize mining," reminded Key.

"Oh yes. Quite. I recall him. He was truly an enigma. Indeed. We had a couple of follow-up visits where I thought we were on to something. We were just about to draft an LOI on his behalf."

"And?"

"And one day he stopped returning my phone calls—just like that. Rather rude actually. Didn't seem in character for the chap, but then again, he was from Berkeley."

"That would be the People's Republic of Berzerkley."

"To be certain. I even drove by his flat one day to see why he dropped the dialogue so abruptly. I had genuinely perceived a transaction there."

"Uh-huh?"

"He didn't live there anymore. The landlady said he had perhaps skipped town. He simply stopped paying rent and summarily departed. In fact, she said he left many of his belongings and they were picked up by some Middle Eastern gents."

"Could these guys have been Iraqis?"

"Well, yes. In actual fact, that is the nationality she stated. I thought I'd be somewhat more general as to details, however."

"You know, for a fellow who is as demanding on painstaking details as you are, you certainly slip easily into generalizations," chided Key.

"Right you are. Guilty as charged. Do as I say, not as I do and all of that rubbish."

"Did anyone suspect foul play?" asked Key.

"No. No. He was, according to his Landlady, a bit of an odd duck anyway. This behavior was consistent with his past. She reported that he drifted from one California University to another, following R & D grant money. She was relieved that he left his apartment clean and tidy. She said you could even still smell the Clorox. He did take his computer, just not his CDs, clothing, pots or pans. He probably just ran short of capital and succumbed to the sweet alluring song of the next university grant-funding siren."

"Maybe … so," said Key with halting speech. As he said this, he methodically lit his cigar with cedar and rolled it between his right thumb and forefinger. He was studiously listening for any telltale crackling that would suggest the tobacco was too dry. He breathed the flame in and then blew it back out through the cigar, while rotating it to ensure a proper lighting. He walked closer to the railing on their deck and mused that the fire marshal would have a nosebleed if he caught him. But, fuck 'em.

"Do you remember when your last chat with him was?"

"Oh, let's see, it's been almost a year ago—a year ago last April," said Wentworth, tugging at his mustache. "Why have you taken such an interest in the lad?"

"Just curious," responded Key.

"Well I know why you did not audition as a Shakespearean actor. Lord, that thing stinks," remarked Stanley as he waved his hand with disdain in front of his face to ward off the growing plume emanating from Key's stogie.

"Ain't it grand? 'Shit salesman with a sample.'" cracked Scotty.

Wentworth opened the door, went back inside and strode off, muttering something about being unprofessional and lacking consideration. Key finished the cigar and retired to his richly wood-paneled office to finish his pro forma. He worked long into the evening as he was pressed to complete the financials and have the package out the next day.

TWENTY

Whistler Resort – British Columbia, Canada
September 2010

ON A HIGH-COUNTRY LAKE NESTLED in the Blackcomb Mountains near Whistler Resort, British Columbia Canada, the prime minister and his aides were fishing for trout from four small boats.

Whisp, whisp, whisp. The casting of the nine-foot-six-inch, Winston Boron IIX, dark bottled green, six-weight fly rod interrupted the perfect silence. There was an occasional wind, which would build up and then just as quickly die down amongst the pines. Not a great deal of talking going on. Fly fishing was considered the "quiet sport," and the prime minister enjoyed an economy of speech during these occasions. His aides accommodated his request for solitude, albeit in a crowd.

After executing excellent form and fashioning a tight loop, the official punched his forward casting stroke to the proper ten o'clock abrupt stop and let his cast fly. The energy transferred seamlessly to the running line, unfurling out smartly in front of the angler.

"A sporting cast to be certain," remarked his aide.

"Enchante," said the French guide.

A fine cast of almost twenty meters, it plunged into the depths of the thirty-nine degree water. It promptly sank with authority, as the 420-grain line was designed for just that purpose. The line took the fly down to the depths where the larger fish dwelt. Where they felt safe. Deep enough where even with the trout's eight-powered binocular vision they felt secure.

Strip. Strip. Striiiiiip. Pause. Strip. Strip. Striiiiiip. Pause. Stripping the sinking line back with his left hand under the bottom of his right hand's forefinger with intermittent pauses, the PM provided animation to the number 18 soft hackle wet fly that he had affixed to the end of his tippet. He'd tried swinging it slowly earlier, as they were near the confluence of a small rivulet, however he had just recently gone back to stripping, as this had been productive in the past at this lake. The rhythmic motion continued uninterrupted without another sound for five minutes.

There was no other disturbance—nothing in the water, nor in the air— even though there were twenty-three eyes riveted on this single lime-green running line. This "stillness" had been perfected for the last ninety-three minutes, save being pierced by the call of the erstwhile loon. Non-fishermen felt as though they were being punished in this setting. The effect was not unlike an intimate golf gallery awaiting the Great One's putt. After all, the prime minister of Canada was fishing—clearly newsworthy.

"Bit of chill in the air, eh?" asked his aide.

"Yes. Isn't it grand?" responded the prime minister.

The official was angling near Whistler Resort, up high in the mountains of British Columbia, in a cobalt blue, remote alpine lake. There were nine other security types monitoring his actions intently. One wore an eye patch, two were bald and six were armed. The lattermost group was assiduously glassing the tree line for any signs of movement or something out of the ordinary.

Bam! Solitude was broken. The fly was hit with the extreme brutality known only to fly fisherman and men who have been unfaithful to their wives. The prime minister received the fifty-five-foot, electronic handshake and follow-on spasmodic, acrobatic tugging affirming success.

"Believe you've disturbed his nap, sir!" quipped the guide. A twenty-one-inch Rainbow trout fancied this buggy piece of metal, thread and deer hair, festooned with just a bit of flash. Experts had never been quite certain if fish strike at these objects out of hunger, or irritation the way one would swat at a gnat.

"Reel! Reel! Reel!" barked the guide, so the PM would keep tension in the line. The large, broad-shouldered muscular fish streaked swiftly toward the boat, constructing a large loop of slack in the angler's line. Steelhead are notorious for this maneuver as well, as it was an artful way of getting its freedom back. This tactic made it very difficult for the angler to keep his fly line taut, with all the newly configured slack in his lap.

The fish exploded out of the water, thrashing his head to the right and left violently, while dancing on his tail clockwise one hundred degrees around the boat in an additional effort to dislodge the hook from his mouth.

"You certainly have him on the run, sir. Fine job," patronized his aide.

The prime minister, being acutely aware of this tendency to water walk and dance for freedom, raised the rod tip high above his head and stripped line in frenetically with his left hand, while pulling it under his right forefinger. This kept his line taut, mitigating the dreaded slack loop and kept the small hook lodged firmly in the fish's jaw—all to the keen disappointment of the trout.

"This beauty is coming to hand," said the determined official, as the last two had broken off and publically humiliated him. With a good level of tension in the line, he broke water for the third time and emulated Stevie Wonder's head movements at seventy-eight rpm. The fish still could not quite throw the hook, due to the prime minister playing it skillfully and not attempting to get too horsey.

After a great deal of harrumphing," and a few smatterings of "good show!"—with a single "Mon Dieu" from the French guide—the prime minister adroitly landed the fish. Providing just enough side pressure to exhaust the fish and yet still not break his 5X tippet, he brought the fish to hand adjacent to the boat and bent over to collect it.

"Look up and smile, sir!" suggested his aide.

The official smiled magnanimously for the photo op, then gently arrested the fish's motion and artfully removed the hook, without ever completely lifting the fish from the water. He then slipped the trout back into the cold, clear, glacial green-blue waters, where the fish paused briefly, took two recovery breaths and then swam off indignantly with a flourish of its large dustpan tail.

"That's the ticket!" exclaimed the prime minister. The eleven other observers broke the silence with a properly understated, gloved "golf clap," which would have fit in nicely at high tea, with the brandishing of highly varnished humidors thereafter. This was just about as giddy as this group got.

"A storm's approaching, Prime Minister. We should go," cautioned the French guide, as he pointed to the ominously dark-bottomed cloudy front approaching fast from the west.

"Au contraire," responded the prime minister. "Today is a masterpiece! The Lord has made this glorious day ideally suited for fishing. There is nothing man nor nature could possibly do to ruin this picture-perfect day. Angel Lake and her bounty have brought us as close to heaven as mere mortals can experience." In so saying, he hoisted his champagne bottle to the darkening purplish skies. They were heavily laden with blustery, high-country snow as they continued to gather overhead. He threw his coat hood back to expose his face to the biting cold and thrust his glass heavenward with a flourish. "To today!"

"To today!" all accompanying him repeated in rapt, governmental lockstep unison. He popped the cork ceremoniously skyward.

Simultaneously, as if on cue, a primitively malevolent, very low, almost sub-ultrasonic guttural hammering started deep in the distance. Then, in reverse Doppler effect (as it swiftly became closer and closer) it ended with the punctuation of a blinding light. The flashpoint engulfed the entire tiny mountain lake and its occupants, both above and below the waterline.

The number 18 soft hackle fly vaporized, as did the champagne cork in midair.

As well as the hand holding it.

TWENTY-ONE

THE FLASH BURNED THE TOP portion of the trees on the eastern side and belched forth a voluminous billowing steam cloud where the lake had been just moments before. The heat was suffocating and unworldly. The blinding light obliterated all things physical in the tightly confined, high mountain lake area.

As the flash ebbed and the disturbance subsided, in its wake was a series of nothingness. The single fish was gone. The prime minister was gone. The twenty-three eyes and their bodies were gone. And the lake was gone. In its place, was a modest-sized simmering abyss, which seemed to drop to eternity. A loon flew overhead and warbled its forlorn cry, concluding this time with an unusual shriek.

There was no sound but for the solitary charred remains of a conifer to the south, as it cracked at its midpoint and crashed to the forest floor below. This moment in time was frozen. All in an eight hundred yard-diameter ring was devoid of life. The fishing party was truly...

Over.

The earth continued to gurgle, belch, steam, hiss and bluster in protest of its recent violation.

The news hit the Canadian UP wire service swiftly, but the facts were garbled. One report stated, in a rather pedestrian way, that the royal's fishing party was lost. Another, as if to buy time, rather cavalierly mentioned that all was fine, great fun and sport were being had by all and the group expected to take an extended stay as the fishing was *fabulous*. The third intimated that not only was the royal party lost, but even their lake was lost. This last remark drew a single raised eyebrow from the news commentator, who was looking directly toward the camera as he concluded the story.

Rescue helicopters had been dispatched promptly when the security group's walkie-talkie line went inexplicably dead. Paramedics, a Canadian Forestry official (mapmaker), a local tracker and a half dozen stalwart Canadian Mounties lined out multiple search teams. Six choppers were manned with search and rescue experts, who had packed into this wilderness area many times previously. They were not strangers to the harsh weather or its unforgiving terrain.

As the first helo circled the area, the map maker and tracker were in complete agreement as to where the small mountain lake should be, due to triangulating precise coordinates on independent GPS. Mystified with its absence, the rescue team kept having the chopper pilot circle higher and higher to gain a better vantage point and to encompass a greater line of sight. This first chopper bore a youthful American pilot.

The tracker spoke. "I don't know what to tell you. I was just up here fishing myself three weeks ago to the day, as a scout, to be certain the fishing would be acceptable to the prime minister. I would wager my finest bamboo fly rod that Angel Lake was between that saddle"—he pointed to two upcoming sister peaks— "and back over that draw." The tracker ran his fingers thoughtfully through his well groomed gray and brown beard in astonishment, bewildered.

"I totally agree," chimed in the mapmaker.

"It's crazy. It ain't right," said the tracker. "Sure. We've lost man, beast, horses and an occasional trail to the weather. But we've never lost ... a lake." He spit Skoal in disgust on the floor.

The *ak-ak* sounds of the twin helicopter rotor blades reverberated through the pass with sympathetic disdain, as the craft banked hard left into the wind.

Much of the day passed with two refuelings for the choppers, as the gathering storm arrived in full voice.

"Well. What do you propose we do?" shouted the mapmaker to the Mountie.

"Our job," responded the Mountie curtly.

"We've been at this for ten hours …"

"My clock-reading skills have not atrophied during that time," said the Mountie crisply.

"We've been through two tanks of petrol."

"Yes. And we'll go through two more and two more after that if that's what it takes," rebuked the Mountie sternly.

"Well," stated the map maker, "there comes a point …"

"A point where conversation is unnecessary. I believe we're at that point," gritted the Mountie between his teeth. He had never taken his eyes down from his binoculars throughout the entire exchange. His epaulets were straight. His gaze was straight. His jaw was straight.

The mapmaker was mute. The Mountie was an imposing figure. Apart from his regal, colored garb, he sat overly erect from a bout with scoliosis as a child. His jaw was as square as a lantern, with similar proportions along his muscular back and shoulders. He was 'deezed' as they say in Canada. His gaze never wavered. His eyes were smallish, from squinting in the sun over the years. This was a man of purpose. In his early forties, he stood well over six feet, weighed two hundred thirty pounds and had graying hair. This Mountie always got his man. He would be damned if he was going to "lose" either a lake or the prime minister on his watch. That was simply unacceptable.

The Mountie, Willingham, turned to the mapper. "Have you the coordinates of Angel Lake?"

"Yes."

"I'll have them now," stated the Mountie, taking a tone of simultaneous demand and request.

The mapmaker gave the coordinates in degrees of longitude and latitude.

"I require the precise coordinates of Angel Lake," barked the Mountie.

"Including minutes?"

"Including seconds." snapped Willingham.

The mapmaker stared intently at the map in front of him and methodically gave out the degrees, minutes and seconds of both longitude and latitude.

Willingham promptly turned to the pilot. "Lock on those and drop to within fifty meters of the tree line."

"What?" asked the pilot incredulously, as the wind was starting to howl again and visibility had headed way south.

"I used small words. Do it!" The Mountie was taking control. Complete control. His tone was not in the form of a question.

"No disrespect, officer, but while these tactics may work well on the ground at twenty miles an hour on horseback, if we so much as brush up against a tree, it'll make for a *real* bad day."

"Make your point," demanded the Mountie.

"With just this stick and less than a quarter-inch of metal separating my keister from my Keeper, I'd rather not be introduced to trees at 225 knots, if you get my meaning. Have you ever had a one hundred-foot-tall, thirty-inch diameter Redwood teach you physics at that speed? It's a very brief lesson. Not many repeat students. One I'd like to avoid."

The Mountie pulled out his baton and slammed it against the dash mightily. He was grinding his molars and speaking between teeth that were large, straight and clenched. "Sir, this is not a discussion. This is an announcement. Either you take us down to fifty meters above the tree line with some degree of grace, or I'll do it lacking that same grace. Your decision." He glared defiantly at the pilot.

"Simply for the record and perhaps our tombstones, let me mention what's going on aeronautically here," shouted the pilot over the sleet, which was now raging outside the cockpit." We are in a helluva storm. Understand, we cannot see squat. These ranges are tough to traverse, even on a calm day with good viz. We're also looking at some major-league downdrafts."

"What are they shouting about up there?" asked the mapmaker to his companion in the back of the craft. The other back seat member shook his head sideways.

The pilot continued, "If we go in tight to those saddles, we could catch one, which will suck us downward four hundred feet in a half second. We're talking a blink. We won't be able to recover and I won't be able to do spit. It will crush us like a bug against that granite windshield over there!" The pilot gestured wildly in disgust at the upcoming saddle range's sheer, granite walled face, peppered with ice and spring-fed waterfalls.

"Fascinating." whispered Willingham. "We're going down now." In so saying, he grabbed a hold of the stick and forced it gently, yet firmly down.

The pilot took back control and accommodated the Mountie toward the inevitable.

Arrrraugh-ak-ak-ak! The craft yawed severely to port, causing the rivets to groan. The pilot had concluded that, as long as this Mountie was going to kill them all, he was going to extract some personal pleasure in the process. He would enjoy witnessing this dignified Dudley Do-Right with starched tighty-whiteys engage in projectile vomiting all over his gold maple-leafed clusters. The chopper descended at an elevator free-fall rate, which left everyone's stomach in their mouths.

Arriving at a fifty-meter ceiling had the rescue troupe dodging and weaving treetops. The steep turns of the craft made it feel like a Mach 1 slalom course. They were shouting louder to be heard above the sleet being driven against the windshield as they were buffeted at sixty-five knots.

"When will we be there?!" shouted the Mountie to be heard.

"On my mark. Three. Two. One. Mark," responded the pilot.

"Good. Make ever increasingly larger concentric circles from this point's origin."

"Roger that."

"What's that?" shouted the Mountie above the fray, pointing down at a dark spot on the ground.

"What's what?" said the mapper.

"That dark spot. It almost appears burnt. I don't recall a fire being reported in this area."

"There wasn't one reported," said the Forestry official dryly.

"What?" screamed the Mountie.

"There *wasn't* one!" came the Forestry official again, this time at full voice to be heard over the thunderous roar occurring just outside their window.

"Pull in closer, they've cooked it," ordered the Mountie. "Closer still."

"To pull in any closer, we should sit 'er down, as the downdraft will slam us into the ground!" screeched the pilot above the earsplitting wind. The pilot continued shrilly above the deafening den. "With this much snow in flat light, there's no definition. Can't see squat. We can't see if our landing surface is horizontal or stable enough to accommodate us. We could tip over or capsize in deep snow."

"That's a chance we'll take," growled the Mountie.

"Roger that." The pilot caved and took them down. As a plumb bob knifing through air, the helicopter dropped into a white snowbank with a *wooosh*. It was a slow-motion sinking effect into a large down pillow, as if in an aerial pillow fight—with one end open and down feathers billowing out from the other. The snow was circling in mid-air and climbing up the craft's walls, enveloping it.

"We're hovering in snow!" shouted the pilot. "If I cut the engine, we'll go over!" The Mountie was busily taking pictures of the former lake, now cavern, whose rim was peppered with freshly fallen snow. "No hard surface! We'll have to come back at the end of the storm. We're outa here!" exclaimed the pilot.

The Mountie said nothing but kept taking pictures. *Click. Zzzzzt.* He turned. *Click. Zzzzzt.* He took another. *Click. Zzzzzt.*

The chopper's air manifold strained under the weight of the heavy, moist snow it was inhaling in an effort to get to fresh air. It continued to complain. Suddenly, the high wind sent a stray, flying conifer's limb into the tail rotor. *Ding.* The craft half in, half out of snow begin spinning. Bogging down.

"Mayday! Mayday!" screamed the pilot into his radio. He pressed his ID button so his transponder could be located more easily on radar.

"This is Bravo, Tango-C-Zed-R. We are in trouble and going down hard at the following coordinates," barked the pilot.

"How many souls are on board?" squawked the tower.

TWENTY-TWO

"FIVE SOULS ABOARD. REPEAT. FIVE souls."

The unflappable Mountie kept taking pictures, as if unconcerned by the goings-on around him. The tail angled down sharply and came in contact with the ground. It snapped neatly in two, driving the main fuselage deeply into the powdered snowbank, as the torque's sudden stop savagely ripped the entire chopper in half. The Mountie and pilot were thrown free and were cut up pretty good, though their injuries were primarily cosmetic.

"Jesus," remarked the pilot, surveying the carnage.

The paramedic, map maker and Canadian Forestry official did not fare as well. The paramedic was introduced to the five hundred-rpm main rotor blade, whereupon he was pureed. The Forestry official gazed down as his feet felt warm. His right shoe was filling up with blood.

"Sacre bleu," he groaned. To his horror, he discovered a large, sixteen-inch, glass, spear-like projectile buried deep in his groin. It was in the shape of a comma. A period-shaped projectile would have been more fitting, as it was his undoing. He fainted and did not regain consciousness.

The mapper was thrown over the ledge down to the next granite shelf twenty feet below, resulting in his left leg and arm being broken. His leg suffered a compound break, as was readily apparent due to the startling angle of the broken bones' grotesque geometry completely penetrating the flesh.

"Down here!" he cried.

The precipice was icy, steep and milky translucent in color. Fifty degrees from vertical, the injured mapper, navigating the edge in ragdoll manner, kept trying to drag himself up with his good arm closer to the side of the embankment for safety.

"I'm down here!"

Each time he tried, he would gain a foot or so and then slide four feet backward, closer to the edge, chattering along the ice as he slid. He looked up at the Mountie pleadingly.

"Hold still man, we'll send you a rope!" ordered the Mountie. "Hold still!"

"No. I'm okay. I can pull myself up." The mapper had gone into shock and was feeling no pain.

"Hold still, I say!" The Mountie realized the mapper was not going to do any such thing.

Crack. A single sound. It didn't sound that menacing. The ice sounded as if it was simply relieving itself—which, in a way, it was. The precipice was a cornice, or ice cliff, cantilevered out some seven feet. This could not be discerned until it broke off cleanly under the mapper's weight.

"Shit." whispered the pilot.

The man never screamed. Instead, he lunged for his backpack, which carried his prized maps. He got them, just as he disappeared silently over the ledge to his final resting place, 847 feet below, clutching the cherished tools of his trade to his chest.

The Mountie said nothing. He grabbed two pain killing syringes from the paramedic's bag. He quietly drove one deeply high into his left thigh and he handed the other to the pilot.

"Here. This will keep you from going into shock," he said, extending his leathery, weathered, outstretched hand.

The pilot stared at him with large, vacuous eyes. He held the shot limply in his left hand. He was having difficulty focusing and self-administering the needle.

"Here." said the Mountie, as he grabbed the pilot's belt, hoisted him up sixteen inches and drove the needle squarely into his buttocks.

The closest commercial airport was in Vancouver, which was still a great distance. A regional forest fire-fighting FBO unit was not as distant. Their makeshift tower got a clear fix on the SOS and another chopper was already en route. They couldn't land for the same reasons that had cost the former three their lives. However, they could drop a basket to safely transport the two survivors to the leeward side of the mountain.

The wind was shrieking. It would rage, gust and then reverse unto itself, not unlike an Eskimo puppy shaking its head wildly, trying to yank its towel from its master. The sleety snow was biting and drove as a thousand pins against their faces with each gust. The pilot went up first in the basket. It yawed uncontrollably one direction, then another. The Mountie was still glaring sternly at the smoldering hole, which had disappeared, as it was now mostly snow covered.

What in God's name happened here? thought the Mountie, searching for a shred of anything that would make some sense. The scene appeared homogenous with the rest of the landscape. His turn came. Up he went, straining his head in all directions to get a better last view of what appeared to be a great white nothingness to all other observers.

"What were you looking at?" asked the pilot.

The Mountie did not respond.

The pilot helped pull the Mountie out of the sling. They both took their seats, while alternately stomping cold feet, shaking their heads and slapping the melting snow off of their parkas. The new chopper pilot turned to them in the back.

"We understood there to be five of you!"

"There were. There were five. Now there are two," answered the Mountie. He did not look at the pilot.

"We'll come back for the bodies after she settles down a might. Couldn't find the prime minister, eh?"

"Nope. Not a sign," said the rescued pilot.

"We found him," said the Mountie quietly, while staring blankly out the window. "We found him."

Twenty-three

Menlo Park, California
November 2010

SCOTTY BOUNDED DOWN THE STEPS outside his office and jumped into his restored MGB. He had just knocked out a deal which had taken him almost two years to close. He had known from the start this deal had legs.

What a rush, he thought. He leaned over and slid "She's Got Legs" by ZZ Top into his CD player. He cranked it and accompanied them with soaring animated air guitar riffs, in between pounding out the backbeat on his steering wheel.

He redlined first gear and rapped hard through second. He buried it in third, as he merged into traffic on Highway 280 out of Menlo Park. He was thump, thump, thumping his way across the San Mateo Bridge when he heard the radio report that the prime minister of Canada and his fishing party were missing and feared dead.

A little early to be locking down the casket, thought Scotty wistfully, not having yet heard all the details. Later that night, after his workout, he lay down and elevated his odiferous socks and three-holed sweats up high on the sofa's arm to drain the fluid from his ankle. Though much improved, it would still swell when used aggressively. He slowly and menacingly lowered his remote at the TV. He clicked it on while announcing with his strongest epiglottal push, "Set for stun, Scot-eee." *Zap.*

The 10:00 pm news came on. The headline story, as quoted from *The Province,* Vancouver's most widely read newspaper, was the disappearance of the prime minister. The casual, almost pedestrian, mention of a large, snow–covered, steaming cavern witnessed by one of the rescuing Mounties caused him to sit up quickly on the couch. The hairs on the back of his neck tingled. He leaned forward, straining for every word.

"While no foul play is suspected, the entire party seems to have literally vanished into thin air," said the news commentator. "This happens occasionally, given the freakishly swift front that came in as a debilitating blizzard, which caught everyone unaware."

Still, the bodies were yet to be recovered. In light of the high wind and temperatures plummeting to single digits in the last thirty six hours, it was considered doubtful if the party could survive.

Scotty was numb. Was he overreacting? Powerful politicians died all the time. But not like this. And not two in a row. Why should this cause him so much interest? This wasn't his problem.

Fuck it, he thought. *My dog ain't in this fight. I should take Ali's advice and back off.* He still felt it more than a little odd that two powerful, neighboring North American leaders just happened to expire within a few months of each other—accidentally or otherwise.

He also felt it strange that while no foul play was suspected, much less confirmed, both deaths included caverns of moderately sized, gaping holes near the site where the dignitaries were last seen. Sure, the Mexican president died in an earthquake and those things do have the propensity to serve up large fissures with the occasional abyss, but why all the Mexican military at the quake site thereafter? Shouldn't there be the Mexican equivalent to FEMA types instead of armed Federales poking around?

Key also noted the snippet of footage he saw of the Mountie interviewed after the fact in Canada. It wasn't so much what he said, rather, how he said it.

"I know there's nothing concrete to make allegations with, but my sniffer"—the man pointed his forefinger to his nostril—"tells me there's more to this," said the Mountie on camera.

Key wrote the Mountie's name and badge number down, as well as the province he was stationed in: Mountie Sheridan Willingham, Vancouver based.

Key tossed fitfully that night in bed. He had recurring dreams of the college student from Berkley and his Throughput device. *What was his name?* He asked himself. *Oh, yes, Butterfield—Milo Butterfield.* Sounded a bit corny, like he belonged in a Dickens novel.

"Ichabod Crane!" He startled himself as he awakened shouting this character's name. He wondered if there was any connection to these two events. While Butterfield had not seemed malevolent at the time, he recalled learning of his untimely curious disappearance. Key pondered whether the design flaws had been solved and whether the device had fallen into hands of others less inclined toward mining.

At home, he was pensively feeding his blue tangs in their two hundred fifty gallon salt water aquarium when he looked up, exasperated. The fish darted up for the food then down diligently to the bottom for consumption behind a pinkish-orange piece of coral.

"Screw it." He snapped up his cell and dialed an international operator. "Yes, operator, in Vancouver, looking for the Canadian Mounted Police, post #153. Yes … That's it."

"153 here!" rapped out the polite but curt reply at the other end of the line.

"Yes. I'm trying to speak with an officer, one of your Mounties in particular—a Mr. Sheridan Willingham. Is he available?"

"I believe he just may be. I'm looking at him. Hold please."

Pause.

"Willingham here."

"Officer Willingham?"

"Yes."

"You don't know me from a load of coal. But it may be appropriate for us to speak, to speak in person." Scotty was pacing impatiently back and forth in front of his second-story bay window.

"Regarding?"

"Regarding the death of your prime minister."

"If you've got something to say, let's have it," responded Willingham.

"Well. I'm not going to astound you with hard, evidentiary material."

"Mmmm. Go on."

"It's more a series of hunches really that things … about things that just aren't right."

"Specifically?" snapped the Mountie.

"Are you familiar with the president of Mexico's death, which happened just a few months ago?"

"I heard about it, yes. Not aware of the details, however."

"This is not hearsay as I personally visited the site. There supposedly was a micro-earthquake with a hole opening up in the earth, just where he and a handful of his staffers were standing. They and their vehicles completely vaporized, with no bodies found."

"Take off, eh? Did you say hole? Was it a large fissure, or crack?"

"Well, that's one of the things that was curious. It should have been a crack, but it was a hole, entirely too circular in shape for my taste. Moreover, the damage was extraordinarily localized. Normally, a quake does not perform surgical damage the way a tornado might."

"Not normally."

"Additionally there were a goodly number of Mexican militia present. Federales. It would be natural to have some disaster relief people on site, but these guys were very long in the face, armed and loaded for bear. Do you see any correlation as to what occurred with your prime minister?" Key asked.

"I'm duty bound not to discuss the particulars of a case over the phone, even less inclined with a stranger. You made this call. What's troubling you? Why have you taken such a personal interest?"

"I'm a venture capitalist."

"Right. Quite. I've heard all you Yanks are venture capitalists, eh?" taunted Willingham.

"This is out there, but well over a year ago, a college student came into our firm and introduced us to a concept that would have revolutionized mining."

"Yes?"

"It supposedly had the ability to surgically burrow through the earth with a small, nuclear device as propellant. There may also be a tie to Red Mercury."

"And?"

"He disappeared. Gone from the face of the earth. Poof."

"What was the lad's name?"

"Butterfield. Milo Butterfield. A Berkley grad."

"Let me run that to ground," said Willingham. "What's the location of the pay phone you are speaking from?"

"I'm not at a pay phone. I'm at my residence on my cell."

"Good Lord, man. What's your name?"

"Key, Scotty Key."

"Phone?"

"415-649-0968."

"Listen closely here, Mr. Key. I want you to get off this phone immediately. Do no tarry. Schedule permitting, it would be grand if you could fly to Vancouver BC day after tomorrow. We chat, you see the Island and we'll get you a nice Kraft dinner. We'll have e-tickets under your name waiting for you at the San Francisco airport. Is that the closest one to you?"

"Yes."

"Our station is the downtown Vancouver police station at 4th and D Street. However, if possible, I'll pick you up at the airport around Noon. Can you make it?" pressed the Mountie with his call to action.

"Yes, I'll do it." Key had a flashback of his childhood friend Oliver being thrown up against the cold, gray, concrete walls at the circus and his face warmed.

"And above all, talk to no one about this—your thoughts or suspicions—absolutely no one. Is that clear?"

"Got it."

Scotty hung up. grabbed his Carhartt jacket and ran, sticking only every other stair. He was virtually flying. At the base of his townhome, he noticed a small, thinnish Iranian or Iraqi huddled near a bush across the street.

It was dusk and all he could make out was the occasional glowing red ember of what was, perhaps, a cigarette. That alone was certainly not unusual in San Francisco. What bothered him, though, was that, while the guy seemed to be staring, his posture suggested he was also trying to conceal the attention he was paying to Scotty.

Shit! That guy could be Stink Eye's double, the Iraqi from Cozumel who'd confused his ankle with prime rib. thought Key. He turned his gaze away and when he looked back, the glowing cigarette and its end-sucking host were gone.

Not possible. That guy's three thousand miles from here, thought Key. Scotty went outside, pulled the top down and poured himself into his low-slung roadster. Once inside, Key picked up his phone and called Pig.

"Cornelius?"

"Who wants to know?" taunted the redhead.

"The mother of your illegitimate child, asshole. It's me," snapped Key, feigning an annoyed tone.

"Did we lose our innate ability to identify ourselves, Mommy? How are you this morning?"

"Too early to tell, still running diagnostics. Listen, I'm on a cell phone and I want to keep this brief and just between us girls."

"Okay. Astound me."

"I need to talk to you."

"As opposed to this current activity?"

"Yeah. Face to face."

"When?"

"Now."

"Not in ten or fifteen minutes, but right-the-fuck-now? News flash, Key, never apply for work at the diplomatic corps. Ever."

"Can you do it or not?" clipped Key.

"Call it."

"Meet me at the Clift Hotel, the place with the big chair, the Redwood Room, in an hour. Tell absolutely no one about this. Okay?"

"Yes, mother. You're not bringing along Alfred Hitchcock, are you?"

"No. But if you keep running your mouth, Norman Bates is not out of the question." Key hung up on Pig midsentence.

He proceeded to drive in ever larger circles to confirm that he was not being followed. At one time, he thought a dung brown, older model Saab was dogging him a little too close, but then it turned off. He would flit from feeling he was being cautious, evasive and smart to chortling out loud at his own paranoia.

Honnnnnk! blared the horn of another driver, as Key ran a red light to make it difficult to follow him. Up and down the steep hills of San Francisco, he motored, watching the steam belch out from the early-morning restaurants vents.

Once at the hotel, he heard the high-level revving of Pig's Maserati downshifting into the parking lot. Key quickened his stride out the front door of the hotel to greet his friend, as it was still completely dark. It was a damp morning and his heels made for a sharp, hollow clicking sound against the wet, glistening walk, which was still bouncing off the full moonlight.

Click-clack, Click-clack, echoed the sound of heels on concrete, picking up speed close behind him.

Like the circus.

TWENTY-FOUR

KEY STRAINED HIS EARS, BELIEVING his steps were being mimicked in staccato fashion behind him. Stopping when he stopped. He turned quickly once and looked, so quickly he could hear his coat vent snap. He strained his eyes to dissect each and every mottled alleyway, which were all bathed in gray and sepia tones this time of day. Nothing. Probably his imagination.

Key's cell phone rang as he approached the restaurant and he answered it, "Mr. Key?" asked the stranger.

"Yes?"

"This is Mountie Sheridan Willingham in Vancouver B.C., whom you just spoke with moments ago."

"Yes."

"We ran a quick Interpol search on your Mr. Milo Butterfield. He expired about ten months ago, all but in your back yard. An apparent accidental death from blunt force trauma resulting from a skate board accident."

"Hmmm."

"The autopsy reports he was loaded with meth at the time."

"Really?"

"Yes. I've text messaged you with the mausoleum address and crypt number where he is entombed. Actually, it's not far from you. I've not linked it with his name nor offered any other content in the message."

"Good."

"You don't have to say anymore. Just thought you'd like to process this before we met." said Willingham.

"Thanks."

They hung up.

Pig waved aggressively and smiled at Key broadly as he bounded up the eateries steps. He and Scotty went inside to the maître d's station.

"Well, Sherlock, Mr. Watson has arrived," mocked Pig. "Oh and seeing this weather clearing reminds me I owe you a car wash, after you unethically lured me into a girly-man's over-under bet on the last Giant's game."

"Keep your voice down," barked Key. "Let's grab the booth over there." He motioned to a large, red, leather six-seater over in the extreme northwest corner for privacy. It was in tight against the heavily draped windows and adorned with highly ornate, gold filigreed lamps.

Cornelius veritably threw his body into the booth and banged his fist down, sending a pretzel skyward, which he then quite neatly—doglike—snatched out of the air with his open mouth. Key looked at him in exasperation but knew he wouldn't have Pig's attention until he acknowledged the feat with a quiet, understated golf clap.

"Why is it that all people important to me snatch shit out of the air with their mouths?" asked Key.

"It's a gift." said Pig. "My mother's side."

"How proud she must be," responded Key.

"Nurse!" Pig roared at the waitress. "Two coffees, black."

"Cornelius, do you remember the lad from Berkeley who came and pitched us a year or so ago?"

"Nope. Did he have nice tits? Failing that, what would ever make you think I'd remember him?" asked Pig with his mouth full, while steadily powering down a handful of pretzels.

"Butterfield, Milo Butterfield, the young man from Berkeley, who had a way of revolutionizing mining. Do you remember the exchange?"

"Yes, yes I do. And for the record", Pig paused to snatch another pretzel in midair with his mouth, "he had lousy tits."

"Okay. Do you remember his Throughput device, which he said still had some bugs? Issues with how to keep it cool or some such thing?"

"Yup. This steel trap" Pig said, tapping his forehead, "records every kernel of salient information. I'm pretty fucking amazing that way," exclaimed Pig smugly as he congratulated himself. "Pretzel?"

"Pass. Do I have your attention?"

Pig nodded. "Well. I literally just learned our Mr. Butterfield woke up dead a few months ago. Apparent accidental death involving drugs and a skate board."

"It happens."

"Yeah, well, true. But perhaps there's more." Said Key. "But really, did he strike you as a tweaker—I mean, *even a little?*"

"No way."

"A skater-dude or snow boarder?"

"The Flying Tomato he ain't."

"Doesn't make any sense. I want to scratch around some more under the covers."

"Stealth mode, eh? Well maybe what really happened was he first tried Throughput as a suppository and it flew up his ass."

"Simmer down, Pig. This could be some serious shit."

"Okay," said Pig, lowering his voice an octave, hanging his head and bouncing his chin twice in mock shame.

"Do you recall the death of the Mexican president a few months ago?"

"No. Yes. Maybe. Yeah, I mighta heard something like that."

"Did you hear the circumstances surrounding his death?"

"No. I don't recall." mumbled Pig, again with his mouth full. "Nurse! Can I get some eggs Benedict swimming in Tabasco sauce? And make the yolks real runny would you, doll?" exclaimed Pig, half shouting at the waitress across the room.

"He and a few of his staffers were swallowed up by an earthquake that possessed a very tight pattern."

"Hmmm."

"In an area that did not possess many fault lines. Also, did you hear on the news yesterday about the prime minister of Canada? He and some of his party are missing and feared dead."

"Let me guess. This whole incredible earth-eating thing again?"

"Matter of fact, yes. They fear it is death from similar, albeit not linked, circumstances."

"And you're convinced our Mr. Butterfield had something to do with these?"

"Well, the method of both dignitary's eventual demise was eerily similar and in keeping with what Butterfield said he was trying to develop."

Pig continued to listen, while he scrunched up his rotund, reddish face and shoved in two more pretzels, gushing another greeting at the smiling server who brought his eggs Benedict. She had a skirt that exercised a great deal of brevity and sported nice pins.

"So now our Mr. Butterfield also suffered a highly unusual and uniquely terminal fate, that's not at all in keeping with who he appeared to be— on many levels."

"So who do you suppose we take this up with? All officials interested in loosely correlated coincidences with absolutely no evidence?"

"I propose we get it straight from the horse's mouth," said Key.

"What horse?"

"Butterfield."

"I thought you just said he was dead."

"I did. And he is. But do you recall him claiming to have imprinted the key data on a microchip and putting it under a filling in one of his back molars?"

"Yes, I enjoyed that, pretty Dr. Fuckin' Strangelove, if you ask me. So you're saying, like, you … you truly believed him? So what do you suggest, a séance?"

"No. We dig his ass up, reclaim the molar's microchip and play the hand out."

Pig did not respond but looked genuinely horrified. "You can't be serious. You're shittin' me! You're outta your fucking gourd. Count me out."

"What have we got to lose?"

"Oh I don't know, ten years of our freedom, for one thing. I may be going out on a limb here, but I believe the great state of California still frowns big time on the average schmuck exhuming bodies for sport, in particular, without a court order," pushed back Pig.

"First off, *pussy*, do I sense a breakdown in action over a little thing like ethics? This is not the Cornelius Brandon III, Esquire, I know and love. What happened to *it's not the principle; it's the money?*" poked Scotty, goading his friend on. "Pig, take your right hand. Stick it high in the air." In so saying, Key violently thrust Pig's right hand straight up heavenward. "Thrust it down deep into your right pocket. Move it slowly to the left. If you can't find *any*, it's because you haven't got *any*."

"There's no guarantee this is going to make us any dough. It could just get us a few nights in jail and an arrest record, while you so artfully explain, 'oh I had no idea this was Mr. Butterfield's tomb, I thought I was digging up my great-aunt, Edie,'" said Pig.

"We're in luck in one respect."

"How so?" asked Pig.

"I just learned the address of the mausoleum he's in. No digging. We just have to deal with a guard, maybe a lock. Maybe a guard and a lock—worst case," pointed out Scotty.

"Ooooooh. This is just too easy then. I feel like I'm cheating," responded Pig sarcastically. "We'd only have to shoot one guard ..."

"We know which *drawer* he's in. We can be there in forty minutes. We'll go tonight, well after dark. I've got to get this done, this evening."

"Well," said Pig, as he slammed down his last cup of coffee. "Bring on Boris Karloff and let's go rob a fuckin' grave. Then I can take that off of my bucket list!"

TWENTY-FIVE

"ATTA BOY!" CELEBRATED KEY AS he gave Pig a crisp high five, realizing he had closed his friend on the adventure.

Later that night, on the way over to the mausoleum with Pig in tow, Key thought he caught a glimpse of the dung brown Saab again. He was so resolutely certain this time, he asked Pig to twist his outside mirror and stay on "high dung Saab alert."

As if out of "central casting," when they approached the mausoleum, the owls began hooting their beckoning calls to mates nearby—two short and one long blast. *Hoot-Hoot-Hooooot.* And on cue, the misty, moist marine layer gently rolled in, eerily enveloping the entire area and further dampening any sounds. The top of the wispy cloud's layer was moving faster than the bottom. As such, when craning one's neck and staring straight up for a lengthy period of time, the viewer got a vertigo sensation.

Upon reaching the graveyard Scotty killed his lights. Driving through the headstones, the moonlight danced uneasily off the clammy cement. When gazed at too long, the trees seemed to morph together forebodingly and form long, frowning faces. It was all too easy to conjure up shadowy, ominous forms where there were none.

"Hold my hand," whispered Pig.

"Bite me."

Ponds with a bit too much vegetation were being suffocated by their lily pads. Damp grass promenades, recently mowed and wetted by the *spritz, spritz, spritz* of the Rain Bird sprinklers, were all meticulously manicured and perfectly trimmed for the scant viewing pleasure of the few. All combined, they painted a canvas which bespoke of being where all things dead resided. The pair approached a prayer circle equipped with a four-tiered, turquoise, tinkling fountain. Ornate benches and other spiritual artifacts heralded a presence seemingly more religious then the area initially suggested.

The two could hear their tires, nervously crunching the gravel beneath them. When they slowed down further, the volume seemed to, in fact, increase. Pig was sweating a lot. The small, wooden bridge's single-lane planks and struts complained and groaned in a wavelike chorus as they passed over them. It was an elongated, multi-tonal groan, as if vividly reminding them they knew what they were about to undertake was forbidden. Verboten. As if gently harkening them to flee. One last chance—leave, leave now. This was just wrong.

"The Alpha & the Omega," said Scotty, looking up at the stone engraved inscription in the top of the crypt. "Yup, that's the one."

"The dumb and the dumber," countered Pig, making two vulgar, rapid, up-and-down hand gestures high in the air.

Key slowly eased his car between two exceptionally tall Russian pines on the south side of the structure, in an effort to totally mask their presence.

"Do you think there is a night watchman or security of sorts?" asked Pig.

"Probably and no. The watchman should be out here roaming around on his thirty-minute rotational circuits. But, with all likelihood, he is either asleep, watching porn, or texting his girlfriend," Key said dismissively.

"Wow. Those all sound much better than this. I think I like this guy!" chortled Pig in a whisper, as he leaned his head to the right and blew his nose with one finger on the ground.

Pig and Scotty furtively exited the car and looked around cautiously to ensure they were alone. They entered what was, fortuitously, an open mausoleum without an exterior locking door or gate. They could hear their heels clicking against the damp, granite foyer floor as they rounded the corner. Each click was like a final admonition: *What are you thinking?* Their small Maglite's beam bounced up and down among the drawer's labels, searching for the correct sequence.

"Hmm … 2405. That's the one. This is his drawer," said Key, coming to an abrupt stop in front of it. "Listen!" commanded Key in a whisper.

"What?"

"Shhhhh."

Approaching with almost catlike silence, far in the distance was a golf cart. Visible first atop one mound, just vaguely through the mist, the cart slid completely away from view behind the next. Its electric battery-powered engine was all but silent. Upon coming closer, the wheels started to make the grinding sound against the same chat on the roadside that Key recognized instantly.

Inside the cart was three hundred pounds of sweating, unkempt, gelatinous humanity, with a gray, short-sleeved security guard shirt two sizes too small. The garment was digging into jiggly arms, which were antique white in color.

"Shhhhh, he's coming closer," cautioned Key.

The guard's ensemble was punctuated in front with a short, black tie, possessing one gravy and two large queso stains with a single, vertical run on the left. The tie's conclusion was five inches above the guard's belt and resided at an angle thirty degrees from the vertical due to the resident's paunch.

His very large, black, leather belt showed prior wear marks on the second, third and forth notching holes. It was now tethered precariously onto the last. The belt appeared to be threatening exhaustion, with the tensile strength of that much cowhide being tested by the heft of; an oversized baton, the largest Maglite money could buy, one set of handcuffs, a taser, a black and silver, shiny mace canister, a hangared magnum-sized energy drink in-a drum, and a holster, which did not have a gun as an occupant. Rather, in the holster was a movie theatre-sized box of Junior Mints nestled up next to and accompanied by the smallest box of white powdered doughnuts that could be purchased, packaged and aligned in a commercially viable manner.

"Shit," whispered Scotty.

"Wanna try and make it back to the car?" asked Pig.

"Nope. No time. He's on us."

Coincident with the conclusion of those words, Key grabbed Pig's arm and pulled the prior linebacker on top of himself while wedging the two into the darkest corner. They were slammed between a meditation/prayer area and a statue of someone who looked extremely earnest and was undoubtedly at some time quite important.

"Not a sound," whispered Key.

As if on cue, following his last word, the inside of the structure was completely bathed with light, the intensity of which could only be afforded by a Maglite whose size rivaled the back limb of a Great Dane and was clearly coming off a set of fresh batteries. The cart came grinding to a halt, which caused its occupant to lurch forward as a single doughnut rolled out onto the ground.

"Anybody there?" asked the guard in as stern a voice as he could muster. The tone was as authoritarian as anyone whose respiratory system was challenged with morbid obesity and exacerbated by abject fear could summon up.

The guard did not dismount. He stayed in the cart. He took the exceptionally large Maglite and panned the structure top to bottom, inside and out, in a very thorough manner—at least, as thoroughly as one could pan from a remote, fixed position. He leaned forward and backward gradually. He groaned.

Creak. His leather belt made the single sound.

The cart beneath him yawed and groaned. He did not get out of the cart. He shut the engine off. Pig looked at Scotty, rolled his eyes and shook his head to the left and to the right while slowly, silently mouthing, "Fucking. Fuck."

The guard reached toward his holster, which initially alarmed Key. This concern was soon abated when he saw the guard was just retrieving his movie-sized box of Junior Mints and ingesting them leisurely as he studied off the structure. He would take one from the box, rest it on his tongue and suck. He'd suck just the top half of the chocolate off to get to the mint. And then he'd chew it, swallow and repeat.

With every other mint, he'd additionally suck air through his teeth for that cooling sensation and then run his tongue methodically along the outermost layers of his top and bottom teeth to suck off and secure every last morsel. Key felt the dining cadence was eerily reminiscent of a National Geographic special he had seen many years ago on gorillas as they preened the mites and ticks off each other's backs.

The guard did not get out of the cart. After what seemed like twenty minutes and, in fact, was but three, the guard reholstered his Junior Mints, started the golf cart back up, summarily turned the cart around and headed back to the cemetery's administrative building. He punished and crunched the path's gravel unhurriedly again as he weaved his way back.

"Mother of God," sighed Pig in relief.

All the way back, the guard's Maglite would intermittently violate all serenity the darkness had once afforded those confined corners. The beam invaded nooks and crannies that begged to be left alone. It permeated all while the guard remained in a seated position.

"Why am I here?" asked Pig.

"Because you love me. Quit your fuckin' bellyachin' and hand me those tools."

"Nothing quite says I love you like a rotting corpse," bemoaned Pig, as he handed Key the heavy bag they had brought with them. Pig could smell the mausoleum's moldy air as he breathed deeply when he bent over to help. Pig had extraordinary olfactory abilities. Yet, for all his gritty toughness, he also had a weak and queasy stomach.

Key promptly dropped down on one knee and opened his dark brown tool satchel, which he'd recovered from his car's bonnet. He brought sufficient implements to remove any locking mechanism they might encounter with dignity. Or, failing that, the lock was coming off without that same dignity.

After a few unsuccessful attempts, he turned to Pig and said, "Give me the beater."

"The beater?" inquired Pig.

"Yeah. The two-pound-fucking hammer. It has a tremendous amount of persuasion when other, more conventional methods have failed."

"Ohhhhhh. The 'beater,'" mocked Pig.

Key also took out an old chisel and poked it in between the narrowest of openings between the lock and the drawer. With a quick *rap-rap*, he smote the end of the tool until a high ear-piercing, singular *chink* was heard, signifying the end of the chisel as it snapped in two. Pig just looked at him, big eyed and sweaty faced.

"Hey, if this was easy, they'd have accountants doing it," said Key.

The good news however, was that even in its failure, the chisel had opened the smallest of cracks a quarter of an inch or so, to invite a further and even larger intrusion.

"Where is that son of a bitch?" said Key, looking for a tool.

Key reached back into the rucksack and this time removed a rusty, cast-iron pry bar and wedged it between the ever so slightly larger opening in the lock. He commenced to whack the shit out of the other end with his "beater." *Ping. Ping. Ping. Splang!* The lock ultimately yielded to the fusillade of Key's punishing blows and threw itself on the floor in disgust.

"Well. We're in," whispered Key.

"Happy fucking birthday," quipped Pig.

Key and Pig grabbed both sides of the drawer and quite rudely, interrupted Mr. Milo Butterfield's dirt nap, sans the dirt. They slid his drawer out and peeled back the top thin, metal mantel covering after removing another, yet smaller locking mechanism.

The top mantle's aging, discolored metal complained vociferously as it was pried and bent back and forth, back and forth. Ultimately it yielded through metal fatigue and was forced completely back to reveal its occupant.

Key and Pig cut their way through yet one more Visqueen moisture barrier, which was present not only as a vapor shield but also as a neighborly courtesy, or form of communal odor control. Now that the barrier was penetrated and the sealed Visqueen was no longer intact, there was no longer any form of aromatic courtesy to be had.

"Jesus! Fucking Christ. Fuck me!" whispered Pig in his most ardent whisper yell, as he brought his hand sharply to his face in an attempt to block the vapors entering his nostrils. His head snapped back, reacting to the acrid, pungent fumes and struck a ceremonial stand behind him.

"Tempting. And pass," responded Key to his friend's second suggestion, keeping his head down and staying on target, albeit with tissues stuffed up each nostril.

"Can you believe the stench on this bad boy? Wheeew. We're talking ripe!"

"Yeah, they do that. Come on, give me a hand getting his mouth open."

"Getting his mouth open? You aren't going to slip him some tongue are you? I will bitch-slap you like a two-dollar whore if you do!" threatened Pig.

"Just hold his head still and shut the fuck up," commanded Key. He just wanted this unpleasant business done.

Pig steadied Milo's rotting skull. It still possessed uneven, crusty patches of skin, in some spots present and in others already decomposed. Scotty grabbed the iron bar once more and pried open the skull's obstinate mouth, while Pig struggled in close with both hands to keep it motionless. So stubborn was the jaw however, that at the fulcrum's maximum leverage point came a singular: *Click*.

Key had broken off two of the rotting corpse's front teeth. Rapidly resolving the pent up pry bar's pressure, one of the teeth reacted promptly to its newfound freedom by shearing off, heading skyward and shanking right toward "out of bounds."

The tooth release was so quick, it caught Pig unaware. It came to rest without fanfare on his outstretched lower lip. At first, Pig tried to shoo it away, thinking it was an insect. The realization however, that a meaningful portion of Butterfield's yellow, dead and rotting tooth was resident on his lower lip quickly triggered a gag reflex.

"Awwwwwkgh!" Pig choked. He spun violently to his right, while throwing up between his hands, which were making an automatic, albeit impossible, attempt to control same. He tasted the bitter, vinegary bile contents of his last meal and then he smelled it again in his nostrils.

"Perfect. I smell it, now I taste it." Pig spat and spit again. "Shit."

"We'll be out of here in a minute," said Key in hushed tones.

He then pulled out his small Maglite and twisted the end to engage it. Shoving the dark end in his own mouth, he moved in much closer to the corpse's face and pushed the illuminated end deep into Milo's grotesquely gaping mouth. He swept the cavity to the right and then the beam panned to the left.

Scotty still couldn't quite see. He placed his right knee up on the drawer to push himself fourteen inches higher and extract a better viewing angle. The smell was overwhelming and nauseating. The heavy evening air seemed to exacerbate the stench that was getting hung in their nostrils. The light was searching, back and to the left. He swept the light again.

"Do you see that!" whisper-shouted Key.

"See what?"

"That left back molar. It's gone. It's not there. It's the only tooth not there."

TWENTY-SIX

"IT's THE ONLY TOOTH NOT there," said Key again incredulously, as he dismounted the raised drawer's ledge with a thud. He slap-brushed the dust off his pants.

"Help me here. This is clearly a bigger deal to you than me," lamented Pig.

"Don't you recall? Butterfield shared that he trusted no one with his device's proprietary design—not even his computer. He told us he'd placed it on a chip and embedded it in his left back molar for safe keeping."

"Yeah, Yeah. No, you're right," said Pig, raising slowly and brushing off his coat's arms more solemnly than usual. You mentioned that Nancy Drewism factoid earlier."

"Okay. I've seen what I need to see."

They slid Mr. Butterfield back into his prior resting place with a resounding clunk. This action broke his skull clean free from his shoulders at a very brittle neck vertebra. They returned the vapor shield, gently hammered back the exterior skinned metal mantel with the beater, while muting the racket with three layers of damp musty green towel between the beater and the beaten.

They left. Back over the vine-covered, single-lane pedestrian bridge, they drove. The wood struts complained yet again as to the hour of the intrusion. Lights off, they circled their way back around the four-tiered, turquoise fountain, the prayer retreat station and out the main gate. Fortunately, the guard was just concluding being deeply engaged in his cavalcade of porn, following a thoroughly comprehensive session of abusing his SMS text messaging, as well as himself.

The next morning, Key was awakened by a call from Ali.

"You never write. You never call," she teased.

"And that is the punch line of the old nun joke after she's raped by an escaped gorilla," chided Key. "Say, changing gears here, do me a favor and don't call me for awhile."

"Okay. Sure, Scotty, sure." She paused. "Everything Okay?"

"Today, yes. Not sure this line is secure. Until I sort out some of the last few weeks' events, let's only talk in person. We can meet where we met for our first dinner at 8:00 am tomorrow. Okay?"

"You mean the one on …"

"Yes," interrupted Key, "the one with the mailbox out front. Please don't say the name or address."

"Okay, got it."

Good to his word, Pig swung by at 5:00 am the next morning to pick up Key's MGB for the car wash Pig owed him due to the loss of the Giant's bet. It was still dark out and Scotty was packing for his trip to Vancouver. The darkness was rendered all the more impenetrable by the low clouds that had yet to recede that morning. Key and Pig briefly shared steaming hot coffee, white powdered doughnuts and insults as they discussed their next steps based on the information they'd gleaned the night before.

"Well, I'd better get to the office, make a cameo appearance and greasepaint up some whiteboards so as to dazzle our erstwhile employer," cracked Pig.

"Got it. Thanks for cleaning up the car. Fast pay makes fast friends, you know." With that chiding, Scotty winked and threw Pig his keys.

"Key, you're such an asshole," countered Pig. Not raising his head, Key smiled and blew the steam off his coffee.

Pig clamored down the stairs and out the front door to the MG. Scotty heard the throaty roar of his car engage as Pig started it in his driveway. Pensively for no reason, at the same moment, Key walked over to his bay window, gently pulled the curtains back and peered out upon the thick, pea-soup foggy morning's streetscape.

There. Across the street, down some eight cars—was it the same dung brown Saab that had been dogging them last night? He strained his eyes. He couldn't be certain, due to the distance and conditions. Maybe it was brown. Maybe it was gray. Maybe it was a Saab. Maybe it was an old restored Peugeot.

Directly across the street, a single glowing ember, previously concealed behind an abandoned public phone booth appeared. It ebbed and flowed with the drag from its owner.

Shit, thought Key, as he sprinted downstairs, leaping each half flight in a single bound.

"Pig!" screamed Scotty, running to his front door. "Piiiiiiig!!" He cried out more loudly this time.

The MGB had stopped revving its engine. It was still running, however. *Thank God Pig hasn't driven away*, Key thought to himself. He ran outside, slipping on his moist front stoop and falling resoundingly on his ass. Recovering quickly, he picked himself up and went around to the driver side of the car. Seeing Pig's silhouette, he felt relieved and bent over, talking.

"Listen. I don't want to overreact here," said Scotty, out of breath and smiling, "But you may want to …" But then, he stopped. He stopped smiling. He stopped talking.

Pig was still there.

Slumped.

There was a single bullet hole in the driver side window. The bullet employed was a hollow point. Key recognized the carnage. It appeared to be from a Winchester Black Talon or Ranger "T" series. The ordinance was intentionally designed with a reverse tapered jacket. This jacket was deliberately weakened to allow the cuts to open into six petals upon impact, fanning out for maximum devastation. When spent, it formed a talon. The round had caught Pig right above the left eye and taken the entire top of his head off. Brain tissue and blood were sprayed generously across the dashboard, the seats and the other passenger window.

"Fuck!" shouted Key, as he slammed both fists on the hood of the car and spun to look around, straining his eyes in the fog to see if the assassin was still present. He looked across the street at the abandoned phone booth. No glowing ember. He jerked back around and cast his gaze down the street. The dung brown Saab was gone.

And so was Pig.

He opened the car door. Pig slumped into his arms. He felt his friend's neck with two fingers. No pulse. It was over. Glancing at the grotesque remnants of his friend's head, whose skull was unwound like you'd half-peeled an orange, he realized there was nothing left to resuscitate. Key choked back the emotion that was rolling over him. His eyes became moist and his face warmed. He wiped his mouth.

"I am so sorry, buddy," lamented Key, holding Cornelius in his arms and rocking him back and forth as he spoke. "I am sooo sorry. I shouldn't have drug you into this." He was breathing heavily and his heart was beating as hammer and tong. "I'll square this for you, buddy. You have my word. You have my word. I'll square this for you." Scotty hugged what was left of Pig's head.

Reaching for his cell phone, he noticed it was not on him. He returned back inside to call from his hard line. He was in a trancelike state—zombified. He walked back slowly to his front door and stumbled up the last step, almost missing the riser entirely as if he was in a coma, numb with disbelief.

He got to his bay window and faced east, shoulders slumped. A catch was in his voice as he placed the 9-1-1 call. Halfway through the report, he turned to look back out the window at the horrific landscape and saw that Pig's body was gone. In less than two minutes, the shooter's shells and Pig had been policed.

TWENTY-SEVEN

As PROMISED, THE NEXT DAY Key met Ali in the morning early for breakfast at the Max's Diner where they'd first met. Key was late, due to completing the police report on Pig's death.

"Wow. Why so glum?" asked Ali.

Key slid crumpled into his seat, downtrodden. "It's Pig, Ali. He's ... He's dead."

"Oh my God! Was it heart related?" asked Ali, putting her hand over her mouth, thinking of Pig's temper and his proclivity toward alcohol and obesity.

"No. It was bullet related. He was shot in my car. He was shot in the head in my car, in my driveway this morning. It was a 'hit.' He was taking my car to get it washed to square up an old bet. Jesus, I still can't believe it."

"Oh Scotty, Scotty, Scotty, I am so sorry for you. I know you two were very close. You worked shoulder to shoulder with him for quite awhile, didn't you?"

"Yes, yes I did—five years." Scotty held both hands in tent fashion over his mouth and nose with his thumbs under his chin and breathed through the hand tent. "I just can't believe it. He didn't deserve this. And I got him into it."

"Into what?"

Scotty brought her up to date on Vinnie's G2, the possible existence of Red Mercury and the shadowy Stink Eye.

"Maybe you should just let it go," said Ali, wiping her eyes with her sleeve, as she had liked Pig as well. "Let the police handle it and just walk away."

"Not happening. Nope. Going to see this through till the end." Key set his jaw with conviction, those muscles flexing and relaxing again. This was a call to action he was not going to shrink from. He was flooded with images of his childhood friend Oliver and now Pig.

"I still can't believe it. He was so vibrant, so alive, always laughing, always teasing. I just saw him. Do you think they thought… he was *you?*"

"He was in my car, in my driveway and it was dark."

Key went on to reveal his phone exchange with Mountie Sheridan Willingham. He spoke of Sheridan's desire to fly him promptly to Vancouver the next day. He debriefed her as well on last night's affair with Pig in the cemetery. Ali's eyebrow raised slightly when she learned that Butterfield's left back molar had gone missing.

She listened intently but then again expressed concern for Scotty's personal safety. "I don't think this is a good idea," said Ali. "It's dangerous and taking your eye off the ball."

"Thanks for the concern."

"Maybe diluting your focus on closing one of the largest LBOs you've ever chased, Scotty." The pursuit was code named "Raptor." The transaction had consumed about nineteen months of his time and it had a high profile with Wentworth.

"They killed my best fucking friend, okay?" he replied in an uncharacteristically elevated tone of voice. A reply so loud the neighboring two booths stopped talking abruptly so they could eavesdrop better. "Nothing I can't handle," said Key. "I owe Pig. I'm going to square it for him."

Ali saw there was no changing his mind and yielded before the disagreement became more heated.

"Watch your six Ali, they know you are an 'associate' of mine," said Key.

She knew he was right.

"Any of this have intersecting sets with your line of work?"

Scotty knew she would never surrender anything "classified" or on a "need to know" basis. He was simply casting about for a reaction. However, if she reacted in a way that suggested the NSA might be aware of what he'd discovered over the past twenty months, he might have some insight as to the scale of what he was dealing with.

Another patron entered Max's. "Ali!" shouted a GQ handsome man, who had just walked in. He was lean and tall, with all fashion accessories matching perfectly in an understated manner. The gent was a silver gray-haired Brit, with hazel eyes and a broad smile.

"Scotty, I'd like you to meet my boss, Burton Buttons," said Ali, standing to introduce him as well as distance herself emotionally from their last exchange.

"My pleasure, Burton." Key rose and shook Buttons' hand firmly, staring straight into his eyes.

The men locked gazes, neither turning away. They nodded and smiled, yet both were studying the other's countenance, while expressing limited authentic emotion themselves.

"Likewise. Indeed, indeed. Heard many good things about you," replied Buttons, playing with his cufflinks and then shooting them both out from under his jacket to heighten their visibility. "Tried to cajole Ali into meeting you earlier, threatened to have her guts for garters if she kept putting me off, however she is quite clever at corporate dodgeball to be certain." Said Burton with another expansive smile.

"To be certain," said Key, making his face pleasant but telegraphing no real, telltale smile or expression.

Ali extended an invitation to Buttons to join them at their table by gesturing to a nearby chair. He accepted. Buttons drug his chair out, making a loud squeaking noise on the tile and took a seat as he directed his dialogue to Scotty.

"So. You're over at PacRim Ventures?"

"Yes."

"Menlo Park, Sand Hill?"

"Yes, Sand Hill office. That's the one."

"VC's are like flies over there, aren't they? Thick, like moths to a flame." Buttons pursed his lips, sat up overly erect and sipped his coffee while holding the cup's handle in a rather effeminate manner, from Scotty's point of view.

"A number have made their address there without a doubt."

"And I understand from Ali you code name your work just like the DOD?" asked Buttons.

"Also correct. The larger deals, loose lips and all of that." Scotty was beginning to be mildly agitated by the rapid-fire questions from a guy he'd just met, especially knowing his background. Still, he was Ali's superior, so he had to offer up the illusion of civility.

"Precisely. And is it ... Well ...," Buttons hesitated. "I also hear you have been involved in some recent amazing events with some rather fantastic island adventures."

"Not certain what those would be," deadpanned Key, offering no ricocheting feedback, either verbally or visually.

"Oh, understand. Quite right. You're much too modest. And our relationship is still in its infancy. How rude of me to drill down. Shouldn't pry. Hazard of the trade, you know. Simply be assured, we are quite vigilant and you needn't be concerned about any of those matters on our watch."

"I'll sleep better tonight." said Key flatly, as he broke his gaze and addressed this last remark to his coffee cup, which now had his full attention.

Ali glanced at him while flashing disapproval out of the corner of her eye, not turning her head away from Buttons, however. She sensed a bit of attitude growing in Key's retort and body language.

"Well. I should run. Francis, enjoyed meeting you." Buttons stood up abruptly. "I'm sure we'll be talking again in the future."

"My pleasure." responded Key, not knowing exactly why or on what occasion they'd be talking again.

Buttons left.

Key turned to Ali, whom he directed his full gaze. "Young lady, precisely what did you tell him?" he asked hotly.

"Much less than you think. He was wanting to see what you would volunteer up on your own. Relax. You passed the test. You didn't run your mouth. Some people, when they meet NSA leaders, are so chatty they tend to delegitimize themselves. They are all convinced they've just found Amelia Earhart, solved the Kennedy assassination or the next conspiracy theory. They can be long-winded. You were not. You done good."

"Nevertheless," said Key in disgust. "In the future, just tamp it down. I mean *really*. Why did you tell him anything? *Anything at all?*" Scotty was shaking his head stunned with disbelief.

"Well. Let's see. It's kind of *my job* to keep him current with 'chatter,'" responded Ali sarcastically, as she squared her shoulders back at the affront.

"I trust you did not mention any personalities, names, or facilities in your 'chatter' debrief?"

"No, I did not. Your friends' identities are safe with me. You're upset," said Ali.

"Yes, yes I am. Burton Buttons? Not a fan."

"Wow. That came out of left field. What provoked that? Is this meet-another-alpha-male, snarling-dog syndrome?"

"Nope. He's just a bit too familiar on sensitive topics with someone he's just met. And, someone in his business, you'd think, would be the last one to broach those topics so soon after meeting someone—especially in public."

"I think you are being a bit harsh," chided Ali, attempting to calm him down.

"Perhaps. But it really steams my clams. Pig isn't even in the ground yet and this overly smarmy, smiling spook feels the need to grin-fuck me—as if he expected me to run my mouth on personal matters the first time we've ever met," said Key in righteous indignation.

Ali looked down, as she knew there was no calming him down at this point. She regretted making the introduction.

TWENTY-EIGHT

AFTER COFFEE, ALI MENTIONED IT would be good if Scotty could drop briefly by her place on the way into the office, as Hoppy had made Key a gift for his birthday.

Upon arriving at Ali's townhouse, Hoppy was holding her virtual court from the top of the fire hydrant, doing a faux lip sync into the non-business end of her mop. Her boom box was booming at full throttle and belching out Lady Gaga's "Poker Face," which was one of Hoppy's fave fives. Her face was beat red with intensity.

"Mento?" asked Ali of Key, cocking her head back and smiling as this one was vaulted low from her under left thigh high above her head in an attempt to put the past heated discussion behind them.

"Pass."

Ali ignored his petulant response and put another coat of Burt's Bees gloss on her lips. She kicked off her Casadeis and threw herself onto the sofa, having grown weary of trying to get Scotty out of his funk.

The sitter was in the rocker on the porch, intermittently rocking, knitting and reading the *San Francisco Times*. She glanced at Hoppy over the top of her glasses to ensure the little girl adhered to the do-not-*ever*-cross the-sidewalk-as-you're-too-close-to-the-street rule.

Upon seeing Scotty, Hoppy jumped down from the hydrant, summarily dropped her "mic," seamlessly performed two flips, a cartwheel and slammed her face into his thigh at full throttle. The move was in concert with her exceptionally large glasses being relocated forty degrees clockwise and a bit further down her nose, such that her right ear now had twenty-twenty vision.

"Hey, hey, hey! What do you say, munchkin? 'Sup? Word to your sistah!" He held his fist up high and his elbow at a right angle in mock rapper salutation. "How's my favorite hip-hop star!"

Hoppy responded by throwing a peace and an okay sign, cocking her hip to the side and busting a move with two body thrusts and a prompt dive back to Scotty's thigh, where she assumed the role of the moist human tourniquet. Moist, as she was silently giggling and drooling down his leg. She ran behind the hedge outside the house to perform the amazing human blowfish routine again for Key.

Smoooooooofth! came the sound off the glass as she pressed her lips to the other side of the pane. She'd puffed her cheeks up and blown hard, which made a water buffalo farting sound with the expulsion of air against the pane. Then she laughed very hard, although without making a sound. It was a bit like watching an old Chaplin movie.

From around the corner roaring in full voice that got louder and louder as its owner grew nearer came the exclamation, "Motherfucker! Motherfucker! Motherfucker!"

It was Alex rounding the corner with his purple and green, plastic dinosaur in tow. Hoppy immediately ran over, applying her tourniquet arm-hold to his left thigh as well. Remarkably, it in no way slowed down or impeded his progress. He just kept walking, with her attached like a starfish, stuck to his leg.

"Alex! What's up, buddy?" asked Key with a warm smile.

"I told you not to do it!" exclaimed Alex loudly. To put a fine point on it, he hurled three bags of single-portion Cheetos at Scotty.

"Ah Hah! Looks like a new manager at the Shell station is still getting schooled up as to just how much a dollar can buy!" laughed Scotty as he bent over and picked up the bags.

"Well, there are US dollars and there are Alex dollars. The latter possesses infinitely more purchasing power," said Ali.

"No doubt." He grabbed Alex; tussled his shock of thick, red hair and threw him in the air, exclaiming boisterously, "How many times have I told you not to take advantage of the grown-ups!"

"I have a new part-time job, Mr. Key!" exclaimed Alex.

"Really. What is it, buddy?"

"I'm a Not-Macer."

"Ah ha. And what, pray tell, does a Not-Macer do?" asked Scotty.

"For one hundred dollars, I won't mace you," replied Alex solemnly as he held up a small canister of breath spray at a sinister angle.

"Whoa. Well, here's a buck to keep me off your list for at least a couple hours anyway."

Alex quickly pocketed the dollar, laughed and continued at the top of his lungs to enjoin the entire neighborhood with his harangue, "Motherfucker! Motherfucker! Motherfucker!"

Alex's mother appeared, looking exasperated, peering over the fence, shaking her head while wagging her finger and saying, "I don't know where he gets it!"

It was uncharacteristically warm for November and the sprinklers had just come on next door. Key took it upon himself to set Alex down, bend down on one knee and draw him in close, saying just barely audible, "Alex, how hot is it today?"

Alex paused briefly then exclaimed, "It's a hot somm-bitch!"

Ali tried to stifle her laughter and Key guffawed, much to Alex's mother's lack of amusement.

Key then looked at Ali and said deliberately too loud, "I don't know where he gets it!"

Alex's mother stuck her tongue out at Scotty, flipped him off, turned and walked back into her house as the screen door slammed behind her.

"Okay, Hoppy," cajoled Ali, "what have you gotten Scotty for his birthday?"

Hoppy opened her eyes exceptionally wide in recollection, made a silent mock shriek and hopped up the stairs to retrieve the gift.

In the meantime, Ali brought Key three Pill Pockets, so he could amuse himself with taunting Tang into securing a Pill (or for that matter anything that smelled like a Pill) and watching him stalk, snatch and scurry back to Hoppy's book bag with plans of savoring the treasure later. Stalk. Snatch and scurry. Stalk. Snatch and scurry.

Hoppy came down the stairs, clutching her surprise for Scotty. She was taking the stairs two at a time, even with her diminutive size, and making up the gaps by executing a half vault with her arm against the staircase banister. She hit the bottom stair with a double-footed stomp, which made both of her dog ears bounce. At the landing, she reached into her voluminous purse and pulled out the gift. She was holding it out in front of her with a pride-filled expression.

"What have we here?" asked Scotty.

Racing over to Scotty, Hoppy extended both arms straight out with his bounty. He saw enough anticipation in her eyes that he knew, whatever it was, he was going to have to summon up an Oscar-winning performance of appreciation.

"Well. Open it. The child will explode if you don't," encouraged Ali, fluttering her hands.

"This is truly an honor," said Key to Hoppy. He bent down to be at her level so he could gaze upon her eyeball to eyeball. His nose was but two inches from hers. He spoke very slowly and sincerely, like to a spooked horse. "I appreciate this. This is very special to me because it comes from you."

Hoppy beamed.

He carefully removed the wrapping paper one fold at a time, fawning all the while with alternating "ooohs" and "ahhhhhs" until he discovered a custom-made, kiln-fired saucer nestled within. It was a heavy, one-inch thick plate, some nine inches in diameter, with an overly large oval toward the bottom and a depression in the middle. Then it struck him.

"Is this … Is this—you?"

Hoppy nodded yes enthusiastically, pleased he could discern her puffy-faced likeness, which she had pressed into soft, wet clay before kiln-firing it into perpetuity. The image was the same bloated cheek, open-mouth blowfish she had just shown him fifteen minutes before and some three dozen times previously. The manic expression, which had always sent him initially into overly dramatic mock horror, was always quickly followed up by raucous laughter.

"Well you know, I didn't have one of these. And, since it's of your face, I will cherish it forever. Thank you very much, Hoppy. I'm touched." He bent over, kissed her forehead and tenderly gave her a hug.

Hoppy curtsied in her multi-plaid outfit, did a cartwheel and then hit a frozen starfish pose in celebration. She held it for five seconds then ran back and gave Scotty a crushing neck hug with squinting eyes. There was just a little bit of drool making its way down the left side of her mouth. Ali announced it was time to gather at the dining room table. It was a bleached white pine affair with bright white and delft blue Scandinavian tile insets around the border.

Key was presented with a large, twenty-inch diameter oatmeal birthday cookie with the word *Scotty* in large, green and white icing script smack dab in the center. "Happy Birthday" was written around the top of the cookie and a single candle stood in the center. The three sat at the table, sang and held hands while bouncing them up and down to the beat of the perennial Birthday song.

"Happy Birthday toooooo youuuuuuu!" two of the three sung. "Happy Birthday" culminated by a moment of silence for Scotty's wish. He blew out the candle and much clapping and cheering ensued. The obligatory "tickle match" unfolded between Scotty and Hoppy, with the event concluding by Hoppy grabbing the restroom's bath mat and slinging it over Key's back while he was on all fours, to simulate a saddle.

"Careful, that could be a bucking bronco," cautioned Ali.

Hoppy all the while was being steadied on Key's back, by spreading his necktie as reigns. Then the bucking would commence, resulting in the compression of Key's Adam's apple and the elongation of his tie—well worth it when watching the mime shrieking and giggling Hoppy's face projected.

After twenty minutes or so of this nonsense, Scotty noticed his watch and knew he had to get back to the office and kiss Beetleman's ring and various other sundry body parts. En route to the office, he was struggling with how in the devil he was going to get up to Vancouver the next day without attracting undue attention and still satisfy the needs of his managing director.

Moreover, during the police report about Pig, the sergeant had said he may be circling back with more questions for Key later in the week. Scotty knew what that meant. Next click, he would become a "person of interest," whereupon he would not be allowed to leave the country. He had to avoid that exchange at all cost. Key and Wentworth had previously expressed their heartfelt mutual condolences for the passing of their workmate on the phone. The toughest initial discussion on the topic was all but behind them.

"Terrible about Pig," said Wentworth, acknowledging briefly how close Pig and Scotty had been.

"Yes." was all Key responded, as he settled into his office chair.

Wentworth entered his office and confronted him at his desk. "On a separate matter—Raptor?"

"All good, Chief," replied Key.

"No. Hear me, Francis. I'm looking for more than the auto-perfunctorily dismissive response here. A correct and proper, workmanlike report is what I am seeking. When is the last time you spent some time with their board? I haven't seen a status write-up on this deal for over a month. Is this for real? Or is it just a grand exercise in expense account puffery? Kindly resist your innate propensity to bullshit me."

"Saw the principals two weeks ago, write-up is on the northeast corner of your desk under the fruit basket. You are in a bullshit-free zone. It's the real deal."

"I want to see an overall 20 percent cash on cash return here."

"That's pretty strong, isn't it? Considering we're also making 16 percent on top with the mezzanine debt alone?"

"In today's frozen market, Scotty, me lad, we can get 16 percent out of a vending machine. No bank is going to touch this transaction. This new administration and its 'Great Recession' has parochial business loans DOA. LBOs are all but impossible to effect.

"But don't you think …," started Scotty.

"Let me finish," said Beetleman. "And, if the banks ever did consider it, they'd also require 30 percent equity up front from Raptor, which clearly will not materialize in our lifetime. Their permanent rate would not be in single digits. So. We pretty much own them." Stanley amplified this point by first making a fist, then with a single lip lick, raising his chin and pulling his suit coat down in the front with a snap.

"I have your point." Scotty had his chin resting on his fists as he sat motionless with his elbows resting on his desk. It was quite clear to him this was not a discussion. It was an announcement. And he knew from having dealt with these instances previously that Wentworth would be agitated if he debated or offered up anything other than immediate compliance. Compliance, with just a dash of obsequious and fawning behavior.

Wentworth had his thoughtful moments to be certain. They were normally heralded in by his being seated at the conference table with other partners in shirtsleeves with his coat off. The last part was important. In the coat-off position, Wentworth seemed almost as if his battle armor was down and, in like fashion, so were some of his defenses. In this position, he offered up the perception of vulnerability to his staff.

Alternatively, if the coat was on and he was standing, the corporate antennae signaled something very different. If he'd just stopped by your office to do a data dump or the D.A.D. acronym (*delegate and disappear*), only the foolhardy would stand in front of his verbal fusillade. In that mode, there was never any ambiguity as to the outcome.

"Francis, Raptor. They're headquartered in Vancouver, BC, yes?"

"Why. Yes—they— are," replied Scotty emphatically, giving each word its own beat, wryly realizing his problem was about to be solved for him. "In fact, I was planning on getting up there tomorrow, informally initiating the socialization of our term sheet so there are no surprises when the team meets with them to codify this in a couple of weeks."

"Terrific! That's the spirit. I knew I could count on you. Get back up there, you junkyard dog and rip their throat out!"

Beetleman dug doglike at the ingrown hairs on the back of his neck. He licked his lips as if preening away mites, pushed his thick, black, horned-rim glasses up from the end of his nose, turned and walked out in a flourish. On the way out he didn't look up. Rather, he took his right hand, whose fingers had amazing individual girth and slammed it against the door's frame so hard the three-by-six pane of glass bowed, flexed and bowed again. Halfway down the hall he shouted back, "Let's get this done, Scotty. Put a bow around it!"

"Will do, Stanley. Glad we had this time together. We'll defecate or dismount. Looking forward to yet another chance to over perform chief," muttered Scotty mechanically under his breath in an insincere, robot-like monotone.

Wentworth did not acknowledge Key's sarcasm being half-way down the hall already, however they understood each other perfectly. It was part of the dance. The Arthur Murray footsteps had been thrown down on the floor too many times previously. All knew where they started, all knew where they stopped. The rest was but Kabuki theatre. Beetleman strode off and continued down the corridor, pincers pincing, hands shoved backwards through his black oily hair, on the warpath to tune up another one of Key's colleagues with a pacing akin to the recent drive-by direction.

TWENTY-NINE

Vancouver, British Columbia
December 2010

ON BOARD THE PLANE EARLY next morning, Key threw himself into the deep leather appointments of his business class seat and fell asleep after takeoff. Upon awakening midflight, Key recalled that he'd always enjoyed visiting Vancouver. With a bit of European flair, the people were friendlier than across the pond. He remembered the smiling faces at the fish mart where they threw the fresh salmon, laughed and sang overly loud without the fear of reprisal in the middle of the day.

Inasmuch as Hong Kong had slid away as a British protectorate, Vancouver had become a true melting pot. True, there was some initial resentment of the massive Asian influx, resulting in seeing some "No HongKouver" T-shirts being worn back in the day.

He recalled his father, after visiting the '86 Expo in Vancouver, had told him about the throngs of illegal Vietnamese immigrants who'd arrived in their dinghies in the seventies and who Carter had let into the United States. These people were hard working but destitute. For those reasons, they were called "the boat people".

His old man had always admired the Canadian government's solution to immigration. Their program was a bit different. To become a Canadian citizen, someone had to:

1. Form a company
2. Employ at least one Canadian citizen
3. Pay C$165,000 to the Canadian government for the privilege of becoming a citizen

Voilà! Welcome to Canada!

These folks, aptly so, were called "the yacht people." A marked contrast, he thought, as opposed to how the United States dealt with immigration, with its porous borders and continued federal policy of nonenforcement. US "chain migration", whereby an illegal's baby, if born in the US automatically became a US citizen, had spiraled out of control. The total of this class had now ballooned, resulting in an estimated 15,000,000 illegal aliens nationwide.

They were getting free drivers licenses and health care, without paying one dime in taxes. Some states were even allowing them to vote. With these entitlements, the national debt was growing off the hook. He'd read a Los Angeles Times article that concerned him deeply about the trends surrounding illegals in California and the US.

- *95% of all murder warrants in L.A. were for illegal aliens.*
- *67% of all births in L.A. County were to Mexican illegals on Medi-Cal whose births were paid by taxpayers.*
- *35% of all inmates in California were illegal Mexican nationals.*
- *FBI reports that half of all L.A. gang members were illegal aliens.*
- *In L.A. County, 5.1 million speak English while 3.9 million speak Spanish.*

He also learned less than 2% of illegals were picking our crops, but 29% were on welfare. Perhaps most disturbing was 70% of the total US' annual population growth and over 90% of California, Florida and New York's growth was resulting from illegal aliens. Ironically, one of the angriest groups at this trend was the 'legal' alien. Those good, God-faring, folks who had taken their time, done the right thing and worked the process for entry into the US lawfully.

So it wasn't the people, as Scotty had no issue with them on a personal level, he wasn't a racist. Rather, he was an "experiencist". He paid attention to what people did, collectively and as individuals. It was the lack of an orderly assimilation process, no requirement to learn English and any follow-on requirement to contribute or add value, versus sponging off of free entitlements that ate at him. The increased; violence, drug and human trafficking, as well as the soaring national debt were out of control. But no official at the highest levels in government seemed to be genuinely concerned. In Key's view, we were flat losing our country.

Willingham met him at the curb in Vancouver's airport. He gave the baggage handler a Twonie for his trouble. Lush municipal landscaping graced most hard-scaped edges and bordered the walks, giving off their sweet smell to all. Off the beaten path were massive amounts of dense, fill your nostrils, dark green ferns.

"Flight okay?" asked Willingham, making small talk as he extended his hand in welcome.

"Uneventful. Wheels up, head to pillow, wheels down. None of that irritating metal against concrete sound upon landing," smiled Scotty broadly as he shook the Mountie's large hand firmly.

"Excellent! A proper landing then," snorted Willingham. "Let's install your baggage in the bonnet and we'll be off. Need the biffy beforehand?"

"I'm good, thanks."

Willingham was an imposing human. He was quite fit and towered six foot four. His head was the size of an Alhambra water bottle with a squared-off lantern jaw. He was the poster boy for the Royal Canadian Mounted Police. As they drove, Scotty filled Willingham in on the events that had happened in Cozumel and provided more detail on the encounter with the small Iraqi.

"May we spend a moment more as to your expressing concern about pinkeye," said Willingham.

"That's Stink Eye," corrected Scotty. "Insult him properly, please."

"Quite. *Stiiiink Eye.* Yes. You Yanks tend to immediately blame the Iraqis or Iranians for any problems that come up any more."

"Perhaps. But don't forget *South Park*'s 'Blame Canada' ballad, you're not completely off the hook yet." Key instinctively liked this guy and felt comfortable enough to cut up with him, even though they had just met.

"Well. Yes, quite. There's that. But truly, why are you so convinced the issues are always emanating from the Middle East? I believe you to be wrong."

"And I try so hard not to be wrong."

"Indeed."

"Apart from most of our challenging issues having been involved with or performed by Middle Easterners, nothing. And I don't have any attitude about that." Scotty put his sunglasses on to dampen the sun's glare. He noticed the freshly painted and exceedingly tidy, quaint housing they passed as they continued on into the city.

"With your permission, I have a bloke who's a colleague of mine I've invited to lunch at Canada Place, not the thing one discusses over the phone. He claims he has a couple of interesting pieces he'd like to vet for our mutual puzzle."

"I'm in," said Key.

Neither Scotty nor Willingham possessed the stripe that required mindless chatter when there was nothing to say. There were lengthy periods of silence as they made their way toward downtown Vancouver.

As they drew closer to Canada Place, Key gazed upon the exceptionally large five tepee/sail structures that made up the facility's roof. They were constructed to be reminiscent of extremely large white sails. In fact however, they reminded many of American Indian's tepees, due to their extreme slope and triangular, conical shape. The comparison was not made in a bad way, it was a unique and imposing structure whether you subscribed to the sail or the tepee doctrine.

Key and Willingham had collected their briefcases, checked in with the restaurant hostess, and procured a small, round patio two-top with a good view of the water. The sea surrounded the structure on three sides.

"Francis."

"Call me Scotty, please."

"Righto. Scotty it is. By the by, Stanley Park, the island is to the north." said Sheridan as he pointed at the island just across the water. "If we solve all the world's problems today, you should consider visiting it."

"Oh?"

"Yes. It's about four hundred hectares, or one thousand acres and is 10 percent larger than you Yank's Central Park."

"Indeed?"

"Yes. And almost half the size of London's Richmond Park. Trees can get to be seventy-five meters in height with two hundred kilometers in trails and almost a nine-kilometer sea wall. It's a splendid place to take in the sights."

"For example?"

"For example, sea otters, amazing flora and fauna, dolphins, beluga whales and a positively remarkable display of historical totem poles."

"Sheridan, I believe that's the most excited I've seen you. You should work for the Canadian Chamber of Commerce!"

"Actually, in my line of work, we essentially do work for the Visitors' Bureau. Anyway, down to business; enough of the chitchat."

"So, Sheridan."

"Hmmm."

"Got to ask you straightaway."

"Shoot."

Both men lowered their voices and leaned in toward each other.

"Do you believe it was a naturally occurring earthquake that did your prime minister in?"

"I do not." retorted the Mountie without hesitation.

"*The Province* is publishing it that way," said Key.

"I was there, both air and ground. I saw people die trying to find the prime minister's body. I saw a lake …a lake … just disappear. I'm no geologist however, that's highly irregular, eh?"

"Quite irregular, eh. Sorry. Now that I'm here, I'm picking up the lilt."

"Not to worry. It's contagious," responded the Mountie.

"I heard a Canadian comic once ask why, when addressing a Yank, Canadians always ended their sentences in *eh?*"

"And?"

"She said it was short for *asshole.*"

"Charming."

"Back to your prime minister."

"Yes."

"If it's not a natural quake, what possibly could have done him in?"

"I have no earthly idea. Do you?"

"Well, yes, as mentioned on the phone, I met this student a year or so ago who talked up the notion of developing a small fissile burrowing device which could revolutionize mining. Sort of like Red Mercury in a commercial setting."

"I thought Red Mercury was but urban myth."

"Me too. But he had a rather convincing story to tell about how, when employing a modest-sized canister, using fusion then fission, it chewed threw earth like the mother of all moles."

"Sounds like rubbish."

"In actual fact, we were surprisingly high on the concept initially, but then lost contact with him. "But then, you run the recent Interpol search on our guy—Milo Butterfield—from UC Berkley and he wakes up dead. And he dies of all things, from a *skateboarding accident* while loaded with methamphetamines? You needed to meet the gentleman, Sheridan, however you'd be almost as likely to be out whacked out on drugs skateboarding as Mr. Butterfield."

"Just wasn't his cup of tea, eh?" said Willingham. "Anything else peculiar?"

"Yes. I'm a bit embarrassed to admit this impropriety, however, that buddy of mine I mentioned who was executed in my driveway day before yesterday, he and I frequented the mausoleum where Mr. Butterfield's remains reside."

"Yes?"

"Well, he was there, but his left back molar wasn't."

"And how could you possibly know that?" he asked leaning forward with feigned sternness.

"Welllll …," mumbled Key, looking down at his drink.

"Wait!" interrupted the Mountie, holding a hand up toward Key with his palm out. "We're not having this conversation. I don't want to know or foreswear later I ever had any knowledge of, nor encouragement towards these shenanigans. So, what is so improper about a missing tooth?"

"When Butterfield was in our offices, he was more than a little spooky as to his invention. He knew he was on to something big. He was very, very goosey however."

"Okay."

"As such, he trusted no one, no computer with his data, algorithms, or source code."

"Yes." The Mountie sipped his warm tea while signaling to the waitress they were ready to order.

"He put it all on a small flash chip and placed it under the filling in his back left molar."

"Preposterous."

"He told me personally. His lips to my ears. When he was in our office, the man even opened his mouth and pointed to the exact—now missing—molar."

"So you're suggesting that some Muslim element, some collection of Middle Easterners, has dispatched Butterfield, taken the chip from his mouth and harnessed this thing for evil?"

"You know, I have never said that, not once. Been thinking it, but yes, I am saying it now." Scotty rapped the table gently coincident with the last word.

"What earthly good could come of killing the prime minister of Canada? That's akin to attacking Sweden."

"I know. It's goofy. But as we mentioned briefly on the phone, you shared you recall a similarly irregular death for the president of Mexico awhile back?"

"I do. You're surely not suggesting those two elements are linked?" asked Sheridan, leaning forward even more.

"I feel the two events have strong components of linkage, yes. You were at your prime minister's site. I visited the president of Mexico's 'natural earthquake' site in Mexico City en route to the dust-up in Cozumel I shared with you on the drive over."

"And?"

"And. It didn't look like any earthquake aftermath I had ever seen and I've seen a few living in California. For one thing, it was surrounded with about fifty Federales and there was this extraordinarily deep cavern, which by my calculation, was over four thousand feet deep."

"Intriguing. Earthquake in a bottle aside, to imagine anyone attacking Canada and the same consortium of hooligans attacking Mexico is a stretch. What natural resources do those two countries mutually possess that are so bloody valuable to another?"

"Exactly," replied Key.

"I can't imagine the timber and tequila concession being that sought after. One always thinks of money however, neither has loaned you Yanks funds of consequence. Going after the US with a coupe is far more believable. We are acutely aware of your President Rasheed's handling of your recent economic affairs and how upset he has Republicans, Independents and Democrats alike."

"Exactly. Although you mean 'King Rasheed, that would be more like it."

"I get that."

"And what is up with his using the 'red star' symbol of socialism or communism in so much of his marketing material?" asked Key.

"Sometimes fact is stranger than fiction."

"I respect the office of the president, however, this guy is doing everything in his power to run roughshod over the Constitution and dismantle two hundred plus years of governing. We're drowning in a sea of red ink that our children, and our children's children are going to be saddled with paying off. Rasheed's trying to create an oligarchy and immerse us in debt to the point of bankruptcy."

"No disagreement. Then what's the link between Canada and Mexico?"

"Unclear."

"Let's think. What do the US, Canada and Mexico have in common?"

"Borders. They all border the US," said Scotty.

"Precisely. Therefore, they have NAFTA in common. Which is the very topic my Mountie colleague was going to advance. Odd. He's not normally late. Calendar integrity is a strength of his normally."

"You raise an interesting hypothesis. Some feel Rasheed is attempting to unwind that agreement at the behest of his union cronies who pretty much have him in their pocket." Key grimaced in disgust at the multiple examples of corruption that had seen daylight in the last few months.

"The US unions would benefit greatly with the agreement unraveling, yes?" said Sheridan.

"Oh yes, without a doubt. They would be able to bring it all back to the US under their control and extract higher union wages. They'd get their 'vig' on everything as they'd accelerate a regression to isolationism, as they fund their Cadillac medical plans and unsustainable pensions. It's pretty much the same playbook they used to ruin the steel and airline industries thirty years ago. They just recently spread that same government infection and affection to the auto and financial industries."

"You sound as though you know something about the topic."

"Advanced degree in economics. A bit compulsive, forgive me," said Key.

"No worries. Continue."

"As a consequence, we flat don't make *anything* anymore. All manufacturing is all outsourced. It's scary. In fact, 70 percent of our economy is based on spending. There are precious few steel mills to speak of and no large foundries left. We've got no more shipbuilding facilities and surrendering our automotive industry to government control is nuts."

"Just read that myself the other day in *Financial Times*."

"Boeing is not making near the planes they used to. And the new hot, en vogue energy industries have the bulk of the solar panels made in China, with most of the wind turbines being made in Europe. We simply have no heavy industry of consequence anymore. Just media. If Canada were to invade us, we'd simply have to throw CDs back at you—rap, or blog you to death."

"There's a visual."

"Or maybe we'd put the war on a reality television show, until ratings fell. Only then would we pull our troops out. We'd clearly have an edge in that theater of combat."

"Novel concept. I just want you to know I can get Canada behind this effort and perhaps influence some Brits over at MI6 who we're friendly with."

The words had barely left his mouth when …

SSSSsssssst. Thwapp! SSSSsssssst. Thwapp! Rudely interrupting their exchange, two twenty-inch-long, jet-black, metal darts buried themselves in the brie they had been enjoying just moments earlier.

THIRTY

IN AN INSTANT, WILLINGHAM UNBUCKLED the leather restraining strap on his holster, stood and pulled his weapon while scanning the outdoor veranda. In the same moment, Scotty lurched away from the table while knocking over the pitcher of tea and a chair. As he stumbled, he noticed the angle of the dart. It was quite vertical in nature—some sixty degrees up from horizontal. So there was no sense scanning the horizon line. He looked up.

SSSSssssssst. Thwapp! Another dart arrived. Only this one found its home and buried itself deeply into Willingham's chest. He lurched, went limp and fell face forward, flat onto the table, arms askew. Signaling his tabletop arrival to all, the silverware and plates bounced a full three inches skyward and two glasses shattered on the concrete floor. This caused a bit of a buzz and much scurrying about for a ten-yard radius around them. Key looked heavenward and saw a black blotch on the second "sail" from the end. Key reasoned correctly that the darts had been launched from a high-powered crossbow with a scope.

Scotty rolled behind an enormous Boston fern, just as the fourth dart announced its arrival, shattering the floor-to-ceiling window behind where he was standing. While the plate glass broke into thousands of small pieces, a few shards still cut his shirt sleeve and forearm.

"Can you see him?" he asked a neighboring diner scurrying for the exit.

"No! And I'm not sticking around to look either!" said the stranger, bolting for the exit.

Key leapt over to Willingham's sprawled, motionless body and grabbed the pistol from the man's hand. As a SEAL, Scotty had had a reputation for being the best in the last five classes as a pistol marksman. In fact he'd been awarded a medal. It simply stated "Pistol Expert." A warning to all who viewed it on his uniform that to tease this cobra could be fatal.

Key drew down on the black form, which was a good one hundred twenty yards away and squeezed off three quick rounds. The distance was too great to assure any accuracy with a pistol, as his target was moving rapidly. Key could not make out the aggressor's face, as he was cloaked totally in black. His garment was so snug it might be a wet suit, including a face mask of sorts.

Scotty saw his prey do a remarkable arabesque and make an enormously large pendulum swing toward him. The man looked like a very large spider tethered by thin, long cables that had been laid out well in advance of the attack.

Key kept moving swiftly, as he knew a high-powered crossbow, when fitted with a scope, could be deadly accurate. In support of that view, the next dart arrived: *SSSSsssssst. Thwaap!* It hit the person to Scotty's left, dropping the man like a pair of dirty socks.

Scotty ducked behind a short wall, which was slightly curved at the top, thereby providing him some measure of cover from above as well. He turned his head to view the last dart's victim and noticed there was a tranquilizer dart delivery system at the end.

My God, he thought. *They're not trying to kill me. They're trying to 'bag and tag' me. As an insect to mount on their board*, he imagined.

They'd undoubtedly follow up with an extraction team soon to snatch him out of there for God knows what.

"Shit."

He kept on sliding down behind the low wall on his belly to secure a better position. At the same time, Spider-Man was swinging from yet another weblike cable to reposition on another sail—the southernmost one, which was closest to Key. From behind a small potted tree with thick foliage, he pushed the pistol and both hands halfway through the growth, thereby concealing his position.

He breathed out, steadied both hands atop the stubby wall and slowly squeezed off a round. *Crack!* The spider slid down his last cable some fifteen feet before arresting his own fall. He'd gotten his target. It wasn't a kill shot, however, the wound appeared to be in the leg.

Taking advantage of his newly gained upper hand, Scotty squeezed off two more rounds in quick succession. He was conscious of the fact that he was coming to the end of his clip. He'd have to conserve ammo and shoot with a higher degree of precision.

Spider-Man had recomposed himself and had slipped out of view. Key could see a couple of thin cables bouncing, suggesting his mark was still moving around and hiding behind one of three makeup air units, regrettably, he was not certain which one. By now the entire veranda had cleared as the local Mounties had been summoned.

Briiiiiing! Someone had set off the fire alarm to aid in notifying help. Key knew he had but three minutes tops to capture or kill his prey, as shortly thereafter, he was going to be surrendering control to the authorities.

SSSSsssssst. Thwaaap! This one caught Scotty in the calf. The burning of the tranquilizer solution commenced immediately. He became warm all over. He tried to fight it, to no avail, as everything slowed down. He realized that in a brief moment of concealment, Spidey had slid down to his very edge for a closer shot and had hung over upside down to execute it.

He saw his shooter—while still hanging inverted—salute him, pull a knife from his ankle sheath and cut his own nylon cord, as he plunged headfirst into the ocean below. *Hence the wet suit.* This was Scotty's last thought as he lost consciousness.

Over the top of the Canadian Mounted Police clattering up the penthouse stairways with dogs barking and riot gear, one could hear the *ak-ak-ak-ak* of an incoming helicopter rotor closing in rapidly. Extending from the chopper was another black nylon cord, with yet another figure in black dangling from its end. The snatcher.

They were now clearly after Spidey and foregoing Scotty. The helicopter slowed, as it approached sea level and drew up to a brief hover. The new black figure never left his suspended perch, it was going to be a grab-and-go.

The Mounties kicked the veranda door open and started shooting at the helicopter. The chopper yawed hard right and quickly dipped across to the other side of the tall, five roof sails. Dropping down lower again, the black dangler simply bent over, attached an additional harness around the swimming wet-suited Spidey, sucked it up at three connection points and signaled to the pilot to ascend. They were off. Banking hard right, the helo spun out to sea, accompanied by the Mounties' hail of bullets.

Key awakened in a Vancouver hospital bed next to Willingham. This hospital was dime bright and spotless. Orderlies were whisper quiet as they scurried about with unrepentant energy. Outside their room were stationed two Mounties guarding the door. Whether they had been dressed in Mounties' uniforms or not made no difference. Their austere expressions said it all. In addition to their normal armaments, they carried machine pistols, tasers and a K9 was present. This was not SOP for the Mounties, but then again neither was the recent indignity foisted upon one of their finest and their prime minister.

Key and Willingham alike were disoriented. Drooling and slurring their words.

"Shhhoow. Wash it as gude for you as eetch wash for mee?" asked Key. "I shink I'll harve a sheegarrettte, as I feel like I jusht goth fokked."

"Merican hoomer. Humthh. Lord, I'm wobbly. Feels like I'm totally pissthed."

THIRTY-ONE

San Francisco, California
December 2010

BACK IN THE UNITED STATES, Ali was debriefing her superior, Burton Buttons, on what had just transpired in Canada. She'd received a call from the Vancouver hospital and heard a Key update an hour earlier. She was searching for some clue from Buttons's response (or nonresponse) that would tie this in to current or past Black Ops projects. Buttons was not serving up any content in that area, however, he was giving her more than enough direction in the personal advice column.

The NSA chambers were antiseptically sterile. A dull sheen metal finish on most of the appointments, with muted gray-beige interior walls was consistent with the sparsest sprinkling of furnishings.

"Ali, you need to dispense with your attention to this affair and perhaps to this gentleman altogether ..."

She interrupted him midsentence curtly, "Odd to drift into personal waters here, Burton. Why would you suggest that?"

"Firstly, I wasn't that impressed with the gent."

"You met him but one time and only briefly. And?"

"And secondly, if he is attracting this reprehensible element like a lightning rod, then my counsel is you don't want to be anywhere near him the next time lightning strikes. It could put you in jeopardy." Seeing he was starting to get her attention he upped the ante. "It could put Happi at risk."

"Hmmm." Ali wasn't buying it.

"In fact, it might make a lot more sense for you to go to a safe house with Happi for a week or so until we can sort this out. If they were, in fact, targeting your friend, then they know his associates and they know his associates' associates—like your daughter."

"Riiiight," said Ali wistfully.

"Make sense? I'll summon the car," clipped Buttons with a discussion's-over tone.

"I don't know, Burton," said Ali equivocating.

"You are too close to this. You should know the drill by now. You can't go home. Don't make it easy for them to harm you. We can get two weeks worth of clothing and toiletry articles to you, add that to your at-the-ready go-bag and you're set. We'll outfit Happi as well."

Ali *was* too close to it. She knew what Buttons related was correct. She did know the drill. However, as the drill was all about her now, she was struggling with compliance. *Classical*, she thought.

But then again, there was Hoppy.

"This all seems a bit rash, Burton, pretty hasty to me. Perhaps we just hang at the Center for awhile…"

"Ali, give me your cell phones." Buttons was interrupting her and becoming quite directive. "We've got to dump these. Now." He opened the back of the phones, unfolded his pocketknife and plucked out the GPS chip with his smallest of blades.

"Wait," she objected.

"If not, they'll be shining like a tea service in a dumpster. We'll get you some prepaids at the safe house. Better yet, we'll call and update your friend that you'll be underground for awhile. That way no signal can be traced to you, once we bounce it off of a dozen other servers. Once you're there, we'll 'read you in' as to what else we know."

"So you'll call Scotty?"

"Indeed. I'll need his number."

"Okay … Here it is: 415-649-0968," said Ali reluctantly.

"Perfect. Off to your chariot and your driver will collect Happi on the way. We'll sort this out in the meantime."

Ali hesitated. "Listen, Burton, this all still seems a bit premature. The more I think about it, let's hold off a few days, triangulate the chatter, check out our listening posts and align more data points."

Ali, listen, I am on tenterhooks on the matter. I didn't want to go here, but would you come into SAT-COM with me for a moment? Please?" said Buttons, not waiting for a response and directing her down the corridor somewhat reluctantly.

Buttons ushered Ali down the hall past the card scan security area, which was followed up by an iris, palm and voice imprint. The area was manned by two armed guards. Behind the gleaming six-inch thick, blast-proof doors which slid open quietly along their rails, was an octagonal room, resplendent with technicians and technology.

The Satellite Communications Center was teaming with computers, monitors, large translucent big screens and cordoned off rooms where decoders, encryption and exacting listening devices were housed. The largest screen covered the entire northern wall of the windowless room, displaying images the satellite was currently focused upon.

"Cosmo, Pull up Ms. Woo's home coordinates please on the north wall," barked Buttons.

Cosmo, the flat-topped satellite chief operations officer instantly banged in the requisite coordinates on his keyboard. The sweep refocused, narrowed and truncated repeatedly until, after a few iterations, it zoned in on northern California, just Menlo Park, then Stanford Shopping Center, her street and house with two neighbors, then finally just her house and front yard.

"Ali, we have been paying attention to your residence and a few others in the last couple of days, due to a tip we secured when we broke through their encryption. The algorithm was a blend of Morse code, Yiddish and old histograms taken from Cherokee smoke signals. Notice the brownish Saab across the street?"

"Yes. Yes, I do," Ali fidgeted uncomfortably as she recalled Scotty's multiple references to that very car.

"Well it matches the same vehicle description your boyfriend put in his police report of the chap who dispatched his friend."

"Not many brown Saabs around," muttered Ali, looking down.

"Not many brown Saabs of that vintage," agreed Buttons, shaking his head knowingly, seeing he was starting to get her on board. He then turned to instruct Cosmo to return the scan back to the prior coordinates, just when some fresh activity appeared on the screen.

Her neighbor's back screen door opened and Alex's mother could be seen ushering him out the door to play. He was dragging his purple and green dinosaur with his head cocked back uproariously. He was quite probably shouting out loudly to the neighbors and proclaiming the obscenity of the day.

Alex rang the front doorbell for Hoppy. He rang it again. No one responded, as Hoppy was at school. After a moment, Alex gave up; stepped down the stoop, dragging his dinosaur by the long piece of brown twine as he liked to do, and peered into Ali's front window. His head jerked up, almost as if someone had called his name. He then walked over to Ali's car.

En route, he started swinging his purple and green dinosaur faster and faster around his head in a circle. Then, the terminal knot on the brown twine yielded to centrifugal force and launched his plastic companion at a high rate of speed toward Ali's car. It hit the car door handle firmly. In an instant, the visual landscape totally changed.

A UPS truck-sized ball of flame erupted spontaneously in Ali's driveway where her car and Alex had just been previously.

THIRTY-TWO

"OH LORD!" EXCLAIMED BUTTONS.

There was no other sound, save Ali gasping and holding her hand to her mouth. The scene felt surreal due to the silence. Image only, no audio. You could see Alex's mother open her back door and run at breakneck speed over to the burning vehicle, which was completely engulfed in yellow-orange flames and human carnage. Her head was spinning around. She was turning in circles in their yard. She was shouting Alex's name. You could see her shouting for her son. But he was not going to reply. Not this afternoon. Not ever.

"Mmmmmph." Ali made a mousey, unintelligible, forlorn noise, dropped her Mentos, and squinted moisture from her eye. Ali deliberately didn't wipe the tear, fearing it would encourage more. She sat down hard in the chair to her right. The room had become quiet, pin-drop quiet. All eyes were bouncing from the screen to Ali, to Buttons, then back to the screen. Soon all became aware of the morbid event.

The nothingness was soon filled again by the flurry of muffled keystrokes, as data was manipulated and satellites withdrawn, dispatched and repositioned.

"Ali," said Buttons quietly as he touched her shoulder.

"Don't," she said, jerking away from his touch. Ali sniffled, wiped her nose choking back emotion and demanded, "Take us to the safe house now."

As she took the elevator down with the driver to the limo, her head was reeling. She couldn't get the image of the car bomb out of her head. She also felt Burton had been more than a little harsh with his appraisal of Scotty. He barely knew the man, it was personal and none of his business. While Buttons seemed to genuinely care about their well-being, why, she wondered, was he taking such a dim view of Scotty after meeting him but once?

Her driver escort, Dave, was a tall, older black man who was clearly ex-military and still fit. Although his teeth were crooked, they were strikingly white against his caramel-colored skin. Everyone liked Dave. He beamed a toothy, infectious smile, which was friendly. It helped relax her.

"Don't worry, Ms Woo. We've got your six. You and your daughter will be tucked in safe like a vault before nightfall."

"Where's the safe house?"

"You know I can't go there, Ms. Woo. We'll go fetch your daughter and then we'll all be buttoned down in a couple of hours—four tops."

"Okay and yes, I do know the drill."

They arrived at Hoppy's grade school. She was waiting out front, swinging a Dora the Explorer lunch pail. She had just struck a frozen starfish pose for one of her girl friends, when the nondescript limo drove up with her mother and Dave. NSA had called ahead, so no one had to enter the school. The collection was going to be quick.

It had been show-and-tell on Tuesday and Hoppy had brought in Tang. As a result, he and his condo (Hoppy's book bag) unintentionally made the limo's passenger "A-List." Hoppy entered the limo and Ali hugged her neck with a sniffle.

Hoppy shrugged her shoulders and, without speaking, looked inquisitively at Ali, as if to ask "What's the matter, Mommy?"

"Nothing, honey. Just allergies," Ali couldn't get the fireball image out of her mind. Alex was gone, just gone. His poor mother. She'd tell Hoppy and deal with this later when her jangled nerves weren't quite as raw.

Dave's limo entourage also included an undercover motorcycle cop, who would escort them. He was undercover in scruffy biker clothes and bore a few faux, albeit authentic-looking, Henna tattoos. His nose had been broken twice and looked as if it had never been repaired.

"Check two three," said the patrolman into his mic, confirming audio.

"Roger that on the check. You are loud, clear and green-lighted for Grandma's House. Over," Replied SATCOM crisply. His helmet had an internal microphone to stay in communication with NSA's regional office and Dave at all times. The cop would alternatively lead and then lag behind a quarter mile or so, so as not to attract undue attention or make it clear that he was linked with the limo. He was, however, always within ten seconds of his assigned payload.

Back in the limo, Hoppy wanted to learn what was going on. She took out her pad and paper and wrote: "Why the vacation, Mom? What about Friday's recital?"

In fact, Hoppy had the number two role in Friday's production. She was a mime and was looking forward to it. The role was clearly not much of a stretch, but she had invested countless hours in front of the mirror in preparation. She focused on the popping out of "jazz hands" from her hips. Her jazz hands *simply had* to pop.

"Well, honey, Mommy's got to go on an out-of-town business trip and we thought it would be great for you to see what Mommy does. Also, it's very important for the next few days to stay within sight. Always. Like hide-and-seek in reverse."

Hoppy turned her hands up forty-five degrees, lowered her eyebrows while shaking her head east and west and offered up the typical obstinate child look of amazement. It corresponded to the adult version of "what the fuck?"

"Yeah. I get it, Hoppy, it's a bit unscheduled. And I wanted to see you in the recital too. However, this could not be avoided. Sometimes in life priorities get reshuffled. Thanks for understanding."

Well. There wasn't going to be any understanding. Hoppy folded her arms and crossed her legs tightly. The peewee slammed her back into the deep, rich, black leather and sat up stiffly in the seat. She stared straight ahead in defiance. Her short little legs did not make it to the floor.

To release some of her frustration she commenced kicking the baseboard under the seat with her heels. She knew better. She kicked away regardless. Her mother would have routinely nipped that in the bud but didn't this time. She knew how hard Hoppy had been practicing at home and rehearsing at grade school. She new if Hoppy could speak, her response would have certainly been the perfunctory, "Okay. Fine."

True to Dave's words, the limo headed North on Hwy 101. They crossed the Golden Gate Bridge, with its majestically soaring, muted orange columns, each just barely penetrating the bottom of the morning's fog. That familiar scene was the beacon and glowing harbinger announcing each and every daybreak to Bay area residents.

"It's a beautiful bridge, isn't it, Ms. Woo?" Dave asked, making small talk.

"Yes. Yes it is."

They rolled by Sausalito where the clouds were just starting to recede. They came to the Stinson Beach exit and took it. Heading west, the small, two-lane road hit the junction with Pacific Coast Highway 1. The entourage snaked along the coastal highway north for well over an hour with the undercover motorcycle leading then trailing, trailing then leading.

She had thoughts of Scotty and wished she could speak with him. She didn't care what the topic was, she just wanted to hear his voice. She wanted him to hold her and assure her it was going to be all right—assure her they were not going to be like Alex or Pig. She had thoughts of Scotty's safety and of her daughter's, which was clearly job one. Then there was that billowing fireball in her driveway ...

As they drove by small town after sandy, windswept town, Ali recalled a happier time. She reflected upon the time she had spent with Scotty and Hoppy at the Fitzgerald Marine Preserve near Moss Beach off the PCH.

Scotty was diligent about paying keen attention to when low tide was "in," so they could reap the maximum benefit from walking in the tide pools.

With the tide out and with aquasox on, they could safely visually delve into the marine world 'below" without getting any more than their feet, ankles and calves wet.

She remembered how Hoppy had shrieked with glee as she'd come across an orange starfish, which in but twenty inches of water would actually appear deer hunter orange. She recalled Scotty saying that same starfish and all other things red would appear black at eighty feet of water while scuba diving. In Cozumel, she'd witnessed that very phenomena and knew it to be true.

On the day they visited, the shell collecting was just fair, as many had previously frequented the beach earlier, scrubbing it clean. Each day would awash the beach with new treasures, new booty available for young and old alike. While it was a reserve, things still seemed to get legs and trot off.

Ali and Scotty alike had drilled into Hoppy that she should never turn her back on the ocean. Initially Hoppy thought it was another tale of the Easter Bunny or Santa Claus to be debunked in the future. However, both adults had made it a point to share very real stories. Stories from the news about the uncharacteristically large rogue wave, which would catch people napping and literally drag them out to open water. And if they couldn't swim or if there was a rip tide of consequence—next stop, Cancun.

While at the beach, they'd kept their eyes out for the occasional harbor seals, which would perch, sometimes motionless à la a backyard patio sculpture in true seal repose. These were one hundred yards off the beach. Sometimes they would serenade you, sometimes not.

Aquasox were a lifesaver. If they weren't saving you from the occasional strawberry on the bottom of the foot from a coral rub, they were protecting you from a small shard of glass, a cigarette burn, or the infrequent hypodermic needle. This last item used to make Scotty grind his molars down a sixty-fourth of an inch, as it wasn't an issue when he was young.

Ali had enjoyed pointing out to Hoppy the anemone's swinging gently in the surf when they were both bent over close to the sea's surface. Some green, some yellow, some yellow-green, their tentacles swayed, trapping the tiniest of organisms for dinner. Most of them were non poisonous, however, there was always the problematic maverick. As such, they were all on the don't-touch list.

The breeze had been moderate and pleasant, with just a hint of salt. Small schools of tiny, bright fish would dart in and out of the corals and anemones. They'd zing to the right and left, as if a flock of birds had been disturbed midflight. Their brilliant yellows and electric blues never ceased to amaze Hoppy, as she would always appear startled, gasp and point with glee. Surely there was an extension cord somewhere nearby to make these iridescent colors so vibrant.

Damp, bright green sea grasses, odd, hump-backed hermit crabs, black urchins, sculpins and inquisitive shrimp had the entire area teaming with life. It was a good idea to hold still long enough for their natural camouflage to melt away, so as to discern the finest treasures in the clear shallow pools.

On they drove, past Bodega Bay. Ali wondered if they were going to go as far north as Mendocino. Ali and Scotty had fond memories of a very long, drizzly weekend there once. They had secured a cozy room with a fireplace and hot tub. A room they'd never left. A grand bay window provided a spectacular view of the ocean. The other two corners boasted multiple flowering plants in hues of purple, red and yellow, filling the room with their fragrance.

She remembered staring endlessly at the sea. It had a hypnotic effect on them both. They'd drunk a little too much wine and had a little too much sex in the windowsill. He'd been seated, she hadn't. The bay window's sill had a large plate with overstuffed, fluffy, floral pillows. The plate had to go however. There had been no plan, announcement, or discussion of the follow-on event. It just unfolded naturally. No words really, clothes had come off as the rain continued, with its cadence never changing.

The memory also stuck with her due to Scotty being frustrated as an avid fly fisherman. While the trip was for her, Key had optimistically brought his gear along and was considering wetting a line in the Russian River. It had rained nonstop and blown the river out, however— chocolate milk blown out. It shouldn't have been a surprise, as the rain didn't let up much in California's monsoon season.

The receptionist at their small bed-and-breakfast said there was no smoking (as Scotty liked the occasional cigar) in the room or, for that matter, on their entire twenty acres. This last nugget made Scotty wince. Upon checking in, they felt as if they were nestled in a box of cotton, as it was so very, very quiet.

Whether this was an undocumented feature or the unintentional result of the fog's insulating factor, in conjunction with the heavy surrounding foliage, was unclear. One felt, however, as it they were in the library of libraries. No loud noises, herky-jerky motions, or quick movements would be welcomed or tolerated.

Their greeter had a very deep, throaty, overly calm, almost theatrical, voice. It was a bit over the top, suggesting a great deal of local dinnertime theater performances, or maybe too much ingestion of a bold cabernet with Demerol. Her drippingly slow, almost humorous, initial greeting of, "Gude evening" was a bit reminiscent of a cross between Greta Garbo and Bella Lugosi. As she engaged, she'd float up tight into your grill until you felt intruded upon—smell-her-breath close kind of intrusion. Conversations oozed, as if from a tube a toothpaste. Speech was ethereal and spoken in overly hushed tones, earning the establishment Scotty's moniker of Prosaic Inn.

As such, Key and Ali had exchanged many "Gude evenings" in jest with each other, while toasting the other with mawkish drama or bowing deeply, as if they'd just been knighted. The rain had continued nonstop. Not hard, just non-stop.

As a result, Scotty had teased unmercifully; the word *Mendocino* was actually short for, "Men don't see no," as in:

"Men don't see no fishing,"

"Men don't see no cigar smoking,"

"Men don't see no sun," and

"Men don't see no fun."

Reality cruelly snapped Ali back to the present-day tormented thoughts of Alex and the fireball.

Jesus, she thought.

The limo was pulling into Jenner. They were slowing and the sound of gravel crunching under exceptionally large, reinforced, solid rubber tires announced their arrival. They were stopping for lunch. It was quite dusty when but one door opened. The limo driver had elected not to announce his intentions to turn in advance and had come to a quick hard stop.

Dave went inside to the roadside diner to secure the meals. The motorcycle cop left his bike, took the wheel of the limo and drove it toward the middle of a field across the street.

Climbing inside the vehicle, he tipped his hat and said with no expression, "Ma'am."

Ali nodded. That was all that was said by either party.

There was nothing in the field but sixteen-inch tall grasses, which were blowing, bending and swaying in the sea breeze.

From this vantage point, the patrolman had no visual obstruction for three hundred yards in any direction. The limo had bullet-proof glass and solid rubber tires. They could not be shot out. No one was stopping this limo. Pity on those who tried, as they would have to deal with Dave and the crooked-nosed patrolman.

Dave came back to the middle of the field with lunch. He took back his driver's seat from the patrolman. They stayed parked toward the middle of the vacant field, while the escort drove his bike some fifty yards away to afford an even longer line of site up and down PCH 1 for anyone or anything approaching. A goose-like sentry watching over his flock. They ate.

"Been with the company long?" asked Ali of Dave.

"This is my twenty-fifth year. I'm out in six weeks."

"How do you feel about that?"

"Oh, you know, excited for the next step of leisure with Mama, however, I will miss the action and the people. Especially the people. There's a great class of people who work in this organization, like Mr. Buttons; he's top drawer, yes, sir."

"He seems to be …" She caught him studying her, smiling and nodding, while looking at her in the rearview mirror.

"He brought me out here from Detroit fourteen years ago. And you, Ms. Woo?"

"Just five years. Lots more time before I melt into the sunset."

"Ummmm. Well our shadow just started his bike. I guess we should continue on moseying on to Grandma's House."

"Probably. Could I make a brief call from that public phone at the corner of the gas station?"

"Now, Ms. Woo, you already know the answer to your own question, don't you?"

"Mmmmmm," she growled in Marge Simpson mock disgust.

"You don't want to blemish a flawless twenty-five year record with a frowny face in my jacket, do you?"

"No, Dave, no. I would not want to do that," she said.

Dave laughed a belly laugh, which started guttural and then ended up wheezing. He put the limo in gear and drove slowly through the dirt to get back on to PCH 1 pavement. He looked in the rearview mirror to see Ali again with his gentle smile. It was her job to try, it was his job to say "No." Everyone knew his job and everyone knew each other's job.

Tang poked his bleached orange head out of the book bag. Just his head. He then popped right back in and then came right back out, with an almost jack-in-the-box cadence, as if trying to cheer Hoppy and Ali up. He receded briefly and just barely peered back out again.

The car hit a bump, which startled him. He exploded clear out of the bag and circled around the back seat's floor and back-most windowed area twice before settling down in Hoppy's lap. Ali laughed gently, smiled at Dave and tossed her long, blue black mane over her left shoulder, as she breathed deeply in an effort to relax.

Hoppy reached into her purse pocket and grabbed two Pill Pockets. With no encouragement required, the brightly colored animal raced over to them, looked quickly to the right, then up, down and left again. All motions rapid. Furtively glancing around for any potential interlopers who might interrupt his feast, Tang snatched the morsel up from the ground quickly.

After a brief bit of his front paws proudly parading the possession, he quickly took it back to his book bag condo for the requisite safekeeping and follow-on hoarding. Ali then sent a Mento skyward for herself.

On they headed north on PCH 1 with the sea's waves to the left lapping and lulling, lulling and lapping. It was a warm day, a bit more humid than normal, not sultry, just heavy and warm, which made for heavier still eyelids. The western sun streamed through their limo's window unabated and the wave's endless, hypnotic rhythm had a soporific effect. The sea's white noise cadence ultimately put down first Hoppy and then Ali. They slept.

Ali was awakened by a rather large and remarkably clean eighteen-wheeled vehicle rumbling past them. It was almost shiny. It was odd that this large of truck was on a remote, two-lane section of PCH 1. Surely there was a more direct route to its destination then drifting through the backwaters of turista-ville. The truck was not only long, it was wide, tall and exceedingly clean.

They entered another small town. Pulling up to the only four-way stop-signed junction, another large truck, heading west from a small, rural feeder street, turned right and north, right in behind them. It had the profile of one of those Central Valley trucks, which would normally be heavily laden with tomatoes. Seeing it empty and a bit out of place made Ali antsy.

She glanced into Dave's outside mirror. She could see the patrolman back around the last curve, his speed increasing in an effort to catch up. She saw the front of his bike bouncing up and down as her escort was clipping through the gears aggressively to close the gap.

Ali looked in the rear view mirror to try and catch Dave's eyes. He was coughing and starting to wheeze again, a bit anxious. With two hands on the wheel, he was focusing on the shiny truck in front of him, which seemed to be downshifting and slowing down, as the truck behind them was speeding up. Then, with surgical precision, the tomato truck to the rear locked all its breaks up. It made that bawling, bouncing, semi-sliding, wheel-lurching cry as it skidded sideways to a halt.

Blocking both lanes behind them.

THIRTY-THREE

THE SEMI'S SIDEWAYS SLIDE MOVE not only prevented their retreat, it also provided a wall of separation between them and their biking escort.

As if on cue, the rear door of the large, covered, shiny 18-wheeler in front of them was thrown open. It disclosed two men behind a heavy gauged, solid panel of steel. Beyond that was what appeared to be a full-bodied, four cable pulley system, which was advancing forward rolling on rails. This was a system Ali was not familiar with.

Dave spoke, "Don't you worry, Ms. Woo. We eat guys like this for lunch every day, every damn day and today is no exception."

Without hesitation, he flipped the console open and rapped off a burst from two embedded machine pistols buried in the limo's grill, each of which fired at one thousand rounds per minute. This setup had been designed and approved for dignitary transport use in Afghanistan.

The bullets ricocheted off the heavily armored panel which protected the two masked men. Ignoring the bullets, they were busily turning cranks and dials on the four pulley system. One was hunched over as if looking upside down in an inverted periscope, arming it, or aiming it.

Flop. Flop. Flop. Flop. The system's drums and pulleys engaged, each making this loud noise and cycled over to display a spear. A very large harpoon was on each end of the four cabled drums.

Fwiiiiiit Clank! Fwiiiiiit Clank! Fwiiiiiit Clank! Fwiiiiiit Brangkt! All four harpoons were fired in quick succession at the limo. Dave had a system to "double lock" the doors, which he engaged. It slammed two additional heavy, internal steel rods through each door as further redundant protection.

Three of the harpoons found their mark.

The first two hit the lower front quarter panels just below the grill and penetrated securely to arrest the limo's frame. The third one, on top and to the left, hit a strong framing connection where the backmost corner of the hood met the lower end of the windshield. The rightmost shot struck the vehicle a glancing blow and was deflected off. Three was enough, however.

With positive connectivity achieved, the pulley system engaged and a high, shrill piercing screech kicked in as all four started to retreat and advance backward on their rails, back internally toward the forward bowels of the truck.

The system was literally sucking the limo into the truck.

A seventeen-degree ramp dropped down out of the truck's rear. The ramp grated loudly, bounced twice and energetically sparked off the pavement. The truck was reeling the limo in.

Like a fish.

Dave hit his brakes, to no avail. The tomato truck had his retreat blocked to the rear. The three harpoons were pulling the limo into the back of the covered 18-wheeler with a force that exceeded the limo's braking power. The brakes would fail before the four drums would.

Tang was running figure eights throughout the vehicle in abject fear and reacting to the ear-splitting noise from the shrill whining pulleys and the screeching brakes. Hoppy was screaming, albeit silently. Ali pulled her weapon and was demanding the windows be lowered.

"That's not protocol! Stay in the car! Stay put! I got this!" screamed Dave.

"The hell with protocol!" responded Ali, trying all door handles unsuccessfully in quick succession.

She tried to break out the glass with the butt of her gun, but couldn't.

It was too thick. The gun bounced back so fast it hit her in the head smartly and left a small cut.

Behind them, the patrolman laid his bike down on its side due to the deliberate fishtail swing-out deftly performed by the tomato truck driver. This was no ordinary tomato truck driver, he could have driven in tomato-truck-NASCAR.

The patrolman slid in under the truck. He was lying prone on the pavement. He gathered himself and peered out from behind one of the large, paired truck tires at the cab, weapon drawn. No one was on the left side of the cab.

He heard shots. They were ricocheting off the pavement and back up against the bottom of the truck. They were close. His machine pistol crisply bah-rapped off fifty rounds in the direction of the cab. He laid back down, looking under the bed of the truck.

The crooked-nosed escort ripped his helmet off, so he could clear the sweat from his eyes and get closer to the ground for a better view. He saw a single set of legs and fired, this time hitting his mark, exploding the calf and bringing the Iraqi shrieking to his knees on the hard pavement. The patrolman touched off one more burst and finished another attacker with an "S" spray combination to the face, upper torso and groin.

Hearing yet another series of shots ricocheting in his direction from the other side of the truck, he attempted to position himself behind a set of the truck's large dual wheels. This time, however, the angle was working against him. This arrangement would not provide adequate cover. He considered making a break across the street to secure safety behind a hulking, faded green, rusted-out, abandoned John Deere tractor. He thought he could make it. As he bolted for it, the spray of gunfire followed him, barely missing its mark. The officer was breathing heavily—part from fatigue, part from adrenalin. He felt undergunned and outnumbered.

Just before lurching across the street, he attempted to call in the incident to NSA command. Regrettably, his lapel microphone had been crushed during his slide and was inoperable.

Ali could see what was unfolding out her rear window. She covered Hoppy's eyes with a blue plaid blanket so the child could not. She thought of the image of her car as a fireball. She thought of Alex. Were they going up in flames too?

The patrolman rolled through the cockleburs and stickers, barely noticing their prickly venom as he was focused on a much higher priority. Coming to rest behind the aging tractor, he realized this was a coveted vantage point. He found he could angle himself for protection behind the vehicle and yet still barely poke his machine pistol out between the undercarriage or spaces between the tractor wheels' spokes. This afforded him significant cover as he returned fire.

The trooper's confidence was increasing, as he liked his new position. Then, out the top of the bed of the tomato truck popped two more heads, albeit briefly. He shot and missed both. They popped up and down with the rapidity of a Whack-A-Mole game at Chuck E. Cheese. Their head popping was not without purpose, however. As they popped, the northernmost one lobbed a stun grenade, or flashbang, to the front end of the tractor. The southernmost assailant parroted this action by directing his grenade toward the tail end of the tractor.

With a military background, the trooper knew quickly what came next. These maneuvers were designed to flush the tomato truck's quarry. While they were only flashbangs they left the patrolman dizzy, temporarily blinded and disoriented.

Whisk-Whisk-Whisk. Three fly fishing lines came from the distant bushes. Their terminal tackle were large #2 hooks. One caught him behind the neck, one in the left shoulder and lastly, one gathered firmly in his left buttocks. With unyielding, triangulated pulling, they ground deeply into the patrolman's hide, which aided in separating him from the cover of the tractor and pulling him in to land him.

Like agitated ants pouring out of a fire ant hill, three Iraqis spewed out from the bed of the truck with machetes. Ali wanted to turn away but couldn't. The gruesome, magnetic draw of not being able to look away from passing a car wreck's carnage had her in its grip.

With eerie precision, as if they had done this many times before, the patrolman's assailants threw down a large sheet of Visqueen, pulled the screaming patrolman over on top of it, and stood him half way up on his knees. The first machete lop took his head cleanly. They severed the hands and feet almost in a pedestrian manner. Ali turned away, there was just too much blood, even for her. This was not an execution, it was the butchering of livestock.

From the tomato truck came the sound of a portable engine. *Whirrrrrrrr*—the whirr of a 35-horsepower, 850-pound flywheel wood chipper. She heard it firing up.

She chose not to look this time.

The Fire Ant Three poured the chipper's liquefied remains of the trooper into a large metal block, barely poking out of the bed of the truck. It was a previously crushed car in the form of a large cube. They cemented their efforts closed into the cube with a plug. There was not going to be any trace of the trooper or his DNA, nor would there be any trace of what had just occurred.

The limo had now been completely swallowed up into the shiny 18-wheeler. The back door rolled completely closed. It had two-inch-wide rubberized weather-stripping around its edges. The two aggressors had vanished. It was pitch black in the forward bowels of the truck.

Dave shouted, "Don't you worry, Miss Woo. I got this!" He turned on an inside light.

"Turn that light off!" screamed Ali, as she jerked up and down violently on the car handles. The double lock absolutely kept intruders out. It also positively, absolutely kept occupants in.

"Open the fucking door!" screamed Ali frantically.

"That's not protocol! Stand down! They can *not* get in. I got this!" cried Dave again, as he was fumbling under his coat for his .9mm Glock.

Then, through the vents came the gas. It started slowly seeping through the front floor vents, mushrooming and enveloping the entire interior carriage of the vehicle. The limo's occupants passed out.

THIRTY-FOUR

Mexico City, Mexico
January 2011

AIR FORCE ONE WAS LANDING in Mexico City. The smoke puffed up from its landing gear as the bird touched down, just as the mariachis and welcoming bands began to play. US President Rasheed (which meant *Rightly Guided*) was making an appearance to kiss babies and take bows after his prior advance envoy had laid the groundwork.

In stealth mode, rumored and not yet formally vetted by any media, the envoy had actually stood up the notion of disbanding NAFTA. The governments of the United States, Canada and Mexico had signed NAFTA, or the North American Free Trade Agreement, creating a trilateral trade bloc in North America. The agreement had come into force in 1994.

Economists on both sides of the aisle wrangled about whether NAFTA penalized or benefitted the United States. As a high school debate project, there were equally eloquent arguments to be advanced on both sides. There was no equivocation, however, as to where the United States' union leadership and its army of K Street lobbyists stood. They wanted the bloc gone. Wanted it gone now.

They felt the treaty was artificially depressing wages and increasing the unemployment rate at the lower end of the economic strata. It was no secret they were welded to Rasheed at the hip, in thought and deed. There were those who even advanced the notion that *they were* the very thought, leadership and mouthpiece behind the president, thereby effecting the most powerful ventriloquism act to ever perform on the world stage.

Rasheed had been silent on the matter early in his presidency, glossing over it with his one hundred megawatt smile to focus on other matters. Matters like Stimulus One, Stimulus Two, taking over the banks, governmental firings of public companies' CEOs, taking over auto companies, cap and trade and lastly, universal healthcare, with its $2 trillion price tag. En toto, Conservatives (and now even moderate Blue-Dog Democrats) were genuinely concerned as to whether these programs and their associated debt burden were sustainable. They feared they would drive the country into bankruptcy.

Key had even coined a phrase for the phenomena, the U.S had a bad case of *indebtgestion*.

Many pundits observed that the spending, adjusting for inflation, had exceeded the combined total costs of WWII, the New Deal, both the Iraqi Wars and the Louisiana Purchase.

Rasheed had inherited just over a $200 billion budget deficit and in two short years, he'd increased it over sixfold to $1.4 trillion. Further, the new deficit would exceed all prior presidents' administration's budgets, dead or alive, in the aggregate. Remarkably, the rather outrageous platforms still were being advanced successfully due to the leader's winsome ways and magnetic charisma.

A striking individual, with long, black, wavy hair, Rasheed was handsome and rather unique, as he was only the third president of the United States to ever be elected as a bachelor. It had been 125 years since that had last occurred. Grover Cleveland was the second bachelor when elected in 1884, although he married during his first term. James Buchannan was the first, elected in 1857 and he remained a lifelong bachelor.

The current Mexican president's name was Juan Francisco Villarreal. He had been thrown into office quite abruptly following the prior president's untimely demise due to a temblor. The interim president's formal office title was Constitutional Citizen President of the United Mexican States. In Spanish, he was known as Ciudadano Presidente Constitucional de los Estados Unidos Mexicanos.

Villarreal had neither the inclination, grit, nor temerity for the office. But he was there. After military service and until late, his post had been mostly ceremonial in nature. His legacy was one of compliance, peacemaker and lubricant when there was any sand in the formative gears of Mexican policy, graft, or corruption.

"Buenos tardes," said the US president.

"Buenos tardes, mi amigo. Welcome to our country," said Villarreal.

All the señoritas adored Villarreal's powerfully dark, handsome face and regal carriage. He walked as if dancing a dramatically slow waltz. His reputation, however, was not akin to his deceased predecessor. The prior president had an iron will. He was considered to be of high integrity and had made a reputation for himself by cleaning up corruption in Mexico, focusing on its drug cartels and corrupt military. Villarreal on the other hand, was considered soft on drugs and crime, so soft, he was thought willowy and acquiescent to almost any new legislation, for the right price.

As the US president continued down the open-air gangplank to deplane and through the receiving line, President Villarreal's entourage met him graciously with forced, warm smiles. Villarreal was dressed smartly in an exceedingly bright white ruffled shirt, blue suit, and a smattering of gold and silver military medals on a blood red sash. This validated to all that he was beyond a doubt El Presidente. Equally importante, brandishing his medals provided proof certain that he had previously been El Jefe—a general in the Mexican Army.

In his heart, Villarreal had warmly welcomed the US president's intentions. This was not so in the case of the deceased president, to whom the treaty dissolution was previously advanced.

Mexicans were normally a very warm and ebullient lot, friendly and always looking for a reason to celebrate. The newsmen and women, cameramen and locals on that day, however, were not as joyful. They viewed the United States' visiting dignitary with a bit of disdain, some with a jaundiced eye. Rasheed had developed a reputation as an exemplary public speaker, who rarely followed through on his soaring rhetoric, in too many instances, doing precisely the opposite of the bulk of his most steadfast campaign pledges.

The two left with their cavalcade of dignitaries to motor off to Los Pinos, Presidente Villarreal's official residence. Los Pinos was nestled inside the Bosque de Chapultepec, located within a lovely sixteen hundred-acre park at the outskirts of Mexico City.

THIRTY-FIVE

Fort Ross State Park, California
February 2011

ALI AWOKE THE NEXT DAY in Fort Ross State Park. She was out prone on a bench in the middle of a public park with her head throbbing. Throbbing undoubtedly from the gas she'd inhaled, which had put her down for the last eighteen hours.

Groggy, she felt a large lump in her right front jean's pocket. Feeling around, she determined it was a hand-written note on exceptionally thick paper, wrapped around a stone. It was made intentionally thick, so that she would not miss it.

The note was brief and to the point. "To see your daughter alive, have Francis Scott Key traded and confessing to Father Johansen at 5:00 pm tomorrow." The note went on in a smaller font, as if a legal disclaimer, to say "Sonoma Mission Catholic Church 1858 La Cienta, Sonoma, CA. Do not inform or bring others, or the child will suffer what you saw yesterday."

Ali winced visibly, as she envisioned Hoppy's limbs being smote, stricken off one by one. She couldn't get the image of the trooper or that same fate for Hoppy out of her mind. She sat up abruptly, wiped her eyes while choking back tears and pulled herself together.

Ali couldn't call Buttons, as the note was quite specific. On the other hand, protocol was to promptly inform NSA and they'd help her sort it out. But damn it, they had been in the act of "sorting it out" when it had become fucked up. This situation needed some serious un-fucking.

Ali gave Key a call from a public phone collect. He was relieved to hear her voice.

"Scotty?"

"Ali! My God. Where are you? Are you all right?"

"I'm okay. They've killed Alex however."

"Jesus! How'd that happen?"

"They blew him and my car up when he accidentally struck its door handle by swinging his dinosaur this morning. Buttons showed me the event live on SATCOM." She whimpered.

"Buttons? I'm telling you. There's still a big question mark over that guy's head in my mind. I'm not sure which team he's playing for …"

"Scotty, he was simply showing me our house was under surveillance from that Saab when it happened out of the blue. He was trying to convince me and Hoppy to go to the safe house and I was resisting. He's a good guy. I wish you'd get off of it!" she shouted. "And …" She sniveled to force back tears and remain brave. "They've taken Hoppy. They want to exchange her."

"Exchange her? What? For a ransom?"

"No. No. They want. Well. They want *you*. They want to exchange Hoppy for you. I don't expect you to do this. I just don't have anyone else I can talk to about it. I can't talk to anyone else without feeling I'm signing her death certificate, but I don't want you hurt either," said Ali, trying to choke back her emotions.

"Ali, it would be my honor."

"What?"

"It would be my honor to be exchanged for Hoppy." Key was trying to square with the demons he couldn't shake from abandoning young Oliver.

"Oh … kay."

"Where've you been? Where are you now?"

208

"Buttons told me he'd call you and explain it to you. He didn't?"

"No," said Scotty.

"Buttons pulled the rip cord on a safe house move for me and Hoppy yesterday. The trip to the safe house headed south. Way south."

"How so?"

"I'll update you when we speak. But Scotty, it was awful. Horrible! These are despicable people you'd be turning yourself over to. Know that. They are insects who do not value life at all and relish in taking it in horrific ways. I don't want to see you hurt. I don't want to see Hoppy hurt. I don't know what the hell to do."

"It's all right, it's all right. We'll figure it out. Don't worry about Hoppy. We'll get her back."

"Scotty, I am petrified. I want her back, but I don't want you to get killed in the process! They hacked him to pieces with a machete and pureed him! Butchers!" she screamed.

"Him?"

"The patrolman they sent along to protect us."

"Not to worry. I'm too mean to kill. No one can digest Key-Jerky."

Key did what he could to prepare and went to Sonoma as instructed at the appointed hour of 5:00 pm the next day, Tuesday. Ali trailed closely behind in a second car.

"You okay?" he asked her in a reassuring tone upon their arrival.

"Fair. Will be better when this is all over."

"Don't worry. Have a Mento."

Key entered the richly appointed church and made his way up to the front, approaching two altar boys lighting tall, thin, white candles amongst the large, stained-glass windows and heavily veneered dark walnut pews. He circled back to the left where the confessionals were located. Upon approaching one of the altar boys, he pointed toward the confessional and stated blandly,

"I have a 5:00 pm appointment with Father Johansen. Would you kindly let him know I have arrived?"

"Of course." The boy gestured to Key to wait off to the side.

Father Johansen entered and stood briefly with him outside the confessional.

"Yes, my son. How can I help you on this glorious day? What is weighing upon you? Have you come for confession?" asked the Father.

"I'm here for the trade."

"The trade?"

"Yeah, the trade. I don't know if you're personally involved, however these are my only instructions."

"So. You have no confession for me today, my son?"

"No, I'm here for the trade. End of line. Me for the little girl."

"I don't understand."

"That's it. That's all I've got, Father. The little Asian girl. Me. For her." Scotty's responses grew more curt as he speculated that the good Father may be yanking his chain.

"Apologies my son. I am very confused. My schedule was penciled in for an urgent confession at this time and yet you have none. I am at a bit of a loss. Wait a brief moment, please and let's see if Rebecca can spread any light on the matter." The Father left the room and walked across the aisle to telephone Rebecca, his assistant.

In leaving, he motioned to Key to wait in the confessional. Around the corner, not visible to Scotty, where Ali was directed to wait came Hoppy.

She didn't appear to be harmed however abject fear was written all over her countenance—it was drawn, pale and somewhat pinched in appearance. It was also smudged and soiled. Prior tear tracks stained her dusty, angelic face.

She smelled musty, a bit damp, almost salty. She did not have her book bag or lunch pail with her. Ali rushed to greet her, knelt and hugged her neck while sobbing. She turned to Scotty to thank him, but he wasn't there. He was gone.

In the meantime, with the altar boy's encouragement, Scotty had taken his seat in the confessional.

With no warning, a small trapdoor opened directly beneath where Scotty was seated and his body weight promptly shuttled him downward. Downward through what appeared to be an old combination laundry/dumbwaiter chute, which had been built and abandoned decades earlier. After a single-story free fall, Scotty was summarily chucked on his back into a dumpster filled with soiled white uniforms.

As he looked up from his new resting place, he saw Stink Eye glaring down at him. The Iraqi had a gold tooth where Scotty had taken the previous one in their first introductory meeting in Cozumel. He had the original tooth on a string around his neck. It had remained as a constant reminder that these two would meet again.

Struggling to right himself, Scotty found there was no solid footing in the dumpster and he simply sunk deeper in the dirty linens. Stink Eye's gold tooth glinted as he smiled. With a bang, he slammed the two lids closed on top of Scotty as he thrashed about to free himself. Stink Eye quickly slipped a thick, steel pin through both hasps, which effectively locked them down—and Scotty in.

Swwwwwwwwt! Stink Eye whistled between his teeth and motioned to the exterior loading door as a large, unmarked, white, windowless van with lifting forks begins to emit a sound: *Ding, ding, ding,* rang its backup bell, as it jockeyed into position to consume its new load.

The laundry dumpster was hoisted high overhead as Stink Eye jumped on the back end of the truck to greet it. Once it was completely inverted and hanging, Stink Eye took a hammer and with a single stroke, knocked out the long pin he had just inserted. This action promptly opened both lids, plunking Scotty and about three cubic yards of clothing and dirty rags on top of him, down. Flailing and unable to navigate through the rags and cloth quickly enough, Scotty saw the truck's top again slammed closed. The hydraulic arms that had just picked up the dumpster groaned as they returned slowly to their original position on the slab.

THIRTY-SIX

Fort Bragg, California
February 2011

AFTER A FORTY-FIVE MINUTE DRIVE, the truck deposits all its contents, including Key, in a pile on a cold, damp and uneven, stone floor in a cave-like setting near Fort Bragg. Toward the end of its journey, the truck had driven through two inches of seawater. Scotty could smell the salt spray and even hear the waves as they made their final approach. *Ding. Ding. Ding.*

Key was greeted by three Asian gentlemen who were rather thin on manners and heavy on compliance administration. They immediately struck him twice in the mouth and rapped him once smartly behind his head with a set of nunchucks.

They bound him onto a sturdy, straight-backed, wooden chair. Tying his hands, they arrested his feet to the front two legs of the chair. The chair did not creak. It was old, yet very sturdy in its double oak, glue and dowel construction. Key found it odd that his caretakers were Asian and not Iraqi, although now did not appear to be the proper time to have a genealogical discussion with them on the matter.

"I've come here for the trade," said Scotty.

His captors simply grinned at him. The grotto was cold, dark and dank.

It was about 52°F. While not currently shivering, Scotty was acutely aware that, if he remained here long, he would be. To Key's right was a forty-two-inch high table with shiny, bright surgical tools, which appeared to be an eclectic collection from a dentist, an orthopedic surgeon, or perhaps a vet. His imagination ran briefly as to their potential uses and then he pulled himself back to present day.

His hosts started off more politely than expected, with but two questions:

"Who knows?"

"What have you told them?"

Key responded with his name, his occupation and his military rank. They repeated the questions. He repeated his response.

The shorter of the two went over to the table and picked up an instrument. It appeared to be a curved and pointy dental pick, which he holds close to Key's right eye. He picked at Scotty's lowermost right eyelid. He picked again. They ask the same two questions:

"Who knows?"

"What have you told them?"

Key's response was unwavering. He was attempting to look unfettered by their methods. Suddenly, the back of his chair was hoisted five feet in the air and Key found himself in midair, leaning slightly forward. A small floor crane had swung over, connected and effected the lift with a hook to the chair back's strongest framing member.

The chair and Key were swung over in a single motion toward the opening of the cave. The tide was starting to come in and the cave's floor was two inches deep in seawater. The two Asians slogged through the water, the questions were repeated, as were the responses. Key looked around the room pondering an escape route or any sharp ledge he could work his lashings against.

The lift swung Key and the chair another one hundred twenty degrees counterclockwise over a large bath, the kind that resembled an industrial horse trough. Key sniffed. He didn't smell any acid or caustic odors. Relieved, he noticed, however, that large blocks of ice were floating on top of the bath. *Perfect*, he thought.

Splash!

The clutch had been engaged and with a free-fall descent he was dunked into the icy bath with barely enough time to catch his breath. Underwater, he could hear his heart beating, initially very rapidly, perhaps eighty beats per minute. Scotty judged the water temperature to be just under 40 °F. Every fifteen seconds he was under he could feel the cold biting at his face, the small of his back and deep in his ears. After thirty seconds underwater, his heart had already slowed down markedly. He thought he may actually listen to it stop.

Whoooosh.

After seventy-five seconds, he and his chair were plucked from the icy bath and swung up and back clockwise to his original position by the table. Dripping, Key began to shiver uncontrollably. The questions renewed:

"Who knows?"

"What have you told them?"

The back-and-forth questioning and dunking continued for another couple of hours, with no perceptible progress on either front. The cave was completely dark and silent, save the occasional drip, drip, drip familiar to these damp environs.

Key's eyes had adjusted to the total darkness. His shorter host (the one who always smiled) strode over and inserted plastic brackets in each corner of Scotty's eyelids. The brackets were designed to keep his eyes open continuously post installation. Key reasoned that his torturers had gotten this technique from *Clockwork Orange*.

A screen in front of Scotty was thrown on, offering up nauseatingly, horrendous images of all genre. At that same moment, blood was dumped on him and he spat the remaining residue out of his mouth. Close-up images of hundreds of tarantulas, cobras and black mambas were flashed back and forth. Simultaneously, two dozen real spiders and six snakes were thrown on top of him. While, fortunately, he did not have an enormous fear of either of these creatures, it was admittedly unpleasant. After two more hours, three-inch-long, mottled brown leeches were placed on Key's body, some in sensitive parts and others less so.

Hunger and hypothermia crept in as he continued to shiver. His ordeal had gone on for over twelve hours. He'd witnessed graphic images of beheadings, mass graves, truckloads of corpses. Dachau, Sachsenhausen, Buchenwald, Flossenbürg, Mauthausen, Ravensbrück, Auschwitz—all were shown in horrifically grim detail. Every third image was followed up with the arcing, blinding flash of a welder's rod and:

"Who knows?"

"What have you told them?"

Images from Vietnam, World War II, The Iraqi War, the Chinese Civil War and Afghanistan flooded the screen. His hosts came every fifteen minutes to squirt saline solution into Key's eyes. The hydration allowed the images to remain in crisp focus.

Every so often without warning, an air horn was touched off right behind his head, close to his right ear. An exceptionally high, piercing shriek would come from overhead, just as he would start to pass out. Startling him by design, it kept him awake. Seeing the ESE tattoos on both of his host's calves, he found it strange they were Asians, as opposed to being Stink Eye's kindred Iraqi spirits.

Key felt his focus draining, as he was thinking of Ali and Hoppy. Thoughts of Pig and Alex helped him keep his resolve. Between those thoughts, he was constructing an entire building in his mind.

He went over the process he'd used in a summer job in his youth. He marked off the four corners, struck them square with string, rough grading, fine grading and he laid down a base coat of gravel. He dug the foundations, placed #4 rebar twelve inches on center each way, tied them off and was pouring the footings. He was keeping his mind occupied. In fact, his fantasy building was being constructed in a very hot, muggy place, so the cold felt rather good. *Sell it.* He had to sell this notion to himself to stay lucid.

Although they'd poked and prodded at him with their glittering surgical steel tools from the forty-two-inch high table, he had not yet shed a meaningful amount of blood. Not yet. This was to keep him conscious, to ensure he would stay aware of the pain while creating anxiety and fear.

"Say, if those are your party favors," said Key dryly, "take me off your next invitation list."

The sarcasm was met with an immediate back-fisted blow to his face and an equally broad grin from the gentleman who delivered it. Scotty bent over and spat another mouthful of blood.

Key was now assured they were not going to take him out quickly. Rather, they wanted to break him mentally, as opposed to physically. They absolutely wanted the answer to their two questions and it was obvious they were not going to stop until they had them.

He heard them making whispered comments about "the Fisherman" coming soon. The context never made sense, however. He was uncertain if this was a proper noun or how they were using it. He was confident however, the Fisherman's arrival would not be a good thing.

The images, the piercing noises, the ice bath dunkings and the picking at his hide continued for another six hours. The repetition of the two questions was mind-numbing. Then a new, darker form appeared from the southwest corner. Key had been drifting in and out of consciousness, so he was unsure how long this new aberration, or person, had been there watching. In the corner.

Watching him.

Out of the corner strode this new, darker, sinister form, who was much shorter, more muscular than his fraternity brothers. He was somewhat stooped over. Like a troll. His face lacked animation and his eyes were flat and lifeless, like those of a trout left to die on the shore. However, he had two significant, rounded scars, one under each cheek. They all but followed his jaw line as slits. Almost like gills. Perhaps this was the Fisherman.

The new player was dressed in a frumpish frock of sorts on top of a kilt-like affair. He retreated back to his corner. There, he retrieved a fly rod, on the end of it was a small #20 Yellow Sally. Key knew this as it was one of his favorite dry flies.

From the corner, some twenty-five feet away, the Fisherman started casting. He false casted twice and the third time, he hit Key's ear lobe and pulled off just a bit of flesh. It stung like a wasp but demonstrated the Fisherman was quite accomplished in his casting skills.

The Fisherman's two minions tied Key's head firmly to the back of the chair, which carried a makeshift wooden extension for this accommodation. Successfully immobilizing his skull, the Fisherman then skulked back to his fly rod. Key saw the rod glint as it began its rhythmic back and forth motion.

He heard the *whisp-whisp-whisp* of the fly line through the air on each false cast and felt the sting upon its arrival. The Fisherman was upping the ante. He was now attempting to pluck the four small brackets from the corner of Key's eyes. Key had casted to hula hoops successfully in the past and had seen plate and tea cup demonstrations of fly casting accuracy. He'd never seen anyone cast to three-quarter-inch brackets. Never to eyes.

The questions came again:

"Who knows?"

"What have you told them?"

It was going to be in his self-interest to hold very still and accommodate Asia's answer to Buffalo Bill meets Lefty Kreh. *Whisp-whisp-thwack!* The first bracket was pulled out crisply. It was uncomfortable, but he'd not been blinded. That was a win. This same back-and-forth motion continued three more times with surgical precision. On the fourth try, however, the blunt end of the hook hit the very corner of his eye, which sent Key reeling backward. This flipped his chair over, whereby he hit his head on the stone floor and blacked out.

Some time later, Key awoke, disoriented and shivering. His face was hot. It was extremely hot, hard and swollen. He felt his puffy face pumping blood. Pounding—there was a thunderous pounding in his ears. His sinuses had a drumbeat from his hammering heart. Blood thumped through the back of his head and high on his neck. His cheeks felt as if they would explode and there was this stench. *My God, what is that stench?*

THIRTY-SEVEN

UPSIDE DOWN. HE WAS SUSPENDED in the chair and hanging upside down. Held in place by the small dolly lift, which was keeping his nose but two inches above the incoming sea, he had been left to dangle, inverted in the chair, upside down. Discarded without ceremony, he had been abandoned to cough, spit and choke—choke on the water that was becoming deeper each minute as the foaming tide rushed in.

Had they given up? he wondered. Were they simply going to drown him? Pain. Dull, throbbing pain in his right lower jaw. An aching nausea overcame his every fiber. Had they roughed him up some more while he was out? The acrid ammonia odor from the capsules they'd used repeatedly to revive him still filled his sinuses. Throbbing—he turned his head to its maximum ability and looked down and out the corner of his eye in the direction from whence the ache came. There was a half inch-thick, steel cable with six flat, oblong hooks that could slide freely up and down. One, however, had been pushed up and through his chin, up through the bottom of his jaw, alongside his teeth and then back out of his open mouth. A stringer. They had put him on a stringer.

Like a fish.

He ran his tongue along the multistrand cable, discovering this was the root cause of the newfound metallic taste in his mouth. The steel clicked against his teeth. Not being able to close his chops for hours had made them as dry as cotton. He was parched and filled with phlegm. He glanced again skyward—toward the ceiling. The dark, moss-laden canopy over him continued to trickle down moisture and left a gritty film in his eyes. He smelled the lichen-coated rocks and heard the dripping overhead just before a large drop hit him in the eye. His head reeled back. Blinking out the residue, he saw the half inch-thick, stainless steel cable was anchored firmly overhead. It continued back deeper and ultimately disappeared into the pitch-black bowels of the cave.

There were other objects, blurry objects—other things hanging on oblong hooks behind him. He had to strain. Without a clear visual he had to arch his back and twist his neck whereupon he felt the immediate electric shock of level-ten pain in his mouth reminding him that he had been impaled. He arched, bounced once and turned again spasmodically in the other direction.

That stench—what is that god awful stench? he wondered. The odor was so pungent and oppressive it almost blocked out all others.

And there—there he saw six more oblong hooks, suspending six more oblong things, six more forms. They reminded him of the butcher's shop in Menlo Park where his father had taken him as a child to have the salmon they'd caught steaked out for their barbecue. They were all gently swaying together in the cold. Swaying in the moist, numbing cold, as if on display. There were no fingers, no hands, no feet, no heads. But they were all moving gracefully together in the sea breeze that was gliding into the cave.

Squinting to focus his eyes better, again he turned his head sideways and struggled to blink out the ceiling's excess moisture, which mixed with the blood running in a small rivulet down his face. He spat out more clots. The headless body nearest him had something on the small of its back—a marking of sorts. *It's a skinny triangle,* he thought, as he strained to get a better look. No, it was a skinny triangle with ragged edges.

What in the hell was that?

He knew that image. It was a skinny triangle with ragged edges shaped like a tree. No, it *was* a tree—a thin pine tree. It was the logo of the Stanford Cardinal.

Jesus. It was Pig! He recoiled. They had hung Pig, sans appendages and head, right next to him. They had run one of the oblong stringer hooks up his rectum and pulled the other end out his belly button. What was left of him was just hanging there. Suspended. The pride of the Stanford Cardinal hung, dangled—upside down—like a piece of meat.

After ten more minutes of hellish swinging punctuated by the last-minute snapping back of his jaw, he realized his options were constricting. He would either drown or pass out— then drown. Guess this was it. Lights out. Good night, nurse.

THIRTY-EIGHT

SCOTTY DID NOT GET THE feeling that either the Fisherman or his two henchmen were returning. He reasoned their union probably gave them breaks.

"Heh heh," he laughed nervously, trying to allay his worst fears. His mind drifted back to Ali and Hoppy, Ali's gentle laugh, Hoppy's smile and window blowing shenanigans. He thought of her starfish, of Pig in his car, in his driveway with the top of his head blown off. He recalled the brains, skull and blood sprayed over the passenger side of his car and now...

Pig hanging upside down.

Next to him. Ass up and penetrated by a large, sharp, unforgiving hook. Pig, his five bunkmates and now Key were all tethered from an overhead stringer. As fish. Everything was getting blurry, he was going to pass out. Scotty fought the blackness overwhelming him as the tide noisily rushed in, crashing against the jagged stone walls. He knew he may not have another chance.

Then, over in the northeast corner he heard a scurry. A very large rodent ran two feet up the wall, across the floor and back down to its starting point in a figure eight. The rodent's appearance was appropriate. As long as he was going to drown like a rat, he wanted to be judged by a jury of his peers.

The animal darted out again. This time, instead of retreating to the corner, it came much closer to his face on a nearby elevated rock that had not yet been submerged. The animal was an extraordinarily large rat and it was orange.

Shit! It was Tang. He thought. *How in the hell did he get here? Is this where they held Hoppy? Was she still here? Tang must have gotten out of Hoppy's book bag.*

Tang continued to run in circles. He came up on a safe, dry rock to sniff Key's face then retreated to the darkened corner to reconnoiter. Key felt like he was drifting in and out, however he wasn't sure. Had he seen Tang? Or, was it an illusion?

Just then, his right hand touched his right rear pocket. He'd kept Pill Pockets in a small watertight pill box in his right cargo pants' pocket to amuse Tang in the past. Was it still there? When sliding his hands around to that side, he felt the lump. Scotty managed to open the box and find four Pill Pockets.

He handled them gingerly, being careful not to drop them into the rising sea directly under his face. Swinging gently, he took them and awkwardly rubbed them all over the ropes binding his hands behind his back. He rubbed aggressively, pushed and drove the Pill Pockets' goo completely into the twine's fibers.

He waited.

Swinging. Breathing. Pain. Swinging. Breathing. Pain. Scurrying. He heard a scurry. He definitely heard another scurry. This helped sharpen Scotty's focus and heighten his awareness. Tang had smelled the Pill Pockets and was tearing across the lower wall to get to the elevated, lone dry rock nearest Scotty's face.

"Hey, buddy." Key was more than happy to accommodate him. Although it caused the stringer to pull the wound even slightly larger in his face, he contorted his body, twisting, turning, bending and fuming, until his hands were close enough to the ferret to serve as a bridge for the animal to climb aboard.

At first tentatively, but then more aggressively, the ferret moved toward

Scotty. It recognized Key's odor and it certainly recalled the strong musky-sweet smell of the Pill Pockets. Tang was quite hungry. The ferret leapt over to Scotty's shirt, clung on and started licking the ropes.

Recognizing it was not going to get all of the goo that way, the ferret began to chew. He began to gnaw on the ropes with his sharp teeth. One at a time he would bite through the individual corded fiber wraps of the rope. He wasn't going to sever them all. He didn't have to. With each cord loosened, Scotty felt the hold on his hands relax a bit and the circulation in his hands returning.

After the fourth one snapped, Scotty wiggled his hands free. First things first. He reached over, still upside down and opened the stringer that had punctured him and gently removed its hook from his face.

"Awwwwwww!" He screamed during the extraction. "Mother of God!"

That was a pain he would remember and perhaps impart to others in the future. He swung unfettered by the stringer, widely enough to grab the side of the wall with one hand and push off with the other, making his new arc significantly higher. At the apex of this new, higher swing, he grabbed the rock ledge, arrested his motion, bent up and untied his legs.

Splash! Upon removing the final binding from his legs, he fell face down into the water. It was now sixteen inches deep. Still shivering, he stood up on his knees and retrieved Tang, who was frantically swimming in circles around him.

"Gotta take care of you, little buddy. I owe you big time."

Tang just looked at him expectantly, as if to say, "If you really loved me, you'd be handing over some more of those Pill Pockets."

THIRTY-NINE

Menlo Park, California
February 2011

SCOTTY MADE HIS WAY TO a nearby farmhouse to receive succor and a ride from the kindly older gentleman. Key, the book bag and Tang hitched a ride with him back to Menlo Park in the indigent farmer's rusted-out, faded green and wood-paneled truck. His last adventure had left him haggard, filthy and shop worn.

En route, he'd borrowed the farmer's cell phone to call Ali and leave a message that sounded like an innocuous telemarketer. That was her signal he was OK to go meet him at the previously agreed upon location. During that same ride he'd also called Vinnie to suggest they get together, albeit obliquely as the farmer was listening.

Upon seeing him, Ali's eyes went immediately to the oozing puncture wound under Scotty's jaw. "Thank heaven you're alive! Lord! What happened to your jaw?" she said as she shuttled Hoppy over to the side of a large tree out of ear-shot.

"I met the Fisherman and he strung me up. We engaged in a little 'catch and release,' although he was initially fuzzy on the release part, so Tang pitched in." Key ran his tongue over the wound inside his jaw and mouth. He winced. Turning his head to the side, he spat puss, mucous and several soft scabs to the sidewalk below.

"Jesus," exclaimed Ali, as she realized the severity of the wound and that it was a through and through puncture. "You've got to get that taken care of, get it stitched up."

"Right. I've got an investor friend who's a plastic surgeon. I'll call him. I'm sure he can hook me up and return my 'godlike' body without a lot of fanfare. But most importantly, do you have a safe place that you, Hoppy and my new-found personal hero (handing her the book bag containing Tang) can lay low for awhile?"

"Yes. I have someone in Portland who perhaps we could spend time with."

"Okay. Good."

Now, however, it's time for me to go," said Key.

"Where? Go where?" asked Ali.

"I'm heading back to Cozumel to hook up with Vinnie, Sheridan and perhaps another who can help unravel this. But you and Hoppy need to get gone, pronto."

"You're probably right as this is getting just too hot to go through channels," said Ali.

"Channels? Like your English Channel? As in that duplicitous fuck you report to who almost got us killed?"

"Calm down. You don't know that."

"Yeah? That two-faced, smug, overly perfumed limey? I didn't like him from the jump."

"Scotty." She paused. "Scotty, you don't know that to be true."

"And you do not—not know it. Isn't it odd that only three people, other than yourself, knew about your double secret departure and only one of them is still converting oxygen to carbon dioxide?"

"I have your point. I just don't want to think that. Because if Burton sold me out …"

"You're a big girl. A big girl who works for a big nasty organization that does not have a conscience. You know I am a flag waver. Hell, it's in my genes, I have no choice due to my lineage.

"Yes, I know how passionate you are about this country and its future Scotty."

"The NSA can shoot its mother, balance its milk and cookies on her stone cold belly and sleep like a baby."

"Harsh."

"Accurate."

Ali said nothing. She looked down at her lap and said nothing.

"Look Ali, I'm just trying to help you string these beads together. I want you and Hoppy safe but you're going to have to keep your guard up in particular around people who are paid for a living to deceive people. You can stick around here and play mumblety-peg with Machete Man, or you can protect yourself and your daughter."

"You've made your point. Let's move on." said Ali.

"I'm heading off to the island. Not sure from a visibility perspective it's in your self interest to accompany me, but you're welcome to."

"No. I agree. You're right. I'll head north. And if I need you, I'll call the pay phone across the street from La Ceiba. Beginning to see why you were so maniacal about saving that number off earlier anticipating this cloak and dagger routine."

"Bingo. Get your cloak. Avoid the dagger."

Key bent down, gave Hoppy a firm hug, assured the little one he'd be fine as she was staring aghast, fixated on his wound. The three parted ways. This time Ali took Hoppy without an announcement, without fanfare. She was distraught. Was it really possible that Buttons had sold her out? Was it a burn notice? Was this a Buttons thing, an Ali thing, or an NSA thing? Or did this run deeper, as Scotty speculated?

On television that morning at the farmhouse, Key had seen President Rasheed speak. He was stressing publically how he was trying to make NAFTA work even though, as a practical matter, he felt it was ineffective and unraveling.

So, Key thought to himself, *which is it? Is our president truly trying to salvage this thing with Presidente Villareal? Or is he conditioning his US constituents 'this dog won't hunt,' as he tanks it behind the scenes and spends us into bankruptcy?*

If the latter was the case, he wondered, did that strengthen the timing connection between the recent demise of the Mexican president and the Canadian prime minister?

Later that same morning at the airport Scotty continued to watch the news at his gate just prior to boarding. He witnessed part of what was exacerbating NAFTA's unraveling. New food embargos had just been placed on the table by the US between the United States, Mexico and Canada. The embargos were installed under the auspices of curbing a potential H1N1 virus outbreak, which was rumored to soon approach bubonic plague proportions by the Center for Disease Control. Was there truly a pandemic? Or was it just a ruse?

Key thought, *Why is everything so urgent with this administration? Crisis after crisis. Why is it always a doomsday, end-of-days scenario? Or, is it just a head-fake—a cattle prod to move the livestock along?*

These crises were happening frequently enough to start to challenge the legitimacy and authenticity of the very Office. Some suggested they were a contrivance to accelerate the promulgation of policy at terms that were desirable to the administration—and to a few special interest groups. For example, the unions were often weighing in (and wading in) deeply at the front of the line for each Bill's "pork."

Key knew the unions had benefitted mightily when the automakers were broken up. They ended up owning a significant controlling interest of the newly government-owned concern when they heretofore had none. The unions also had a keen interest in lobbying toward the dissolution of NAFTA, even though the administration had promised not to retain any lobbyist on his staff. While it was natural and historically accurate to have the Democratic Party favor the unions, this term they were so close you could not fit a dime between them.

He was mulling these thoughts over as he boarded the plane. He reflected again on the upcoming meeting with Vinnie, Willingham and another in Cozumel. He recalled how sober the usual jocular Vinnie was when he spoke with him earlier and yet was greeted instead with:

"We need to chat. In person." clipped Vinnie.

Rodriguez also wanted to introduce him to one of his prior SEAL buddies who was in the graduate class right after Scotty's. His area of expertise was marine biology, exotic weapons and demolition, or, as Vinnie said, "all things that bloom and boom."

FORTY

Cozumel, Mexico
February 2011

UPON LANDING IN COZUMEL, SCOTTY was met by Vinnie, Sheridan and Mr. *All Things Which Bloom and Boom.* The latter gentleman's name was Chris P. Ritz, aka "Cracker."

"Scotty," said Vinnie, "I'd like to introduce you to the dishonorable Chris P. Ritz, aka 'Cracker.' Be sure to habla real slow now, although he was born in Llano, Texas, English is his still his second language!" To galvanize the insult, Vinnie slapped Cracker on the back with a braying laugh.

"Nice to meet you, Chris."

"Call me Cuh-rracker."

"Cracker it is," replied Key.

Llano was a small, charming Texas town about three hours south of Fort Worth, where at the mini-mart's checkout counter, one could buy deer corn, breath mints and thirty-ought-six shells. There was a luminary statue in the town square that out-of-towners affectionately referred to as "Llano-Lynn."

Cracker was starting to put on weight. Although young and still strong as an ox, he had the propensity to fry pretty much everything. He used to boast he liked to fry up butter. A mountain of a man, he approached six feet six, tipped the scales well over three hundred pounds and was shoe-leather tough.

Legend had it when cat fishing in sweltering heat, he'd carry his catch in a burlap tow sack. To keep them from puncturing his calf with their fins (as they'd bounce back and forth when carried) he'd first bite their fins off with his teeth just before chucking them in the sack. Without a blink.

He said he liked to suck on a radish afterward to get the bitter taste out of his mouth. Squared off like a fireplug, his shaved head had a "hot dog roll" at the base of his neck, which grew to a "foot-long" when he jerked his head back laughing. Which was often.

Cracker had a crooked half frown, half smirk, which was at times engaging and at times, irritating. It was mostly irritating to anyone who attempted to bullshit him. His accent was thick and slow. All bulbs burning in his mental chandelier, it was difficult to discern how much of his accent was trumped up to sneak up on his unwitting prey.

He enjoyed throwing people large conversational latitude, just so he could slowly tighten the noose, exposing to all just how fucking stupid the guy running his mouth was. Oddly enough, he had become quite thick with MI6 in the UK. This association allowed him to keep his fingers in the international intelligence pie, as well as giving him access and wide latitude to secure things that go boom in the night.

Cracker said, "The real reason I talk soooo suh-low around Vinnie here, is so this spic can keep up." With that riposte, he sent a hardened, razored hand strike with blinding quickness toward Vinnie's groin. Cracker pulled the punch at the last minute and then ran it back sideways alongside his ear just to fuck with him. "Comprende, ese?"

"He knows a thing or two about your science project, Scotty." said Vinnie. "Give him his way at first. Kiss his ass a little and let him think he's real smart. Play him like a fat honky cracker."

"Thanks for the tip."

"Let's go to some place a bit more private."

"We want this off the church PA," said Scotty.

"Doesn't suit," drawled Cracker.

Vinnie, Cracker, Willingham and Key threw snorkeling gear into *Atsa-Moray*. They motored out to an isolated atoll that had a shallow reef, bringing along sandwiches and the obligatory dozen cervezas. The crash of the waves against the gentle rocks masked any attempt at high tech eavesdropping. Additionally, if glassed, the location provided ample line of sight, heralding any who would approach within a half a mile.

They were gently bobbing back and forth in the surf with sandwich and beer on belly. Bobbing up and down as a fraternity brother charm bracelet on break. Rising and resting his buttocks on top of a beach ball-sized brain coral, Cracker remarked, "I wonder if this is how 'Enema In' got started?"

"That's Eminem. And the answer is no," said Key.

"These are the things we come to you for, Gringo!" roared Vinnie.

"Yeah. Well whatever. Okay, partners, listen up, rahtnaow," commanded Cracker. "I'm fixin' to school you ladies up.

"Right before the Mexican honcho met his maker through 'death by earthquake,' the locals were talking up some weird glowing lights at sea, out toward the east end."

"Near Palancar Reef?" asked Vinnie.

"Zackly. Well, all southerners and damn few Yankees know bioluminescence is a form of luminescence, or 'cold light' emission. Less than say 20 percent of the light generates thermal radiation, though it is not fluorescence, phosphorescence, or refraction of light."

"Is he making this shit up?" asked Key.

"The man knows his stuff," asserted Vinnie.

Cracker continued, "So, some 90 percent of deep-sea marine life produces bioluminescence in one form or t'other. Those lights are mostly blue and green. These are the colors that pass through seawater best. However, certain loose-jawed fish emit red and infrared light and the genus *Tomopteris* emits yellow bioluminescence."

"*Tomopteris*? You boned her in Portugal during SEAL training, didn't

231

you? Wasn't she the skinny Latvian who later turned out to be a transvestite?" mocked Vinnie.

"Keep running your mouth and I will knock you down, Poncho! Concentrate. I know it's hard for a Mexican. Pretend it's a shrub, anything that needs pruning—something you're good at. Focus."

Cracker went on, "At first, the locales thought it was large schools of luminescent jellies, or maybe the second coming of Christ."

"I like colors," mocked Vinnie.

"The two best-known forms of land bioluminescence are fireflies and glowworms. Other insects, larvae, annelids, arachnids and even some of fungi have been noted to possess bioluminescent abilities. They've gotten a lot of attention recently, as we've learned some of these jellyfish are darn near immortal."

"Immortal?" asked Willingham.

"Yup. During a crisis, they can age backward, over and over again if necessary. They can transform all of their cells into a younger state, spawning hundreds of prett' near identical blobs. This applies only to *Turritopsis dohrnii* however."

"Praise the gods Mama Ritz did not have that same capability," said Vinnie. "Say, your whiteness, I'm just about to break out in a drool cause this is sooooo fucking exciting. Could we package and sell this speech as white noise? Is there a point in here anytime soon?"

"Ignert, just plain ignert. What'd I tell you? The shrub, Poncho, the shrub. Be one with the shrub. Ya'll focus, you hear? I'll use smaller words for you, Vinnie. So the point: The locals saw a red glow coming way out from the sea near Palancar Reef and red just ain't right. Not natural. No sir."

"Not natural?" asked Key.

"Nope. In close, maybe, maybe sometimes. Like the sometime when there was a bioluminescent red tide beach in Carlsbad in '05. It was real bright like. Glowing, crashing waves containing billions of *Lingulodinium polyedrum dinoflagellates*. But those were all in shallow water, like a beach. Not deep water. Not like Palancar," exclaimed Cracker as he spat out a plug of Skoal.

"Talk dirty to me, Cracker. Dangle those dino-flag-ellates," ragged Vinnie.

"Will you please shut the fuck up and let the man finish?" said Key.

"Sorry," said Vinnie with a hurt, clipped tone as he looked down.

"No worries. I knew I should have drove over here with some shiny spinning rims, sparkly three-stage paint, and dingo balls to keep your attention. It might be best if you just don't talk," fired back Cracker with a smile, but placing his hand firmly on Vinnie's shoulder to let him know he was also serious.

Willingham grinned silently as he shook his head from side to side.

Key brought them up to date on Pig's and Alex's demise, Ali's safe house, the kidnapping and his ordeal with the Fisherman. He said he found it curious that most of his prior problems with Stink Eye and company seemed to be with Middle Easterners, however the recent 'rave' band members were all Asian. He mentioned the ESE tattoo. He concluded by summarizing his concern about exactly what direction President Rasheed was taking the country with all the debt.

"Indeed," chimed in Willingham. "My contacts, who also have affiliations with Britain's MI6, have focused on another interesting thing in the US."

"Leave it up to Canada and the Brits to be out in front as to what is happening on our own home turf," exclaimed Scotty.

"Quite. We won't tarry long on this; however, it might pique your interest to expand a bit on what Rasheed's Chief of Staff is doing in trying to bring the US Census inside his domain and wrest its control from normal channels with the customary oversight."

"Go ahead. You've got the conn."

"Originally the notion was that if the US relaxed all immigration policies, granted amnesty and/or, at a minimum, looked the other way, there would be millions more of a particular persuasion looking for entitlements and a free lunch. Lump their numbers on top of the current fifteen million illegals and soon it becomes such a large voting bloc there'd just be a single party. There'd be no defeating them ever.

"Yeah. I'd heard speculation about that," said Key.

"Quite probably Democratic, Socialistic, or Marxist. Who knows? Whigs or Tories could perhaps get another seat at the table. But it would be the permanent undoing of the balance the two-party system has afforded the US for over two hundred years. Most advanced civilizations normally last only a few hundred years anyway. So, you Yanks' turn in the barrel is about up," said Willingham jutting his jaw out a bit while he scratched it.

"Interesting factoid," said Cracker.

"So additionally, if the Chief of Staff does wrest control of the census, the administration will ultimately be allowed to redraw, gerrymander, or redistrict all key areas of the country to ever so conveniently benefit whichever political entity is in power. Today, it's the Democrats, tomorrow it could be someone else. If this were to occur, it would be the first time in US history this power was taken from the Census Bureau," said Willingham.

Scotty chimed in, "Yup. An oligarchy. They are looking to foist that unsupervised power of measurement and implementation through a group called Buckeye. This is the group who was found to have forty-four individual counts of voter registration fraud in the last election, two thousand complaints in Texas alone. So they can hide behind a corkscrew, if they need to. They're out of Ohio, a key election state."

"Maybe we should let this one go," suggested Vinnie. "We could wake up dead turning these rocks over."

"You know the story of the frog in a pot of water on the stove that is slowly being heated up, right?" asked Key as he drew a large and a small circle in the sand to make his point.

"Shoot."

"They say he never jumps out, even though he could at any time, because he is being made uncomfortable *a little at a time*. He gets used to it."

"Right up to the point where it boils him alive," said Cracker.

"Let's man-up and do the right thing for our countries. I'm tired of pussing-out and being part of the silent majority. Fuck 'em. Let's make some noise," said Key. "Inasmuch as the largest majority of ethnic groups in the nine-county Bay area is Asian, it would be no problem to influence that entire region and control the vote. If immigration is allowed to continue in an unbridled fashion, along with gerrymandering, Mexicans could ultimately control the popular vote in SoCal."

"Lookie here Vinnie, there's hope for you!" said Cracker.

"So maybe the end game is to break off SoCal from NorCal as its own state. God knows that conversation comes up every five to ten years anyway. One thing for sure, whoever wins California, Missouri and Ohio wins the election 95 percent of the time."

"It was shared on talk radio that the financial spoils of the Stimulus Plans are being distributed at a rate of two to one to Democratic districts, versus Republican districts, with absolutely no correlation to unemployment or population density." said Key.

"They discovered the same thing as to which auto dealerships were closed when you Yanks took GM over," said Willingham. "Essentially, if the owner had donated to the Democratic party, he got to keep his shop."

"Yup. What is the old military saying? Once is an accident. Twice, a coincidence and the third time is *enemy fire*," said Key, grimacing as he shook his head.

"So is this something to turn over to the CIA now?" asked Willingham.

"No. The NSA was the only group who knew about *both* Ali's issues—and mine. Then someone did a stab-and-grab with her crew. I'm goosey. Not certain anyone can be trusted right now until we figure this out," lamented Scotty, using a stick to toy with a small crab.

"Yup," said Cracker. "We'd be way off the reservation if we tried to push this up through channels right now as no Black Ops are currently funded or approved."

"Are these tidbits you picked up from *Black Ops Weekly Digest* while on the crapper?" taunted Vinnie as he waved his hands overhead and ended with a single finger point toward Cracker.

"We had a mind to monitor some NASA images and found three sea horses, each with a story to tell," said Cracker.

"Oh?"

"Yes, sir. When their images were digitally dissolved, it was determined that each and every pixel was made up of hundreds of tiny Chinese Buddhas."

"No shit?"

"No shit. And initially, unbeknownst to us, each one of those was later dissolved again and they were encrypted with these and other Wrigley's Fun Facts."

Cracker continued, "So anywho, listen up. As to Vinnie's insight into Red Mercury, it's uncertain if it is fact or fiction. There were a number of 'go fast' boats hanging out at Palancar however."

"Go fast boats?" asked Willingham.

"Right," continued Cracker. "Real speedy, cigarette, *CSI Miami*-looking rigs, at a time that sure didn't look like any fishing or diving was going on. Thought it might be interesting to get some boy toys and check out our glowing sea monster at Palancar Reef. We'd be real quick like. We'll just give it a lick and a promise. Any interest?"

"Boy toys?" asked the group in unison, as they stood up and hand-spanked the sand from their limbs.

"Yeah. Nothin' too fancy. I'm thinkin' invisible cloaking devices, high intensity underwater lasers, infrared underwater masks and STUDS."

"STUDS?" again in unison.

"Stunning Transcontinuous Ultrasonic Defense System—STUDS."

"So amigo, is this one of those if you like the acronym, you're gonna love the toy?" asked Vinnie.

"STUDS sends out a series of extremely low, ultrasonic sound wave pulses. They are propagated nicely through air and even better through water. The pulse is isolated in a forward direction to mitigate it coming backward and tearing you a new one," said Cracker. "Also, It don't beat up anything physically, like a bomb—which is a bit disappointing to me personally. However, any life form, human, fish, or the like is flat taken out. The pulse induces extreme nausea, vertigo and vomiting. Even though the pulses are sent

forward, it is still a good idea to plug all orifices with these baffled devices."
He spread open his palm to display the objects.

"*All* orifices?" asked Vinnie.

"Yup. Especially the pooper. Recognizing in your case, O-B-Juan, this will seriously restrict your ability to communicate."

"And the invisible cloaking device?" asked Key.

"It's a three hundred sixty-degree video screen that records visually what is behind you and projects it on the screen that is covering the front of you. Presto. You're not there. They've used this in Afghanistan for a couple of years successfully on a classified basis. I just saw it talked about in a fictional movie, so I know they're for real."

FORTY-ONE

Palancar Reef, Cozumel, Mexico
February 2011

OVER THE NEXT THIRTY SIX hours, the four men prepared the logistics and assembled their toys, things that go boom in the night and dive gear. They commissioned a speedy, blue black, low profile, "go-fast" boat from a friend of Vinnie's who owed him one. It bore large, white skulls on each side, requiring ample electrician tape to be placed over both to obscure them.

Donned fully with rebreather scuba gear, they headed out at 2:00 am in the low-slung, radar-avoiding craft. They chose rebreathers as these left no telltale bubbles when the wearer exhaled and, as SEALs, they had used a closed circuit underwater breathing apparatus (CCUBA), which was similar. It was a breathing set that allowed one to scrub, reprocess and reuse his exhaled gases—or rebreathe. Its design made it significantly lighter, which was also valuable for tactical missions requiring endurance.

There was just a toenail of a moon, making for a dark, inky night. This was compounded in a good way by mild seas and low-slung, black-bellied cumulus nimbus clouds, which added to the sinister backdrop. The trip to Palancar Reef did not take long due to the craft's speed.

They tied down and concealed each side of the vessel with the projection cloaking cape. Upon arrival, the group determined that the Mountie would be the man to remain topside and discharge a small O-Ring-sealed pistol underwater as a warning to surface in the event of trouble. Sheridan had made a concerted effort his entire career to stay on top of the water.

As they approached the reef, Cracker pointed to the east and said, "See. Do you see that glow? It's the muted red glow I use-ta see. Those other nimrods were trying to tell me it was just jellies! Horseshit. Let's go. Let's go rahtnaow!"

They marked the waypoints on their GPS to allow a precise return. The three divers, summoning up their SEAL heritage, grabbed their regulators with one hand, held their masks to their faces with the other and flipped over backwards with the vessel still motoring at ten knots. They took to the water like otters.

"Okay?" signaled Scotty silently underwater.

They gave each other the okay sign and ignited their personal locator devices by snapping small, red glow sticks on their buckles. This enabled them to distinguish each other from any threat. At the same time, with a single hand, they could easily conceal the small glow. By design, with black wetsuits and no bubbles, they would be challenging to see in the pitch-black inkwell they had submerged themselves in.

There was no anchor line to follow down. They stayed in a tight formation, descending on a sixty-degree plane downward. This allowed for a workmanlike clearing of their Eustachian tubes and it put them on the appropriate vector to reach the long-distance glow looming in the distance.

As they came closer, they noticed a few hammerhead sharks. The animals' eyes were extremely wide set. Each eye was offset outwardly a full foot from the center of their skulls, as if on opposite ends of a hammer's head.

"Tighten the formation," signaled Scotty.

All divers knew these were man-eaters. That was their job. That was their job before they were ever provoked. Fortunately, there was no blood in the water to excite them.

As the men swam closer to the faintly glowing red light, the shark's agitation markedly increased.

Scotty pointed to a buoyantly bobbing cage three feet in diameter, which was suspended by cable from the bottom. It was deliberately tethered there. The orb-like vessel appeared to have steam, vapor, or something oozing off, or rising from it.

Shit, he thought. *It's chum.*

They swam in closer. "In fact, it was human chum. Scotty could see parts—feet, hands, fingers and heads. Pig could be out here. *I could be swimming through parts of Pig right now*, he thought. Key bit down so hard he severed the right side of his regulator's mouthpiece.

These bastards are going to get their comeuppance, he thought to himself.

Looking around, the men noticed they were swimming into a grid of permanently placed, actively seeping chum ball cages. These had been meticulously placed at thirty yards on center in each direction.

"There, there and there," pointed Cracker silently towards the boundaries of the grid.

The closer they got to the opaque structure's dull, maroon light, the more hammerheads they saw and the more frantic the sharks became due to the chum. The pelagics began to snap and bite at the chum balls and at each other's tails. Initially motionless, they'd dart to take a nip out of their neighbor's dorsal fin with no warning.

All three men engaged their STUDS. A high-pitched, accelerating whir commenced as their weapons spun up and a small, green penlight came on, signifying they were fully armed. All reflected on having earlier plugged their orifices. All orifices. Would they actually be immune to the ultra-low frequency sonic pulses? Vinnie laughed through his regulator, as he clinched his butt cheeks together, confirming his baffled suppository was firmly in place.

In tight formation, the three swam in a protective back-to-back-to-back, triangulated configuration, so they had each other's six. Then, two eight-footers darted toward their dark triangle. Without hesitation, Scotty discharged his weapon. *Vuuuuuurrrrrroooouuughhhhh!* The subsonic pulse beamed out toward the man-eaters. The first pulse pushed out with another following not a second behind. A gentle kick from the weapon was dampened by it being surrounded with water.

Instantly, the sharks were stunned. They started gagging on their own vomit and began swimming in flat, wobbly, circles. They were circling on their sides while drifting aimlessly up toward the surface, ascending awkwardly as if their internal altimeters had been disabled.

The large, usually graceful, slinky animals barred their teeth in disgust at their inability to converge on dinner. Their legendary closing speed was rendered ineffective this time. Frustrated, they shook their heads violently back and forth, while gnashing their teeth in a futile attempt to shake the overwhelming nausea.

Disabling man-eaters in a feeding frenzy was pretty cool, apart from, the brief "gayness" of navigating their suppository's placement, which would never be spoken of again. Ever. No wonder the locals had not been able to get close to this previously.

The trio continued swimming toward the hemispherical structure, which they could now see more clearly at the ocean's floor. It was a large physical plant, eighty yards in length, thirty yards in width, with three distinct levels, rather ziggurat in its design.

Gray black and windowless, it was covered in green sea kelp, staghorn coral, anemones and other marine organisms, suggesting it had been there awhile. Eighteen-inch, purple blue filefish and triggerfish darted in and around its surface. Trumpetfish swayed back and forth vertically on top and two schools of yellow, gray and white sergeant majors guarded its apex. There were no doors or openings. It was foreboding and at the same time awe inspiring in its stature.

Without warning, the top portion of the sphere began to open slowly. It startled and ran off a green, five-foot moray eel, as it belched out three enormous steam bubbles. Each bubble was thirty feet across.

"Get down, get down," motioned Scotty to all, as they dove behind a large outcropping of staghorn coral. The aperture narrowed again, like a camera's lens and constricted down to its previously closed state.

Looking again, the men found no other openings—no windows, doors, or appurtenances of any kind. The three were writing notes on their slates regarding the sphere's seeming impenetrability when, from the distance, they heard the discharge of an underwater firearm.

Was this Willingham signaling it was time to shoot and scoot? No. It was a bang stick being used by one of six men in yellow wetsuits approaching them swiftly on underwater scooter-sleds. These sleds propelled them through the water at three times the rate of a normal swimmer.

The men in yellow were dispatching members of their own natural security system with twelve-gauge, touch-and-go bang sticks. The single-shell slug was positioned at the end of a five-foot, stainless steel rod and discharged upon firm contact with any predator.

They were closing in on the SEALs swiftly. The three resumed their back-to-back-to-back defensive posture, as the six men in yellow approaching were heavily armed with both double-banded spearguns and bang sticks. There was no ambiguity as to their intentions. This time as the six came within range, the three fanned out, rearmed their STUDS and sent off three ultra-low frequency pulses. *Vuuuuuurrrrroooouuughhhhh! Vuuuuuurrrrroooouuughhhhh! Vuuuuuurrrrroooouuughhhhh!*

Not unlike the sharks, the six in yellow began to erratically struggle and float upward off their scooters. Disoriented as they rose above their sleds, two in yellow held desperately on to their handle bars with one hand, struggling to resist the inevitable.

Cough, hack, choke, gag! The other four were coughing and gagging on their vomit, frantically trying to clear regulators, masks and lungs to extract their next clean breath. The fresh vomit in the water excited the sharks further and three hammerheads swiftly de-legged two of the yellow wet-suited intruders. Another was literally torn limb from limb by two of the larger sharks. Vinnie, Scotty and Cracker swam over and, with one quick slice each, slashed the other three's regulator hoses.

And then their throats.

As the six mutilated forms drifted lifelessly to the bottom, some three dozen hammerheads coalesced, as if from no where. They had their way with the remnants of fresh bloody meat as a killer whale would with a seal by throwing it in the air. The sharks played with their food like cats before consuming it.

Scotty barely made out the "ESE" on the top, back panel of each wetsuit.

The SEALs watched as all six were ravaged savagely by the most efficient killing machine known to man. Teeth and tail, tail and teeth. Ripping. Pulling. Gnawing. Gnashing. A blur. A bloody blur.

The muted grinding noise of the roof-mounted aperture came again, signaling the top of the sphere was about to reopen. All three SEALs had underwater cameras at the ready anticipating this event. They kicked their fins forcefully to quickly get into position. They'd have but one more chance, as the absence of their six visitors return would surely not be tolerated for an inordinate period of time.

They surrounded the dark gray, coral-encrusted octagonal aperture from all angles, each about one hundred and twenty degrees from the other. They were all floating at a slightly different depth. The aperture relaxed and opened, belching again three thirty-foot bubbles. There was a single instant between each bubble where one could, for just an instant, see inside.

It was during this instant that the autowinders on the three underwater cameras ground away at fifteen shots per second. Moreover, at the openings' maximum diameter, two of the crew additionally fired in "camera balls." These spherical projectiles were initially encased in an inch of dampening (low bounce) rubber. This cushioned their arrival upon impact, whereupon the rubberized skin was automatically shed. An eye opened and continuous video feed was streamed as the sphere, slowly rotated and captured it all. The digitized footage was monitored from their remote web site, monitored by Willingham upstairs.

The three had what they needed. They checked their gauges. Their bottom time was relatively brief. Still, they chose to hang for a single one-minute safety stop at twenty feet and then three minutes at ten. This should be ample time to off-gas, clean up and avoid nitrogen narcosis, or the bends.

Their decision was made on a balance beam. Dawdle and they'd be descended upon by three times the number of the prior scouting party. If they didn't clean up, however, they could be "bent," paralyzed, or even killed from the ravages of the bends.

True, they could take a ride in a decompression chamber to mitigate this, but there was only one on the island. To remain vulnerably stationary in a predictably monitored location would surely make them an easy target.

Hanging and being mindful of their surroundings, Cracker noticed a clump of some eerily luminescent jellies hanging in the distance, the very kind he'd earlier emphatically stated would never be glowing or even present at this depth. He pointed towards them and the three chuckled through their regulators.

After the last safety stop, they ascended slowly, following their bubbles up to avoid an air embolism. Ascending too fast would induce a pulmonary barotrauma, where tiny bubbles would enter the bloodstream, causing gross trauma to the lining of the lung's alveoli, worsened by speed and even more so if the diver holds his breath. There is scant advance warning until the alveoli ultimately burst. If the diver made it to the surface, he'd arrive in pain, frothing, foaming and spitting blood. Drowning or death by stroke would normally follow.

The SEALs slammed their bodies against the go-fast's hull and Willingham aided in pulling them back over the side and throwing them onto the deck like freshly caught tuna.

Willingham struggled a bit with Cracker's weight. Two hot dogs bulged out on the back of Cracker's neck as he wiggled to pull himself up and over the side. Although hefty, he was still yoked. With Willingham's assistance, he ultimately bulled himself up and over. Sheridan winked and buried the throttle forward. The four roared off into the pitch.

FORTY-TWO

THE NEXT MORNING, THE TEAM met for breakfast at a sister of Vinnie's in an open-air back porch overlooking the ocean where they were concealed from all except an errant gull. The air was warm and moist, so it provided the bird sufficient updraft to swoop, hover and shuttle back to sea after making its rounds. The gull had dark gray feathers around its eyes, almost like a mask.

Scotty brought some troubling articles with him to share. "Bear with me, as it's a bit long, however I believe it's worth bringing this global audience we have gathered before us", he pointed to himself and his three cohorts, "up to speed on the current state of the United States financially. I'm uncertain if there's linkage, but I need you to be the judge."

He read out loud:

> Due to political unrest in the US, the states of Montana, Arizona and Texas have begun to advance secession from the United States. As a barometer of the depth of the unrest, somewhat remarkably, the idea is gaining traction.

"Unbelievable," remarked Willingham.

"Oh, I'm just getting started," said Scotty.

> Secession has been glossed over and has never been able to gain legs until the early 1990s, when the Soviet Union, Yugoslavia and Czechoslovakia, experienced a dissolution. Dissolutions spring from the concept of political philosophy, moral basis of the state's authority

(God's will), people's consent, morality of goals, or the appropriateness to cling to these goals.

"Texas is a good state with good, solid people Señor," said Vinnie.

"Then you'll find this next part intriguing," said Scotty.

Texas is the second largest state with over 268,000 square miles, second only to Alaska, it is 10 percent larger than France and about twice the size of Germany or Japan. In 1845, it became the twenty-eighth state, which sparked the Mexican-American War of 1846. In 1848, the Treaty of Guadalupe Hidalgo ended the war with Mexico. The US paid Mexico $18,250,000 in exchange for the property.

"Never been there. Had no idea it was that large," said Willingham, as he leaned backward in his chair and ignited the business end of a large Cuban cigar.

The Compromise of 1850 perfected Texas's boundaries. During the same period, Texas ceded land, which later became half of New Mexico, a third of Colorado, and small portions of Kansas, Oklahoma and Wyoming, to the federal government. In exchange, the federal government assumed $10,000,000 of the old republic's debt. In 1861, Texas seceded from the US to briefly join the Confederate States of America. Tea Party members allude to this event with their banners today, saying, "We've done it before. We can do it again."

"Your president refers to members of that movement as 'Tea Baggers,' does he not?" asked Willingham.

"He does. And that's not a mouth-a-graphical error. That's a backhanded insult, as the term actually refers to an activity normally relegated to sexual deviants," said Key.

The bandit-masked gull splashed in the nearby fountain's water, attracting and diverting a smaller bird's attention, while it spun and took off with the largest piece of bread crust from Willingham's plate.

"You mentioned Montana. They're considering it too?" asked Cracker.

"Yup. Listen up."

Montana, east of the Continental Divide, was a piece of the Louisiana Purchase in 1803. After Lewis and Clark discovered gold and copper, it became a territory in 1864 and the forty-first state in 1889.

"Isn't it almost as big as Texas?" asked Willingham, tapping his stogie against the ash tray.

"Funny you should ask," continued Key.

Montana is the fourth largest state in the US at 145,000 square miles. Forty-fourth in population, it has the third lowest population density. To the north, the state borders the Canadian provinces of British Columbia, Alberta and Saskatchewan.

"Near God's country, eh?" said Willingham as he blew three large smoke rings. "Montana, Big Sky country is a state I can relate to and dearly love. So how does Arizona fit into the mix?"

"Arizona on the other hand, with almost 114,000 square miles is the sixth largest state in the US. It shares three hundred and eighty nine miles of its border with Mexico, which is where a key part of their dissention is today. During the Mexican American war in 1847 the US pursued its claim of much of northern Mexico. The Treaty of Guadalupe Hidalgo in 1848 had the US pay the Republic of Mexico $15,000,000 to culminate the purchase. In 1862 Arizona became a Confederate territory. It was the last of the contiguous states admitted to the union in 1912. In the aggregate, Montana, Arizona and Texas comprise seventeen percent of the total land mass of the contiguous continental United States.

"They could actually legally do this, amigo?" asked Vinnie, while pulling at his ear and sliding his asymmetrical coffee cup back and forth in front of him nervously. Surely this is just people upset, caliente?

The US Constitution is silent on secession. The Articles of Confederation stated the union of the colonies "shall be perpetual." In 1860 and 1861, eleven states seceded, however came back after the Civil War during the Reconstruction Era. The justifications advanced two theories in the 90s. The first is "Choice Theory," or "Just Cause". The latter applies to remediating grave injustices.

"So what are Montana, Arizoona and Texas pointing to as a reason—or their grave injustice?" asked Cracker.

"Montana and Texas feel the current administration is trampling on the Constitution. They argue, the Constitution is a contract between the federal government, the state government and the people. And

they feel that the federal government is not holding up their end of the bargain.

"Can I have an amen?" asked Vinnie.

"Fuckin'-A," said Cracker.

Unnoticed, the gull had swooped back from the sea and dropped his load right at Willingham's feet.

> *This is the key argument for "dissolving such union when goals for which it was constituted are not achieved." They feel it injurious to their right to liberty, free association and matters of private property. The auto manufacturers and financial services industry takeover was the lynch pin for their taking the "private property position." The two states also cite "will and self-determination of the majority to secede." Texas recently circulated a petition where 52 percent were in favor.*

"Indeed. I had no idea it was heating up to this degree," said Willingham as he reached across the table for more tea and to shoo the gull away.

> *Also fanning the flames is the administration's recklessly burying the US in additional trillions of dollars debt. Some reports estimate this oppressive debt at $14 trillion; others range as high as $15 trillion. Previously, $12 trillion was the lid, as the "Debt Ceiling" limit was raised, as required by law, to that amount by the American Recovery and Reinvestment Act of 2009 (H.R. 1).*

"But there's strict oversight, is there not?" asked Cracker. "Besides, in fairness to your president, wasn't he handed a bag of worms from the prior administration?"

"There should be oversight, but no one was minding the store. And he's going to wear that record out of blaming the prior administration. He's had the reigns now for over two years. Half a term. When's he going to man up? He's made the debt six times worse than the prior president, none of his programs have worked, so he's looking for an excuse as he has no constructive successes to point to. Besides, a full Democratic congress has controlled the US messaging since 2006. We're going on five years now of their own special brand of Nirvana. " Key continued:

> *In late 2009, the legal debt ceiling was raised again another third of a trillion. This Band-Aid only postponed the federal government's*

"unlawful behavior" by thirteen weeks, whereupon it was breached again. Just weeks later, the ceiling was raised yet one more time to over $14 trillion. According to Texas, Arizona and Montana representatives, this unlawful action is made worse by the fact that the national debt is almost $1.5 trillion dollars more, or six times greater, than the debt President Rasheed inherited from his predecessor. The three states feel this is completely unsustainable. In 2009, interest payments alone to foreign entities were approaching $1 billion dollars per day. Many fear that in 2011, the payments (in interest alone per day) could approach almost $2 billion and by 2018 estimates are that interest alone annually will exceed $1.0 trillion dollars. If this debt remains unchecked, it will pass 100 percent of the US GDP for the first time since WWII.

"That's a fine howdy-do," said Cracker.

The Heritage Foundation showed publicly held debt as a percentage of GDP was 41 percent in 2008, about five points below historical average. Rasheed's budget promptly doubled this amount and the percentage is projected to rise to over 81 percent by 2019. This puts on full display the notion that the Rasheed administration is steamrolling the country toward insolvency.

"People are flat pissed off," said Cracker.

"Yup. Deficit reduction was recently rated as number one on most citizens' agendas, yet their plea fell on deaf ears. This president forgets who he works for. Fox News's survey showed 78 percent polled in 2010 felt the national debt was so large it was hurting our country's future. Rasmussen and CBS both found that 41 percent strongly disapprove of this president. The Rasmussen Poll found 45 percent are very angry at the government's policies, or 125,000,000 and 170,000,000 people, respectively." Scotty turned back to the reading material:

Seniors will lose $500 billion in Medicare coverage and younger voters who'll have to foot this bill are coming together in their outrage. National health care was originally pegged at costing $850 billion. The administration, according to naysayers, gamed the system by attempting to collect first without any benefits starting until years later.

"Yeah, I heard most pundits felt the true cost over ten years would be $2.5 trillion," said Cracker.

"Exactly. To effect a 'head fake' to the American people at the same time they're mounding on debt, the administration was suggesting a mini-campaign of deficit reduction."

"Priceless!" said Cracker as the group roared. "They were trying to use the leftover $200 billion from Stimulus One to reduce the deficit with much chest puffing to brag about their fiscal responsibility. That insignificant reduction, when viewed as an overall percentage, is mice nuts.

"As this was borrowed money in the first place, this premature ejubilation was akin to declaring a faux victory of principal reduction if one were to borrow from MasterCard to repay Visa."

"That dog won't hunt," said Cracker as he blew his nose in disdain with one finger. "Whether from multiple stimulus plans and bailouts, refusing to enforce immigration laws, nationalizing industry sectors, or pushing the national healthcare agenda and 'Crap and Trade,' those in power are steadily dismantling the bedrock of this country."

"To the point of soft tyranny, hyperinflation and ultimate bankruptcy," said Key.

"They think we're fucking stupid and just going to sit here and take it!" bellowed Cracker, as he threw his coffee cup against the fireplace shattering it over the seawall to the rocks below. Cracker continued "Pundits exclaimed that if there was a checklist of one hundred things to do to undermine this country, this administration was steadily checking them off, one by one. With the US Treasury printing currency willy-nilly, many experts feel hyperinflation is just around the corner. Hyperinflation hit Ukraine to the tune of 960 percent in '09. It can happen here."

"My grandfather told stories of his father talking about the crazy inflation in Germany." Is there a piece on that?" asked Vinnie.

Key nodded.

"In pre WWII Germany, hyperinflation was at "300 million percent (sic)." People were being paid twice a day so they could run to the store to buy a loaf of bread. If they'd waited till day's end their paycheck would have become worthless. Individuals were carrying their cash in

*wheelbarrows to barter for alternative goods, goods that bore real value
in contrast to their worthless currency.*

"On a separate topic, I will tell you it has become the wild-wild west
in border towns between Mexico and the US, mi amigo," stated Vinnie.
"Particularly Texas and Arizona."

"They mention that in this article as well. Give me a minute," Key
said, running his finger down the page. "This next piece is quite relevant to
those two border states of Arizona and Texas. Together, their southernmost
borders comprise 83% of the 1969 mile US border with Mexico, so they
reason they should have something to say on the matter. Did you know it's
the most highly crossed border in the world averaging 250,000,000 *known*
crossings per year? With the feds recently trying to shut down the new Arizona
immigration law which was derived simply to validate the enforcement of the
federal immigration law, folks in Arizona are hotter'n a freshly-fucked-fox-
in-a-forest-fire."

"It didn't help that Mexican cartel drug lords are shooting ranchers and
placing million dollar bounties on some of your US sheriff's heads," added
Willingham as he crushed out his cigar.

*Key kept after it, "With immigration traumas and escalating border
town violence along the Arizona and Texas borders, the residents also
cited a reason to secede as "self defense." This applies as a bona fide reason
for secession when the state can not (or is not permitted) to adequately
defend itself and the larger (federal) entity is not assisting.*

Scotty put the article down and said, "Montana, Arizona and Texas looked
at this administration's socialistic agenda with disdain and reasoned we'd lost
our way, drifting too far from our framer's vision of the Constitution. We'd
lost our historical grit and backbone. Abandoned the very tenacity which
pioneered the formation of this great nation."

"We've become a nation of "Pussies." Said Cracker.

"Rasheed's a bright guy," said Willingham, "wonder what his true
motivation is for his reckless behavior?"

Scotty spoke. "Strong men who previously were action-oriented are becoming listless, dispirited and despondent due to the worst unemployment since the great depression. They felt helpless. They were not rising up in outrage, in fact the term for this phenomena had been coined by a talk radio host as the "Chick-A-Fication" of the US. Everything's 'PC' to a fault. Dissent—you're demonized and labeled a racist—which is code for *'I have no logical rebuttal'*.

"Zackley. Name calling. That works about as well on me now as it did in third grade." said Cracker.

Key spoke again, "Perhaps the pending action of these three bold states will be the catalyst for people nationwide to finally awaken to Edmond Burke's famous quote of:

> *"For evil to flourish, all that is needed is for good people to do nothing."*

FORTY-THREE

SCOTTY WENT ACROSS THE STREET to the pay phone at 7:00 PM each night as agreed upon with Ali. She'd call at that precise time from another pay phone. Or, she would not call at all. Proper nouns were never exchanged. On this evening, they connected.

"Mr. K."

"Hey there, Lotus Blossom. How is Ms. W?"

"Missing my hunk of overgrown otter."

"That's seal."

"Whatever."

"You and your dwarf faring well?"

"Well, we are faring. I am concerned for some of my relatives in Urumqi however."

"Where is that?"

"It is the capital of Xinjiang, a northwest province of China."

"Is that where all that barbaric rioting is occurring? I'm seeing videos of clubs, meat cleavers and long steel rods being wielded by the masses. Ugly," said Key.

"Yes. That's it."

"I saw something about it on the news. One hundred fifty killed and ten times that number injured? Near People's Square."

"That's what's being printed in the papers and on the Web. With the Communist Party leader Ah Zho shutting down the Internet, Facebook, Twitter and cell phone texting however, deaths and injuries are feared ten times that."

"Wow. That can't make Zho feel good about just passing the sixtieth anniversary of communistic rule. What's the rub?" asked Scotty.

"Mainly between the Hans, who make up the majority of the Chinese and the Uighurs. A strong ethnic cultural clash is occurring. The Hans are upset the aggressive Uighurs are moving in and trying to take control. Zho has pledged to swiftly execute any who he feels are behind the uprising."

"Really. He's a pretty nasty dude isn't he?"

"Zho is described as an overly ambitious leader who is completely ruthless and will stop at nothing. He's been compared to Genghis Khan or Pol Pot of Khmer Rouge, totalitarian in his ruling and an iron hand. As you know, in Cambodia in the late '70s, Pol Pot and his regime killed over seven million citizens, one in five of every Cambodian. It was one of the most lethal regimes in history, as to percentage of populace killed."

"My God. I knew it was bad however, that's a chilling statistic," replied Key.

"Yes. Asians are conversant with his brutal communist legacy all too well. They tried their 'social engineering' overt control in agriculture and medicine, even anti-intellectualism. They advanced torture and executions against subversive elements, even in their own ranks. It's essentially genocide."

"I've seen pictures of Zho. Unpleasant-looking fellow," said Key.

"Yes. He has the intensely burning eyes of Charles Manson, coupled with an otherwise dead, expressionless face. There is absolutely nothing this man will not do to advance his cause."

"Sometimes these things are just psychologically driven. 'X' rats in the box—they're happy and coexist, ten 'X' rats in the box piled on top of each other in destitute economic squalor and they're at each other's throats. The Uighurs have a Muslim background and heritage, yes?" asked Key.

"Correct. Same Muslim background as our US president."

"Hmmm."

"In fact, part of the rub is they are accusing the US of stirring the pot, due to a prior exiled separatist female. She has however, secured asylum from the US She is a very vocal Uighur protagonist."

"Pity. Our prez met with Zho recently, did he not?"

"Yes he did. In fact many of my relatives were outraged over the photo of Rasheed bowing deeply to Zho. "Dunno. It's truly a head scratcher." said Ali. "Not used to seeing that."

"That's creepy. Reagan and Lincoln have got to be spinning in their graves over that one. Curious the image didn't receive more ink over in the States. What's that all about?"

"Unclear. Unaware of Rasheed bowing to any other leaders however. Just Zho."

"Didn't he also just authorize millions in funding for fifty-five out of country mosques? Where's the rationale in that as the US goes bankrupt?"

"As well as totally ignoring the separation of church and state doctrine." said Ali.

"Wonder if that behavior has any correlation with his out-of-left-field endorsement of that ostentatious mosque overlooking 911's Ground Zero in New York City? Essentially an edifice celebrating a Muslim victory as has been their practice for hundreds of years. That is not engendering large applause." said Scotty.

"Nope."

"Shoot. While we're at it, let's erect a memorial to Japanese suicide bombers tall enough to cast a shadow over the sunken USS Arizona. Hell, let's make a day of it." said Scotty sarcastically. In so saying, he recalled at that very memorial in Hawaii how his grandfather, a WWII vet, had almost bitten his pipe in two after seeing a Japanese man pointing at the sunken vessel and laughing.

Forty-four

California, USA
March 2011

Back in California at 12:03 pm that same day, a tremendous bolt shook the very bedrock of the entire state. Nauseatingly deep, the 8.8 quake shuddered the earth's mantle and propagated the shake efficiently so that fifteen hundred miles away, in Texas and Kansas, people felt the shock. But right before anyone felt it, tens of thousands of people vomited.

One hundred twenty-three kV lines were snapped like twigs. Their large distributive power cables did a tantalizing death-dance on the ground in search of any passing life-form to French fry. Thick columns of smoke were rising and power in all metropolitan areas was downed. Downed in an instant. The grids, trunk lines, feeders and distribution lines had all failed. It was uncharacteristically warm that day.

Many Californians prided themselves in being haughty, smug and blasé during these occurrences. This sub-segment of the populace enjoyed passing these quake stories off in a backhanded manner to friends afar, whose home bases did not enjoy this oddity of nature. It was this same smaller segment of Californians who would quake in absolute fear during a Midwestern tornado or would become paralyzed as to how to deal with a hurricane in Florida.

On this occasion however, even this die-hard segment was having difficulty summoning up a listless, pedestrian attitude, as this occurrence was so spectacular, so pervasive.

Many of the taller structures in San Francisco and Los Angeles alike had been retrofitted to withstand a 7.7 quake. An 8.8 was a different matter altogether. On the Richter Scale, an increase in scoring by just a single digit meant the quake had increased in severity tenfold.

The Richter magnitude scale, has been around awhile and assigned a single number to quantify the amount of seismic energy released. Newer measurements taken by the moment magnitude scale offered up even more startling comparisons however. This newer scale focused on the actual energy released by an earthquake, which better stated its true devastation.

Specifically startling, the energy release of an earthquake is *exponentially magnified* by (and scales with the 3/2 power of) the shaking amplitude. Its amplitude is the degree of vibratory movement measured between its mean location to its extreme position. So a difference of 1.0 is actually 31.6 times more destructive in the energy released. And since the difference is exponential in its growth, a scaled difference of but 2.0 larger is *1,000 times more devastating* in the energy released.

As a consequence, many structures, even those retrofitted with significant "X" bracing and had their foundations placed on massive rollers or dense rubber plugs to allow the structures to flex, roll and sway—failed.

Library Tower in Los Angeles. Down. Transamerica Tower in San Francisco. Down. San Mateo Bridge in San Francisco, tallest five spans. Down. Richmond Bridge in the North Bay area, top eastbound decks—70 percent down. An 8.8 quake was estimated by some to have the energy equivalency release of one hundred thousand atomic bombs, with each single bomb akin to what was dropped on Hiroshima. It was cataclysmic.

All major California cities were paralyzed and burning. Fires everywhere. 1,847 in Los Angeles County alone, while a total of 15,000 fires raged statewide. The quake's impact at 8.8 was well in excess of the December 16,

1811, New Madrid, Missouri 8.0 quake, which caused the Mississippi River to literally run backward for a period of time.

East of Highway 5, the event ignited miles and miles of brush fires, which raced toward Yosemite Park. All birds flushed first. Then, smelling the smoke well in advance, the animals began to stampede.

Horses, moose, bears, elk, deer, raccoon, badgers, mountain lions, rabbits and squirrels thundered across the park's meadows. They no longer feared "Man." And if "Man" was in their way while they were racing at breakneck speed from an assured flaming death, then it was at "Man's" peril.

Loss of life was initially too high to be calculated. Some felt it could exceed three hundred thousand. No one knew, as all forms of media were down. As had happened on 9/11, many chose to leap from the taller buildings for a swift conclusion, rather than face the slower, agonizing fate at the hands of walls of flames licking up the skyscrapers' five stories at a time. Some leapt two at a time, holding another's hand. Some leapt grasping pictures of loved ones. Some just leapt.

The stench of death was everywhere. The smell of burning flesh was acrid and exacerbated by the heat, unusually high humidity and a general lack of oxygen. It was mixed with the foul, choking sulfur vapors, which belched out intermittently from sand blows.

Sand blow plumes could be sixty feet in diameter and one hundred fifty feet high. These Old Faithful-esque spewings were caused by the Precambrian layer being ruptured along the faults below. The plumes released the extraordinary pressure pent up deep down under the earth during soil liquefaction. The sky was completely blanketed with smoke. Black smoke. Gray smoke. White smoke. If it could burn, it was burning.

Fortunately, San Francisco had learned its lesson well from the earlier Loma Prieta quake. Instructional it was as to the ineffectiveness of downed water and hydrant lines to combat such an event. One of the more surprisingly effective warriors emerging to battle the conflagration in the late eighties had been the small, highly robust fireboats moored in the San Francisco Bay. Ironically, it was but weeks away from being formally decommissioned at the time. It slurped up a never ending supply of sea water to quell the Marina District fires, in contrast to the more traditional hydrant-based systems—all of which had failed. So the city had kept the little fireboats around.

Los Angeles was not as fortunate. Not only was their infrastructure more spread out than San Francisco's, much of it was inland. Its geography did not enjoy the lengthy access to seawater through a large Bay as did San Francisco's. The inferno-like heat of thousands of fires spurned the Santa Anna winds to new heights, fanning the already out-of-control flames.

From a telecommunications perspective, hard lines were down and most phone towers had been compromised. Chip sets were shorted out and receivers were fried. Instead of dial tones, one was greeted with the uncompromising fast beeping of "trouble" on all trunk lines.

In large and small towns alike, pets were on an "early-release program." Pets of all sizes, stripe and color were dazed, frightened, howling, growling and wandering in circles. Much like the general populace. They were choking on abject fear. Were they going to be safe? What just happened? What was going to happen?

There were thousands upon thousands of animals in the streets. Large boa constrictors, pet alligators and other exotic darlings were finding refuge in startled neighbors' trees and pools.

Dogs began to band together in packs, howling and barking. They snarled and cried out as they scavenged for food and water. With their hunger and nightfall advancing, they became increasingly aggressive. They would tear at orange juice-coated cardboard cartons, or flesh. Sometimes each other's flesh. Or they would shrink in trembling, primitive fear into the nearest corner, much like the general populace.

Elderly women, who heretofore had been shopping in tony, luxury neighborhoods in Orange Counties' Costa Mesa and San Francisco's Nordstrom, would run to an adjacent car for perceived safety. That safety was only perceived. Most of the structures had been so severely weakened, this was only a temporary safe harbor. It was the troubling precursor of even more devastation, as scores of aftershocks swept over the state killing even more.

Thousands of auto theft and motion detecting devices beeped. Car horns engaged, stuck and blaring. Incessant blaring. The noise was maddening, deafening. Screams. Initially millions of screams. Then after the first, heart-stopping, nauseatingly low pulse, the silence was broken by the occasional shrill outburst of a mother finding her child alive, or the bawling shriek of a mother discovering her child deranged, de-limbed, or worse.

Those driving felt like they had received four flat tires due to the extreme undulations. Confusion was normally the first emotion. Gazing out at the California highways, raw, primal fear came next. Highways, which heretofore were smooth, undulating ribbons designed to stream traffic at seventy miles an hour, were now laid out as crumpled, buckled-up quilts. Asphalt appeared as corduroy. Miles and miles of corduroy. Broken glass was everywhere.

Soot, smoke and grime were in the air, as all things flammable burned. Rails were snapped and natural gas pipelines were ruptured and burning. Images reminiscent of Iraq post-invasion found grunge covered faces staring with dead eyes down at their feet cut from broken glass. Ash and microscopic shards of broken glass veritably snowed into people's eyes.

Gang colors had banded together in packs, like dogs. With faces smudged, they proudly brandished their colors. The event had a divisive and galvanizing effect on its members. Half went to the pack-like state, while half seemed to abandon their pledge to violence and were helping those less fortunate.

When rubber or butyl was present, the resulting smoke was dark, choking and cloaking. Oftentimes this cover was used by vandals to set shops on fire or loot. Looting, plundering, maiming, killing, raping and sodomizing were all done under the cover of smoke.

Local area hospitals moved to a triage mode. The tents set up in parking lots were filled, with the overflow spilling out into the streets. There were not enough gurneys to accommodate all. Not all elderly or severely injured could get help. They lay on the grass to avoid the sweltering heat of the buckled asphalt.

When shade could not be found, facilities used patio umbrellas to offer the wounded aid as they awaited their turn in the endlessly long lines. Lines whose wait time thirty minutes earlier had been measured in minutes now had wait time measured in hours, days for those whose injuries were anything but life threatening.

Those in bumper to bumper traffic who had the misfortune of being under an overpass never saw the end coming. It was swift and resolute. Ton after ton of concrete rumbled down with an unforgiving finality. Physics could be a cruel instructor.

Monstrous, jagged blocks of concrete, some the size of a bus, fell freely. Twisted structural I-beams and horizontal lacing members littered the sky-scape, horizon line to horizon line. An artificial, leafless forest of bent, twisted rebar and contorted structural steel landscape was eerily reminiscent of *Terminator* movie sets.

Seismologists were trying to locate the quake's epicenter to no avail. It seemed uniform. Never before had such a long, elongated quake shook so violently and for such a lengthy period of time. It affected both Northern and Southern California. The shaker lasted 137 seconds, just a bit over 2 minutes.

To those involved, it seemed to last over two days. Watching property, pets and loved ones perish evoked that singular vision that slows itself down tenfold when catastrophic events occur. God must enjoy watching car wrecks too, as he wanted you to recall them.

Forever.

Devastation was beyond comprehension. The violence was so epic it broke off a significant piece of California, physically separating it from the balance of the state. The quake commenced in the north along the Mt. Diablo thrust and portions of the Hayward fault. It headed south through the Calaveras fault and on to include over two hundred miles of the San Andreas fault. It concluded in the far south, along the lesser San Gabriel, Sierra Madre and Elsinore faults.

With this self-digestion of California, the state did not slip into the sea as predicted previously rather, the entire section opened up along the aforementioned fault lines. The lengthy rupture was quickly filled from the

Bay and ocean alike, as a brackish salt and freshwater mix violently rushed in, creating an encircling canal.

Land heaved violently, buckled and subsided instantly, creating new pocket lakes. Scores of levees up and down the state breached, sweeping away hundreds of thousands of houses.

Lake Shasta's thirty five mile long, 4,500,000 acre feet of water moments before had been resting placidly 500 feet above the nearby city of Redding. With the failure of its 600 foot high dam, a wall of water hundreds of feet tall was released with such a fury that it consumed the city of 100,000 in an instant. All moving water statewide, caused over 180,000 to drown.

The canal was from 50 to 100 yards wide and it created a new island. The geographic phenomenon was 50 miles wide at its narrowest to the north by San Francisco. It widened as it made its way inland following I-5, along the San Andreas fault and it became almost 70 miles wide toward LA. In total, it was 450 miles long.

The new island was bordered on the north by Geyserville, on the northeast by Mount Diablo and bounded on the east and southeast by the San Andreas fault, with its southernmost border being Del Mar. It was 20,000 square miles of land mass, or one-eighth of the prior 156,000 square mile-area of California. It consumed however, well in excess of 90 percent of the state's property value. Although the island was a thin rectangle, if "squared out" it would be 80 percent the size of West Virginia.

People were stunned. Most were unaware of the "new island" formation and how pervasive the damage was, as the infrastructure was completely disabled. Word was spreading fast by mouth, however. It was also personally witnessed by airplane passengers, whose approach had been waived off at the last minute.

The new island controlled two-thirds of the California coastline and with the exception of San Diego, contained the bulk of their largest metropolitan areas. The isle enjoyed the same longitude as Barcelona, Spain, making the climate one of the most enviable in the world.

FORTY-FIVE

Cozumel, Mexico
March 2011

CRACKER PARLAYED HIS CONNECTIONS AT MI6 to have a detailed analysis of the photos taken at Palancar Reef. The photographic evidence was indisputable. "They" were manufacturing a spherical end product that went into canisters. Content varied in size from softball to bowling ball to beach ball.

Cracker relayed to MI6 the story of Milo Butterfield. While the Agency did not have Butterfield's chip for analysis, they agreed that, between what was witnessed underwater and Scotty's advanced mining description, Red Mercury was being manufactured at the reef.

Cracker debriefed others while pointing at a variety of images. "Where y'at? Get your ass over here. Prepare to get schooled up," said Cracker.

"Were you thinking, amigo? I thought I smelled rubber burning," said Vinnie.

"Another six or seven years of that and you'll hurt my feelings."

"Let the man talk," barked Willingham.

Cracker continued. "These pictures confirm the commercialization of Red Mercury. The area to the west is devoted to canister production, which is consistent with Scotty's description of Butterfield's process."

"They got his molar," said Key.

"Zackley. Additionally, the large, belching steam bubbles through the aperture also suggest they finally figured out how to cool it down during production. They took the last stage underwater. They're literally using the entire ocean to dissipate heat in this last critical step, prior to canister insertion."

"So, why don't we send in the Marines right now and be done with it?" said Scotty.

"Rahtnaow? No. Beings how all of this is happen'n within three miles of Cozumel it's not international waters. Not our country. If we made a military move internationally, we'd be invading a Latin country unprovoked. Wouldn't suit. With no proof, no hard evidence, other than these pitchures and some vacant left molar hearsay from a geeky dead guy's mouth, we'd look pretty fuckin' stupid globally. And, they haven't really *done* anything with it as of yet. We need a crime, a discrete incident. And Vinnie, my friend, rest assured you'd look the stupidest, the fastest," said Cracker.

"Thank you for that, my blanco, hot dog-necked gringo!"

"De nada," Cracker countered. "So. It doesn't matter how we really feeeeel about US President Rasheed and it's no never-mind how we feeeeel about what's going on at Palancar Reef. Until we get some hard evidence and tie it to a specific group, we'd just look like the typical conspiracy-theory nut jobs."

Willingham received a call from his HQ in Vancouver. He was apprised of what had just occurred in California.

"Well, mates. Here's a new wrinkle," said Willingham.

"Whatta you got?" asked Cracker.

"It seems as though the western edge of California has just experienced the mother of all quakes and has created a new four hundred fifty-by-fifty mile island where its western border used to be."

"Holy shit! So, it slid into the ocean as predicted?" asked Vinnie.

"No. It broke off along the San Andreas fault and has created a big-ass new island, complete with a hundred meter moat all the way around."

"Wow. Did they determine the size and epicenter?" asked Key.

The Mountie continued, "Well the size is one of the largest on record, some saying high 8s, 8.8 maybe. Death and property destruction are ... well ... they're legendary. Maybe hundreds of thousands are dead. The whole state is either on fire or underwater, as Shasta Dam and most of the levees breached. The epicenter is the interesting piece. Depending on who you speak with, there are either multiple epicenters or no epicenters at all, suggesting ..."

"Suggesting multiple, identical, simultaneously timed quakes all up and down California's fault lines," said Scotty.

"Precisely."

"What are the odds of those events occurring simultaneously?"

"Looks like we may have just found our 'discrete incident.'"

Forty-six

Portland, Oregon

March 2011

Ali and Hoppy had headed a great distance north to Oregon. Near the Deschutes River north of Portland, they were relatively unaffected by the quake, however, they felt it. It was early in the salmon season so the visiting fisherman population was still a bit thin. It was raining in Portland, as it was want to do, so individuals with common sense (other than fly fishermen) and those possessing IQ's above room temperature were inside.

Hoppy became bug-eyed during the first shock wave. It was bone jarring, with an initial "bang" or car collision feel followed by wavelike undulations. Those wave forms had both her and Tang running in circles through the house. Her mother chased after her and the ferret from room to room in a futile attempt to calm, corral and cajole them.

FORTY-SEVEN

Cozumel, Mexico
March 2011

BACK IN COZUMEL WITH CRACKER, Scotty and Willingham, Scotty said, "Someone is not who they seem. We've got to get the third leg of this stool figured out."

"Otherwise, we just have 'stool,'" lamented Cracker.

"Righto," proclaimed Willingham while fidgeting with his collar. "I've run it up the flagpole through our connections with MI6."

"Yes."

"We have some G2 as to where a prominent, under-the-radar union leader will be meeting with someone representing your Mr. Rasheed in but two days."

"Really. This is reliable data?"

"Who knows? However, MI6 has someone in deep who coughed up this chicken bone."

"Respectfully, why in God's name would they share it with you?" asked Key.

"As a practical matter, they recognize most of our operatives already, whether it is a Brit or a Canadian. Whilst with budget cuts we don't have the legions of players to make the sky go dark with parachutes the way we once could in the eighties. Quite frankly, we were thinking of you, Scotty."

"I'm honored."

"You should be, as this is highly irregular. I did make them aware of your SEAL training, as well as your stint as a sniper or pistol expert, whatever that was you were doing when you were dithering about overseas. I certainly held my hand up for you on a get-it-done basis. If you are up for it, here is a disposable phone. You know protocol. Dial 1-888-484-3328, they'll read you in. Then destroy the phone."

Scotty called and secured the meeting logistics. The meeting was to be between two individuals—Mr. U, who represented the unions and a Mr. Caesar. Both names were obvious aliases. Caesar was an oft-used acronym for these affairs to represent the president of the United States.

The physical meet was to be in Washington DC, near the northernmost WWII Memorial's fountain. It was to occur out in the open, so both sides would be well aware of any onlookers or the far too casual passersby with earbuds. Relatively close to the fountain's cascading water, the spot would also make it easier to mask the conversation. The cherry blossoms were falling, falling onto the ground and into the fountain. Briefly beautiful, but quickly dying.

Scotty shared the details with Cracker, who had a couple of ideas. For starters, he'd use the projection/cloaking tarp they'd employed earlier. To listen and record the event, a miniature camcorder was coupled with a twenty-inch diameter, high-end parabolic dish for the audio.

The dish, when formatted with military-grade audio circuitry, twelve-band equalizer and noise-cancelling technology with an ultra-high sensitivity shotgun mic, would allow Key to be three hundred yards away and still capture sound and image. His objective was to lay up the night before in the large stand of trees that overlooked the memorial's reflection pond. He'd additionally bring rope to tie himself off in the event he fell asleep before daybreak.

FORTY-EIGHT

Washington, DC
March 2011

Two DAYS LATER, AFTER SLINKING out to his tree of choice at 3:05 AM and avoiding the unusually attentive park guards with the cloaking tarp, Scotty set up shop two-thirds of the way up one of the bushier trees. A cherry tree. He found a conveniently robust secondary central fork, which allowed him to distribute his weight on one trunk, with the other being a stable mount for gear.

There was no air circulation and the tarp cut the occasional breeze from offering any relief from his tree-stand cookout. While waiting, his tongue had ample opportunity to explore the puncture wound to his jaw, rolling over it again and again. This reinvigorated him as he started to doze off.

The two came together at the base of the fountain as pre-ordained by the informant at 0900 hours. They had never met before and in all likelihood, would never meet again. Each was seated separately for at least ten minutes before giving each other any direct eye contact. They were assiduously studying their surroundings, looking for an out-of-place FedEx delivery boy on a UPS guy's route, a bum with too expensive of sneakers, or donning a Rolex.

Looking for the little things.

It was the little things that made a difference in this trade. The difference between taking a warm breath or taking a cold bullet. They eyed each other warily from alternate locations facing the bench. The two continued to monitor their environment, in, around and overhead in an unassuming, low-key manner. One read the paper. One tossed coins wistfully into the fountain.

Mr. U's double chins were sweating. Not a fan of the gym, lobbying was his full-contact sport of choice. Still large, imposing and strong, he had a doughy face and heavily folded jowls that swayed as he strode to his seat. He blew his large bulbous nose so loudly it startled the small child in red plaid shorts down the bench from him.

Normally festooned in heavy jewelry, cuff links, finery and Armani suits, today U was dressed as casual as any tourist. Unable to personally part with the oversized nugget jewelry and remarkably heavy gold chain around his neck, he was sporting sand-colored pants, a navy blue Polo and a large-brimmed Panama straw hat to cut the heat. His overly prominent glasses caused his nose and the top of his cheeks to sweat.

His counterpart, Mr. Caesar, appeared to be of Muslim descent, or at least some portion thereof. He was swarthy and rail thin with close-set eyes. In his late thirties, he was tallish and had a nervous tick. This tick appeared when he tried to signal his understanding of a shared concept as his head would jerk up overly fast. It was almost like a parakeet's upward head bob after just completing a quick drink in his cage. He was anxious.

Mr. Caesar spoke first. "Quite hot today, eh?"

"Hotter than blue blazes," responded Mr. U.

"But not so hot one couldn't build a snowman … if he really put his mind to it?" said Caesar.

"Can't build a snowman without two pieces—a lump of coal and a carrot." As if on cue, Mr. U lit an exceptionally dark, seven-inch-long Cuban cigar. It was torpedo shaped and enormous. Torpedoes are not usually that long. This one was. It had been handmade especially for him and a collection of his cronies in Cuba. He blew the bluish white smoke politely away from Mr. Caesar as he adjusted his large, thick glasses.

Reciting the seasonably unlikely lines known only to these two men and two others affirmed each other's identities. Only in so codifying would they now advance their hypersensitive dialogue. Scotty's parabolic dish was fanned out and open for business, even though perspiration was running profusely down his back and off his face, dripping onto the black, plastic back of the video recorder.

"Nice to meet you, Mr. U," said Caesar as he opened his large umbrella, which would ward off any attempt at snooping imagery from overhead satellites.

"Likewise, Mr. Caesar," responded Mr. U.

"My benefactor has advanced the ball handsomely along the lines established earlier and wishes to accelerate the timeline to receive his Super Bowl trophy."

"As you know, those terms were set from the get-go and they're already buttoned down," said U.

"Yes. I know."

"Super *Bowl* is with a *B*. It's a big single *B*. As in one."

"Agreed," said Caesar. "However, my benefactor wants the balance up front, as he is experiencing quite an erosion in popularity at his neighborhood barbecue."

"And tea parties?" grinned Mr. U in a smarmy manner.

"Precisely. And tea parties."

"So sad." retorted Mr. U with feigned concern. He blew the cigar's smoke directly into Mr. Caesar' face. "No one likes to be skewered at a barbecue. However, it does beat being on the grill personally for attempting to re-trade, if 'yous' get my meaning?"

FORTY-NINE

"Perhaps you are not fully aware of who you are addressing," said Caesar.

"Fully aware. And that is why I am speaking slowly for you—so as to resolve any outcome ambiguity whatsoever. There's been the propensity for your 'benefactor' in the past to attempt to re-trade and count field goals as five points at halftime. That shit won't fly dis time. The trophy is too large. Either he wins the game, or he doesn't. The deal was one-fourth of the trophy up front, one-fourth at the fifty yard line and the balance due when he's in the end zone. Capisce?"

Scotty's left leg started to cramp after being flexed for almost six hours. He was hopeful this would be the conversation Willingham alleged MI6 said it would be. He glanced for the fifth time at the dish and recorder to confirm the red needles were indeed bouncing so content was captured.

"I'll take that back for his consideration," said Caesar, attempting to summon up his most haughty and arrogant tone.

"Yeah. You do dat." Mr. U took a stubby steel-rod-firm forefinger and drove it directly into Mr. Caesar's sternum. "You take that back for his consideration." Mr. U was now sneering. "Or you can shove that bright shiny fire hydrant", Mr. Caesar pointed, "up your ass and spin. Alternatively, you can return the first half of the *B* trophy, which your benefactor already possesses."

Caesar winced. "Now you're angry. That was not our intention," said Caesar.

"Yeah. Well fuck your intentions. I know how your guy deals. His words are turds. Set your fuckin' watch. He should lead with deeds. No head fakes, no juking, no end arounds. This ain't no Gallup Poll. Do this or don't. Decide in twenty-four hours. Finito." Mr. U punctuated his last word by fanning both hands open wide in a jazz hands fashion and thrust them up and away from his face in disgust.

"Okay, okay. Please calm down, you are attracting unnecessary attention." Mr. Caesar was sweating. He wiped two cherry blossoms, which had drifted down and stuck to his forehead, from his brow.

"Cute. Ya know, you're cute? If we don't hear from you, we are going to assume we are on track with the original deal. If you go sideways on us … well." Mr. U laughed. "Let's just say, you don't want to go sideways on us. In thirty years, when they break the rest of the seals on the classified JFK file, just ask him how he feels now about going sideways on us."

"I get your point."

"You know, we've never had a long line at our complaint department."

"Again, I have your point."

"Good. I want to button this down, for 'bochyous guys."

"Shall we review progress and the game going forward?"

"Shurah." Mr. U sent skyward a globule of brownish colored cigar spittle some three feet away and onto the sidewalk. Subsequent to that, he thrust his right forefinger deeply up his nostril to clear it and without cleaning the end, pointed it in Caesar' face. "We only need two things from your … from your—what'd you call him? Oh yeah, your *benefactor*. Just two things really. Number one, protect and enhance. Grow *my* benefactor. And number two, we all remain 'sociable.' Simple. Now that's not too hard, is it?" asked U.

"We have the protection pieces in place," responded Caesar. "Our friends to the north and south have become more cooperative. Check that box."

"More cooperative, as now there are different butts in seats."

"Correct," responded Caesar tersely.

"Yeah, we gotta give you props for that. Those earthquakes—very creative. Don't know how you did that, but very creative. But in addition to NAFTA being unwound …"

"Kindly do not use that word," rebuked Caesar.

"Have I offended your sensibilities? Relax. No one is close enough to hear us and if they were—fuck 'em. They can't stop this train, it has left the station. In addition to your friends to the north and south, you were going to also make it easier for our associates to … to get together. Do you recall that? Do you read me?"

"Expand on that."

"Getting rid of the secret ballot, card check. Easier to unionize."

"Don't …"

"*Do not* lecture me again on how *not* to spell these out. Do *not* take advantage of my good nature," exclaimed U, shouting while adjusting his glasses and then calming back down.

Mr. U was driving his forefinger again into Caesar's face.

Caesar could smell his breath. It wafted over to him with a beefy maduro cigar-laced bloom. A pungent, sweet but sour overtone, which concluded with a nice sinus finish. "We didn't call this meeting. You did. There was a bow around all dis, all very neat and tidy. Do yous guys need paint by numbers? We've been over this. Twice. Now, your benefactor comes back to us hat in hand. He wants to retrade the deal and it ain't even halftime. Tell your benefactor to quit his fuckin' whinin' and get it done."

"What else?" asked Caesar.

"Being real 'social' like. It had four pieces."

"Hmmmm," Caesar did a parakeet head bob, signaling understanding.

"Yeah. Get in two more czars and another judge friendly to *my* benefactor, take control of the car and money people on the Monopoly Board so we own 'em."

"We got that done," trumpeted Caesar.

"Yeah. Well Congratufuckulations. That's one of four. Also, have your friends at Buckeye get their crayons out and color real nice lines so your chief of staff can take over control of the census in a manner pleasing to us. Between that and relaxing immigration enforcement, we feel those districts will be more warm and welcoming to our people. You wit' me?"

"Got it."

"Honest, fair-minded citizens who know how to divide the pie for the working man and vote for the right guy. They'll do the right thing. You know what I mean?"

"Yes. I get your meaning." Head bob.

"Lastly, push through health care reform *with* the government option. That would set the insurance and pharma power players to the side and put us right in the middle. We get our vig, our rightful share. Just enough to wet our beaks. Read me?"

"Yes, I follow. We feel the other pieces are all but in hand."

"Why don't I get dat same feeling when I watch TV or read the newspaper? We're seeing too much push back. You gotta move faster on this before it unravels."

"Not to worry. It'll get done. We had to push health care through quickly, albeit somewhat diluted, as it took fewer votes to get it done with our procedural reconciliation ploy." Caesar winked. "Failing that, it could have taken six more months. Perhaps never. But we got it through. Now, we just need to broaden it to include the public option later through scope-creep and incrementalism."

"Six months, okay. A second term? Not okay. Yous guys are breaking a lot of glass. There may not be a second term. Do we have perfect clarity now on whose playing in your Super Bowl, how we all count and how you get your trophy?"

"Yes. Perfect clarity," head bobbed Caesar.

Before Caesar could thank Mr. U for his time, U wiped the sweat from his face, threw the balance of his torpedo cigar in the fountain, turned on his heel and strode off. There was starting to appear a thin, darker vertical line on U's sand-colored pants on the rear between the buttocks—from sweat.

Caesar head bobbed again, as if to formally conclude the meeting according to Roberts' Rules of Head Bobbing.

The meeting was over. To ensure the nothing-going-on-here mode Caesar sought, he took his seat again, acting disinterested in all things for a few more minutes. Upon rising, he leisurely read some copy on the memorial, stared into the fountain and smiled at small children who were visiting. The children frowned at Caesar and looked concerned. Their parents smiled.

Jesus, thought Scotty, *if just half of this comes out audible, we may be able to get some subpoenas.*

He knew however he was still a long way from the end game. How did the Iraqis fit in? What was up with the ESE tattoos?

FIFTY

The White House, Washington, DC
March 2011

"Mr. President, we have a caller for you in the front rotunda. They are not on your schedule, though you do have some time available. Shall I send them away?"

"What time is my golf game?"

"Not for three hours, sir."

"Who is it, Winston?" asked President Rasheed.

"She says her name is Mrs. Green, although the moniker does not appear to match her nationality, sir. She claims she represents a philanthropic group and knew your mother," responded Winston dryly.

"It's okay, Winston, she's cool. Send her down. Do go ahead and wand her for weapons and bugs as customary however. And when that's done, you may relax the Secret Service to a five hundred-foot perimeter."

"Are you sure, Mr. President?

"Well just how big is she? Does she look that tough? Don't you think I could take her?" laughed Rasheed out loud while throwing his head back.

"No, Mr. President, she's a small Asian woman in her mid fifties. You should have the upper hand. She's on her way."

★

"Mr. President, presenting Mrs. Green," said Winston.

"Mrs. Green, Mr. Rasheed, the president of the United States."

"Thank you, Winston," said Rasheed. "Mrs. Green! How long has it been? I can see time has been a friend to you." He turned to Winston. "That will be all Winston, as you can see, we have a lot of catching up to do."

"As you wish, Mr. President. "Winston left, closing the door behind him. They bowed to each other.

Mrs. Green spoke first. "As-Salāmu ʿAlaykum." (Peace be upon you). "The Muslim community thanks you for your support, understanding and patronage."

The President responded. "aSalaam ʿAlaykum." (Upon you be peace).

The Arabic spoken greeting is used primarily by Muslims and Arabs. They both smiled warmly and performed a two-handed hand shake solemnly pumping their hands up and down twice.

"Forgive me," Rasheed said. Then he personally took a secondary wand and wanded her for the third time.

"Sorry about that. A bit unseemly. Make no mistake however, I can't be too careful these days," he said as he fired up a small localized eavesdropping jamming device by his desk.

"I understand, Mr. President. No offense taken," replied Mrs. Green smiling a thinly pressed, forced smile. "The Fisherman and Ah Zho send their kindest regards."

"Thank you for that. Kindly send my warmest return salutations in return." A bit narcissistically, Rasheed languished a bit more than briefly in front of the three-quarter length mirror to look at himself, paused, then continued walking.

"Sit. Sit." He motioned toward one of the two primary visitor chairs facing his desk. "Cigarette?" President Rasheed lit up and put his feet up on his desk, scratching the Presidential Seal slightly. His hands were behind his head and his fingers were interlaced. He smiled broadly.

"No thank you. Regrettably the 'loose cannon' matter in the SEAL department did not have a successful conclusion," remarked Mrs. Green.

"Yes." He sat back in his seat and moved forward slowly. Fidgeting, he paused and pulled at both lapels before speaking. "That is regrettable. And while we are always proud of our SEALs' tenacity… He is but a single man." replied Rasheed. The president crumpled up two pieces of paper off his legal pad, squashed them into a ball and shot across the room toward a wastebasket, which had a hoop around the top. It fell short.

"This whole presidency thing is seriously messing with my game!" smiled Rasheed like a Cheshire cat, as he waved his hands in the air in mock horror at his missed shot. "I need some more vacation."

"Understandable."

She had come to continue negotiations with Rasheed for the parties' mutual interest. She was togged up in a light green dress with matching hat, which exhibited just a bit of lace peeking out from under one corner. Her jewelry was all but nonexistent. She was very proper in dress and decorum.

Known to precious few, Mrs. Green was the Uighur female separatist whom Ah Zho exiled from his country. In fact, unbeknownst to all, Green and Zho were *both* Uighurs and Zho's feigned allegiance to the Hans was merely a charade to the Chinese populace. This in turn provided a legitimate cover story for Green's entry into the United States, where she could be used in a covert manner as Ah Zho's operative, all in plain sight. The arrangement did not suggest any impropriety to the Hans between Green and Zho, as, at least publicly, they appeared to be in opposite camps.

"Ah Zho sends his regrets to the people of Xinjiang, China. As well as his thanks to the president for his involvement in that disturbing event."

"Pretty spectacular, wasn't it?" asked Rasheed, feet back up on his desk and once again leaning back until his chair creaked loudly.

"Amazing. Those dreadful Uighurs are so contentious."

"So contentious," Rasheed paused and flashed his megawatt smile again. He added nothing more.

"It is feared the unrest fomented by neighboring territories could spread well beyond Xinjiang and cause those governments to topple."

"Look. That would be most unfortunate, but let me clear. I know what a strong leader Chairman Zho is and he would be there to pick up the pieces in the good name of the People's Republic of China if that were to occur." Rasheed leaned way back in his chair, which creaked noisily again at the intrusion. He studied her off and avoided her expressionless gaze.

"So gracious of you to say so, Mr. President. With your permission, I will pass that most flattering compliment along."

"You have my permission." He thumped the top of the desk for effect. He flashed a broad smile, as if proud of himself.

"Thank you, Mr. President. On another matter, it appears the Red Mercury prescription for your onslaught of the flu was just what the doctor ordered in Mexico and Canada."

"Yes. That dreadful H1N1 flu is behind us and we have tidied up any broader border issues. Please send our regards to The Fisherman and Chairman Zho for that as well. You know, while on that topic, curious if you'd care to comment on the recent catastrophe in California."

"Well, horrible. At the very least, it is dreadful, Mr. President."

"Yes. Well it certainly was that, but was it more than just a dreadful natural disaster, which killed over 242,000?"

"How do you mean, Mr. President?"

"I believe you know exactly how I mean, Mrs. Green." His tone now more stern. He leaned forward in his chair in an effort to intimidate and stared unblinkingly into her flat expression, which offered no emotional ricochet. It was as if he was looking at drywall.

"If you are suggesting a larger denomination in aid to philanthropically assist in the recovery, I can take that back ..."

"No. No. Look. Let me be clear. I want to speak with the highest degree of precision. Neither you, nor Mr. Zho, nor the Fisherman—*none of you*—had a hand in assisting that catastrophic natural disaster along, did you?"

FIFTY-ONE

"WHY, MR. PRESIDENT, WHILE I do not believe you are trying to offend us, I am somewhat taken aback by your question."

"Not my intention. Not my intention. Just had to ask the question. I'm relieved, very relieved." He leaned back summarily, put out the first cigarette and promptly lit another. He took a long drag and inhaled deeply and more slowly than before.

"Yes. As am I." Her back stiffened somewhat and she sat up just slightly straighter in her chair. "Chairman Zho thanks you also for the rightful attention to Iraq, Iran and Afghanistan."

"Yes, make no mistake, they were heretofore officially dubbed the 'Axis of Evil' before my arrival. I inherited this mess. We have to protect the American people."

"I understand, Mr. President. No one has had it more challenging than you," she replied.

"Having said that, we're doing all possible to bring order to those regions and galvanize, mobilize and effect nation-building with our overseas contingency operations. But it's a game of finesse, we can't be too heavy-handed. We don't want to be perceived as going in there as jackbooted thugs. Look. Let me be clear, we'll get out of there as fast as we can, leaving them better citizens of the world."

"I know you will, Mr. President, as it takes focus off of the Muslim Uighur community. Those nations which you rebuild will love you for that. They will honor your name for all time."

"This is less about love and more about fair distribution of income and equal rights for everyone, Mrs. Green. Just doing the right thing for the American people. It's all I am capable of doing. Whatever is in their best interest, my constituents are the sculptor and I am but clay on the potter's wheel."

"Of course you are, Mr. President." She continued staring with no inflection in her voice, hands folded in her lap, not blinking. Pleasant.

"Thank you. I and all the American people appreciate your gratitude."

"You're welcome. And the third Stimulus Plan—it's coming along nicely?" she asked.

"Coming along nicely, yes. Our economy desperately needs that third stimulus as well. The American people deserve it, 'from each according to his ability, to each according to his needs.'" In so saying, Rasheed reached over, took a small bronze key from his key chain, unlocked the bottom right-hand drawer of his desk and grabbed an etching pushed way toward the back. The etching was of the complete Marx statement of the creed in the *Critique of the Gotha Program*:

> *In a higher phase of communist society, after the enslaving subordination of the individual to the division of labor and therewith also the antithesis between mental and physical labor, has vanished; after labor has become not only a means of life but life's prime want; after the productive forces have also increased with the all-around development of the individual and all the springs of co-operative wealth flow more abundantly—only then can the narrow horizon of bourgeois right be crossed in its entirety and society inscribe on its banners:*
>
> *From each according to his ability, to each according to his needs!*

"Mr. Zho will be so pleased to hear you keep the passage in the Oval Office."

"Glad to hear it. I value all points of view as a citizen of the world. I'll keep my view broad and will select what is in the best interest of the American people. Sometimes they don't know it at first, sometimes it takes a little nudging. But let me be clear, they all depend on me and the US government to be fair and make this a better place globally."

"Such a wise sage you are Mr. President. To your point, Chairman Mao once said: '*Once the correct ideas characteristic of the advanced class are grasped by the masses, these Ideas turn into a material force that changes society and changes the world.*' We have found in China that it is good to have the masses depend more on the central government."

"We are just, albeit slowly, arriving painfully at that same conclusion," said Rasheed, grimacing a bit. "There is always a painful pregnancy just prior to a beautiful rebirth." A whisper thin smile flitted over his lips and disappeared as quickly.

"So true," she said, sitting up even straighter.

"As an aside, I might also pass on our appreciation for Ah Zho's acceptance of the other trillion in debentures, warrants and debt. That will help our government get through these challenging times as we stimulate the economy back to prosperity."

"You are quite welcome. We saw the $500 million-debt interest per day is making quite an impression in the press, however. With trillions in debt to China and Japan alone, we are hearing concern this will bankrupt the US, as the plan has no long-term solution."

"Nonsense. You are dealing with the United States of America. We are too big to fail."

"Perhaps. But with your national deficit increasing sixfold, this heightens the concern. With the world starting to discover your debt addiction in plain view, it may be difficult to contain and blunt this much longer."

"Just one media house. We can co-opt them. They can be managed. The rest have fallen into line." Rasheed crushed out his cigarette butt forcefully to make his point. "We will bring back the Fairness Doctrine and drive this country to 'net neutrality' to better manage the communication process."

"Yes. We had to briefly suspend our texting capabilities when the background noise was too loud or boorish at our end as well," she said.

"There will be fewer shrill voices bleating and clouding the issues—clouding the truth, that for which reasonable minds will not stand. There will be fair and equitable views, sanitized and presented by the federal government so they are more suitable for consumption. It's what the people want, it's what they deserve."

"Zho saw your unemployment rate has doubled from 4.9 in June '07 to well over 10 percent in '09. Some suggest the number is closer to 20 percent when one considers discouraged workers who have stopped looking. How should I characterize that to Mr. Zho?" she asked softly.

"That's just a blip. We will spend our way back to prosperity. FDR did it. It's not a long-term concern," he said, snapping his fingers dismissively as he got up and took a Johnny Carson faux golf swing over the presidential seal.

"The advancing BRIC countries," she said, referring to Brazil, Russia, India and China, "have added materially to the global labor pool, substituting their outsourced FTE's for yours. We know this depressed compensation and caused more layoffs with a global power shift away from the US. This puts global unemployment above two hundred million for the first time. That might be a powder keg for you, Mr. President."

"A one time anomaly. Our chief economist analyzed that with the newest of algorithms. By exponentially accelerating federal programs for pull-through and perhaps, adding another stimulus program as a catalyst, we have confidence the jobs we won't lose, or won't save, is decreasing at an increasing rate."

"Good. We know that weighs heavily on you as well."

"To be certain."

"Hopefully the fine American people do not lay this entirely at your feet Mr. President. So much of this is outside of your control. Yes? On the bright side, it has made it easier for China to invest in the US and purchase resource-based companies."

"Yes. Good, good. While the US is experiencing higher unemployment true, it's a temporal thing. Last year's Summer of Recovery is working. Recall we received this heartburn from the prior administration, we inherited this mess. Don't forget that! This is not a problem of our creation. Even before then, the Clinton era redefined full employment from 4 to 6 percent. It was handled in a real low-key, page-three article way."

"That recalibration means it was acceptable to essentially have six million people perpetually relegated to the ranks of the unemployed," said Mrs. Green. "Some critics suggest this is by design, a blueprint for a march from capitalism to socialism."

FIFTY-TWO

"ABSURD," SAID RASHEED, REMOVING HIS hands from behind his head to light his third cigarette. "Sure you don't want a smoke?" He shook one out of the package and stretched his arm out as he offered it to her.

"Quite."

Both smiled and laughed gently with their heads bobbing together. Green's head was moving up and down tenderly, while the president's was swaying right and left stridently with his nose twenty degrees above horizontal.

"In Communist China, we found the will of the people can be broken when taxes and unemployment are high enough. In fact, if memory serves me, the Cloward-Piven strategy from your Columbia professors in the sixties espoused much the same thing."

Rasheed paused to speak, then said nothing, steepling his fingers and peering out just over the top of his forefingers at her as she continued to speak.

"Spiking welfare enrollment would make a political crisis where the choice could only be anarchy or a guaranteed low national income. It would promote disruption and deepen the divide among races and socioeconomic classes. Extreme poverty, therefore, must be eradicated first through the redistribution of income."

"Well, to your point, jihadists consider 'taxpayers' to be the moral equivalent to imperialist soldiers. That's the very reason taxes need to be raised to provide programs that promote equality and to get these people jobs," said Rasheed.

"Some suggest the US moral decay is already so high the unemployed will move to drugs, prostitution and violence to get by—just to eat. A recent statistic shows a future half of all US children will be on food stamps at some point in their lives."

"Absurd."

"The degeneration and unrest could necessitate the move to a police state to avoid anarchy. This is what occurred in the Soviet Union. As a result, the government is now run by the Russian mob," she said.

"Well, we all hope that won't happen here. This moral decay however, is the very thing the 'Axis of Evil' highlights as an excuse for their evil jihadist deeds against us. As Muslims, we both know this degradation is a travesty on our soil that must be reversed. Hence my personal endorsement of the New York City mosque. This monument will serve as a guiding international beacon, aid in slowly introducing Sharia law and lubricate the healing process."

"Of course, Mr. President. You are so 'rightly guided.'"

He laughed knowingly. "We would have to protect the greater good of course with marshal law in the event of anarchy. The 'tea parties' are already showing the green shoots of violence and racism brewing. We've seen example after example of that. It's only a few, well-orchestrated, bleeding-heart radicals, mind you. We can manage them."

"Confident you can, Mr. President."

"On a different matter, in light of the high unemployment, we cut the COBRA charge 65 percent to make it easier on the unemployed, as well as to extend their unemployment insurance," he said.

"How humane. Mr. Zho applauds that. He laughed recently during a recent US visit when he saw a bumper sticker that stated, 'Sheeple Win.' It's working. There will be less incentive to work, with higher taxes and medical benefits all but paid for by the central government."

"They deserve nationalized health care. It's a right."

"The masses should then be more compliant. They'll work more for the … Uighurs and the unions. The US will soon experience a more cooperative and malleable populace, as they continue through the stagnation of protracted unemployment. They will become more open to new ideas."

"That's what we've hoped for. New ideas. Hope and change."

"Like new forms of government. In lieu of a tea party, it will be a three party. The triumvirate shall rule, making for a more efficient and peaceful proletariat."

"Hmmmm," murmured Rasheed as he steepled his fingers together yet again in prayer fashion on his lips, just under his nose and covering his mouth.

"In China, our constituents simply do not know what is best for them."

"I couldn't agree more," stated Rasheed. "As here, we're helping them with that."

Both laughed gently.

The president flashed a fleeting micro-smirk from behind his hands.

"The money supply."

"Yes."

"We understand that before inauguration, it was at $800 million and it is now $2 trillion US."

"Those numbers sound about right."

"Are there not concerns about the hyperinflation the printing of all that money will cause? It concerns us, as we want repaid in currency that has a global value of consequence."

"Look. That had to be done to fund the first and second stimulus, cap and trade, the American Recovery and Reinvestment Act, as well as the bailouts of the banks and the auto companies. We had to save the American people from the banks, Wall Street, insurance companies and big pharma. They were running roughshod over the American people," he said. "We've had to better regulate them, bring them into line with watchdog oversight for the American people."

"Those bankers are the money changers of the temple." she said.

"Precisely. That referendum, as we nationalize health care, could require another short-term trillion-dollar loan. We had no choice—let me be clear—no choice at all. We'd have been plunged into a great depression otherwise. I saved this place. Without my swift, decisive actions, this place would have gone down in flames. Finito!"

"Well, Mr. Zho values our relationship with your government, however, he also wants assured he will be paid back for the large notes we've incurred. China has advanced the largest unsecured loan in global history.

"Hmmmm."

"We currently hold over $1.5 trillion in debt and almost another $1 trillion in securities and debentures. You owe the Japanese another $1 trillion and with your outstanding obligations this total is soon to exceed $5 trillion globally. And we both know that is but a fraction of your overall $14 trillion national debt."

"Look. You are dealing with the full faith and credit of the United States of America. We have *never* defaulted on a debt obligation—ever."

"Well aware of that. It was on that basis we granted the credit in the first place. And you personally received the other 25 percent of your stipend?"

"Stipend? I don't know what you're talking about?"

"I believe this time you know exactly what *I mean*, Mr. President. If you don't wish to discuss it in this forum that is fine."

The president twirled around in his chair and stared out the window. For a moment, nothing was said as he affixed his gaze across the lawn at the cherry trees. Seconds passed.

He rose to his feet, continuing to face the window. "Did you know there are over sixteen hundred cherry trees in Washington, DC, Mrs. Green? Eleven different types?"

"No. I did not know that, Mr. President. That's remarkable."

"Indeed. Truly remarkable."

"In China, the cherry blossom characterizes feminine beauty," said Mrs. Green.

"Really."

"Yes and in Japan, it is associated with Buddha. The concept of 'mono no aware,' or one of extreme, fragile beauty and a quick follow-up death, suggests mortality. It is for those reasons much constant pruning needs to occur."

"Interesting."

"Isn't it? The beautiful, fragile tree needs to be meticulously cut back, controlled and managed, or if left on its own, it will falter and experience premature death." Mrs. Green half nodded upon completing her sentence and looked directly at Rasheed.

The president said nothing. He continued standing and staring out the window, his hands clasped behind his back and his chin raised more than slightly. He was looking out the window at a singular gull. Mrs. Green said nothing. Ten seconds of additional silence elapsed. Neither spoke.

"Well. This has been a delightful exchange," said Rasheed, getting out from behind his desk while breaking the unbearable silence. Walking while his right hand gestured her toward the door, he exclaimed, with the broad smile he was known for, "We shouldn't wait as long in between visits."

"Yes. It has been delightful," said Mrs. Green, rising. "And I'm confident there will be many more pleasant visits."

"Indeed. Many more. Please send my very best to Chairman Zho."

"To be certain."

"As-Salāmu ʿAlaykum."

"aSalaam ʿAlaykum."

This time both bowed more deeply to each other, without employing the two-handed handshake. This time they did not touch.

"Winston," said the president, speaking into his intercom, "Mrs. Green is ready for her escort."

"As you wish, Mr. President. We'll be right up."

While waiting on Winston, Rasheed showed Mrs. Green some photos of himself speaking from the Brandenburg Gate in Germany, where there were crowds of over two hundred thousand strong. He showed her a photo of himself speaking at a prior convention, where he was first introduced. That was one of his favorite activities. Speaking.

Winston came and collected Mrs. Green. They had a lovely conversation, strolling together down the main corridor and back out to the front of the White House steps. He had remarked how fetching her hat was and how it reminded him of one his mother used to wear every Easter to church, although his mother's hat was pink. She mentioned his carriage and demeanor were so stately, so regal, his ancestors surely must have come from royalty. It was so— pleasant.

FIFTY-THREE

San Francisco, California
March 2011

"GOOD MORNING, BURTON," SAID ALI as she placed the call to her boss.

"Ali! Ali! I thought you had fallen off the grid! So glad to hear your voice. What a relief. You okay?" asked Buttons.

"All good in the hood. Wanted to see if you could meet me today and catch up."

"Well of course, Ali. Anything for my favorite agent. Where's good? Or I have an idea; how about …"

"Yes. I have an idea too. I'll call you with the location, in say, forty-five minutes? That will allow you precisely fifteen minutes to clear the building and take a thirty-minute cab ride."

"Pretty clandestine. Are you taking me hostage?" Buttons laughed out loud sarcastically.

Initially, Ali made no response, then she commented, "No. No. Just want to be certain it's just you coming."

"Sure, Ali. No problem. That shouldn't be a problem. Hey, we're family here!"

Exactly forty five minutes later, Buttons' cell phone rang and Ali directed him to the southwest corner of the Transamerica building to await her call in thirty minutes.

"Fine. Fine, Ali. However, this is a bit over-the-top, don't you think? Don't you trust me? I don't have all day for a surreptitious cloaking of your intentions."

"This isn't going to take all day. And the intentions will soon be self-evident."

In twenty minutes, Buttons was alone at the southwest corner of the Transamerica Tower. A nondescript Yellow Cab drove up with Ali and Key in the backseat.

"Get in," she said.

"Sure, Ali. Sure," said Buttons, trying to appear blasé but in fact becoming nervous.

He got into the back seat between the two and they drove off. Small talk was made over the next thirty minutes, with Ali asking about Buttons' wife and kids. Content was kept artificially light. One could sense an overt cockiness in Buttons manifested through anxiety. Key was silent and looked out the window. The cab left downtown and crossed the Bay Bridge heading east toward the Caldecott Tunnel.

Previously staged, in the tunnel on the eastbound side, were eight more identical cabs standing stationary with their emergency flashers on. The three entered the tunnel and waited sixty seconds to let some four other identical cabs exit in front of them. In another moment, the second tranche of four identical cabs, plus Ali's, disembarked, each leaving some five to eight cars between the other.

They were in the fifth cab. Two were headed north, two were headed south, two east and three west. If observed from a satellite imaging system or helicopter, it would be very difficult to discern which cab was carrying the director.

"Give me your cell phone," said Ali.

"That won't be necessary."

"That was more than a suggestion," said Ali, more sternly this time.

All doors locked in the same instant.

Buttons gave her the phone and Scotty rolled down his window on the left side. Both her fists flew up simultaneously, going in opposite directions. With her left hand, she threw the phone out the left window to the curb. It shattered. In an identical, mirrored movement with her right, she back-fisted Button's face.

"You broke my nose! You broke my bloody nose! I demand to know the meaning of this!" exclaimed Buttons in righteous indignation, as blood streamed down upon his achingly white shirt.

"All will become clear soon," said Ali as she patted him down for wires and threw his watch out the window as well. Key reached down, grabbed both Buttons' shoes and threw them to the curb. The cab continued as Key looked nonchalantly out the window.

"I can't believe you put your niece at risk! You pig!" She struck his nose again in precisely the same spot. This time an audible crunching sound was heard.

Buttons groaned. He spat mucous, blood and a single tooth out the right back window. The driver did not look back and an opaque privacy screen rose slowly between the parties.

"His niece?" asked Key incredulously.

"Yes. I thought I shared that with you. Burton's deceased brother was my ex."

"No. No, that's something I would have remembered. Even with a 64K DOS, green screen memory, that would have stayed with me." Key shook his head side to side in disgusted astonishment.

"You surely didn't bring me out here to break my nose and effect couples therapy?" asked Buttons sarcastically.

"Asshole!" Ali struck him again, but this time Buttons blocks the blow with his forearm.

He motioned as if he was going to strike back and Key grabbed his wrist, twisted it uncomfortably and said, "Bad idea, Scooter."

"Ali, Hoppy was never truly in danger. She was simply a tool to get to your boyfriend. My hands were tied. This was way above my pay grade. If your suitor had just left matters that didn't concern him alone. If he'd …"

"If? If? If my aunt had balls, she'd have been my uncle," retorted Scotty, looking straight ahead as he raised his right arm at a high right angle perpendicular to his rib cage and drove his elbow smartly into Button's already savaged nose.

"He has a name. My boyfriend's name is Scotty," said Ali sarcastically. "We know about the payoff to Rasheed from the unions. We have it documented. He's a petty thief, nothing more. A thug—a small-time, prior Detroit thug hits the big time."

"You have nothing. He's untouchable," grimaced Buttons, wiping his nose on his sleeve.

"We've got enough to impeach him," said Ali.

"It'll never happen. He owns the media, they're in his pocket. And apart from his current loyalists on The Hill, he'd simply buy any shortfall votes to keep it from ever happening. One hundred million to Louisiana here, three hundred million to Nebraska there …"

"We're not going away," Key said.

"Recall, the man owns a currency printing press. Ali, dear, this is just business, don't get in the way of the big DC machine. It will chew you up and spit you out. You, Hoppy and your friend, Scotty."

"We're not letting it go. We've got enough," replied Ali.

"No. No you don't. Listen, by the time Congress is commissioned to consider this and a special prosecutor is appointed, you will have had another birthday. Add on twelve to eighteen months of legal delays and the guy will be out of office. His reign of terror will be over."

"Then we'll go to the police. The DC Police won't wait for a 'special prosecutor.'"

"No you won't. You have more sense than that. You're naïve, if you don't think the DC Police aren't already in his pocket. Ali dear …"

"Do *not* call me dear."

"Ali, the man is an entomologist and you are his bug. Hell, we are all his bugs. I had no choice, my wife is on an overseas assignment with my kids near the border of Iran. It was hinted obliquely that, if I did not cooperate, they could get lost and be imprisoned for 'accidentally' crossing the border. We both know how that ends. I had no choice."

"There are always choices," snapped Ali.

"Listen, you can't stop this guy. He's been schooled long and well at the knee of the Detroit mob and organized unions. He is painstakingly methodical and cunning."

Unmoved, Ali remained silent.

"The man has Freon in his veins. He can say one thing with advance full intention of doing another. What did J. R. Ewing once say? Once the conscience goes, the rest is easy." Buttons sniffled, wiping more blood from his nose on his right coat sleeve. "Have you ever asked yourself why it took $862 billion in stimulus to create but two million jobs? Why it takes $400,000 each to create a $60,000 job? Where do you think the rest goes?"

"Why don't you tell me?"

"To feed the beast. The Machine. It's a war chest for graft, bribes, buying votes and ensnaring all in his corrupt net so he can be king. Hell, so he can be God."

Moments passed with no speech between the parties. Each looked dispassionately out the windows as the rolling brown hills passed, as if but wrinkles on a patchwork quilt. They all quietly searched, as if looking for the silver bullet.

"Everyone makes mistakes," whispered Key into Buttons' ear, looking out the window up high at a helicopter.

"Not this guy," rebuffed Buttons. "He's got watchers watching watchers watching watchers. If there is a Brutus in his camp, he will be drawn and quartered, politically or literally, well before he can ever get at this bloke. Nothing sticks to him. The man is the king of Teflon. "What would you say if I shared I have a sniper's laser scope on Ali and another on your groin right now?" challenged Buttons.

FIFTY-FOUR

"I'D SAY YOU'RE FULL OF shit," retorted Ali.

"If you direct your attention to the chopper, which has been over us for the last five minutes, perhaps you'd feel differently," said Buttons haughtily.

"You mean the one that just banked off to the left to follow the diversionary cab to Golden Gate Bridge? That one princess?" asked Scotty.

"It is of no consequence. It's not like they won't figure it out in two minutes time. This is the way the world works. You'll let me out of this cab, or you'll both be incarcerated for the rest of your natural lives. You have no shot up against the machine. He wipes his bum with the Constitution. The laws don't apply to this guy. He'll have your guts for garters. Get used to it."

"Then we're just going to need more salient details for the next 'meet' to level the playing field, that's all. So we can lock down and ultimately solve our political Rubik's Cube," said Ali. In so doing, she cuffed Buttons' hands behind his back.

"What are you going to do? Shoot me? Waterboard me?" asked Buttons, spitting a mouthful of blood on the cab's floor.

"No. We are bored with water. We're going to go for pinot." deadpanned Scotty.

Ali stuffed a knotted sock in Buttons's mouth and covered it with an eight-inch strip of duct tape.

After concluding his riposte, Scotty took an old-styled corkscrew, from a cheap motel, a single metal screw with a fixed wooden handle number, and drove it into Buttons' knee. It buried at an angle, up and under his kneecap. Buttons jumped straight up into the air violently, banging his head on the vehicle's ceiling.

In his ill-spent youth in sports, Scotty had chondromalicia in his right knee caused by an ulcer under the kneecap. He knew just how excruciating the placement of this cajoling device could be.

"Now, this can come out pretty soon, if you play nice … or," Scotty said, twisting the corkscrew just a trifle clockwise, "if you screw with us, we will screw with you."

Buttons head banged off the ceiling again, while blood, mucous and snot expelled a full three feet from his nostrils, splattering the back of the privacy screen.

Mawwwwwphhhh! He was gagging on the sock and his own bloody phlegm. His shirt and pinstripe suit's pant leg were both soaked in blood. His calf was wet with the new red rivulet trickling down its backside. Buttons was huffing and puffing in pain. He was finding it difficult to breathe in between choking back a gag reflex.

"So what's it going to be, big shot? You and I both know where to put the needle," asked Scotty showing no emotion.

Ali ripped the duct tape off and pulled the knotted sock out of Buttons' mouth allowing him to speak.

"The union goon is from Venezuela! He's with Chavez! He'll be holding a meeting again next week. That's your shot."

Bong! "Wrong answer. Nice try, but too quick. You get points for playing, however you gave him up too easily." With that, Scotty turned the corkscrew ever so slowly another half inch, resulting in an immediate lurch, more blood spurting from his nostrils and tears streaming down both cheeks.

Buttons reached down with his mouth in an effort to remove the corkscrew from under his kneecap. He gave it a single, quick outward jerk, to no avail, as the "screws" had threaded into his joint. He screamed again loudly. He choked, hiccupped and sobbed.

"Sometimes," remarked Key, "the best way to keep a good 'hard-on' is to just not fuck with it." With that, he slammed his palm on the wood handled end of the corkscrew, driving it into the soft tissue and bundled nerves under the patellae another three-eighths of an inch.

"You know," Scotty said, "I don't normally enjoy this, however after a visit to your friend the Fisherman's, 'resort' and the free facial he performed," he stroked his scar, "I rather hope this takes awhile."

Buttons closed his eyes in abject fear.

"Yup. I am officially looking forward to this taking awhile. To manage your expectations, I'm going to move next to the other knee. Then we have something special in store for you, if you hold out for the bonus round."

He took out a very large, striper bass-sized, heavily gauged metal stringer and draped half of it across Button's groin.

"The stringer through the jaw thing was such a creative piece of work, you inspired me. Know however, that many have called me dickhead, so there's no telling where I may choose to string you up."

"Burton," said Ali, "he can be a dickhead. Trust me. You should consider coughing up the 'meet' and saving yourself considerable time, pain and disfigurement."

Scotty unzipped Buttons' fly. He unbuttoned the slack's keeper at the top, exposing Button's briefs. No one spoke. Key was slowly running the separate stringer hooks up and down through his hands. One by one.

They jangled.

Thirty seconds passed, although it seemed much longer to Buttons. Key picked one end of the stringer up and opened two of the last curved, hooked openings. These were both sharpened to a sixty-degree point to penetrate hefty fish scales, lips, gills, or the genitalia of NSA directors who have headed south.

Key remained staring straight ahead dispassionately. Ali was looking out the other window. Scotty then started whistling 'Heigh-Ho, Heigh–Ho, It's off to Work We Go.'"

Buttons started shaking and convulsing uncontrollably, in pain and fear. "Okay! Jesus! Mother of God! For the love of Christ, put that thing away," pleaded Buttons. "In addition to the unions, it's the Chinese—the bloody Chinese!" he sobbed. "Mrs. Green is key to this whole sordid affair. She'll be meeting with Chairman Zho in ten days."

"Who is Mrs. Green?" asked Key.

"We believe she's the Uighur who Zho exiled as an extreme separatist, although it has been confusing whether she is working for or against him. Zho, publically, holds himself out as a Han."

"What has this to do with Rasheed?"

"We're not sure however, she's met with him twice, during which time he's had the Secret Service stand down to a five hundred-foot radius, which is highly irregular," said Buttons.

"So you don't really know her agenda?" asked Ali.

"No. However we feel she is playing both sides against the middle and some have even suggested Rasheed could be involved in a nefarious manner."

"You are suggesting his involvement in more than directing a stealth NSA black ops way?" asked Scotty.

"Yes. We're uncertain if it's bribery, treason, or both. This thing is white hot. If we don't do anything and we know, we're complicit, we go to jail. If we do take action and trust just one wrong bloke, we'll wake up dead. This machine is ruthless. It will stop at nothing to protect the organism. Nothing."

Scotty intervened, "So this 'meet' between Green and Zho, which coast?"

"West. Probably not DC. I have the location's details in my PDA. Chairman Zho of China has been characterized by the CIA as imbalanced with a personality disorder."

"Go on."

"He's unpredictable. There is no telling what he may do at any given

300

moment. There could be enough happening there to put a fine point on this maybe, hard evidence or not. They might just exchange golf scores. Who the bloody hell knows? We'll figure out a surreptitious way for you to gain access."

"To ensure you don't lose this newfound, philanthropic state of mind, you are officially out on medical leave. You could say you've injured your knee, that shouldn't be too much of a stretch. You go back to the office when I go back to the office. Read me?" asked Key.

"Righto. Now can we go patch this knee up?"

"Of course. We have a doc at the ready. We won't make you hitchhike back on a dusty highway, drooling blood, choking on scabs and spittle. That would be unseemly. Eh mate?"

Understanding the complete meaning of all of Key's words and the UK mockery, Buttons glanced sideways with moist eyes out the window and said nothing.

Fifty-five

Northern and Southern California, USA
April 2011

THE ARMY CORPS OF ENGINEERS skillfully dispatched hundreds of teams to reopen transportation and communication arteries in California. They erected ninety-two temporary bridges.

Although first used in WWII, the corps' use and design was honed further to the point of being practicable in the Vietnam War. These bridges enabled traffic to move over the new canal, which encircled the 20,000 square mile island.

The locals were referring to the area as Islafornia. It was already taking on its own identity. Business was proceeding, albeit with many cell phone towers down, at a glacial pace. Rasheed had come out two days earlier to view the area and pledge his support at the capitol in Sacramento. He reinforced his FEMA commitment and renewed his promise for the follow-on disaster relief fund set aside for California. He assured all he wouldn't rest until this was rectified and it would be remediated much faster than the southern coastal, deep water oil leak had been.

Apart from the 242,000 dead, another 660,000 were injured, with over one million displaced. These were put up in temporary structures in San Francisco and Los Angeles alike.

Down south, the Rose Bowl was ground zero. Pepperdine and UCLA campuses were also used. To the north, most of the MASH units coalesced at the Oakland As' Oakland Coliseum and the Giants' AT&T Park, with temporary cots, fresh water, soup lines and clean clothes being dispensed.

The Cow Palace, UC Berkeley and Stanford campuses, as well as the HP Pavilion, were converted to help. Mobile teams steadily removed the dead. The stench was unbearable, with the heat, flies, dysentery and other waterborne diseases becoming the new concern for the CDC.

Fifty-six

Chinatown, San Francisco, California
April 2011

UPON RECOGNIZING THE REALITY OF his newfound "medical leave," Buttons resigned himself to welding Key and Ali into becoming part of the next Green and Zho meeting. The general setting was believed to be in San Francisco's Chinatown.

With Scotty's profile being elevated, the team decided he should drive the operation, but Ali would be the tip of the spear. As she normally worked "back office," her identity should not be as top of mind as Scotty's was to either Zho's or Green's sweeper teams. While they had taken her once, it was reasoned that her diminutive frame and ethnicity would allow her to blend into the Chinatown surroundings much better than Key.

Scotty arranged for a nondescript threesome from MI6, courtesy of Willingham, to hold Buttons in an undisclosed, underground location until this played out.

Under the heading of a routine training op, the NSA was tracking only primary players this meeting. They were not intending to monitor at a proximate level.

Buttons had been gracious enough, thanks to the gentle prodding in the cab, to provide Key's team the scrambled, proprietary radio band carrying logistic details so they could be up close and personal when the meeting occurred.

"The package is approaching the corner of 505 Montgomery. It has gotten out of the cab and is walking. Note: The package is wearing a large, green hat with a prominent white feather."

"Come back," was the squawked reply.

"Green hat with white feather appears to be going into an underground parking garage. Subject is gathering baking instructions as to where to leave the pie," came the bark across the scrambled NSA band Key was monitoring.

Scotty was distrustful of Buttons and had fears of his team's cover being blown." They were running out of options however, so his team was linked to Buttons at the hip. If one went down, so did the other.

He passed the scrambled messaging on to Cracker and Ali, who were on the move. Each was in a separate cab spaced a quarter mile apart to allow for a hopscotch effect. This ensured "the package" would not be flushed and that they didn't lose connectivity.

Ali had donned shopkeeper garb. She was wearing $9.99 run-of-the-mill oriental slippers, an inexpensive black, silk blouse with cherry blossoms, black silk pants and an overly large black, pulled-down visor, which covered the bulk of her face.

Her head remained slightly down and she carried a small backpack. Her long blue black hair was arranged in a traditional Chinese single braid down her back. She appeared indigenous to the area.

With the last communiqué, Cracker's cab lurched forward to the corner of Fifth and Montgomery to either dispatch himself on foot or continue vehicular pursuit. They pulled up to a sudden stop. His hand was on the door handle and he was prepared to disembark. They still had audio, but they'd lost visual contact.

Then, Mrs. Green came up the elevator and out of the underground garage. She pulled her hat down low, reentered her cab and headed north briefly and then west, toward Chinatown.

Cracker passed the information on to Key and Ali, who hop-scotched again. It appeared the speculation as to a Chinatown address for the physical meet could be bona fide.

Ali's cab pulled up ten blocks ahead of Green's in dense traffic and Ali got out. Head down, she took on a slumped-over posture and shuffled her feet just a bit to meld into the landscape. Like a shadow in a sepia-toned photograph, she entered the first shop, bowed and shuttled toward the back to the restroom.

Her team had studied the building plans earlier and knew the layout well. In the restroom there was a singular, small, eighteen-inch-by-eighteen-inch window, just large enough for her diminutive frame to wiggle through. After a few tight corners, it led her to an alley in the back.

The alley was strewn with dumpsters and large, black exhaust hoods belching moist, hot steam and gray smoke. It was also decoupaged with a few puddles of urine and the occasional small, orange-brown heap of vomit.

She hurried down the narrow passageway and was confronted by a large, white windowless van, which careened around the corner. Had she been caught? The van lurched to a stop. The driver opened his high cab door with authority. Instinctively, Ali reached for her holstered Glock concealed under her silk top. The driver jumped down to the pavement. Her holster top un-Velcroed, she paused to pull her weapon.

"Hi there," said the driver.

"Hello," she said.

The driver kept working. Paying her no mind, he walked crisply to the back of the van, swung open its back doors, threw down a ramp and began rolling out wheeled carts of freshly laundered cook and waitstaff uniforms. He went inside through the back entrance, fifteen steps south of where he'd parked.

Ali's tense shoulders relaxed. She picked up her pack and continued down the narrow alley, turned right and entered the back door of a shop that sold a bit of everything. She pushed her way through the narrow cluttered aisles that displayed silk wear, the bobble-headed dolls, and through the eight differing manner of Buddhas. She noticed a myriad of small jade figurines and dusty *How to Feng Shui Your Home* books. She hit her head once on a low-hanging, faded yellow, paper and wire lantern.

She glanced up. No one noticed her. All were busy, either shopping or selling, selling or shopping, as if she was any other patron, any other merchant. She opened the extremely narrow, wooden door to the shallow basement and ducking, crept down the tight cobwebby stairs, closing the door quietly behind her.

The small space below housed a large, vintage boiler for heat. There was supposed to be a makeup air shaft that connected to the next building on the east wall. It was absent. Only through the air shaft could she get through to her destination.

She took a small broom leaning up against the boiler and brushed the cobwebs and soot away from the wall. Not there. She did, however, disturb three large spiders, who jumped. They weren't poisonous, they just looked creepy, each the size of a quarter, dark and hairy. Two leapt away and one toward her. She found herself muffling a primal instinct to scream. While she could reverse a foreign operative's knee who outweighed her by one hundred pounds, these eight-legged bastards still gave her the willies.

She found no makeup air vent. Running out of time, she radioed Scotty.

"No vent in boiler room three."

"East wall?"

"No. Not on east wall."

"Come back?"

"Not on east wall. No vent."

"Is the actual boiler there?"

"Say again?"

"Is a boiler physically there?"

"Yes."

"Try moving the boiler's largest vertical stack."

Ali accommodated the request and there, concealed from a prior remodel, was the coveted opening, large enough for a small Asian woman (and none larger) to slide through. This very restrictive opening size was a key governing element that had driven the team's selection of Ali for the job.

The shaft was dark, dusty and moldy. Ali carried a small Maglite in her mouth to illuminate her passage. She thought she heard a rat scamper away, although she wasn't certain. It could have been her imagination. She took her pack off, hoisted it and herself up on the boiler and slid into the makeup air chase. It was a snug fit. Fortunately, due to its age, the gage of the metal was thick enough that it did not audibly complain with her additional weight.

She slid down the chase-work, dragging her backpack behind her. Turning one corner to the right, Ali lowered herself down an old dumbwaiter, which heretofore had been abandoned.

A ragged, rusty edge of one of the duct's metal corners sliced her thigh open. She grimaced but made no sound. Continuing on, she left a small trickling blood trail. Opening a single louver to the room in question, Ali saw it was still a good twenty-four inches away from the next structure's interior wall. There was but a tiny opening, used as an outlet before, which had been covered up during another remodel.

The opening was but two and a half-by-four inches. Partially concealed behind a dresser, the visual piece was going to be a challenge. This could be remediated somewhat with her fully bendable and periscoping, poseable gooseneck video tube. However, it was still going to be dark and grainy due to the low light. She clawed away more spiderwebs from her face, spat soot from her mouth and pressed ahead.

There was an earthen odor in the air. Perhaps it was the baking of fortune cookies, maybe mold. She held her breath, sweating. She could hear the banging of pots and pans through a nearby kitchen's vent and the prattling of two chefs arguing in Mandarin.

Her radio band was on an earbud. She could not tolerate making any sound whatsoever. Ali signaled to Scotty by flashing her earbud's ID signature light twice that she was in position and would be turning the volume off. She hunkered down to await her guests and downed all electronic signals, anticipating a sweep. As she waited, she heard more scampering.

FIFTY-SEVEN

Mrs. Green and Chairman Zho disembarked to differing restaurants, pushed through curtains of multicolored, plastic beads, and made their way to the back of each facility. Each, in turn, passed through a knickknack T-shirt shop before arriving at the predetermined location.

The waiter greeted them independently. Bowing deeply with gravity, he forced out a half smile and shuttled them both toward the restroom in the back. Next to the restroom was a narrow janitor's closet.

They both entered the closet, one at a time and pushed on a large Pegboard, which had mops and dustpans hanging from it askew. It yielded. Each passed through the opening and down a rickety set of stairs to the shallow basement.

Upon meeting, they bowed to each other, exchanged pleasantries and took his or her respective seat across from the other at a very small, cramped table with three wooden chairs.

Each chair was a different color. There was a small, faded tea set in the middle with service for three. The initials *ESE* were inscribed on the pot. The basement, while dank upstairs, was impeccably clean downstairs. One could still smell the head-jerking aroma of bleach used in preparation for this event.

While sitting for tea, Chairman Zho removed from a large cloth satchel an exceptionally large crescent moon, a highly recognizable symbol of Islam.

"A gift," remarked Mrs. Green, casting her eyes and hands heavenward.

"Yes. For our friend," replied Zho.

"He'll be pleased."

"It is our hope."

Two soft knocks sounded at the small, faded door. A voice from a sandaled stranger, completely robed from head to toe and veiled up to his eyes came from beyond: "Allah is Great, Muhammad, Messenger of Allah," said the stranger.

Mr. Zho responded, "Nothing is worthy of worship except Allah."

The visitor entered. He did not lower his veil. The three exchanged two-handed handshakes and spoke the following:

Mr. Zho and Mrs. Green said, "As-Salāmu ʿAlaykum."

The stranger responded, "aSalaam ʿAlaykum."

"Please be seated," requested Chairman Zho politely.

The stranger accommodated them.

"Appreciate your coming on short notice."

"My pleasure," responded the veiled one.

"Before business, a small gesture of our appreciation," announced Zho.

"Ahhhh," responded the stranger, spreading his arms in anticipation.

Zho slid the large crescent moon across the small, wooden table over to the stranger. "Constantinople and Istanbul used the crescent moon as their symbol in the days of our forefathers. It harkens back to a battle in which the Romans defeated the Goths on the first day of the lunar month."

"Ahhhh." said the stranger.

"In like fashion, we feel this is the harbinger of new beginnings and good things to come your way and ours very soon. Praise be to Allah!" exclaimed Zho, looking skyward.

"Praise be to Allah! You're too generous," said the visitor.

"Please. Open it," whispered Zho, smiling.

The newcomer was unaware there was a concealed, flush clasp. The

311

hand-hammered brass and copper crescent moon was ornate enough to be a stand-alone gift.

Upon releasing the clasp, however, the entire toenail moon opened up to disclose a treasure trove of riches beyond belief. It was stuffed chock-full of banded one hundred-dollar bills, gem-quality diamonds, voluptuous red rubies and enormous sparkling jade green emeralds.

"Allah has smiled upon me," gasped the stranger, admiring his rich bounty.

"Allah is pleased with those who strive to please him," said Zho. "Another quarter. Added up, its value is another quarter of a billion, in appreciation for things that have occurred and all things that will occur soon."

"Allah is too generous. This was not expected," said the stranger. One could perceive the shadow line of a smile beneath the stranger's veil.

Ali's goose-necked video tube was struggling as the light was poor, however some scratchy sound and grainy images were getting laid down nonetheless.

"We come today with resolution to many problems for us both," stated Zho.

"Mutual solutions are mother's milk to Allah," said the stranger. He spread his arms graciously wide open, palms up.

"Today we not only represent the interests of millions of Uighurs and Muslims, we also represent the coalition of the future—ESE," said Zho.

"ESE? Not familiar with that entity," said the stranger.

"Yes. Well most aren't today. However, all will be soon. With your permission, I'll use a brief PowerPoint presentation that lays out this enormous opportunity." Zho booted his laptop and reached to his necklace, from which he removed and installed a thumb drive, which disclosed the following presentation. The first screen had the ESE logo with the second slide showing the many differing Asian country flags as Zho spoke to them.

"ESE is a coalition of most of the Asian countries whose people's namesake end in 'ese'—countries with peoples like, Vietnamese, Japanese, oh yes and Chinese." An ESE logo representing this consortium appeared in the bottommost right-hand corner of each page of the deck thereafter.

"Yes. I see," replied the stranger sitting up.

"In America, it has been known for thousands of years that the ancient tribes of Israel still band together today to conduct business only with each other," Israel's flag and two elder men bartering under an olive tree appeared.

"Yes. I'm familiar with the practice."

"And the Japanese for generations have had their Keitsus, it is customary to just conduct business within one's own Japanese Keitsu, so as to always benefit your Japanese community." An image dissolved of six male Japanese businessmen doing business over dinner.

"Of course."

"And your skull and crossbones of Ivy League universities in America curry favor only upon one another, as brothers in arms in one of the most exclusive fraternal orders on the planet." This scene was also represented graphically.

"Yes. I'm aware of that as well."

"This is but a global extension of that model to a newly formed Asian entity, which will function in its self-interest," said Zho.

"Interesting."

"With the global GDP around $70 trillion dollars, this entity represents $9.5 trillion, or 14 percent, of total global GDP. When the ESE entities' marketplace power is combined, it equals a full two-thirds of the entire US$14 plus trillion GDP."

"This is all very informative, however, how does this effect me and my constituents?" asked the stranger.

"We propose to purchase the small strip of California that was regrettably broken off from its primary mass by your recent earthquake, for $10 trillion."

The stranger laughed out loud. "You're kidding! Right?"

"Not in the least. We calculate that the principal and interest the US

313

owes us will soon be well over $10 trillion in just a few short years. That is, presuming it is ever repaid, which is looking more and more doubtful," responded Zho. "The proposal in this presentation would eradicate and absolve all debt to all ESE nations. It would put both of us at peace—culturally, procedurally and fiscally."

"I hope this is all a bad joke and you've had too much sake," said the stranger, lowering his veil to expose his face.

Ali gasped silently. The stranger was President Rasheed.

FIFTY-EIGHT

"THERE IS NO HUMOR ATTACHED to the offer," stated Zho slowly. "Look at the issue objectively. You lead a powerful nation. ESE's land mass is ten million square miles. This image here shows that the United States is a little over nine. We are similar in size, at 107 percent of the United State's area, yet our populace is 7.7 times as dense. In fact, ESE controls 35 percent of the entire global population."

Rasheed was looking over the top of his steepled fingers.

"On the next slide, you see you have an average density of thirty-one people per square mile. China has over four times that and Japan experiences a density of almost eleven times yours. When we fight tsunamis and typhoons, such as Morakot in Chihpen, we have to evacuate over a million people. Over a million!"

"Respectfully, Chairman Zho, that is not a concern of the United States," said Rasheed. "Our dog ain't in that fight."

"It concerns you deeply. And we believe we will have your dog's attention as well, as we're calling in the note."

"That's absurd!"

"It would only be absurd if we thought you had any intention of ever honoring it. That likelihood lessens every time you speak on television, Mr. President. Every new program you put forth, every new stimulus you can't afford, every new program you expect us to bail you out of makes it clear you are unlikely to pay. We are serving you notice that we are officially out of that business. What you owe China and Japan alone is 44 percent of your total global debt, that should concern you as well. Fortunately, ESE is perfecting our lien with a peaceful solution."

"Let me be clear, you have no right. This will not stand. It will never happen," said Rasheed.

"ESE fiscal policies are tightening to reflect global markets. If you elect not to honor our proposal in a peaceful manner, we will be forced to raise your interest rate from 4 percent another 3 percent every six months until it is back to 12 to 16 percent as in the Carter era."

"You can't do that."

"Respectfully, we can and we will. We will bankrupt your entire country. In that instance, we would ask you for the keys to the entire house, as opposed to just a little piece of the front porch as now. The 'porch' isn't even .2 percent of your overall land mass. This solution is practical and makes the most sense for all."

"I understand that from your vantage point. However, the assets alone in that small strip represent a portion much larger than .2 percent of all US assets."

"Indeed, and they are already 56 percent owned by ESE today. You are, in fact, giving up something you don't possess today anyway. So, no loss, yes? In fact, the largest ethnic population in the nine-county Bay area is Asian, so there will be no trauma, no upheaval."

Rasheed sat speechless.

"It will be a natural evolution. There will be no blood, no scalping, no burning of tepees, as when you took the American Indians' land for your own. You'll simply be repaying a debt. A fee simple land sale, like when you bought the Republic of Texas from Mexico or Alaska from the Russians."

"Look. That wasn't the deal!" exclaimed Rasheed in a raised voice, standing and becoming a bit shrill.

"I'm a movie buff myself, Mr. President. I loved Darth Vader in *Star Wars* when he said, 'I've altered the deal; pray I don't alter it further,'" remarked Zho.

Mrs. Green had remained silent with her hands in her lap to this point. This remark created a faint smile on her lips, although her gaze was still downward.

"Don't worry, Mr. President. You'll still get the rest of your billion. Feel good about this. You are personally solving an agonizing debt for the US, which is clearly unsustainable and squaring the collection of that debt between four great nations. You should be very proud."

"I don't feel proud. I feel duped."

"We were thinking of naming the new island Guanxi, for personal connections and influence. In China, your status is determined not by who you are, but by who you know and can connect to. That's ESE's doctrine." Zho pressed out a leering, sneering smile.

Ali was not making a sound. She heard a scratching, twittering scamper. A modest-sized rat came up nose to nose with her. She blinked. She didn't move and neither did the rat. She choked back a scream. The rat sniffed at her backpack. After no apparent entry was found, it abandoned the search and strolled off as leisurely as it had arrived down the duct.

"You are taking this much too hard," admonished Zho. "You'll get used to it, in time you'll grow to like it. All that debt off your plate. What a relief it will be for you, your children and your grandchildren, yes?"

Rasheed stood up, pushed in his chair and paced. "I understand why the Chinese have been characterized as the Jews of the Orient," remarked the president.

"I'm uncertain if that is a backhanded compliment, if so, then thank you. If it is an anti-Semitic slur, then no thank you," Zho replied, leaning forward and pressing ten straight fingers on the tabletop as he stood.

"Did you have something to do with California spawning its new *Guanxi* island?" demanded Rasheed.

"Let's just say its timing was propitious."

"If I thought for one minute you utilized some of those Red Mercury canisters you sold us to exacerbate that event ..."

"Yes. You'd do what? After using that very same tool to speed along your purposes for the unions to do away with NAFTA in Canada and Mexico. Just *what would you do*, Mr. President?" Zho was jeering scornfully as he leaned forward in a deliberate attempt to confront.

Ali could not believe what she was hearing. She swallowed. During their dramatic pause, her swallow sounded so loud she feared they'd hear it. Listening to the sound of her heart she blinked away the grunge that was collecting in the corner of her right eye.

"Make no mistake, this will not stand. This will not occur on my watch! Rasheed shouted.

"But it will, Mr. President. You are internalizing this and taking it much too personally. Historically, most advanced civilizations only last a few hundred years anyway. In the last generation, the US has experienced moral decay, drugs, prostitution, fat and sloth-like behaviors, drifting from the nuclear family and any form of consistent religion. The US has lost its moral compass. You've traded in your founding father's backbone for some self-righteous, political correctness tripe.

"Hold on there ..."

Ah Zho did not allow the interruption. "Your children's heroes are prior felons who strut around in coliseums. You've become weak, but then again, you want them weak."

"How dare you lecture me!"

"They become easier to control that way, don't they, Mr. President? By design. Otherwise, you'd have burned all the opium fields in Afghanistan long ago. But no, you want that healthy trade to continue until much of the US is zombified and will eat any ridiculous policy you put on the table. Any policy, as long as it is first gift wrapped and spun in a slick Madison Avenue presentation across all media outlets you dominate."

"Look. This will never fly. This will not happen."

Zho's rant continued, "You no longer have any input into *when* it will occur, Mr. President. Your only decision is *how* it will occur. ESE is proposing an amicable, peaceful solution to all. That's why we have made this presentation and brought you a copy to sell it to Congress. On a bright note, it can be your idea."

In so saying, he extended his right hand with an identical thumb drive of the presentation for Congress. Rasheed batted the drive away flippantly and it fell to the floor in the far corner of the room.

"I reject the concept, I reject this conversation and I reject you," stated Rasheed emphatically.

"Very eloquent, Mr. President. However, you are no longer running for office. You may park the bus now. Your words are meaningless to us. They are empty. What did the Tea Party protestors' sign say?" He paused, trying to remember. "Oh yes, I remember. 'Your words are turds; lead with deeds.' If you tell *us* the sky is green, we will politely listen. And then we'll look out the window the next morning. If it is blue, it is blue. We are not as naive as the American people, or what did you call them? Sheeple?"

Standing and wagging his forefinger high in the air, Zho exclaimed, "Where did you think this was going with your involvement? What did you expect us to do? Sit by idly as you print money 24-7 for every capricious, ideological whim of yours and expect us to continue to foot the bill? The whole world is watching as your currency and all US assets experience the follow-on hyperinflation of that predictable, childish behavior."

"We have inflation under control."

"What makes you think you and your nation can escape that fate? It is not about ideologies; it is about the *math*, Mr. President, the math. The laws of nature, economics and mathematics are absolute. They are not negotiable. They cannot be apologized or charmed away with a broad smile."

FIFTY-NINE

"Ukraine just last year experienced 960 percent inflation. They 're-let' the hryvnia two years ago and it is worth but 1 percent of its recent reissuance value today," said Zho.

"They're a Tier 2 country."

"Like Greece? You've seen the bloody riots in the streets recently when the government was attempting to withdraw entitlements due to unsustainable, sky-high debt in contrast to their GDP."

"They're a special case, but a speck on the map. Mice nuts."

"Italy and Ireland are not far behind."

"Hurrumph," said Rasheed.

"Why do you feel the US can escape that same fate with worse fiscal behavior? Consider Germany pre-WWII. You are a student of history. With 300 million percent inflation, people were getting paid twice a day, so their paycheck would not be worthless. These are not make-believe tales. These are historical facts, Mr. President."

"We could have you brought up on charges of international extortion at the UN," admonished Rasheed, leaning over and wagging his finger in the face of Zho.

"Not likely. That body is a den of thieves who don't pay their rent, are ineffective, without testicles and devoid of soul. Moreover, you would be tarred with that same brush. The things you have put in motion, the stipends you have already accepted make you an integral part of this. You will not be able to distance yourself from this. In fact, to the uninitiated, you appear to be leading it."

Rasheed stared blankly and said nothing.

"If you elect to not sell the island to ESE or miraculously forestall bankruptcy, then your recent moves to placate your unions with card check, gerrymandering, rigging the census and redistricting by your Buckeye group—they will perfect our lien for us."

"How do you figure?" asked Rasheed. "That vehicle was installed to effect a one-party system, as you know. We will be unstoppable."

"Quite aware. Same reason why you've deliberately relaxed immigration enforcement. You wish to attract the very element who will vote for you, so they can feed at the trough of income redistribution and move freely to a glittering new world adorned with free entitlements."

Rasheed placed one forefinger to his upper lip and looked slightly up while arching his back.

"You will undoubtedly try to revisit the notion of Puerto Rico as the fifty-first state in your union as an extension of that same ploy."

The president placed his forefingers again to his nose pensively, tilted his head down and glared just under his brow at Zho with no response.

Pacing and waving his hands, Ah Zho said with contempt, "A one-party system would give you a supermajority vote to perhaps change the Constitution and allow you to stay in office for three terms like FDR. Who knows? Perhaps they'll even anoint you king." Zho laughed.

"Humorous," said Rasheed sarcastically.

"However, as those gerrymandering lines are being finalized, recall who owns 56 percent of all *Guanxi* AAA real estate. Please recall the new island's majority ethnicity. Do you feel it would be such a stretch to have them vote for secession from the union in the same manner Texas, Arizona and Montana are pursuing today?"

"That twaddle is simply being fanned by extremists."

"There has been talk of Southern California becoming its own state for decades. Islafornia is a physical island, with its own independent identity, its own homogenous culture, the populace being of like mind and being essentially of one race, is that such a far walk for you to visualize?"

Rasheed sat back down. His forefingers pressed to his upper lip with his elbows on the table. His chin was elevated some thirty degrees to horizontal.

Like Snoopy.

"So you see, Mr. President. *It is going to happen.* You have the historical privilege of being the free world leader to solve this global conundrum in an amicable manner. You may take all the bows, it can be your idea. That way, if things head south then you can bemoan the notion that Congress did not take your suggestion and blame them. Beautiful, yes?"

Zho returned to his seat, admonishing again, "Rest assured, this is going to happen. Either:

(1) you encourage a peaceful purchase of Guanxi, or

(2) the island will secede from the union on its own, or

(3) our interest rates will spike up to Carter era heights with

the follow-on hyperinflation precipitating a US national bankruptcy."

Zho continued. "In the lattermost scenario, the northeast could also be at peril, due to the banking bailout, which is globally unsustainable. Moreover, the beleaguered insurance companies, after being driven out of business from the government run single-payer option for national healthcare, will stop insuring coastal areas, which will, in turn, result in catastrophic defaults in the southeast. We may soon own them as well. These are troubling scenarios, to be certain Mr. President, however they are all quite real."

"This is blackmail," stated Rasheed.

"You were right the first time. It's more like extortion. This should be an art form you are skilled at from your extensive training in Detroit. To ensure you don't equivocate on us, ESE is requiring you to sign this document, which states you will formally advance the sell-off of Guanxi to absolve the US of almost half of its debt, as well as this second document, which speaks to your being complicit."

"What on earth would possess me to consider signing anything as patently ridiculous as that?" demanded the president.

"Recall, Mr. President, I am the dictator of a communist country. I make all the rules. I make all the laws. And if I don't like the laws I made on Tuesday, I change them on Wednesday, with a pen. Over tea. However, you are in a democratic society—today anyway," Zho laughed.

Rasheed paced, head down.

"Purportedly, with checks and balances, if this conversation were to see daylight before first being teased out and spun by you to your media, then quite frankly President Rasheed, either your career or your head would be on a stick. Since some of the methods you've used are outside of the norms of US law, with your not enjoying the same unilateral moral flexibility I have, you may be pondering your fate from the confines of a six-by-nine cell."

Rasheed was now visibly squirming. He stroked his chin and spoke. "Fuck it. Write it up. We'll say the debt load has become a state of national emergency. We have to perfect this sale immediately, or we could experience a catastrophic bankruptcy and depression," he said, as he signed the two documents hurriedly. He threw the pen down in disgust.

Chairman Zho retrieved both documents and rotated the semicircular blotter-sealant roller over them, to seal, affix and make permanent the signatures.

"See. That wasn't so hard, was it? Now, let's have some tea and dim sum to celebrate this new crescent moon," said Zho, smiling as he poured Rasheed another cup.

Mrs. Green had said nothing the entire time, her face alternating between a thinly pinched smirk and an otherwise blank expression.

"Pass. I have to take this opportunity to the American people. It is my duty to advance their self-interest swiftly. We can be the light on the path that shows them the way. Besides, I've lost my appetite," exclaimed Rasheed.

He rose, picked up his crescent moon gift, raised his veil to conceal his face and headed toward the narrow door.

"It is always a privilege to see true visionary leadership in action," remarked Mrs. Green. She bowed her head and slowly sipped her tea.

Rasheed looked at her blankly, paused to say something. Opened the door and left.

Mrs. Green and Chairman Zho finished their tea. Neither one of them spoke. All that needed saying had been said. After a few moments they adjourned upstairs to enjoy some lunch. While leaving, Chairman Zho asked Mrs. Green if he could leave his computer. She said it was not a problem, as there were laser beacons she could alarm to protect the area in their absence. They walked to the door's threshold.

She punched in a code and activated the switch that armed the room with lasers, ten inches on center, spread horizontally throughout the space. They left. Barely visible, the lasers created a slight humming noise.

Ali had taken it all in. Stunned with disbelief as to the globally seminal event she had just witnessed, she had to summon great concentration just to move again. While she needed to get out of there pronto, it would also be desirable if she could do so while remaining alive.

It would also be grand, she thought, to take the computer for hard evidence. The collection of evidence was the mantra for this event to triangulate Rasheed. Otherwise, the body politic, federal and heads of state would circle their wagons and lie to protect themselves, their brethren, or their benefactors. But how was she going to get that computer with the alarm's laser grid enabled?

The computer was off the menu. It couldn't be snaked in the current environment. No way. However, the second thumb drive, which Rasheed had chucked across the room, was calling her name. But how? If it actually had an identical presentation to the one Zho had shown the president, it would create a firestorm in the halls of Congress—if not there, then on YouTube. Although she could see the drive, she certainly couldn't get through an outlet-sized opening and hunker her form down to slide snakelike across the floor under ten-inch laser beams.

"Shit."

This must be why Scotty had encouraged her to bring the book bag backpack. Precisely the reason. Resting inside was her secret weapon.

She unzipped the left-hand pocket and reached deep inside. She found what she was looking for. A gun. Not a Glock. Not a Colt. No, it was a medium-sized, plastic squirt gun. It was filled with water—not just water however, it was filled with a solution of water and mashed-up Pill Pockets.

Ali took the squirt gun, leaned on her side, pressed her hand dead flat against the floor of the duct and squirted through the receptacle's opening which was but six inches off the ground. She squirted and squirted. She missed the thumb drive. But she had the distance. She shot cautiously again, ensuring the spray was at least three inches below the ten-inch, absolute maximum laser ceiling. She got it the third time. She placed the squirt gun back in the book bag and opened the main compartment.

Tang came out of the bag slowly and looked at her expectantly. He wiggled his nose and twitched his ears. His eyes were bright. She let him smell the solution that remained on her forefinger. He licked it off as he stood in the chase way.

Ali rubbed some of the solution on the small electrical outlet-sized opening to encourage his exploration. Tang's nose became hyperactive and went into sniffing overdrive.

"Go get 'em, Tang," she whispered. He placed his front legs on the outlet's opening, cocked his small head into the air and sniffed to the right and the left. The squirt gun had left a trail of Pill Pocket solution that led straight over to the thumb drive.

Then, in an instant, he bolted through the small opening. Across the floor diagonally he raced, retrieved the thumb drive and darted back with his treasure to the safety of his condominium book bag, as he had done many times before. In a flash it was over. Quick and easy.

Ali gingerly reached out and pinched the thumb drive with her thumb and forefinger, while Tang held it upright with his two paws. For a moment, neither budged. A quiet tug of war ensued. He looked at her quizzically, an expression that seemed to ask why he should surrender his bounty so readily. Ali showed him why, visibly flipping two Pill Pockets deep inside the book bag's main compartment. Ah-hah! A ransom. He released the thumb drive willingly and dove back into the safety of the book bag to savor his bounty. She zipped it closed and began to slowly retrace her path backward out of the ductwork.

SIXTY

Northern and Southern California, USA
April 2011

ISLAFORNIA'S RECOVERY WAS CONTINUING AT a struggled pace. It lurched forward three steps in construction and back two in widespread dysentery. Shanty towns were constructed daily under bridges or large groves of trees, anything that provided cover would make do. Sometimes simply throwing up a roof in an urban alleyway where the walls were already close was the makeshift solution for many. It was *Mad Max Beyond Thunderdome.* An apocalyptic aura was everywhere. Surreal, unreal and yet all too real for those affected.

CDC and FEMA were doing an admirable job. Yet the job was just too big. Entire boats lay resident in people's front yards, some upside down, some right side up. There were 242,000 dead, yet disaster remediation agencies did not have the social license in this country to gather the corpses with bulldozers and dispense with them smartly in shallow, wholesale graves as had happened in Haiti or Asia after their tsunami.

The bodies had to be treated with more dignity. DNA and dental moldings extracted, parsed and identified. This made for slow going. This was the United States. The stench and disease was overwhelming, exacerbated by the heat. All was made even more gruesome by the one-time, bright-eyed, tennis ball-retrieving, obedient pets which had now started roaming in packs. Famished, they'd vigorously rip flesh off of corpses, so they themselves would not suffer the same fate.

Looting had become a blood sport. Petty looting and grand larceny, on a scale not been seen before, were epic in proportion. Los Angeles gangs, which previously would require a random killing as initiation, had upped the ante, as a single slaying in the current environment was just too easy. Hardly sporting.

The new initiation requirement into the Bloods or Crips was to slaughter a random individual, film it, evoke the act during a robbery and post the gritty images on YouTube as a grim warning how close we were to anarchy.

Most of the high-rises in urban areas had been abandoned, due to the extraordinarily high percentages of structural failure. Retrofitting aside, these had not been designed for an 8.8 quake.

A quake with this intensity had been exceeded only a few other times globally in the last two hundred years. The largest quake recorded during that time frame was 1960 in Chile. It was 9.5.

The quake itself had only killed 5,700 individuals, as Chile had a sparse population. However, the follow-up tsunami killed thousands more or left them savaged, to a slower more agonizing fate of disease and pestilence. It ruptured seven hundred kilometers along an existing fault and effected vertical slippage of twenty meters.

Quakes that approximate a 9.0 magnitude cause tsunamis up to thirty feet high. This was the case with the Islafornia quake, which sent that devastation toward Hawaii. Tsunamis can travel at six hundred miles per hour and oftentimes have a "train" effect of multiple—three or four—waves of like magnitude in quick succession. The thunderous pounding of repetitive, harmonic motion is why this geologic phenomenon is so deadly.

The 1989 Loma Prieta event in San Francisco was tragic. The quake registered 7.1. The duration of the Loma Prieta's primary shock was fairly brief, at but fifteen seconds. Fortunately, it happened at 5:04 pm, when most of the populace had just emptied out of their places of employment. It killed sixty-three and caused $6 billion in damage. The Marina District near Fisherman's Wharf was affected due to its underlying soft landfill. This exacerbated the shaking tenfold for these older structures, resulting in more pronounced structural failure. Older, unreinforced brick buildings could be the deadliest. It wasn't the quake that took the bulk of the lives, it was the follow-on physics lessons from levees, tunnels, buildings, landslides, tsunamis, fires and flooding.

The Islafornia quake happened at 12:03 PM, catching most at their place of work. It also lasted longer than Loma Prieta and other recent quakes. The 1994 Northridge quake in Los Angeles had a 6.7 magnitude and did not result in the same devastation as the Loma Prieta had. All willingly accepted the quake theory for Islafornia. For years, many had predicted a 67 percent chance of another 6.7 or greater quake in northern California to relieve the fault's pent-up pressure, as well as an 85 percent chance of an even larger shaker predicted for Southern California.

Of interest, after a big quake, the entire earth tends to ring. Like a bell.

Most of the airports had been closed for the first thirty days after the event, save the military's. The sky had gone dark with helicopters, which busily shuttled in supplies, food, bandages, medicine and water. They ferried out the injured and the dead. The choppers operated twenty-four hours a day with three shifts in constant rotation.

There was also a larger fleet to take critical patients beyond the confines of the canal to Red Cross hospital ships anchored in the Bay and other inland hospitals where power had not been interrupted. Story after story erupted of PG&E and Con Edison workers toiling to exhaustion and, in a few cases, death. Similar acts of bravery were heralded by police officers and firefighters. Mobile MASH units erected as a convoy trailed the fire department teams.

A number of firefighters suffered smoke inhalation, asphyxiation, or injuries from falling through burned-out floors, roofs, or ceilings. Entire 737s were filled with blood and flown in from Oregon, Washington, Nevada and Arizona. Doctors and surgeons alike worked pro bono to aid in the cataclysmic event.

Over one hundred thousand National Guard members had been mobilized from California and neighboring states. An additional twenty thousand regular Army, men and women were deployed to evoke marshal law. The curfew was sixty minutes before dark to thirty minutes after sunrise.

Alcatraz was converted back into a mass penal temporary holding facility for the 181,000 arrested, as the prisons were overflowing.

SIXTY-ONE

San Francisco, California
April 2011

"THIS AIN'T NO CONSPIRACY THEORY. This is the real deal," said Cracker.

"We have our hard evidence now," said Key. "We can now take the next logical step. We may only get one kick at this cat." said Scotty.

"Time for the frogs to jump out of the pot." added Vinnie.

"I can't believe it was not the Iraqis at the bottom of this. ESE. Fucking Chinese—unbelievable." said Cracker.

"Shouldn't be too terribly amazing. Two-thirds of these guys are the same good people who brought you WWII and the Vietnam War," remarked Key dispassionately.

Scotty continued, "To think that common thug-like payola is driving this great nation to wobble on its very axis. One of these days, or perhaps the next Constitution, we've got to advance the notion of term limits and raising the pay of the highest-ranking members of government some five to eightfold.

"Raising?" asked Cracker incredulously.

"Yes, raising. While not to excuse Rasheed, they all still have feet of clay. If you're making $170,000 a year, in the case of a senator, or $400,000 as the president and you're offered a bribe that will materially change your life, many think about it. Some act. At a minimum, it gives one pause."

"True," said Cracker.

"Alternatively, if the senator is making $1 million and the president is making $5 million a year, will a bribe really improve their life that much? Just how many oceanfront villas in Ireland can one enjoy at any given time? How much Beluga caviar can you eat in a single sitting? It could slow that down a bit. It would undoubtedly save us money in the long run. Think of the billions in 'pork' that could be cut out if the kickbacks were necked down a bit. You'd also attract a higher quality of candidates."

"You mean no more million-dollar NASA toilets?"

"Egggzactly. Or no more three hundred million-dollar congresswoman bribes to buy the last vote needed for government-backed health care."

"You're talkin' about the second Louisiana Purchase?"

"Yup."

"Don't forget the Cornhusker Kickback."

"You know, on a separate note, I believe I figured out a plan to handle this whole terrorist thing," mused Cracker. "You know, a way to weed out those 'sleeper cells' they've planted over here. I was fixin' to write my Congressman. Yes, sir."

"I'm afraid to ask."

"You won't need to ask. I'm gonna tell you."

"My worst nightmare."

"In particular the group that declared jihad, or the holy war against us. They are all fanatical Islamic extremist right?."

"Ugh-huh."

"It's not like they are hard to recognize."

"Nope."

"So instead of the Japanese internment camps that FDR put in place in WWII after they bombed Pearl, we announce this group has ninety days to gather up what they care to and leave the country for another ninety days.

To get back in requires five pieces of identification—number one, an RFID tag embedded in the back of their necks."

"That should be a crowd pleaser."

"Number two, a picture ID with a hologram. Number three, complete fingerprints and palm prints with a retinal laser scan. Number four, documents showing all their bank accounts and property ownership records."

"Are you done?"

"Lastly, number five, they need to present the written authority that affirms they are a US citizen. If and when they deesplay all of those documents, they are welcomed back to the US with open arms and their prior property can be reinstated. I'm tired of the feds insisting we fight this war with one hand tied behind our back."

"So you said there was a second ninety-day waiting period?"

"Yup. While those in question are out of the country for ninety days, a bounty goes out on any of the rest of 'em. Those who tried to game the system will be treated like a wolf, a bad wolf, or Charlie, a bad Viet Cong. There would be a reward of five thousand dollars per set of ears turned in matching that specific DNA strain.

"So we'd be exterminating them, like roaches?"

"No, just eliminating the ones that were here grin-fucking us anyway—the ones laying in the weeds for us. We'd afford them the same caring and sensitive approach they've been dishing out to us for years. These are the very ones who were not here legally or were plotting to blow up your ass or mine—the ones that will slit your children's throats and let them bleed out on YouTube. You know, the ones who will hide explosives up their ass. Those guys. They're bugs."

"Hmmmm."

"Foolproof," announced Cracker with finality. He rapped the table with his knuckles to make his point.

"Well good luck with that. Let me know how it works out with your congressman."

SIXTY-TWO

San Francisco Airport

April 2011

Mrs. Green and Mr. Zho were at San Francisco airport getting ready to board their plane back to Hawaii. Mr. Zho was going to connect through Hawaii and continue on into China from there.

"I thought this was going to be a 757 today," asked Mrs. Green.

"I understand there was a mechanical and we'll be substituting a 737," responded the gate agent. "It's just as fast."

"But this equipment only has two classes of service."

"Ah yes. However, you will still be arriving on time."

"How long until the next 757 departs?"

"Five hours and twenty five minutes. It's inbound from La Guardia."

"Come on. I can't miss my connection," said Zho.

"Heavy load?"

"Quite light," responded the attendant.

They fell in line behind eight passengers and boarded the plane.

They took their seats in first class. Mrs. Green promptly took her shoes off and ordered a green apple martini, which the cabin attendant was going to do her best to cobble together. Zho reclined his seat and ordered hot tea. A couple of passengers were grumbling about the lack of more pillows or blankets, a service that had been terminated purportedly due to the H1N1 virus.

The cabin door closed what appeared to be prematurely to Green and Zho. Turning their heads, they noticed the plane was almost 80 percent vacant. They had deliberately avoided a private jet to keep their travels out of the public eye. They did not want to attract any more attention to their meeting with the heavily robed "stranger."

"Leaving early?" asked Mr. Zho of the cabin attendant.

"Yes we are," replied the male cabin attendant in clipped English. He was a more muscular man than they were accustomed to seeing in that role.

"Odd the plane is so empty," remarked Green.

"Indeed," smiled the attendant. "Just relax. We've got ourselves a dandy pilot today, Mr. Samuel Adams. In fact, he's my uncle. Really, you can call him uncle—Uncle Sam. We'll have you in Hawaii in no time." The attendant looked back over his shoulder, grinned mischievously and then winked.

Both engines were alternately being revved and checked for functionality.

"Zho was taken aback by the smugness of the cabin attendant. He thought the Uncle Sam crack was a bit too glib. Nervously, he attempted to make a cell phone call but couldn't due to local interference.

Sixty-three

Washington, DC
April 2011

Out East, Mr. U was in his limo careening around DC. He was in a black suit with white cuffs and collar contrasted against a light red, pinstriped-shirt with a bloodred tie. He was steadily puffing on his large Madura cigar and reading a copy of *Financial Times*, as he circled the Hill on the outskirts of town.

They had taken the wider beltway, in an effort to avoid all the construction, which was currently plaguing the city. The American Recovery and Reinvestment Act seemed to target certain geographic areas to emulate WPA as 25 percent of all roads or bridges were either torn up or in the process of being closed down for repair. It was wonderful and terrible, all at the same time.

His bodyguard was seated next to him with a black MAC-11 machine pistol at his side on the gray leather seat. Designed for the smaller .380 round in contrast to the MAC-10, the 11 could still fire twelve hundred rounds per minute. Although difficult to control in full auto mode, it could be highly effective up to thirty yards.

Their out of the way route found them approaching an older, smaller, four-lane wooden bridge, which passed over a small causeway. Not many knew of this road and even fewer took it. That was just the way U liked it. Under the radar.

"Nice day," said the driver.

"Dah best," said U.

The water was not but fifteen feet deep and the bridge was merely four football fields in length. As they approached it, they heard a FedEx truck, which had been dogging them in their left rear blind spot, gun his engine. The right front overly reinforced bumper of the truck dove and clipped the limo's left rear bumper, sending the limo spinning and subsequently crashing through the old bridge's peeling, white, wooden railing. It was popped with sufficient force to send the limo careening clear into the warm muddy waters of the causeway.

The limo arrived in the water rather rudely, first on its side as the impact broke out all left side windows. The bodyguard reached to the right swiftly for his MAC-11, but it was already lost, swept away to just behind his head in the swift, warm, chocolate-colored waters.

He spun around to the left but was choking on the frothy, turbid brown water roaring in violently through the windows. He'd open his mouth to breathe and it was promptly filled with more muddy water.

Choking, Mr. U struggled to open the door, but it was too soon. The external water pressure's force against the door was still too much. A single man could not yet overpower it. He'd not be able to until the limo's cabin was completely filled. They were sinking.

Up above, three black forms with wetsuits and rebreathers were dispatched instantly, with surgical timing. They bailed from the FedEx truck while it was still moving (running backward so their fins could navigate pavement) and were in flight, rolling over the bridge railing but seconds after the limo's entry.

Three almost simultaneous splashes were made with their surface ringing waves still visible. They entered the water near the hydraulic disturbance, which was still bubbling up and fanning out from the limo's initial plunge. The vehicle was now almost completely submerged.

Rapidly arriving at the vehicle underwater, the divers swiftly broke out the balance of the windows and hoisted the driver and bodyguard back to the surface and into the FedEx truck.

"This way please."

Mr. U went with another rather stern-looking individual back to a separate late-model, black SUV with tinted windows. Upon collecting its "package," the SUV sped off. No one was around and the pavement was a little wet. No other visible trace remained above the water as to what had just occurred.

The entire event from nudging to splashdown to recovery had taken less than two minutes. About the duration of the Islafornia earthquake.

SIXTY-FOUR

McClean, Virginia
April 2011

MR. CAESAR WAS JUST COMPLETING his morning three-mile run in the tony suburb of McLean, Virginia. He stopped about a mile from his residence to partake from a neighborhood drink stand, where six and seven-year-old girls were selling Kool-Aid advertised for fifty cents a cup.

"Hi, kids," he said, waving warmly.

"Hello," they responded in rapt unison.

The "$.50" was printed shoddily on a two-foot sign, which was two pieces of cardboard taped together with packaging tape. It was painted with tempera paint in red, white and blue. The children had run out of paint on the zero so they'd finished it up in red Magic Marker. The cups were quite small, their sizing reminiscent of the vessels routinely designated for urine tests.

"Hey! What happened to a quarter a cup?" teased Caesar.

"Inflation. Inflation from all the debt and Stimulus Packages," responded the ringmaster dryly with a smile. "Although Mr. Blimpie said you would gladly pay a dollar a cup for yours because you know a dollar borrowed is a dollar earned!" added the child, grinning ear to ear.

"Mr. Blimpie, eh? Who the devil is Mr. Blimpie?" asked Caesar with an edge in his voice.

"He's the big, red hot dog at the next corner," replied the freckle-faced red-headed Kool-Aid ringmaster. Dimples smiling, she pointed down the street. There, a half block further, between a stand of trees, was a vendor in an oversized hot dog costume. It was rather garish. Standing ten feet tall, it possessed significant girth of over three feet in diameter.

"He did, did he?" remarked Caesar drippingly with mock horror and some degree of righteous indignation. He pulled three dollars from his sock and knocked back three urine test-sized cups of Kool-Aid.

"Keep the change," he grumbled.

He jogged on down the street to confront Mr. Blimpie. Arriving at the aforementioned corner, Caesar spoke to the large hot dog, summoning up all his legislative authority.

"So I understand you are taking advantage of seven-year-olds?" he quipped, challenging the overly large, bright yellow, orange and red, felt-covered performer.

"Mr. Blimpie is here for the weak and all small children," responded Mr. Blimpie, speaking through his bow tie with an obvious smile in his voice.

"And you're telling them I'm an easy mark! Where do you get off with that line of crap? As if fifty cents a cup is not high enough!"

Blimpie said nothing.

"Talk to me! Why are you encouraging them to take advantage of me and extract a full dollar per cup?" asked Caesar a bit arrogantly, as he continued to goad the large promotional character.

"Blimpie hot dogs are good for you! If you like Kool-Aid you'll take two!" sing-songed the large wiener. This was accompanied by xylophone background music befitting the age group and a cartoonishly large frozen smile affixed to the wiener's three-foot-wide face.

Caesar, however, wasn't having any of it. He wasn't going to let the performer off the hook without hearing a damn good reason. He demanded that an explanation was to occur face to face. He was up in Mr. Blimpie's grill, figuratively and literally. He was following the large face and its dinner plate-sized eyes as they turned counterclockwise, in concert with the enormous hot dog's rotation. "No, really. What's up with encouraging the kids to charge just me double?"

Mr. Blimpie sang back with xylophone accompaniment, "*With cap and trade, stimulus bills and government health care too, we put in VAT for kids—as they'll pay it back for you.* Right? After all, a dollar borrowed is a dollar earned." He beamed his large frozen smile again at Caesar. Mr. Blimpie made the remarks while turning slightly away and canting his large form back toward a densely covered stand of trees.

"What? *Who the hell are you?*" asked Caesar with amazement grabbing his arm and following Blimpie back toward the grove's corner shaded area to get to the bottom of it.

Then, facing backward to the street, a large, Velcroed fold at Mr. Blimpie's tie opened up in an instant, revealing a powerful man in shorts controlling the suit's motions. He had a small tranq-gun pistol, which he shot Caesar in the neck with. *Thwaap.*

Mr. Blimpie grabbed Caesar before he slumped to the sidewalk and effortlessly pulled him inside the wiener outfit. The wiener's Velcro flap closed as quickly as it had opened.

He placed Caesar's feet on an internal dolly with rollers, held him up and slid him over beside a large black SUV with tinted windows, which was concealed behind the stand of trees. The flap opened and closed again to unload its cargo. You could hear Mr. Blimpie's amplified music start up again ringing throughout the neighborhood:

"Blimpie hot dogs are good for you! If you like Kool-Aid, you'll take two!" The xylophone continued to play after the announcement.

Two individuals in logoed tennis togs who had been playing on nearby courts promptly stopped, sat down their racquets, gathered up Caesar and summarily loaded him and themselves into the first black SUV. Mr. Blimpie was pulled into the trailer in the back of the second SUV. Both vehicles pulled off at a snail's pace through the residential neighborhood back toward the freeway. Slowly. To protect the children.

Sixty-Five

The White House, Washington, DC
April 2011

PRESIDENT RASHEED WAS IN THE Oval Office at his desk musing over some conflicting dates for his next television address. While he'd just done Letterman last week, and *The View* the week before, he had a one-time opportunity to do Leno, but it needed to be this week due to the network's prior commitments and his golf vacation at Martha's Vineyard.

MSNBC and CNN were after him to return to discuss yet another oil spill, which was well into its fourth month. He had a high degree of confidence they would be quite malleable as to their rescheduling flexibility however. He had just addressed joint sessions of Congress and the UN the last two weeks, but he felt it imperative he stay the standard bearer for the messaging, he must keep it crisp, compelling and clear. Just him.

He heard a rap at his door.

"Come," he commanded.

Winston entered with a singular nine-by-twelve sealed envelope, which was marked "Personal & Confidential."

"Mr. President, apologies for the interruption, however, this was hand carried by bicycle courier with some sense of urgency. It has already been processed and cleared as to any immunological or munitions threat, sir. We have been assured there is no danger to you personally."

"Appreciate it Winston, I know you'll take care of me."

"It has an NSA return address. However, that certainly could be a ruse. We did want to respect your privacy however, as you have insisted in the past that we should not open these manner of things."

"Thank you, Winston. You did the right thing."

Rasheed took the envelope and set it perfectly in the center of his desk. He placed his hands together behind his back and looked at Winston. He did not speak.

"Anything else, Mr. President?" inquired Winston.

"That will be all. Thank you, Winston." Rasheed dismissed him with a flip of the back of his hand toward the door.

It was a bit cooler than normal that day and breezy, with a crystal clear view of the cherry trees outside the president's window.

Winston turned promptly on his heels and left the Oval Office. The president continued to stare blankly at the envelope in front of him. Why did this single envelope concern him so? He'd processed mountains of bills, e-mails and potential amendments for review, however he had a foreboding feeling about this lone envelope.

Nonsense, he thought to himself.

He ripped open the envelope and pulled out three pieces of paper. One was an eight-by-ten-inch photograph of him bowing to Ah Zho, another was a picture of him kissing the ring of Mr. U with one knee bent. Lastly, he found a hastily scribbled handwritten note from Burton Buttons requesting a meeting with Rasheed within twenty-four hours to discuss matters that were best not reduced to writing.

Fuck, thought Rasheed. *Is this guy trying to extort more money out of me? We took care of him already. I thought Buttons was buttoned down.*

This wasn't a matter he could delegate to staff. He picked up his phone, rearranged a couple of appointments with Winston for the next day and requested that the Secret Service give him the five hundred-foot stand-down radius he requested for off-the-record matters. Each time this had occurred in the past, the Service had objected and admonished against this deviation. The president was adamant and always prevailed.

The following day, Winston presented Burton Buttons from the NSA to the president in the Oval Office. Cordialities were exchanged and Winston left.

"How can I help you today, Burton?" asked the President. "Surely you are not here again to try and sharpen your golf game at my expense?" Rasheed laughed at his own self-deprecation. "Thought all of your matters were already bedded down." The President shot both of his white cuffs out, pulled gently at his Armani suit coat turned, sat down and crossed his legs in a languid European fashion.

"Well there's been a change, Mr. President and I wanted to personally give you a heads up."

"How thoughtful."

"Yes, sir."

"Change in what?"

"All things that matter. I no longer believe many of our prior conversations can stay contained and, as a courtesy to you sir, thought you should hear it from me first. I fear things are unraveling."

"Burton."

"Yes, Mr. President."

"Were you familiar with some of LBJ's practices?"

"Well, some. Yes, sir. As they pertain to the Great Society or the Vietnam War, sir?"

"No. Let me be clear, more personal actually. I'm referring to how he'd put things on 'autopilot.' I'm referring to his handling of tedious, personal matters. Matters beneath the surface, small but irritating like a gnat, below his pay grade. Things that wouldn't go away. Do you follow so far, Burton?"

"Not sure that I do, sir."

"In particular, Burton, did you know he had four individual buttons installed on his credenza?"

"No sir. I did not."

"Do you know what they were used for, Burton?"

"I do not."

"He pressed the first if he desired coffee."

"OK."

"He pressed the second if he wanted water brought to him."

"Yes."

"He pressed the third if he had a taste for tea."

"Hmmm."

"And the fourth. Do you know what they brought him if he pressed the fourth button, Burton?"

"No sir."

"Fresca. They'd bring him Fresca if he pressed the fourth button."

"Very good, sir."

"And do you know why I tell you this story, Buttons?"

"No sir. I do not." Buttons was beginning to visibly squirm.

"Are you not curious as to the underlying reason for my wasting both your and my valuable time with such a benign story?"

"A bit, sir."

"Look. Know that I have had two buttons installed on my credenza. Do you see them, Buttons?" He motioned toward the right top corner of his desk.

"Yes, yes I do".

"The first is for coffee, black coffee. And water, cold water. I get both served to me at the same time."

"Very good, sir." Buttons was visibly anxious.

"And do you know what the second button is for, Burton?"

"I do not, sir."

"A very muscular ranger bursts through that door within five seconds and splits the person's head who is standing in front of me with a .40 caliber round or an axe. My choice."

"I see."

"I'm not sure you do, Buttons. Do you have the audacity, the stones, to come into this office and try to shake me down, to muscle *me*—the president of the United States!? Do you think you will have any modicum of success trying to roust this office? Let alone on White House property?"

"Mr. President, I came here primarily out of respect for this office."

"Fuck you," stated Rasheed flatly as he swirled in his chair. He pressed the second button just referred to, stood up with his hands on his hips to signify his loathing for Buttons and prepared to greet the ranger.

SIXTY-SIX

"Please don't do that, Mr. President, not yet. I need to debrief you. A moment more please, sir, to give you a heads up."

Rasheed snorted in disgust out of both his nostrils and looked at his watch. It was an expensive black and gold Breitling he had received from the ambassador to the United Kingdom upon the ambassador's appointment. He was watching the sweep second hand sweep.

Then, just as Rasheed had said, within but seconds, a large, muscular, black ranger burst into the Oval Office. His weapon was not pulled. The door was not closed behind him.

"Close the door, soldier," commanded the president.

"No, sir." The soldier pulled up to attention with no salute.

"I said close the door, soldier! Don't play *you bet your career* by making me have to find another ranger who will!" said Rasheed.

Instead, immediately following on the ranger's heels came the vice president, the secretary of defense, leaders of both houses and the senior-most leaders of the NSA, the CIA and the FBI.

Two more rangers came in and the three in camo had Mrs. Green, U, Caesar and Zho in tow. Lastly, came Scotty, Cracker and Ali. Scotty was carrying a large, bulging, leather rucksack in his right hand. Its contents were obviously heavy, due to the manner in which it affected his gait.

"What is the meaning of this?! I demand to know the meaning of this! This meeting was slated as private—solely between myself and Mr. Buttons," admonished the president, with irritation rising in his voice.

Scotty brought his weathered, leather rucksack over to the president's desk. He'd taken out a weighty object, holding it with two hands and outstretched arms for all to see.

"What is the meaning of this?" mocked Scotty. "What is the meaning of *this?!*" he demanded, adding deliberative drama to the last word as he motioned toward the object.

Coincident with the end of his second question, Key dropped the bowling ball-sized object squarely upon the center of the Oval Office's presidential desk, creating a three-eighths inch dent in the dark, richly oiled walnut.

"Jesus!" remarked a startled Rasheed, while literally jumping backward. "What is that? Are you mad?"

"Well, Mr. President, I believe you know exactly what this is. You have seen this diagrammed before on paper. The Chinese showed it to you. Mr. Zho showed it to you, to be precise," stated Key dryly, pointing over to the chairman. Zho looked down, performing a visual shoe shine on his Allen Edmonds. "This, primarily for the benefit of others in the room, Mr. President, is a bowling ball-sized sample of Red Mercury, but then you knew that. Fortunately, it is but a mock-up."

"Let me be clear. I have no idea ..." started the president.

"Respectfully, for once, Mr. President, would you please just shut the fuck up?" asked Scotty, rubbing his scar, although his tone was not in the form of a question.

"This single object if live, could take down two-thirds of DC, or alternatively, if surgically planted with scores of others like it hundreds of feet below the earth precisely along fault lines, could trigger a manmade earthquake. A quake so large and devastating as to kill 242,000."

"I knew nothing of that, I ..." interrupted the president.

"Whether you had knowledge or didn't have knowledge of that incident is unclear, however, it is abundantly clear, with audio and video, you not only knew but planned and executed the 'death by natural causes' of the prime minister of Canada and the president of Mexico," said Key.

"Make no mistake …" launched the president.

Zho glanced a furtive and irritated look of admonishment toward the president's preponderance toward excessive speech.

"Respectfully sir, stop embarrassing yourself and this previously prestigious office and close that never-park-the-bus piehole," demanded Key.

"It will be impossible to stop this train. It has left the station. It is the height of naïveté to think you can intimidate me, or stop things much larger than yourself already in motion." stated the president, ignoring the repeated demands for his silence.

"What we are going to agree upon today is reminiscent of one of the Constitution's founding framers admonitions. I'm referring to a favorite Benjamin Franklin quote: *'We need to hang together on this, or surely we will all hang separately'*, stated Key looking at the balance of the room.

"You're going to attempt to stop this? Ha! You are going to try and un-ring this bell? Pondering an impeachment, are you? A public lynching? We all know how those things end," laughed Rasheed dismissively again, attempting to shuttle Scotty out.

"You're right, Mr. President. We do know how those end. For those reasons, we are going to employ a different approach. The country doesn't need another scandel. It can't stand the daylight, it would be too painful right now. You only have a year and a half left in office anyway. But we are going to stop your march toward socialism, your never-ending 'unicorn utopianism,' and your spending this nation into bankruptcy."

"Amen," said Ali.

"So what's going to happen is this: You are going to quietly step down and the vice president is going to take over. You are going to suddenly develop a debilitating health condition that will not allow you to continue to govern."

"The CIA is excellent at constructing doctor's notes," chimed in CIA Director Mr. Whitney with a flinty expression and a wink toward Scotty.

"The VP will be the ventriloquist for the individuals on the right side of this room"—Scotty motioned to all, except Green, Zho, Caesar and U—"until the next election, whereby all will return to normalcy." Key continued, "You'll step down to give full attention to your health concerns and there will be three other conditions evoked."

"How dare you attempt to dictate terms to me? I am the president of the United States—leader of the Free World!" proclaimed Rasheed. "Robert, throw this raving lunatic out!"

The SecDef did not move, he made no response, nor flinched.

"First, there will be a prompt and swift return to capitalism and governance by the Constitution. Second, we will become part of the Sovereign Six."

"Who the hell are the Sovereign Six?" roared the president.

"Patience. We'll get to that," said Scotty, "And lastly, we'll embark on a vehicle of debt forgiveness with ESE, which will get us off of this road to debt damnation you have us on, as it leads toward bankruptcy. It's giving the US indebtgestion."

"What makes you think this group is going to go along with your fantasies? You do not know what is best for this country. It is you, sir, that has mounted the only unicorn in this room," chided Rasheed.

"You know," said Key, "I read a book by a radio talk show host recently where he referenced a quote from the British writer-philosopher C. S. Lewis, who wrote:

> *Of all tyrannies, a tyranny sincerely exercised for the good of its victims may be the most oppressive. It would be better to live under robber barons than under omnipotent moral busybodies. The robber baron's cruelty may sometimes sleep, his cupidity may at some point be satiated; but those who torment us for our own good will torment us without end for they do so with the approval of their own conscience.*

"And quite frankly, sir to that end, I'm not exactly certain if you are one of the most self-righteous, megalomaniac, narcissistic, manipulative, conniving, despot wannabes to ever occupy this office; the Antichrist, or simply a small-time, bribe-taking Detroit thug with a highly effective Madison Avenue marketing campaign. I don't know and I don't care. But the one thing that all in this room are in lockstep agreement on is that your steady dismantling of America, brick by brick, stops. It stops today," said Key.

Everyone in the room nodded.

"Mr. President, I was trying to give you a heads up first to avoid the embarrassment of this confrontation," bemoaned Buttons. "Everyone in the room is aware of your surreptitious dealings with U, Green, Caesar and Zho. They all possess hard evidence sir."

"I have the prerogative, the presidential mantle of authority, the federal jurisprudence to adjudicate these matters and to deal confidentially at the—at the highest level..." the president stammered as his voice trailed off.

"Save it, Talk-Show Guest-In-Chief," sneered Cracker. "You ain't gonna' rubber-mouth your way out of this. There's a pony under this one." Cracker blew his nose with one finger in disgust on the presidential seal.

"We have all vetted and approved this plan, Mr. President." said the SecDef.

"So, this is more of a monologue?" asked Rasheed.

"Exactly," responded Key. "We have a document drafted. The high points are a return to Constitutional covenants and the end to your nomination of shadow Czars without congressional approval who behave in a unilateral manner to prop up your oligarchy."

Sixty-Seven

"This will go nowhere. You cannot parade in here with your demands and dictate to me," replied Rasheed as he distanced himself and walked further away from the group to the other side of the room.

"Yes we can. And the part about you refraining from using the Constitution to wipe your ass with—that's pretty important to us too," deadpanned Scotty. "We'll repeal national health care and avoid trillions more in debt, rationing and the government's ability to decide who lives and dies. Your plan is the new millennium's home game version of *Logan's Run*."

"My grandmother saw your health care plan. Not a fan." said Ali.

"Return management of the census to its rightful owner. Take it away from Buckeye and your chief of staff, who's attempting to gerrymander and redistrict lines, which will only benefit your march toward a single-party scheme. Disband Buckeye altogether to blunt the registration fraud. Enforce immigration laws to finally discourage millions more aliens from attempting to enter this country illegally." said Scotty.

"While your at it," said Cracker, "Put down the violence and protect our local borders for once with the same enthusiasm that you patrol foreign borders. Disband your endless quest towards trying to cajole illegals to sneak across for more lollipop giveaway-entitlement programs leading to your one-party system."

"Hah," Rasheed laughed nervously.

"Surrender control of GM, Chrysler and the financial services industry back to the private sector on a no-interest loan basis, which they can pay down over time. Let NAFTA continue and stop card check for your union cronies." said Key.

Mr. U stood up without his hat, puffed up his red face, pointed and shouted. "You can not stop the unions. The Detroit Machine will eat yous alive! You're out of your league, sonny!"

Key ignored him. "Rescind all stimulus funds that have not been spent with clawbacks on companies whose holdings are over 33 percent outside of the US, like AIG, for example. When the Fed and Treasury kept AIG names in secret, that's telling enough. Bragging about a write-down publically from $62 billion to $29 billion but in fact slinking back under the covers to provide another $33 billion in 'phantom dollars' means there was effectively *no* write-down. They received one hundred cents on every dollar. This stimulus chicanery has cost us over $400,000 dollars for every $60,000 job created."

Rasheed attempted to walk out, but Cracker barred his path and stood in front of the tall double doors by the rangers with his arms folded.

"End the prosecution of CIA operatives for doing their job. Stop the first-time practice of giving enemy combatants the rights of a US citizen in a domestic trial setting. Reading a terrorist his Miranda rights within twelve hours of capture is nuts. Lawyering him up forecloses any opportunity to secure other cell information." said Scotty.

"I just pray there isn't another attack," said the CIA director.

"Stop spending and printing money so we may mitigate hyperinflation and bring an audit upon the Federal Reserve so we can all discover where and to whom those two trillion mystery dollars went."

"You think any of this will be able to stop ESE? You cannot impinge upon their global power. You have not thought this through," said the President. "You can dictate to me all you want, they do not have to listen to your drivel."

Ah Zho smiled, gently with a half nod.

"Actually, that brings us to our second point. We have formed the Sovereign Six, which is an association of the United States, the United Kingdom, Canada, Mexico, Brazil and India. We have many other good friends who will join ultimately; Australia and Israel are good examples. But you've poked Netanyahu in the eye so many times recently, Israel thinks we're more anti-Semitic than Mel Gibson. We'll stop shitting in Israel's hat and let them deal with Iran.

The Sec-Def, the sole Jew in the room, folded his arms and glared at Rasheed.

"We focused initially on like-mindedness, the ability to move swiftly and geo-proximity to form a hardened, cohesive coalition." Scotty spread a large poster showing the organization's makeup by country, their by-laws and GDP on his desk. "We formed this set of six as a market maker growth engine as the US rekindles its return to its industrialized roots. There will be new Investment Tax Credits for this vehicle as in the Reagan years."

"We will not allow ESE or anyone like them, to wrest our industrial roots from us any longer, as was the case with the steel industry in the late '70s. The Sovereign Six have a combined market GDP of $24.5 trillion. That is almost a third of the planet and some two and a half times ESE's. Let the big dog eat." said Scotty.

"So," interrupted Cracker, "all we are after here is global 'parity,' Mr. President. And being a *citizen of the world*, we know you're real keen on that."

"Mrs. Green and Mr. Zho, this will be the new message you will take back to ESE. We have calculated the subsidies, or surtax, that the ESE coalition has imposed on imports from the Sovereign Six for decades. They range from 15 to 40 percent on top. China is a perfect example.

"How do you figure?" asked Rasheed.

"They tie their currency to our dollar, giving them an unfair edge. When they impose another 25 percent tariff additionally, this feels like a 40 percent advantage or discount, when contrasted to US producers. The fixed yuan/dollar rate also requires China to hold too many dollar reserves."

"You cannot dictate what we tie our currency to," said Zho defiantly.

Sixty-eight

"Maybe not, but starting tomorrow, until the currencies are disconnected, the Sovereign Six will add back that same amount on a country-by-country basis as a tax on their imports from these nations. That will level the playing field on outsourcing. It will strike parity in; steel, electronics, flat screen televisions, cameras, audio equipment, automobiles, rice, PlayStations, fireworks, oh and those tiny little umbrellas in fruity drinks."

"We will still bankrupt you," said Zho defiantly, his face flushing as he squared off against Scotty.

"We considered that and believe you are probably correct," said Key. "So that brings us to our third point."

He unrolled another set of drawings, showing the complete ESE highway infrastructure. "By the end of this week, the US will own all toll roads in China, Japan and Vietnam. That revenue will go directly against principal reduction on our debt instruments which, by the way, now bear a zero interest rate in perpetuity. We've run the numbers and feel that will clean this matter up in about five years. We've drafted that transaction for you to execute today."

Scotty threw the documents for execution literally at Zho's face. They separated in midair and fell fluttering to the floor in front of him.

"We will never agree to that," scoffed Zho. He was unfazed and did not step aside from the hurled documents. Mrs. Green laughed and pulled at the feather in her hat nervously.

"You know, we anticipated that too," said Ali.

"Yeshure. This is my favorite part!" mocked Cracker, slapping his hands and then rubbing them together rapidly like a housefly.

The CIA director nodded at the three rangers in camo. In unison, the uniforms swept the legs of Green, Zho, U and Caesar, knocking the four to the ground. Each soldier put his right knee in a chest to control the four, with the largest also controlling Caesar and Green. Each soldier reached into their small, black, leather surgical pouch on their belt.

"Get off me!" shrieked Ah Zho.

The four rangers each brought out two different inoculation guns and hit their captives twice, once just behind the ear with the larger, gray gun and once in the throat by the Adam's apple with the thinner, black gun.

"As you might imagine, the listening device behind the ear allows us to hear everything said to you. The one in your throat allows us to hear everything you say and 'see' everything you see. Did I mention they are hypersensitive to vibration? So, if you try and cut them out, they will immediately self-destruct and take you with them." said Key

"Well, that's not entirely true," said the NSA director. "They will cause a brain bleed. There's a 30 percent chance you will die and a 70 percent chance you will have a hemorrhagic bleed into the brain. This will cause paralysis, including loss of speech and the ability to swallow. You will be fed by a peg tube through your stomach for the next thirty years."

"So, you watch your entire life change and are helpless to help yourself," said Cracker.

"Much the same way the American people have felt since you took office, Mr. President," said Key.

Cracker launched. "So while we may be going out on a limb here, we are hoping these pinpricks will help influence your thinking. Boy Howdy! Welcome to the team Partner-san!" Cracker bowed and then picked Zho up off the floor with an overly ebullient bear hug, as Zho squirmed to avoid same. Caesar's head bobbed, like a parakeet.

"By the way, if you decide to type and not look at the keys or write on a white board these devices are sensitive enough to hear that as well. If we get the least bit apprehensive, we will detonate these devices remotely just for sport," remarked Key.

"Why, pray tell, am I excluded from this *robotarian* control?" asked Rasheed.

"Because we all respect the office of the presidency, Mr. Rasheed."

"Just not you." responded the minority leader of the House.

The secretary of defense then spoke. "I'd like to aid in resolving any degree of ambiguity as to how this proceeds if one or two ESE foreign entities get a 'hero complex.' We want to be completely predictable as to how that scenario unfolds.

"Here. Here. And here." said Scotty as he threw down eight-by-ten photographs on the table as the SecDef spoke.

"We have undisputable hard evidence, viewed by all in this room, that ESE and its three-body consortium has, without provocation, attacked the United States on her soil—specifically, California—and killed 242,000 of our citizens. Our treasure. That is almost one hundred times the number slain at either Pearl Harbor or on 9/11."

The SecDef continued, "A declaration of war would be granted within four hours if these photos get out. It'd be as easy as getting it out of a vending machine. We know the American people would be behind us 100 percent. However, we feel the carnage should be avoided, for all. It was not the hundreds of millions of the lower-level ESE populace who performed this nefarious act. It was an act of the few at the top. Regrettably, it also involved our president. Hence, our solution.

"Failing that, we will nationalize all holdings either ESE government owned or controlled by a citizen of your coalition that are in excess of US$100 million. We will then attack your countries with all armaments at our disposal. *All* armaments."

Ali turned to Rasheed. "Mento?"